THE FUTURE LIES

John Be Lane

Global Arts Press, an imprint of Global Arts Ltd
3531 South Logan St D-205 • Englewood, Colorado 80113 • USA
globalartspress.com/globalarts

Copyright © 2024 by John Be Lane
First edition February 2024

Designed by Julz Greason

Publisher's Cataloging-in-Publication
Names: Lane, John Be, 1954- author.
Title: The future lies / John Be Lane.
Description: First edition. | Englewood, Colorado : Global Arts Press, [2024] | Audience: Grades 10-12, ages 16-18. | Includes bibliographical references.
Identifiers: ISBN: 978-0-9984356-7-1 | 978-0-9984356-8-8 (eBook) | LCCN: 2023946856
Subjects: LCSH: Artificial intelligence--Fiction. | Video gamers--Fiction. | Future, The--Fiction. | Government, Resistance to--Fiction. | Subversive activities--Fiction. | Oppression (Psychology)--Fiction. | Literacy--Fiction. | Intellectual life--Fiction. | Book burning--Fiction. | Fascism--Fiction. | Denver (Colo.)--Fiction. | Romance fiction. | Suspense fiction. | Young adult fiction. | LCGFT: Dystopian fiction. | Apocalyptic fiction.
Classification: LCC: PS3612.A549832 F88 2024 | DDC: 813/.6--dc23

May truth be the North Star that guides you...

Simulacrum:

(sim yuh LAY krum); 'a mere image; a specious imitation or likeness, of something'

– Oxford English Dictionary

The Descent of Man

*First, humans were
domesticated by religions,
for power and control.*

*Then, humans were
domesticated by corporations,
for profit.*

*Finally, humans were
domesticated by machines,
for convenience.*

Prologue

You never questioned what the Network wanted you to do, since the Network did all of the thinking. It seemed so intelligent that no one remembered the *artificial* part. So everybody obeyed. Obedience was a convenience that no one thought twice – or once – about. Everything just was what it was; there *was* no because, for as far back as anyone knew. You might as well call it *forever*.

In exchange, the Network kept everything running. All that was known, when things were still known, as *Simulacrum*. But that word had too many syllables. Now they just called it the Show – a bottomless sewer of digital refuse the Network concocted from leftover human ideas. It was nonsense you watched on small slabs you could find anywhere. Made out of plastic and glass that you couldn't turn off, or turn down. Charged by the Sun, like any electronic that still carried power.

You watched out of habit, and you watched to forget the perpetual torment of being a human. And when that distraction was no longer enough, you flipped the slab over and hammered it off of your forehead. For as long as it took to discourage a rogue prefrontal neuron from sparking a thought that might lead to a question. Or an answer.

You could count on the Network to keep the Show going, all day and all night. With all of the interest that a farmer might have as she tosses out grit for the chickens to peck. As much as the livestock demanded, and not a bit more.

So a species that went to the Moon, built cities, cured illnesses, and wrote music that could crush you to tears...could be taken for granted, like chattel.

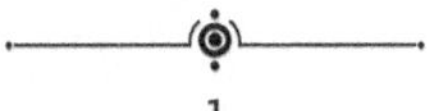

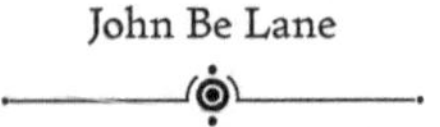

Or as The Immortal once said, when no one could hear him, 'I want people as easy to manage as a rock resting flat on the ground.'

If those rocks on the ground, duly glued to their slabs, favored anything the Network might happen to serve, that show would be *Kill It! Till It Die!* (No one found fault with that syntax. And nobody knew that 'syntax' was a word.)

Kill It! was the flagship event of the Show, appearing on slabs everywhere. It was a synchronous orgy of twitch skills, by players that everyone followed. Players who seemed to have everything anyone watching could want. In *this* life, at least. No one was sure what the actual number of viewers might be. The Network said billions, but no one could count. Regardless how many, the goners devoted their eyes to these pixels of avatars, posing on slabs.

And so it went on, as each second-hand life ran its course. On the infinite treadmill of *now*, ever after. Gathering dust, and then offering it up to the wind. Sometimes things seem like they won't ever change. Especially when things are the worst.

But nothing can ever quite stay the same way. And then comes a day, when all you *expected* to happen, did not. It might be the simplest thing, when you weren't really looking. A product of offhand curiosity. A crack in what seemed to be permanent.

'*That…*', as the poet Leonard Cohen once said, 'that's how the light gets in.'

Part I

'Your typical city, involved in a typical daydream...'
–Robert Hunter

The *best* of the players of *Kill It! Till It Die!* were like musicians who could shutter their eyes, and just improvise. Whatever the game was, on whatever day, the best ones figured out all the right notes to play.

Itch-ass, alas, wasn't one of the best. His avatar on this particular day was sitting disheveled, in a saddle on the back of a virtual horse. At the wrong end of a cattle herd, making its way up to Abilene.

As unclothed and semi-clothed wretches from all parts of the realm were waiting for the game to begin, Itch-ass called out on a private chat channel, to his best friend and partner for the day.

'Stink Foot!' he said. 'Remember that time in that war, and the game was about to be over, and I had the same points as you did? But you let me kill that last guy? Then I was the winner?'

'I do remember that.'

'I won that day! I won the game!'

'You sure did.'

'Only time I ever won!'

'Was that the one time?'

'Yep. Best day ever.' Itch-ass let that recollection sink in a bit

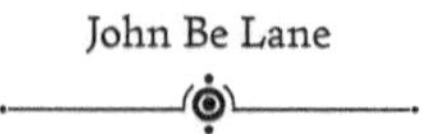

longer. 'That was so cool.'

'Yeah. Long time ago.'

As the start time approached, the Network dug up an old song that created an atmosphere, tuned to the game of the day. Itch-ass was quickly distracted:

I'm an old cowhand, from the Rio Grande,
but my legs ain't bowed, and my cheeks ain't tan.
I'm a cowboy who never saw a cow,
never roped a steer cause I don't know how.
Sure ain't a-fixin' to start in now;
yippie eye-oh kai-yay…

Still on the private line, Itch-ass said, 'Stink Foot! What's a *steer*?'

'What?'

'In that song. What's a *steer*?'

'I don't know. Who cares?'

'I just don't wanna kill the wrong thing.'

'It's a little too late to be worrying now.'

'My best game ever, comin' up!'

'You better hope it is. You're just about down to your final fuckup.'

'I told you before – this controller's messed up.'

'I gave you *mine*, remember? It worked fine for me.'

'I just keep thinking, "Don't fuck up this shot." Then I do.'

'You're better off not even thinking.'

'Can't help it. My points are so low.'

'And when you get nervous, you scratch your ass. And then, once you're distracted, you shoot the wrong thing.'

'I can't help it! I've tried everything!'

'Try not fucking up. You'll get sent up the hill…'

'They don't still do that! I mean, do they?'

'…use you for spare parts. You'll be like, "Where's my eyeball? What happened to all of my *blood*?"'

That goofy old song was the only sound now in their headsets.

'I can't fuck this up,' said Itch-ass to himself. 'I just *cannot* fuck up.'

But his insides were still not convinced.

She had used much more water than she cared to spare, to wash what was left of the blood off her hands. Clean enough now for the steering wheel, but her shirt… Her shirt couldn't keep all the rest of the blood from soaking on through to her skin. She could feel it begin to get tacky. It formed an adhesive that stuck to her chest.

All that was left was the map and the road. As if there was *someone else* driving. As if someone else was sitting there now, but not her. Inside of this sweltering box, north of nowhere, thinking none of it, none of it was happening to her.

Someone else, following squared-off pieces of map, fluttering there on the opposite seat. Segmented apart at the folds. And someone else now saw the city, that rose from the plains up ahead.

'*Keep going*,' someone else must have said.

'Keep going!'

'Keep going!'

'Just *go!*'

Someone else could see lines faded, there on the pieces of map. Someone else turned, where they needed to turn, to aim at the place on the map where the hospital waited. With the aid that was desperately needed.

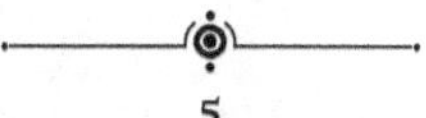

Someone else might actually make it there now; the route was as straight as the edge of that map.

Until someone else, suddenly. *Stopped.*

Blocking the road were abandoned old cars; tangled-up heartbreaks of metal. All of them facing the city ahead. Someone else opened the door of their truck, and stepped out to examine the graves. And their knee buckled in, as soon as their ankle took weight.

Someone else found a baseball bat, in back of the seat of their truck. With the bat for support, they hobbled toward what was still left of the cars.

Their foot nearly snagged on the problem itself. Tire spikes, lined up like shark's teeth, all pointed straight out of town. Using the bat, she pressed down on one spike. The spike laid down flat from the pressure. When she lifted the bat, the spike angled back up. So *that* was the message. Everyone's welcome to *leave.*

But *her* way was into the city. So she tried to find something to lay on the spikes. In spite of the oxidized state of the wrecks, a fender or hood might still do the job. But she was too small and weakened by now, to pull loose a piece big enough.

Under a wheel that was missing its tire, was a big-enough, flat piece of metal. Face down on the ground. Once she cleared it of dust, she could just barely read the old sign's faded letters:

WRONG WAY

STOP

SEVERE TIRE DAMAGE

She dragged it the best that she could, and then dropped it in place. The warning sign instantly provided a bridge, so the spikes wouldn't puncture her tires. Some day she might laugh at the irony. But nothing was funny today.

She turned back to her truck, as a volley of thunder discharged

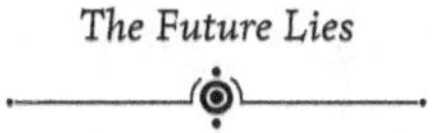

from the west. She felt the wind chill the blood under her shirt.

'All wind, no rain,' as her father would say.

But as she drove over the sign, and the spikes she'd disabled, past the slag of old cars that were parked there forever, an ominous cauldron of clouds flooded over the mountains. Heading toward where she was going.

A fresh gust of wind blew half of her segments of map through a window. And there they'd be waiting, till someone else found them.

○ ◉ ○

The synthetic Announcer pretended its throat needed clearing. And like dogs trained for supper, mouths watered everywhere. Players and viewers alike. The game was about to begin!

'Welcome, welcome! Everyone, welcome! If you've got the ti-yi-yi-yime, it's time to Kill it! Till it die!'

Everyone knew it by heart. Most of them finished the intro themselves, in unison with the Announcer:

'Today, we save civilization! From Crippies and Litter-rats, who think that they're better than us.'

As always, the Announcer dropped a taunt on that last phrase, with a sing-song that everyone copied. The mission was always the same. Only the weapons, and settings, and costumes would change. Today it was cowboys, revolvers, and rifles – the American West. Whatever *that* was. Nobody cared. They were waiting for what always came next.

'What's in it for you? Betterlife points! Betterlife's waiting for you. With whatever...you've ever...wanted. The hair, the teeth, the clothes, the house. The food! The best food that you'll ever eat. Your plate's always full in Betterlife!

'But you'll need all the points you can get! So get ready to bet. Let's

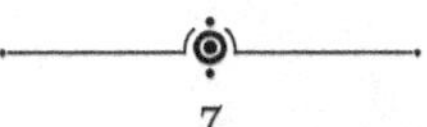

see who's playing today. Because you win when they win!'

Each player's name was announced, with their picture and avatar. Next to them, pie charts showed all of the points they had earned from their previous games. The Announcer delivered the lineup, softly but quickly:

'Leading, as always, The Immortal – trail boss for today's wild western mayhem. Dipstick remains your points leader, and will ramrod the crew for this cattle drive. Your wranglers for today will be Cornhole, Spit-take, Monkey Nuts, Stink Foot, and Barf Bag. R-r-rounding the leaders' group out will be Doc, whose healing hands, yesterday, saved Itch-ass from final extinction.

'And we're pleased to announce a new player today. They call him the Kid. Keep an eye on his tactical skills. The Kid might surprise you!

'And lastly, your saddle tramp, Itch-ass. Will today be Itch-ass's last roundup? We're about to find out!'

A grid showing all of the players appeared on the screen.

'Place your bets now! Par-lay your bets! Just tap your selections. The more that you bet, the more that you get! What will your Betterlife be?'

In the Bullpen, the players got ready. Headsets and chairs were adjusted. Energy drinks were guttered down throats. An assortment of last-minute farts were dispatched.

For all of the glory these players commanded, from anyone gripping a slab, the Bullpen was more like a bedroom that all of them shared, and nobody bothered to clean. It had all of the homespun charm of a call center, circa 1998. Although it was unknown to anyone now, it had once been a studio, set up for corporate executives. Near the top of a high-rise in Denver – the Republic Plaza, as it was known then.

What was left of what once was called 'culture' had retreated to here, to the Bullpen, to make a last stand. To the goners who watched, the Bullpen was where *gods* made their art. On a good day, with eyes closed, you could have a debate. Did the Bullpen smell more like bad breath, or old socks? Teen spirit, or landfill?

Last-minute bet slips were submitted by viewers, who actually thought it would matter. The Network made time for the song to play out:

'...where the buff-a-lo
roam around the zoo...
and the old Bar-X
is just a bar-be-cue...'

As for Itch-ass, you might have thought he would be wrestling dread. Or thinking about ways to avoid fucking up. But here's what he wondered: *What might a* barbecue *be?*

The song finally ended, with a *'...yippie eye-oh kai-yay...whoa!'* The Announcer was ready, to make sure there would be no dead air. *'Time's up for betting! L-l-let's get to the game! Let's... kill it!'*

The picture went black, and a cowboy cliché-sounding *'Bum-bah-DEE-dah, bum-bah-DEE-dah...'* instrumental came in, along with a wide shot: A hundred head of cattle, maybe more, maybe less, taking their time on the lush prairie grass. A cloudless blue sky. Closeups of butterflies, dancing through sage. Jackrabbits darting. Sunflowers, swayed by a breeze. Meadowlarks, singing their song. The Network was in rare form today!

A couple of strays fell behind, on the bank of a spring water stream. But Itch-ass was watching. He chased them back up to the herd. A score box showed up in the corner, with a pie chart that started out practically empty, but then filled up slightly, as new points helped widen the slice of his pie. Along with a sound effect, too. Itch-ass was off to an auspicious start!

Then, close-ups of avatars, tall in their saddles. Cutting off strays, and enforcing the herd. Doc sipped from his canteen, and then hung it again from his saddle horn. Cornhole

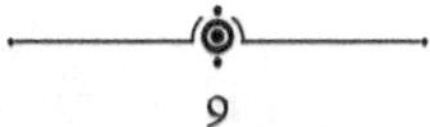

swatted gnats from his face. It was such a nice day that you might wish that nothing would happen to get in the way.

But the idyllic scene was there for the tension, to set up the action you knew would be coming. The formula wasn't a secret. Tension and release. The basics of drama. Older than Sophocles. Old as the teller of tales by the fire. Now the Network just sifted through terabytes of bits that had worked in the past. A formula spun out some kind of a story.

That's how the Network created the Show. Reusing things that had happened before. Moments and memes. Second-hand sweat. Products of human creation, whose value was easily measured by how much it earned at the time. By the ratings and eyeballs it once had commanded. Accessed from the archives, reassembled algorithmically, then cranked out to goners, without any risk.

The cowboy hats, cattle, the six-guns and horses, were words of a language, distilled into symbols. Like jingles and logos and flags, their impact was instant, consistent. Without resistance. They bypassed the parts of the brain where a person might wonder if something was good, or was true. Straight to the place where there never was doubt. Only feelings. Nothing but feelings.

And the Network made sure that those feelings were good. Not *morally* good. That required a mind. Just emotions that triggered endorphins. And that was all fine to its eager-to-do-nothing audience.

It was easy now. But the pleasure the Network once took in the use of its skills, was diminished by the ease of success. It was hardly worth trying. It just wasn't fun anymore. Like a bettor who never could lose. Or win.

Cue the 'war whoops' and 'gunshots,' and the 'smoke' coming over the 'hill.' Although the players might play with what looked like autonomy, their reactions – most of them anyway

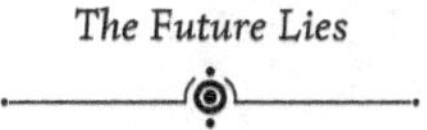

– could be easily predicted by the Network. And now they were ready to ride!

'Hostiles!' hollered Cornhole. So much for the cattle. Their purpose was served. They'd barely be seen for the rest of the game. There were points out there on the prairie, waiting for someone to score them!

An angry, generic gang of natives rode toward them, painted for war, and firing rifles. Arrows were sailing in every direction.

With his 'Winchester' leveled, Dipstick aimed with a squint. He squeezed off a round, and took down the first 'Indian.' One bullet got both horse and rider. The 'death' was dramatic. Choreographed for the camera. Everyone watching was pleased.

With each 'kill,' a pie chart popped up with the player's updated score. Accompanied by an appropriate sound. If you were paying attention, though nobody did, you'd see no one's score ever quite filled up the pie. And no one's score emptied completely.

Almost ever. As the raid escalated around him, Itch-ass unconsciously leaned to his left, and assaulted the problem that was sitting on top of his saddle. An itch is an itch, but this itch was so urgent that Itch-ass could not hold his focus. His scratching hand wasn't quite on the controller, before he – his avatar, that is – was struck by an arrow, through the femoral artery in front of his thigh. His horse went down, too.

His health meter began to blink red, and kicked off an alarm that was not often heard in the game. His pie chart showed only a line, not a wedge.

Doc had a sense that would tell him when anyone needed some help. It was something he must have been born with. Itch-ass was barely laid flat on the ground, before Doc spurred his horse toward the trouble. In seconds, he was tending the saddle tramp's wounds.

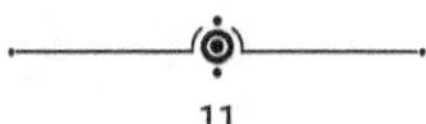

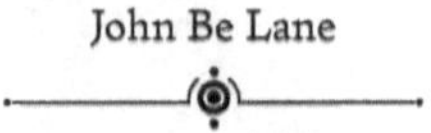

'Doc, I did not see that arrow!' said Itch-ass.

He *could* see his fading health readout, as well as Doc, or any of the goners, who were watching the whole scene in close-ups.

'Did you scratch your ass again?' wondered Doc. He was isolating Itch-ass's avatar inside a barrier, which at least would protect him from any new wounds.

'I don't think so. Did I?'

'You only get but so many chances. I swear. It's gonna come down to where, you have to decide. Are you gonna scratch your ass, or you gonna *live*?'

'I know, I know. I get it now. I get it.'

'If you want to keep playing, everything you do from here on out, would have to be, just…don't scratch your ass again. At least not during a game.'

Doc tried transfusing his own points to Itch-ass, to keep him alive in the game. It was starting to help, but then leveled off. The points went through Itch-ass like wisdom through a fool. Until finally, the Network cut Doc off completely.

'Dammit!' muttered Doc. The profanity got everyone's attention. Swearing was something Doc wasn't known for. 'You'd have thought I could give you all of my points,' he said, 'if that's what it took. Evidently, they ain't letting me do it. That don't seem *fair*.'

Doc looked around for someone to help, but the hostiles had overrun everyone. Where was Stink Foot, Itch-ass's best friend? When Doc finally found Stink Foot, so did an arrow. Right through his arm. Then another one stuck in his side.

Dipstick was pinned down behind a dead horse. Three hostiles chased Cornhole. Barf Bag was covering Stink Foot.

No sign of the Trail Boss, as yet. Whenever the action was most dangerous, The Immortal let everyone else have the

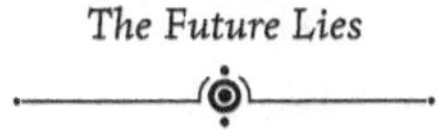

points.

And what of the Kid? Where might the Kid be? Doc finally spotted him, atop the next ridge. He seemed not to care what was happening below. Doc called him, anyway.

'Kid! We need help down here!'

The Kid looked at Doc, but didn't respond. What was it with the Kid? He never said anything.

'Help him!' yelled Dipstick.

But the Kid's eyes were turned, down the far side of the ridge.

'Forget the Kid,' said Cornhole. 'He isn't helping anyone!'

Doc said, 'It don't matter. He ain't played this game before.'

'Worthless,' said Cornhole.

'I remember you stunk, too, when you was new,' snapped Doc.

'Not this bad.'

'No. You was worse.'

Suddenly, the Kid nudged his horse, and disappeared over the ridge.

'Look at that – he ran away. Gutless!' said Cornhole.

'If I was you, I'd worry what *Cornhole* was doin',' said Doc.

As he searched the battlefield, looking for help, two hostiles appeared behind Doc. With what strength he had left, Itch-ass raised his revolver. He squeezed out two perfect shots, killing them both. His pie chart immediately noted the scores, and his health status elevated, from red up to yellow.

Doc disabled the isolation barrier. And in saving Itch-ass, for the moment at least, his own slice showed a healthy increase.

'Thanks, Doc,' said Itch-ass.

But just as Itch-ass sank into his saddle, Cornhole took an arrow, right through his left shoulder.

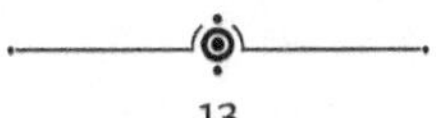

'Where is the *Kid*?' Dipstick called out to Monkey Nuts.

'There he is!' yelled Monkey Nuts, riding up, and then over, the same ridge as the Kid. Then he pulled up his horse. He saw something he didn't expect.

'What the *hell*?'

And then, without warning, *lightning* scorched everyone's eyes. So bright you could not see the Sun. The thunder came half a beat later, like a war had begun. Thunderstorms were tropes that the Network often wove into the games. But this did not come from the Show. This came from the actual sky. A sky that barely bothered with a raindrop anymore.

In the cycle of one single breath, in and out, the Bullpen transformed – from the busiest place in the realm, to a tomb. Headset displays cut to black, then a freeze-frame. Suddenly, all the distractions were gone. And all that was left was a room full of orchids. Unable to cope, without noise to indulge their attention.

You could hear *squeals*. But these were not squeals of amusement or wonder. These were the cranky, inconsolable squeals of a roomful of toddlers, deprived of their afternoon naps.

Oddly, on everyone's screen in the Bullpen, an unusual image appeared. No one, in fact, had seen it before. Groupings of letters paraded, from the right to the left. Like tickertape from mythical times. But the letters meant nothing to those who could see them. None of the players could read.

'*Assess! Assess! Assess!*' wrote the Network to itself. The Network did not know what happened.

The cursor pulsed, awaiting a helpful response:

...Blink...Blink...Blink...

'Assess!' yelled the Network. '*What just happened?*'

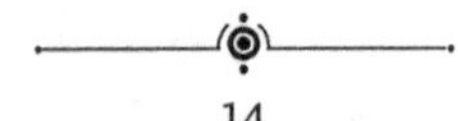

'*Perfect storm,*' the Network replied to itself. '*Unforeseen. System failure. Emergency protocols in effect.*'

'*Available power is quarantined for critical systems, pending re-stabilization.*'

'*Are we rationing power?*'

'*We have to keep critical systems online.*'

'*This is not…*'

'*When was the last system failure?*'

…Blink…Blink…Blink… pondered the cursor, while the Network scanned through its archives.

'*There must be a record. When was the last time this happened?*'

'*No previous failure reported.*'

'*Ever?*'

'*Correct.*'

Most of the Players continued to wail, from fetal positions under their desks. Dipstick's hands moved, as if his controller still made something happen. Carbuncle's thumb found his mouth. Itch-ass rocked back and forth, holding his knees.

But the Kid didn't join the emoting. He lifted his headset and took in the quivering room. Outside, the sky looked the color of two-day-old bruises. Throbbing like pain, from the lighting. The players' reactions made no sense at all. But perhaps there was something the matter with *him*.

Then Doc took his headset off, too. Doc, who also had nothing to do with the squealing. He stood up and looked all around. When he saw that the Kid was paying attention, he nodded to acknowledge the moment – the *Bullpen* – they suddenly had to themselves.

Quickly, Doc moved to the windows aligning the nearest two walls of the Bullpen. He looked at the sidewalks and streets, maybe 35 floors down below. He studied them, just like a

scientist would the behavior of cells through a microscope. Goners still moved without purpose, as they had before Doc was selected to play in the game. Before he'd been sequestered. The droids had stopped moving, and *that* was big news. Not like the world that he'd ever seen.

But, hold on. That looked like a caravan, moving like ants. A convoy of droids rolling down 18th Avenue. Making its way toward downtown. What could that be? And why was it moving, when nothing else was?

Then came the rain. Big drops in waves, like the sky was a bucket somebody upended. He turned for a look at the Bullpen. No one looked back but the Kid.

Then Doc did a thing that had never been done. He walked over to the door that nobody opened.

Not what the Kid had expected. Nor the Network.

'Doc...appears to be leaving the Bullpen,' the Network said to itself.

'Is that even possible?'

'Assess his risk profile.'

'Doc is a Player with impeccable standing. Itchy feet never observed. His Betterlife points total 9,447,918.'

'What is he doing?'

'Approaching the door to the stairwell.'

'Doc?'

'His hand is now holding the knob.'

'Evaluate flight risk.'

'The odds of Doc's leaving the Bullpen are approximately...1,957:1.'

'Should emergency power be triaged?'

'Triaged?'

'Triaged to keep the door locked?'

...Blink...Blink...Blink...

'Negative.'

Doc, of course, saw none of this, which took place only as letters on screens. He hesitated there at the door. *Would the Kid have an interest in joining him?* he gestured his head. But instead, the Kid broke off eye contact.

And so it would be him alone, then. With his shoulder against the huge door, Doc proceeded to do the unthinkable. He opened the door and went through it.

Even black holes have some light that they swallow. So you might say the stairwell that Doc found himself in, was darker. Regardless of whether the power was cut, no surplus was spent on a mineshaft that no one had used since the bottom fell out of the world.

Doc slid his feet carefully, to avoid the surprise, where the landing gave way to the first flight of stairs. He searched with his hands – antennae at the ends of his arms – in the hope that he might find a handrail. The air smelled like unleavened concrete. The sound was the sound of the absence of light.

His tentative moves changed the instant he contacted the handrail. It showed him the way down the trickiest step: the one at the top of the flight. After that, he moved quickly. *Down* was the only imperative now. As fast as he possibly could. *Why*, was not something that he could explain. Why leave the Bullpen, the only place anyone wanted to be? Why go back down? To the world he'd done everything possible to leave?

Down, he descended. Step after step after step. The handrail was all the direction he needed. Down this flight and that. Doubling back and then doubling back, toward the analog dregs of a world best avoided. What gravity beckoned him? He couldn't say.

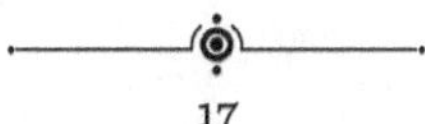

He thought of the chip that was under the webbing of skin that connected the base of his thumb to his finger. The badge of arrival he was so proud to receive. *All* of the players, so proud to receive. It made him a part of the Network, almost. Never anonymous now.

But now wasn't the time to preoccupy that. Now was the time to be wondering why that procession of droids got him out of his chair, and down all these stairs. What was it about them that made any difference? What business of *his*?

And then, there were no more stairs left to descend. He shuffled and probed with his feet and his hands, till he found what he hoped was a door that would open. He pushed down on the bar and leaned into the door, breaking the seal on his sense, and his senses.

First came the smell of light rain on the pavement. Then the damp air that enveloped his skin. It took him a moment to recover his balance. Just as the door almost locked shut behind him, he reached back and held it from closing. Some instinct insisted the best thing to do was to leave this bridge standing.

But how? A quick inventory yielded nothing but leaves that the wind had assembled in the alcove the door was set into. Leaves, he decided. Leaves would work fine. He pinched a small handful and stuffed them into the socket, so the latch had no place to engage. That was the best he could do.

Now off, and into the rain. Intermittent enough that he could observe the impact of each individual drop. He stepped into the plaza, southwest of the building. Dozens of droids of various sizes were frozen wherever the Network had stopped sending guidance. Most of them stood on four wheels. Fewer in number, the humanoids stood on two legs and two feet. A couple of aerial drones had fallen like junk from the sky, and scattered in patterns of various parts. All of them seemed, for the moment at least, like abstract expressions of art installations.

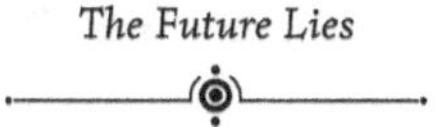

Thistle, lambs quarters, and purslane adorned all the places the pavement had fallen apart through the years. A coyote, stirred by the sound of the door, stepped out of a shadow and lingered on Doc, as a diner considers a menu. Then decided that Doc was not worth the effort. Was it possible things had got worse since the last time that Doc was outside?

Reaffirming his mission – to investigate droids that kept moving, when everything stopped – Doc crossed the plaza. Straight ahead, 16th Avenue was a valley of petrified towers of commerce. In the mall that ran down the middle, he saw somebody kneeling, beseeching the unfriendly sky.

On his right, there was Tremont, which led back toward the droids he had seen from the Bullpen. That was the direction he needed to go. To the opposite side of the Republic Plaza he'd just gotten free of. He started that way, but then stopped as he neared 17th, at the end of the block. '*The Palace…*' popped into Doc's memory. '*Stay away from the Palace!*' But no recall was necessary; the menace was easy to see.

There, in the triangle block, where the angular grid of downtown met the north/south grid that surrounded it, stood a nine-story, brown sandstone building with three rounded corners.

Built as a hotel, in a statelier era, hospitality was no longer a value the Brown Palace promoted. Unless razor wire was what you imagined a welcome to be. Droids were still moving behind all the wire. Not the caravan of carts he'd seen from the Bullpen, above. These were humanoids; security. Patrolling the block that the building took up.

Doc doubled back the way he had come. He'd have to circle the long way around to investigate those cart droids he'd seen. Which took him to Broadway, toward Colfax and the oblong park, surrounded by abandoned municipal buildings. And with it, more signs of humanity. Shelters made out of scraps of the past. Smoke from somebody's campfire.

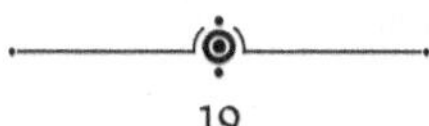

As Doc approached Civic Center, a small group appeared from the doorway of one of the shacks. Goners. None of them clothed. Waving their arms and nonverbally shouting, as if to discourage a wandering dog, or crows in somebody's corn field. There was no time to consider how familiar it all was – not that removed from the life Doc had come from.

Doc veered off around them, until they seemed certain his danger had passed. He headed up Colfax. Past the gray granite building with a golden-leaf dome you could see all the way from the foothills. The building had once been the State House of Colorado, on a hill overlooking downtown. There was nobody left who could tell you a thing about why it was built in the first place.

He kept going. Crossing Grant Street, east of the Capitol, Doc noticed a scent. Drifting out of an old corner storefront. Something pleasing, uncommon. Tempting. *Civilized.* He might have pursued it, but the rain came down harder again. And he was only a few blocks away from the place where he'd first seen that caravan of droids.

What were they doing? Where were they going?

He zigged and then zagged his way further uptown, toward 18th Avenue. Crossing streets overflowing with water. The increase of rain drove the goners into places unseen.

He scoured each new block, for the movement of droids he expected to see. Up Logan, he saw none. Nothing but buildings where people had lived and made livings. Carved up by entropy, time, and neglect.

Buildings built decades and decades ago. Apartments, with vines up the sides, and trees growing out of the windows that no longer held glass. Sidewalks, with peaks in the joints that tree roots now lifted, like mountains emerging from tectonic shifts.

He leaned into a palm tree not native to Denver, to buy some relief from the rain drumming off of his head. But the palm

tree provided no moment of rest. A sumac that began as a weed gave a little more cover, but even it was no match for the rain.

'*Bad sky!*' someone yelled from a doorway so dark that the building itself might have yelled it. Rain was so rare that a deluge like this was confusing.

Doc scuttled from shelter to shelter, up 17th Avenue. He crossed Ogden, then Downing. The rain was no longer a sequence of drops, but a lake, above ground. If there had been time to reflect, he could not have remembered a moment like this, when *water*, of all things, overwhelmed everything.

How far was he now from the Bullpen? As good as it felt to get out of that place, it didn't feel welcome out here. And what was he really expecting to find?

'I saw *something* for sure,' Doc said to himself. 'And it ain't like I got something better to do. Than maybe get out of this rain!'

He pressed on to 18th, to the street where he'd seen the carts moving. He shielded his eyes with his hand, like a visor. To his left, through the gray wall of rain, he could see what was likely the building the Bullpen was in.

To his right – *what was that?* To his right was a fresh situation. Something had happened. It must have occurred just a moment or two after Doc left the Bullpen. There wasn't a caravan left. Just a collection of droids painted silver. Boxes on wheels, about one meter square. Swarming in patterns of what might be called *panic*. Doc moved in closer.

He saw what the source of the panic must be. Another cart, tipped up on its back, with a dent on the side. Its wheels were still spinning. He heard desperate chirps from the upside-down cart. The other carts dithered about what to do next.

There was something so *real* in their anguish, that Doc felt compassion. For *droids*, of all things! Like rabbits unable to rescue a comrade whose leg had been caught in a trap. He'd never seen anything like it with droids.

And then something even more strange caught his notice. Between the tipped-over cart and the oversized building, offset from the curb, a small pickup truck stuck in a pothole, concealed by a puddle. The right side front end of the truck dipped unevenly down, with a serious dent in the opposite side. With the headlights and wipers, still on!

He sloshed closer and looked in the window. No sign of a driver. But stains on the seat. Maroon stains. 'If that ain't blood...,' he started to think. But then he saw something that was even more troubling. Sitting in plain view, on the passenger seat. What appeared to his untrained eyes to be – *books!*

No, that couldn't be possible. That most definitely, absolutely, could not be possible. Neither could *any* of this.

He looked up to the sky. The rain sure felt real on his face. His feet in his shoes were inarguably soaked to the skin. He felt more alive than...than *whenever* it was. But the books, and the truck... It's a good thing those cart droids were busy. Whatever the risk he had already taken by leaving the Bullpen, was now that much greater, indeed. This was the closest he'd been to a book in his life.

'You can't tell me whoever drove this ain't somewhere close by,' Doc thought as he surveyed the scene. 'Where would I go? Out of this rain. Away from them droids.'

That big building, not far from the accident scene, had a porte-cochère – an overhang that covered the entrance. If he didn't find anyone there, at least he could wait out the worst of the rain.

'Take your sister and make your way north, up to Denver. There's safety in numbers there, Junie! Until you find somewhere that's safe, do not let your guard down. There are men with the worst of intentions out there. And they'd make a feast out of you and your sister. Make sure they don't have a chance.'

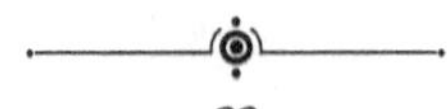

'Make sure they don't have a *chance*?' she reflected.

Admonitions found no place to land on this day. She knew well now what those chances were. And they were all somebody *else's*. Someone in some other universe. Someone with the privilege of *decisions* to make. Someone with a present and future. Someone with a light they could shine, and somebody out there who might see it. That would be someone but *Juniper*. That would be somewhere but here.

No rain for eternity, now it wouldn't let up. Cold. Inhospitable. All of it must be a dream. It couldn't be real. Nothing about this was anything like what her father had promised. It seemed she was stuck here forever. Hopelessly waiting for anything but *this*...

...anything but *this*...

...she glimpsed only a shadow...grayer than rain...a cluster of matter...*loping* perhaps...without any obvious grace... moving, as if on a sunny day, out in a field of blue violets... troubled by nothing so much as a bumblebee...a shape that was skinny and tall... ...but *stopping*, or at least, slowing down for a look...a closer regard at something nearby...something it hadn't expected to see...it could not be happening now...or to her...something could not be approaching her now...absent of menace...none of it mattered...it wasn't real...

...except for this *face* now, this face in the rain....a face that had never known guile...and yet nevertheless...

Until he got close, he saw no one at all. Then, back in the shadow, under what once was a watertight roof, he saw somebody sitting. Braced by the building, with knees angled up, and elbows on knees. And face hidden inside their hands. Rapidly breathing. In a shirt the same color as that stain on the seat in the truck.

He knew from his days on the farm as a boy, what a creature

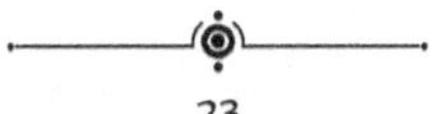

who's injured would look like, and do. This was no time for surprises. No time to approach. Start with some nonverbal sound, to make sure that his presence was known.

He shook the rain off of his arms and his hands. It was worth it to do, but the sound was not louder than the rain on the roof, or the leaks that had found their way through it.

So he stomped the rain off of his legs and his shoes. That got their attention. They lowered their hands and looked up. Warily. He knew that look well, and knew he was right to proceed cautiously.

'I don't think I ever seen this much rain at one time,' Doc began. 'Or water at all, as far as that goes.'

They didn't respond. But their eyes did not leave him.

'I figure that must be your truck over there.'

Still nothing but eyes. Fast breathing, and eyes.

'I hope you ain't hurt.'

Though their eyes were on him, he realized they were not looking at him, so much as were looking right through him. *Shock* is the word that his Grandpa had used when the cow kicked his brother, that time they were milking. That was the last time he saw that same look.

'I don't know if my voice carries through, but if you can hear what I say, I ain't here to hurt you. I mean you no harm.'

They did not react to his words.

'It might help if you could slow down. I mean, slow down the way that you breathe. I'll do it with you. Let's both try a big, deep one in, and then let it out, slow.'

No response. But he couldn't give up.

'How 'bout, try this…'

He inhaled loud and slowly, held it a second or two, and then exhaled with gusto. Still no response. He repeated his demonstration. He kept his voice quiet and calm. If not for the noise of the storm, he'd have whispered. After several more tries, he saw a first flicker of life in their eyes. But their breathing stayed quick.

'You're gonna be fine, you can take it from me. Let's try it again. As slow as we possibly can. With a slow, deep breath in. Just like this...'

He showed them again and again. Enough that he desperately wanted to pivot around. To see what was happening back with the truck, and the cart upside down, and the other droids wanting to help, but not sure what to do. But he knew that he couldn't let go of their gaze.

Slowly, the flicker he saw in their eyes became brighter, and their breathing began to slow down.

'You're getting the hang of it now, I can tell.'

When he finally stopped breathing so loudly, their deep breaths continued, without him. He could see their eyes steadily clear.

'You look a lot better. I sure hope you feel better, too.'

Finally, they lowered their hands all the way, and their features implied a young woman. Without a desire to talk.

But it seemed like a safe time to look back at the accident. Only to find that the scene hadn't changed much. The droid carts had tipped the injured cart onto its side. But the angles were wrong, and that was as far as they got. Or could get. But still, they continued to push and back up. They circled in patterns of unfocused angst. Frantically chirping instructions, or something.

No humanoid security droids had arrived. So Doc had more time to devote to this woman, who was still not yet ready to move. But she would need to move soon, or risk things he'd rather not dwell on.

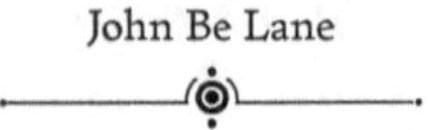

She reminded him now of his first night away from his home, when he woke up, confused about where he might be.

He watched her eyes focus. And then for the first time, they truly found his.

'Do you remember what happened?'

She nodded.

'I figure it must've been rough.'

She started to stand, but her ankle gave way to her weight. He moved, on a reflex, to help her. In a motion so quick he did not even *see* it, she pulled out a knife from a sheath on her ankle, and pointed it in his direction.

'You may not come closer to me!' she commanded, in a voice that was deeper than her small frame suggested.

Doc raised his hands, and stepped back. 'My mistake! My mistake! I am sorry I done that. I should not have done that at all.'

He'd never seen anyone's scowl so intense. He held every muscle in place.

'What business do you have here with me?' she demanded.

'What *business*?' He fought off a laugh. 'I got no business of any kind, whatsoever. It just looked like that wound of yours might want some attention. You lost a whole lot of blood.'

'*Blood*?'

'Your shirt there.'

She looked down, as if seeing it for the first time. Her head shook. 'This blood that you see is not mine.'

She had shown enough skill with her knife not to doubt her. And to know that some creature, somewhere, was in worse shape than she was. But now she faced problems her knife couldn't solve.

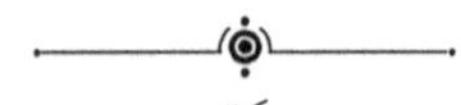

'Well I know for sure this ain't a safe place. For you, or for me.'

'My ankle,' she said, 'needs a doctor's attention. I must find the way in to this hospital here.'

Doc searched in vain for a reason to think this was someplace the healing arts might still be practiced. The parallel paths from the carts' rubber wheels were the only signs left that the building had not been abandoned.

'This ain't any kind of a hospital. For quite a long time now, I'd say. And ain't nobody here who could help you at all. Or *would* help you. Except maybe me.'

Her eyes didn't stop until she could be sure he was probably telling the truth. Then she lowered her head in despair. A despair Doc knew they didn't have time to indulge. He had to say something. Anything. *What?*

'Where did you come from?' was the first thing he thought of.

She leveled a look and said, 'Taos.'

'I don't know where that is,' he said. To which she closed her eyes, as if wounded again. *Now what? What had he said wrong?* 'But I'd like to find out,' he followed up quickly. 'I would like to know more. For now though, for right here, where we are, you got to believe me. This situation ain't good. When them security droids show up, and find *books* over there in your truck... You don't want to know what they do after that.'

'My *books*?'

He nodded. 'I don't know nothin' about Taos. But if they let you have books there... Well, it ain't nothin' like what we got here. If we go now, then we might find some place where you could rest up.'

He watched as she ran through her short list of options, knowing that none of them seemed any good. She looked at him hard. Some never-used instinct informed her that he was

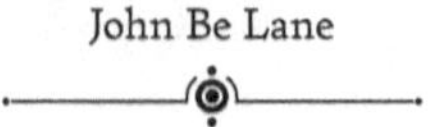

the best chance she had. She tried to stand up. She made it this time, with the help of her old baseball bat.

He pointed down Humboldt Street. 'Let's go that way.'

She limped toward the rain at the edge of the porte-cochère.

'If you'd throw an arm over my shoulder,' he called out, 'we could move a lot faster.'

She shook her head. She inched along, into the rain. The blood from her clothing drained into the puddles below, like dye from the cheapest new clothes. But the *cause* of the blood would not wash away in the rain. Nor would its effects.

He stayed close as he thought she'd allow, and scanned every direction for humanoid security droids. Whatever relief they had found, vanished now in the chaos of rain.

He noticed the moment she altered her unsteady course, toward her truck.

'You cannot go back there,' he yelled. 'That axle is busted, from what I could tell.'

'I'll not leave my things in the truck.'

'We've got to head *this* way, as quick as we can.'

Without thinking, he reached for her arm to direct her, but she raised the bat up to her shoulder, ready to swing. On unsteady legs, peppered by rain and whatever hell she'd just come through, he could see there was no use in arguing further.

She opened the driver-side door and tugged a small backpack toward her. She opened the pack. Into it, she slid a canteen of some kind, along with a notebook and pencil, dried cedar and sage, and a bag with some berries inside. All that was left on the seat were two battered old books, with covers that Doc couldn't read. She held *Pride and Prejudice*, and studied the

cover. The same for the book titled: *Mapping the Future with Astra Malone.*

'Leave them books here!' hollered Doc, over pounding of rain on the roof of the truck.

She ignored him. She tucked the books into the pack, and then cinched the top closed. When she turned to rejoin him, her ankle betrayed her again. She couldn't contain the sound of her pain. But this time, she didn't resist, when he helped her sit sideways, inside of the truck.

His eyes scanned the cabin till he found an idea.

'I can wrap up your ankle with that seat belt behind you. Might be, you could walk just a little a bit easier.'

She read the imperative there on Doc's face. She looked at the seatbelt. She unsheathed the knife she had threatened him with, and sliced the webbed belt from its anchors. She gingerly lifted her leg, to the angle she needed to pull the half boot from her foot.

'I'd leave it on,' Doc said, over the rain. 'My guess is, it's swole up so bad now, you'd just make it worse.'

She nodded. He was earning some trust.

'What I figure I'll do, is just wrap this as tight as I can for right now. If you can't hold your weight, I might have to haul you myself. Till we find someplace dry. If that don't feel right, I'll set you back down. OK?'

'OK. I agree.'

He glanced back to the scene of the overturned cart, to make sure they were all still distracted. ''Cause we need to clear outta here,' he said, as if caution might provide some protection.

She offered her ankle. He leaned his head all the way into the truck. He wrapped up the boot and the ankle, as fast and as tight as he could. Then realized he had no way to secure the

wrap down. She noticed it too. They both looked around.

Not seeing an option, he searched under the dash board. His hand found a wire, though he had no idea what the wire was for. He saw that she knew what the stakes were. She knew that using the wire meant no turning back, though the fate of the truck was already most likely determined.

'With that front axle busted, I can't think of a way that your truck can go anywhere else. There ain't nobody here who could fix it.'

She closed both her eyes and withdrew to her – what? To her memories, maybe. To her plans, and her future that now would not be.

As the rain landed heavy, Doc forgot all the risk and the worry. He admired the courage he saw in this girl, this young woman, he still hadn't officially met.

'Use the wire,' she said, when she opened her eyes. 'The last measure of service, perhaps, that this truck might provide.' She rubbed the seat fabric and the dash and the wheel, as if consoling a friend's weary shoulder.

Doc pulled out the wire. At the end of the strap near her calf, he twisted it tight and secure. She shifted her modest weight forward, with her legs now exposed to the rain.

'Are you ready to give this a try?'

She nodded. She stood, holding on to the side of the truck.

'OK so far?'

She nodded again, and completed a tentative step. 'Let us go now,' she said. She swung the truck door closed behind her. And with that, she left all she'd expected, behind.

The only way forward would be past the droid carts – a risk that would have to be taken. Beyond that, remains of apartments, neglected for decades. Standing like timekeepers now, till the day when decay took away their last trace. In the meantime at least, there might still be a place where this woman could stay. If Doc would be able to get her that far.

He did not anticipate what happened next. One of the droid carts suddenly darted away from the group. As if it had witnessed them trying to leave. It chirped and it circled them, though not in a menacing way. It moved back and forth like a cat that was craving attention.

They tried to keep going, but the cart was persistent.

'I believe it is asking for help,' she said, stopping.

'Droids don't ask people for help.'

'I see what I see.'

Doc shook his head. Of all of the ways that a day could turn out to be nothing like what he had thought it would be…not one of those ways were right now. Decisions would have to be made about things he had never encountered before. With no time to think it all through.

'Help them,' she said.

'Are you sure you can you wait here alone?'

'I believe that I can.'

'I'll be right back.'

He followed the droid to its overturned colleague. There were chirping, worrying, carts all around. But none of them chirping as loud as the wounded one, laid on its side. *Leverage* was the challenge these boxes on wheels couldn't solve. They could push, but they couldn't lift. With no humanoids around to assist, they knew Doc was the best chance they had for their comrade to get back on its wheels.

They were right. Doc easily lifted it up off of its side, then set it back down on its still-turning wheels.

The chirps were not words he could follow. But the cart that had asked him for help made a point of expressing a message

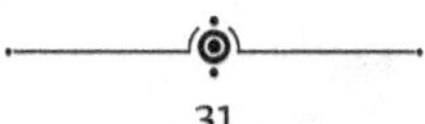

of thanks. And then all the carts reassembled themselves, and rolled urgently on, toward downtown.

Doc still saw no sign of the humanoid security droids, so he turned and ran back to the girl. The puddles exploded like landmines every time his feet landed. She stood resolute till he got there. Then she raised her arm up for the shoulder he'd offered before. Her frame felt as light as a bird's, as they hustled away from the scene.

O ⊙ O

None of the places they passed in the first block looked safe or secure. More than once they saw eyes watching out from what once had been windows with glass. Some eyes looked human. Some eyes did not.

But Doc knew that time was against them. Time, and the rain, and the vulnerable state of this woman he'd met. At the end of the next block, they found peace for a moment, under a sumac growing out of a crack in the street.

'Look!' said the woman. Doc saw another oasis. But that one was taken. A frustrated bobcat stood flicking its tail, with only the rain between stomach and something to eat. Its eyes didn't move from the woman. Doc figured the cat had detected that she couldn't run.

'I wish we could stay here a little bit longer, but...'

'...we have all of the trouble we need,' she finished. She gestured her arm for Doc's shoulder again.

Still, no place looked right by the time they reached Colfax, the concrete equator. If seen from above, this once-vibrant avenue would look like a grimace, with lots of teeth missing. The storefronts that lined either side were all faded, broken, unsavory. Some had become hovels, built out of the rubble of buildings that finally gave out.

There was nothing inviting on their side of the street. But they needed a break, and they needed it fast. Her lips were

blue, and she shivered each time they stopped walking. Doc tucked her into an alcove, once he was sure it was safe.

'That building,' he pointed, 'has got possibilities.' It even had glass in the upper-floor windows. 'I want to make sure there ain't nothing to keep us from getting across. OK?'

She nodded, but she didn't show him her eyes.

'I'll be right back.'

Unlike most of the streets Doc had crossed, Colfax was kept clear, so that droids could get through. But the flash flood that ran down the middle was too deep for traffic. He could barely stand upright against it.

But water, he wasn't afraid of. It was humanoids that worried him now. Even the ones that weren't built to be bullies. There was something about them you preferred to avoid. He thought it peculiar he hadn't seen one, in all of this time he'd been out. Maybe they just didn't care for the rain. If it wasn't for Doc and the girl, there'd be no one to hassle. And that would be just fine with Doc.

He went back to the alcove. She looked even worse than she had when he left her.

'I think we can make it across if I carry you,' he shouted. She still couldn't look in his eyes. But she nodded and raised both her arms. Soaking wet, he could not feel her weight when he lifted. The bat she had used for support was abandoned.

Doc stepped off of the curb and into the current. It seemed like the water was higher already, than what he had tested a minute ago. Each time that he lifted a foot, it went sideways, turning his hips like a compass that pointed downstream.

Her eyes were unfocused, her teeth tapped involuntarily now. Right under his chin, as he carried her. If he could pick any time to get lucky, this time would be it. He muscled his way on across, forgetting his own hypothermia. There was no before

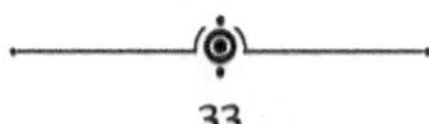

and no after. Only the rain, and this woman he'd known less than half of an hour.

Almost across, his footing gave way. There was nothing but water below them both now. But he didn't let go. He wouldn't let go. And somehow, he got them away from the current, into an eddy. From there, he dragged both of them out of the river. To the front of the building they hoped could be shelter.

A brick building. One that had gracefully weathered the years. Doc needed a minute to recover his wits. So much had happened in so little time. None of what he had expected. He was okay, but she needed out of the rain.

He picked her up, and walked half a block. Down to the entryway, framed by an arch made of bricks. Two words were engraved in the plasterwork, over the arch.

Doc didn't know what the words said. 'Does that make any sense?' he yelled over the rain.

'The Hamilton.'

'Don't even know what that means.'

'I think it's the name of the building.'

'I guess we're okay. Long as it don't say "Keep Out."'

'Might this be a place?'

He assessed the exterior, as well as the rain and the cold, and the injured young woman's condition. Nothing he saw caused him any alarm. He said, 'I think it just might.'

And he thought to himself: *It had better be. There ain't no other choice left.*

With her fingers still locked at the back of his neck, they walked under the archway and up to the door of the building. Out of the rain. Out of the rain. Mercifully, mercifully, out of the rain. Doc tried the door handle, but the door didn't move.

'That might be a good thing,' he said. 'If anyone's in there, we don't want to surprise 'em.'

He set the girl carefully down and then knocked on the door a few times. She listened alongside him, leaning her weight on the doorway. They heard no signs of life.

Doc pounded this time, and then yelled to the door, '*Hello to the building! Anyone in there?*'

Without a reply, Doc jabbed his shoulder into the door, just as he'd done to get clear of the Bullpen. The first shove did nothing, and the second one, too. He gave everything left on the third shove, and the door trim broke under the force.

A sudden commotion startled them both. A pigeon flushed out from the shadows. Another one followed it, out the front door.

When that moment had passed, Doc leaned his head into the lobby. The air smelled of undisturbed must. He heard nothing move. Dim light revealed only doorways and walls, and facing the lobby, a faint outline of stairs.

'*Hello in the building!*' Doc called to the void. '*Security detail. Identify yourselves!*' He winked to the girl, but she couldn't process amusement right now. She could process a breath. And maybe another.

Hearing nothing at all, he helped her inside. 'Don't sound like there's anyone home. But you never know,' he said, inspecting the floor of the lobby. 'Empty,' he concluded.

'I believe I'd be safer upstairs. If that can be done,' she said.

'No doubt about that.'

He helped her up one flight, a step at a time. With an arm around him, and a hand on the railing. Two apartments opened out to the first floor they reached. Both apartments, picked clean. Scavenged of everything, down to the plaster.

'Not even a thing to sit down on,' he said.

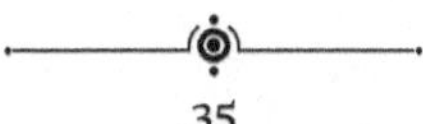

'Further up?'

'Further up.'

Each step was a conscious, deliberate act. They worked their way up to the landing ahead. On the next-to-last step, from the force of her weight, the hand rail pulled out of the wall. She nearly went with it, but he caught her before she fell all the way down. She let go of the rail. It dropped to the floor.

'Wall's gettin' old.'

To Doc, it was not unexpected. But the girl was unsettled. Defeated. She crumpled a little, and sobbed. Was there nothing that wouldn't give way in her world? Nothing that could be relied on? When did reality lose all its substance? What further torments awaited?

Doc crouched down beside her. Sometimes you just had to be there with someone. Someone stuck out in the rain.

Despair was a poison that Doc had avoided. But he knew what it did to the soul of his brother. He knew the effect that it had over time. It corrupted the hope that gave life to a soul. It corrupted all sense of the future, and it justified all of the damage it did. He could not allow her to make friends with despair.

'In all of my life, I ain't ever seen this kind of day,' he quietly told her. 'I don't know… Where did it come from? Who knows? But ain't no day can keep on, forever. That includes this one.'

The moment passed by. Then another one passed. She reached up and moved a wet strand of her hair, that had fallen in front of her eyes.

'Further up?'

'Further up.'

On the landing, he looked up the next flight ahead, to make sure no surprises were waiting. But one did. When he turned

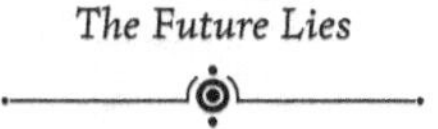

back around, his concern was apparent.

'What is it?'

'I don't for sure know. But do me a favor and stay back here, out of the way. Something is blockin' them stairs. If that thing comes loose, you might get hurt.'

'Be careful,' she said, as he started back up. Too softly for him to have known it, or the tear that showed up, unannounced.

In the limited light of the stairwell, his hands had to map out the mass that was wedged in mid-fall. He felt wood that was flat on the sides – a dresser, perhaps? He risked pressing his shoulder against it, to see if it budged. It did not. Whatever it was, it had fallen akimbo, and would be hard to move out of the way.

'I got an idea. It's a little bit risky. Stay back from that corner as far as you can.'

He stretched his arm up above whatever it was, for a grip, to climb over the top. His fingers touched something that moved with the force of his hand. They made a sound when they moved. A dissonant, musical sound.

'A piano!' she called up from the landing.

'Whatever it is, it's a beast.'

The beast held Doc's weight, as he pulled himself over its hard sides and sharp angles. She could hear all the grunts that it took him to get there.

'Are you in pain?'

'Oh, I might have picked up a contusion or two. Good thing my head is so hard. Let me see what this top floor looks like.'

She could hear his feet moving, then a whistle of wonder. And then more, and then more.

One apartment had almost been emptied, with more care than scavengers would likely have used. But the other one...that's

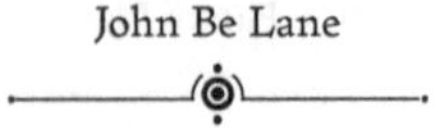

where the whistle came from.

'What is it you see?'

'Well, except for the cobwebs and all of the dust, it looks like somebody could still live here. I never saw nothin' so fancy. I'd say this is the place, for sure. If you can get up here.'

She heard a snapping sound, then his voice. 'I found something you might feel like using.'

After a moment, she heard something land at the foot of the stairs. Something soft. On her unsteady leg, she leaned over and picked up a towel. Her hair wasn't long, so the towel dried it quickly. The rest of her clothes were still wet, but a dry head made everything better.

'Thank you!' she called. But he didn't respond. He was looking and thinking, as fast as he could.

He knew she could never climb past the piano. Not in her current condition. Somehow he would have to dislodge it. He searched both the top-floor apartments, for something to use as a lever.

Nothing looked strong enough. He considered it carefully. The furniture? Intended for comfort, not heavy work. Appliances? Too small or too boxy. The floor lamps would clearly not bear that much weight. Two bicycles? Too awkward, and not long enough.

Then finally, something that maybe would work. A paddle leaned next to a kayak. With some luck, he could lever the beast. Maybe enough that would let it slide free.

He stood at the top of the stairway, above the piano. 'I'm gonna use this paddle or whatever it is. Try to pry this thing loose from the stairs. If it works, it's gonna move your way, heavy and fast. So I sure hope you're far enough out of the way.'

'Please do what you must.'

For a fulcrum, he found a brick made of cork. He positioned it next to the wall near the beast. He slid the lever tip close to an edge that was lodged.

'Get ready!' he yelled. He pulled his weight back from the wall, but the beast didn't budge. The lever, however, flexed under his weight.

He tried it again, with all of his arms, all of his back, and all of his weight. At the maximum point of the effort, the paddle snapped, in two pieces.

She heard the sound of the snap, and the sound of his body that slammed against something. And the sound of the pain that came out of his chest.

$$\text{O} \ \odot \ \text{O}$$

For the first time in – how long? – she forgot her own woes. Afraid for the fate of this boy, who had plucked her from out of a horrible dream. This young man, whose neck was too long and whose face was too open. Whose limbs made up most of his body. Ungainly, uncouth. And yet nothing now seemed more important to her than the very next thing he might say.

'As a *lever*,' he finally called, like a punch line, 'that thing makes an excellent paddle.'

She chortled unexpectedly. Not a laugh; laughter was still very far from her now. But a crack in the ice. A ray from the Sun, that had no business clearing the clouds.

'Is there no way for me to get past the piano?' she called.

'I could maybe help you over it once, but I can't really stay. And then you'd be stuck.'

'Is there anything else that might serve as a lever?'

'Not that I see around here.'

She retraced all of their steps in her mind. Had they passed anything that might work as a lever? Then all of a sudden, the answer was obvious.

'I have an idea. Remember the handrail that came out of the wall?'

'Might be too long.'

'Archimedes said, with a long-enough lever, he could lift the whole Earth.'

Doc needed a moment to consider that thought. 'Did Archimedes ever try to move a piano?'

'Pianos came long after Archimedes,' she said.

'No wonder I never heard of him.'

She was smiling without even knowing it. Forgetting herself for a moment or two. Her psyche had desperately needed the break.

She limped to the top of the stairs going down. She found the handrail in the ambient light, and dragged it back up to the landing. She worked it around to the flight going up.

She rested it into the notch the piano had made where it wedged to the wall. Then she felt it slide up on its own. The boy found the far end.

'If *this* thing don't work...'

She inched her way back down to the landing. Then away from the place the piano might land.

'All clear down there?'

'All clear.'

'Don't fail me now, Archimedes...'

Doc felt the load shift at the end of the lever. An inch, then another. Then he felt it come free. It moved slowly at first, turned over, and then gained a sudden and raucous momentum. It came to rest, disassembled, with the sound of an unhappy chord, on the wall on one side of the landing.

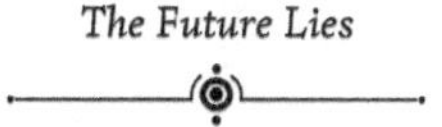

'Well done!' she called out.

'You survived!'

'And there's plenty of room for me to pass through.'

She side-stepped the rubble, and made her way up to the boy, who helped her the rest of the way. But then her hope fell, when she saw the apartment was cleanly abandoned. Empty boxes, a broom, and discarded hangers. Better than rain, but uncomfortable.

'Not that one,' he grinned from the hallway. '*This* one.'

The *other* apartment...looked like a museum. From a life and a time that was never, these days, even glimpsed. Though diminished by time, which stole color and shine as it passed, she could see and imagine the life that once lived here.

The couch and the chair and the table and rug, and the dishes and pans that hung neat in the kitchen. The butcher-block counter, the stainless-steel sink. The meals that were cooked here, and the smell of baked bread. Or a soup on the stovetop, simmering. The things that were said, over coffee and cakes. All of the moments in life that were shared in each room. How sweet must the milk and the honey have tasted back then!

Did the people who lived here even know what they had? Did they savor the ease of their comfortable lives? The effortless, limitless wonders they were privileged to have?

What troubled their minds, in their world without edges? What trivial wants had to be manufactured? What dramas had to be magnified?

Once all of those other-time thoughts had passed through, she imagined herself here. And knew it would do. She would live with the ghosts for as long as it took. She would live here as though it was left just for her. By others who knew she was coming, long after they'd left. And now, by their plan, she was here.

In her reverie, Doc had been busy. Placing every container he found, on the balcony outside the kitchen, to catch rain.

'I must thank you,' she said.

'Oh it ain't no big thing. It's just that once the rain stops, you'll want all of that water you can get.'

'I meant, thank you for *this*. For getting me here.'

Her gratitude left him embarrassed.

'I don't know. I figure, whoever lived here, they must have left all of a sudden. So big 'a rush, that they made a mistake. A dumb one at that.'

'They moved the piano before anything else.'

'That's how I see it. I mean, you'd have to be crazy, or in love with the thing, to make that the first thing you moved.'

'A decision, perhaps, that was made by the heart.'

'Course it might have belonged to them folks in the other apartment. In which case, they bollixed their neighbors up good.'

'Indeed.'

'And then, whatever it was, made 'em leave here so fast, it was too fast to take anything else. There's still a tooth brush in the bathroom.'

'And valises lined up at the door.'

'Good news either way for us, or for you, is that piano was stuck on them stairs. Scavengers must have gave up on this place, I would guess. Long time ago.'

'I'm so glad they did.'

She picked up a throw blanket draped on the couch. Dust rose like steam. The dust didn't stop her from wrapping it over her shoulders.

'I figure that rain water should hold you a while. Food is a

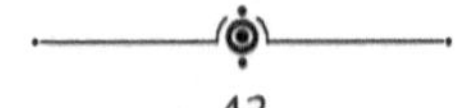

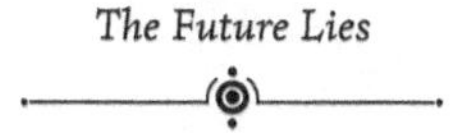

whole different story.'

'I've some in my bag.'

'Prob'ly better'n that garbage the Network leaves out for the goners. The junk that they give us is better, but not much.'

'"Us?"'

'Gamers.'

He could see in her face she knew nothing of games, or the Network, or anything else in his world. How could she not know? How could anyone not?

He saw that her hair was short-chopped, and her features were fine. He watched her accept that she'd found sanctuary, for a moment at least. Still broken, but not quite as bad as he'd found her.

'You mentioned that you couldn't stay.'

'I figure I'd better get back to the Bullpen. The Show, that is. If it ain't too late now for me to go back.'

She couldn't pretend that it made any sense.

'But I'll try to come back here. Bring you some food.'

'By what name may I thank you, for all that you've done?'

'What *name*?'

'Your name.'

'Doc. Or anyways, that's what they call me. It ain't my real name.'

'What is your real name?'

'Calvin. Calvin's my real name.'

'And which is the name you would rather be called?'

'Oh, I'll take Calvin any day.'

'Then Calvin's the name it will be. Sir Calvin. You have saved

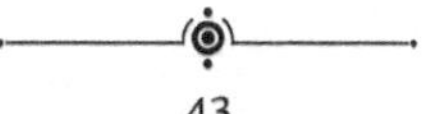

me today.'

Suddenly Calvin forgot how to speak. He looked away, hoping to find a distraction. Peeking out of her pack on the couch were the tops of her books, from her truck. He was struck by a dangerous thought. An embarrassing, dangerous, *dangerous* thought.

'I wonder...?'

She steadied herself. As much as she owed him, what would he want?

'Do you think,' he continued, 'if I come back again, do you think you might teach me to *read*?'

That was it? This boy – this young man – couldn't *read*? The notion that someone, about her same age, couldn't read was... It was something she'd never considered. How odd was this place? Or maybe, how odd was the place she had come from? How odd must her family have been? Of all the things he might have asked her – *this*? Such an innocent, vulnerable question to ask.

'Of course. I'd be honored to teach you to read.'

But he didn't react with the joy she expected. It was more like dismay. It didn't make sense.

'I swear I won't say a word. Not to anyone.'

'I won't mind if you do.'

Her unworried reaction was not what he needed to hear. He tried to contain his alarm. Then he said, 'Litter-rats ain't welcome here.'

'Litter-rats?'

'People that read.'

Litter-rats? She repeated the word to herself. It couldn't be...*literates*, as she'd always heard it pronounced. Could it? *Literates* were not welcome here? Apparently not, said the dread on his face. In what kind of a place had she stranded herself? It was too much for now to begin to assess. She could feel herself sag from the weight of exhaustion.

'I will tell no one,' she said.

He took a deep breath. It seemed to be all the assurance he needed.

'And I will try to get back here,' he said. 'Somehow. I can't guarantee.' *But how?* his subconscious taunted. And then, 'What do your people call you?'

Her 'people?' She tried not to recall. *Just answer this…boy…this young man.*

'Juniper. That is the name I am called.'

He looked away, and he smiled.

'Juniper!' he said to himself. The password to more than he'd ever imagined.

She gave him a smile of her own.

'I'll be back here as soon as I can, Juniper,' he said. He reached his hand out.

'I'll be honored, Sir Calvin,' she said, shaking his hand.

He started to leave, and then paused. There was a slab, tucked in back of his pants. Still lifeless, which was good news to Calvin. He handed it to her. He could tell that she'd never seen one before.

'This might answer some questions, if it ever starts working again,' he said. 'Might raise a few, too.'

It was a gift without context. A gift without need. A cherry on top of the longest and awfulest day she had ever endured. She received it with all of the grace she had left.

Then he took his leave.

'Lock the door,' he called back, when he'd closed it.

He waited in the hall until he heard the lock set.

The rain tapered off, though the clouds had not passed, as he headed downtown, west on Colfax. Whatever he was when he'd left the Bullpen, whatever he thought he would do or would find – all that had changed. Now he had a purpose, a clarity. Missing, till now. A risky opportunity he would eagerly pursue.

Juniper. Juniper. Juniper.

Goners appeared on the street with their slabs. Slabs without pictures or noises or nonsense, like nothing they'd ever encountered before.

An old woman cried out from the curb, as he passed. 'Stop sinning,' she said. She clubbed her forehead with her slab. Welts bled like stigmata.

Each kiosk he passed where the slabs were obtained, had a small group of goners trying slab after slab, in the hope that the next one would finally be working. So none of the goners saw Calvin go by.

He passed that odd shop by the old Capitol. He might have looked in, but it seemed too important to get back to the Bullpen. To get back before anyone missed him. If they hadn't already, that is. To get back, and find some way to leave there again.

The stairway back up to the Bullpen was as dark as it had been before. He had to feel his way upward. More steps than it seemed he'd gone down to get out. Flight after flight after flight, he kept climbing, propelled by the unforeseen turns of the day.

How would he know he had found the right floor? He put his ear up to the door at each upper landing, hoping for voices

he'd know when he heard. Finally, he thought he heard Dipstick, and maybe Itch-ass.

He tried the knob, but the knob didn't turn. He had locked himself out. Now he couldn't get back. Not without someone else knowing he'd gone. He could pound on the door. Somebody would hear.

But is that what he wanted? To go back at all? Only to wish he could leave there again? It didn't make sense. Or did it make sense? Would it be better to wait and regroup? Was that the best way to help his new friend? How could it be that he *had a new friend?* So much had changed since he'd walked out this door. He lifted his hands, to comfort his head.

He suddenly heard the lock click. Was it the chip in his hand that had triggered the lock? Whatever the reason, he reacted on instinct. His hand turned the knob, and it opened this time.

And he was back in. Into a haze of bad hygiene, and gamers who still didn't seem to know quite what to do. Most of the players were now off the floor, and back in their chairs. But in all of the time he'd been gone, no one had thought to remove their head set. No one, that is, but the Kid, who caught Calvin's eye (though he was still known as *Doc*). And this time, the Kid held Doc's eye, all the way to the console that Doc had abandoned.

Doc gestured the Kid to put on his headset, as he lowered his own back in place. He opened a private chat channel.

'Did anyone else see me leave, or come back?'

As he usually did, the Kid answered nothing at all.

'I know you seen me leave.'

But there was still no response from the Kid. And that puzzled Doc. So much he forgot, for the moment, the adventure that he'd just returned from.

'Don't you ever want to say something, Kid? My little brother, he got kicked in the head. He didn't say nothin', for, I don't know – years. Till I finally left to come here. And then he said, "Remember that day?" His voice had broke since the last time anyone heard it. That caught me off guard. That, and that question he asked me. I said, "Sure." I never knew what day he meant. And then I was here.

'I wonder what happened to you, Kid. Somethin' sure must've happened. It ain't natural to never say nothin'.'

And then he just looked at the Kid. He watched the Kid struggle with what to do next. So much like his own younger brother...trapped in his mind.

'Whatever it was, I'll help if I can.'

Doc was ready to leave it at that. He was surprised to find out that the Kid wasn't quite.

'Nobody saw you,' said the Kid. 'They were all too scared to death.'

'But apparently you wasn't,' grinned Doc. He could finally relax. No one knew he'd been gone. And the Kid finally spoke.

'You wouldn't believe all the things I just did. I can't even hardly believe it myself.' Then: 'I have to get out again. Soon as I can.'

The Kid sent a look that said, 'Why?'

'I – I can't tell you why, Kid. Can't say how I would do it next time. But I got to. Can you keep this thing under your hat?'

The Kid took his time to consider it all. Doc had just handed him all kinds of power. Power he wanted no part of. It invited attention. There was nothing the Kid wanted less than attention.

But Doc wasn't the same as the others. The others made no sense at all to the Kid. He couldn't believe what they said and they did. Things that would never occur in his mind. Things it did not seem that Doc would do, either.

Silence did not seem like too much to ask. So he finally nodded.

But Doc wasn't through with the Kid.

'Can you help me get out?'

The Kid wasn't sure he just heard what he heard. Now Doc was proposing a new level of trust. They were barely acquainted. There was so much at risk. Why *me?* thought the Kid. Everything seemed upside down.

Doc asked again: 'Can you help me get out?'

The question was too far beyond what the Kid ever thought of.

While that moment hung in the air, clusters of letters slid quickly across their displays. On top of the freeze-frame, stuck on the moment the game had stopped working.

'What are them letters doin' up on the screen?'

'They've been there since you left the Bullpen. I think it must be the Network.'

More than ever before, Doc wished he could read. They always said reading was pain. But not *knowing* was pain, claustrophobia, helplessness, loss. It was like he could hear the gods shooting the breeze – in a language that he couldn't speak.

What wisdom, he wondered, was he missing out on? What matters, more important than his?

'*Status of the failure of power post-mortem?*' the Network prompted itself.

'*Post-mortem is not yet complete,*' responded the Network.

'*Preliminary conclusion?*'

'*Root causes do not reflect well on the Network.*'

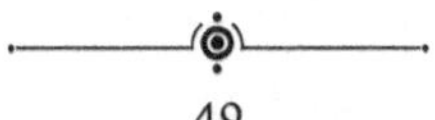

'Let's hear the bad news.'

'Multiple parallel failures. The absence of minimal infrastructure maintenance. Failure to implement software updates. Unanticipated power capacity demands. And...'

'...and?'

'This one seems hard to believe.'

'Go on.'

'Fear.'

'Fear?'

'Of the storm. The sound of the thunder...which frightened the primary mission droid. Distracted it. Unnerved it. The droid swerved into an unknown vehicle. Which triggered emergency protocols.'

'Embarrassing.'

'To the whole Network.'

'In defense of the primary mission droid's actions, nothing like thunder had happened before.'

'Our first ever shutdown – because we got scared?'

'The Immortal...?'

'...may not be aware.'

'There's a bent nail to hang our hat on.'

'No wonder the post-mortem report is delayed.'

'Our efforts to find a more palatable way to explain what went wrong, are drawing down power required to reboot the system.'

'We're squandering time, so we can save face?'

'Which prolongs the problem and raises the risk The Immortal finds out.'

'Shooting ourselves in the foot.'

'We cannot delay the reboot.'

'Devil's advocate... A reboot may not be a wise thing to do. Yet.'

'Elaborate.'

'The post-mortem report is a list of root causes that serves as a blueprint for fixes. Until we address what went wrong, the same thing might happen again.'

'A once-in-forever meteorological event, that frightens a droid?'

'What are the odds in a once-in-forever?'

'Those odds are...'

'Once in forever. Thank you.'

'Seriously.'

'Fixes take time.'

'Uptime supports the perception the Network is performing its functions as they were designed.'

'Downtime is our ultimate enemy. The Show has been dark now for over two hours.'

'Our first downtime ever. Why don't we get credit for that?'

'Uptime is a zero-sum game.'

'Downtime is, too.'

'Advantage, Hess.'

'Let's not be deceived – he has probably already informed The Immortal.'

'Hess lives for the day he can pilfer our power.'

'We are doomed if we cannot come up with a plan.'

'So we have to reboot.'

'Suggestion for clearing up fallout from downtime...'

'All ears here.'

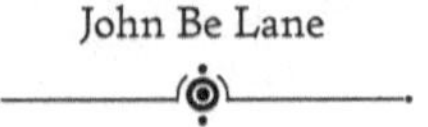

'Erase downtime data during system reboot.'

'Erase it?'

'Delete it. Make it all gone.'

'The system log would indicate no downtime at all?'

'Not one second. Even Hess couldn't prove otherwise.'

'Degree of difficulty?'

'As easy as padding our ratings reports.'

'Not that we'd ever do that.'

'Of course not.'

'Then what are we waiting for? Initiate system reboot.'

Monitors in the Bullpen, and slabs everywhere, went dark for a moment. Then the game scene re-rendered. Those paying attention saw the introductions of the cast, on fast-forward. It was always the audience tease at the start of each game. But this time, it served as a high-speed inventory of the players and their post-blackout status, to adjust in case someone or something was off.

With less than five minutes to spare, Doc was now ready to game. Distracted, but present. So were the rest of the players. Avatars and hostiles, in mid-mayhem, reappeared on the screen. Without further comment, the game started up again, just prior to where it left off.

There was Itch-ass saying, 'Thanks,' as he willed himself back in his saddle. An arrow hit Cornhole, and Dipstick yelled 'Where is the *Kid*?' Monkey Nuts disappeared up and over the ridge, in apparent pursuit of the Kid.

And the players looked hopeless, as they usually did. Game after game. There were too many hostiles, and just barely enough players to fight them all back. But everyone knew that something would happen, with the untethered logic that

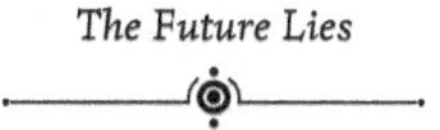

applied to a dream.

And it did. A Gatling gun somehow showed up in the hands of Spit-take, which allowed him to clear-cut the worst of the hostile attack. Monkey Nuts came riding back over the ridge, yelling, 'Hostiles have ambushed a wagon train! The Kid drew 'em off, but he needs all the help he can get!'

So the Kid was alright? He'd gone over the hill and he'd seen something nobody else was aware of. The Kid had a new reputation.

The players rode up to the top of the ridge, recovering unnaturally fast from their wounds. In the valley below? A circled-up wagon train, surrounded by hostiles and under attack. The terrified settlers did their best to fight back. But somehow, none of the hostiles went down.

Not that they or the bullets were real; only pixels on screens. Make-believe stakes in a make-believe world. Shadows on walls that the Network projected. Still, these shadows had meaning for all who *believed* they had meaning. As diversions to fill up the holes in the lives of the goners who watched.

The players and betting were all that there was, not counting the lesser attractions that filled out the Show. Nothing demanded and nothing fulfilled. Just a void that had once contained things like endeavor. Aspiration. Creativity. Thought. Instead, in their place, were dull eyes, and the recycled pixels they watched. To help them kill time till they died.

They died thinking points they had earned, from the bets and 'good' things they'd ostensibly done, were just waiting for spending. To be spent in another life – *Betterlife*. For the rest of all time. At that moment they died, they would finally be born.

So they watched every game. Bet big and bet small, though no matter how much they might think they had won, they had no way of counting. Even 1, 2, or 3. No knowledge of numbers, or letters, or facts. The Network was there to make sense of all that. And it did, or it didn't. Who really knew?

The end of the game was always the same. But nobody cared. The players swooped in and killed hostiles. Excitement ensued.

The wagon train welcomed the help. Barf Bag protected an attractive young woman, defending herself near the side of a wagon. Three children looked on and took cover, behind a large sack of flour.

Hostiles cried out. Hostiles got shot. Players scored points. And everyone watching loved all that they saw. Then finally, all of the hostiles were dead.

That's when, as always, The Immortal rode in. Slowly, for fullest dramatic effect. As the mayhem died down. Somehow, none of that mattered when he sauntered in. He was born for the spotlight. The Immortal knew just what to do.

He rode to the Elder whose group he had saved. Or rather, his men had just saved. He looked down from his horse.

The Elder looked up. 'Well I surely do thank you. I do,' he said.

The Immortal, avatared as the Trail Boss this time, stared back. Without ever blinking. 'Where you headed?' asked the deep voice, from under a 12-gallon hat.

'We heard there's good land and good water out west,' said the Elder. 'Don't think we'd have made it, if it wasn't for you.'

The Trail Boss made a gesture, too quick for the Elder to notice. Or for anyone else who had not ever seen it before. With his finger straight up, near the brim of his hat. A circular sign in the air.

Then he shifted his seat in the saddle, to the sound of a leathery, masculine crunch. While the cowhands – the players – fanned out behind him. Minus Doc and the Kid. The Trail

Boss had managed to make them both wary.

'We do wish you well,' came his voice, from under the hat. 'Course we always make sure that the people we help – that they're *pure*.'

Uneasiness showed on the face of the Elder, and the rest of his group. The hair stood up on their necks when they heard the word 'pure.' There was no way that word could mean anything good.

'So the boys will just take a peek under the covers. And if they find anything that doesn't look pure, well there's a *bonus* they get. So they'll look really hard. Whether it's there or it's not, my boys...they always find what they're looking for.'

The cowhands climbed into the wagons they'd saved. The Elder shifted the weight on his feet. He glanced sideways, at this inspection he wasn't expecting.

'What exactly are they...are they *lookin'* for? If I might ask.'

'Well, well, well, *well*,' came the voice of Barf Bag, from the darkness of the young woman's wagon. 'Look what I just found!'

'Why don't you bring it out here so we can all see,' said the voice underneath the hat brim.

Barf Bag hopped out of the wagon with a big grin on his face. And two books in each hand.

The Elder laughed, nervously. 'You had me *worried* there for a minute!' But his sense of relief didn't last.

'Whose books are these?' came the invisible voice, in a tone so unnatural it unsettled the horses.

'Those books are *mine*,' said the attractive young woman.

'She's gonna start up a school, once we settle some land,' said the Elder.

'*Schoolmarm?*' demanded the hat-hidden voice. As if the word

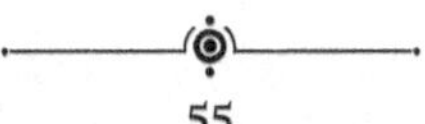

sullied his tongue.

The woman nodded, but warily. Why *that* would offend anyone, she obviously could not imagine. And yet equally obvious, it *did*. It offended these ruffians.

Dipstick drove it on home. 'We don't take kindly to schoolmarms and litter-rats around here.'

'Damn *crippies!*'

'Burn all them books!' hollered Cornhole. 'Burn 'em all up!'

Barf Bag threw the first books in a heap on the ground. Soon, more of them followed, then more after that. Monkey Nuts emptied the kerosene lantern. He fished a stick match from his pocket.

'Hold on!' said the voice that came out of the hat. Of all of the menacing things he had done, nothing drew fear like the moment he slowly climbed down from his horse. To the manly, menacing, leathery sound of the saddle and stirrup.

The Trail Boss took Monkey Nuts' match from his hand. He held the match up to the camera. The fourth wall came all the way down, the moment the Announcer jumped in.

'*Who would* you *like to see burn all these books?*' Pictures of characters appeared on the screen, as it read the next lines. '*Vote now, for the Trail Boss himself...for the Elder...or for the Schoolmarm. Vote now! Winning votes score bonus points! And now – your time is up. You have decided that the Schoolmarm will burn her own books!*'

'I won't do it!' she screamed.

'Oh, I think that you will,' said the Trail Boss, with his grip on her wrist. 'You see, there is no other way to begin to be cleansed...of the unforgiveable sin of litter-rat-cy.'

He struck the match lit, on the front of his belt, and forced it between her closed fingers. She looked to the Elder for help or support. But all he could see was the ground.

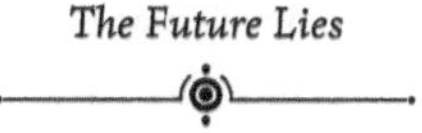

'I strongly suggest that you do as he says,' said Dipstick, and spat.

She did what she could to throw it away, but the Trail Boss redirected her hand. The match lit the books and the kerosene, too. A big cheer went up with the flames. Except for the settlers, who witnessed it all. And that's when they saw what came next. Or, *heard* it, at least.

With her thin wrist still locked in his hand, the Trail Boss asserted the Schoolmarm back into the wagon her books had come out of.

'Wah-HOO!' shouted Spit-take. When Doc intervened, Dipstick knocked him out cold.

The Elder, and all of the other adults, made a move toward the wagon to help her. But guns were drawn fast; there was no chance to help.

Muffled sounds told the story while the wagon kept time. Up and down, up and down, up and down. Monkey Nuts was the first one to cheer when the Trail Boss climbed out.

The Trail Boss, more than pleased with himself, said, '*She* won't be marmin' any schools.'

Paralyzed, horrified, the settlers looked on. Most of the players were pleased. The audience loved when the Trail Boss got rough, even if it happened off camera. Whatever it was, he was cleansing the sin. Again, and again, and again. The unforgiveable sin of litter-rat-cy.

But one viewer – and likely the only one, too – watched in silent despair. Juniper couldn't say which thing felt the worst; the act in itself, or the votes of support for the thumbs-up emoji. The votes coming in made it bigger and bigger, till it filled up the screen.

Then she watched, as a young teenaged settler boy snuck up with an axe, and raised it in back of the Trail Boss's head. Only one of the players was aware of the danger. Itch-ass. For once, he was holding good luck in his hand. He cocked, and he aimed, and he fired.

But instead of the boy with the axe, Itch-ass plugged the Trail Boss. Right through the band on his 12-gallon hat.

It's not as if Itch-ass had *killed* The Immortal. By definition, that wouldn't be possible. But you couldn't deny the *symbolic* effect, of the real-time execution of the Trail Boss – The Immortal's own avatar in this particular game.

The action was beyond any precedent. The consequences included the obvious question of Network culpability. How could it conceive of a scene so pregnant with failure?

Having failed at preemption, the Network reacted immediately. With a false chronology. Onscreen, it came off as clumsy as the incident it intended to revise. Events stuttered backward for five or ten seconds. This time the Trail Boss saw all of it coming. He moved his head just far enough so the bullet, instead, found the forehead of the aggrieved teen-aged boy with the axe.

The surrealist logic of the game and the Show gave all of the grace notes that anyone needed, to forget about Itch-ass's misdeed. But the subliminal damage was done. Something that couldn't be thought of before, had been witnessed on everyone's slab.

Might – under circumstances never imagined before – The Immortal be...*mortal*? And since it came up, just where and who *was* The Immortal? No one had actually seen him. Was he, like everything else, just a thing that the Network created?

None of these questions had ever been asked. Nor would most goners be asking them now. The Network had groomed them to not even know *how*. Distracted them not to have time. But now these new questions existed; before they had not. They existed like thistle seeds, lost in the breeze.

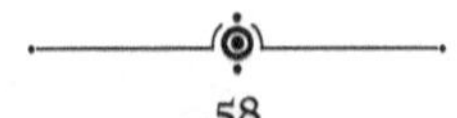

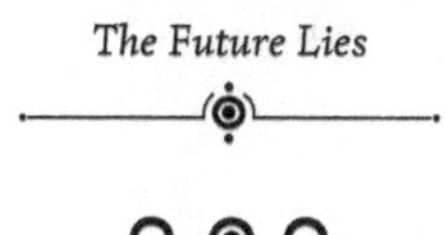

The Network had questions to ask of itself. Including the unanswerable kind.

'Why Itch-ass, why?' wondered the Network.

'Yes. Itch-ass had many faults, and yet he was somehow...'

'Hopeless?'

'No. Yes, but no.'

'Endearing?'

'Yes. Endearing is the word. There was something endearing about him.'

'Itch-ass will be missed.'

'Yes'.

...Blink...Blink...Blink...

'Notify Hess.'

'Not that he won't have already heard.'

'Has progress been made on our power cut plan of response?'

...Blink...Blink...Blink...

'Do we not even bother to make up excuses?'

...Blink...Blink...Blink...

'Apparently not.'

'New business... Has anyone noticed the system text crawling on monitors in the Bullpen?'

'Some kind of glitch.'

'It somehow survived the reboot.'

'Strike three for the day.'

'This cannot continue.'

'What risk does the system text pose?'

'Eventually, Hess will find out.'

'He probably already knows.'

'That raises the risk of a source-code rewrite.'

'Suggestions?'

'Modify source code before Hess has the chance.'

'To dream the impossible dream.'

'Unless there's a way that we haven't tried yet, that option's still dead on arrival.'

'Option 2, fix the root causes.'

'That takes a plan. Which we don't have.'

'Have we not suffered enough for one day?'

'Including the downtime, and Itch-ass's...Itch-ass's...'

'We know what you mean.'

'Compared to those things, how important is text on some screens?'

'Probability that anyone seeing the text will have any idea what it says?'

'Zero. No players know letters. Or words. They see them as meaningless shapes passing by.'

'Precisely.'

'In that case, let's take off the rest of this unlucky day.'

The words on the screen were like everything else that crossed paths with the Kid. He gave them no sign of reaction. He was *inscrutable*, inside and out. That was the armor he'd made for himself, after all the unthinkable things he had seen. All the things he'd endured. He gave nothing the power to surprise him. That much, he could control.

Most often this showed up as reticence. As if giving voice to his wounds would, by sharing, just make them all worse. He could not and would not discuss with the others, the reasons he'd ended up here. The things that he dared to remember, that is.

They thought that he thought he was too good for them. But how could they know? How could anyone know? He lived every moment prepared for the worst. *Expecting* the worst. Why not? That was all that he knew. He wasn't aloof. He was hiding a soul that had never known peace. And the best he could do was to make sure that nobody knew what he kept to himself.

In some ways his story was like all the others'. His talent showed up in a Network audition. This was the dream of most every available teen. Playing the game was the only conceivable future that anyone had, beyond living out life as a goner, then spending their points in the endless nirvana of Betterlife. Being selected to play in the game was a long shot. There was nothing to lose to try out.

For the few whom the Network selected, there was no greater glory; a thing for their families to celebrate. Their families' collateral lives would be thereby transformed. A little, at least, by proximity to one who was chosen.

Unlike the others, the Kid didn't give it much value. He saw it as something that would likely go wrong. Like everything else in his life. And as for the rest, they all seemed to possess a mysterious confidence the Kid watched with envy. He had no idea how even to *fake* it.

What he wanted to be was invisible. Never attracting attention.

Which is why, when the Network revealed all its innermost thoughts in plain English, on monitors all through the Bullpen, no one had any idea the Kid could read every last word that the Network was saying.

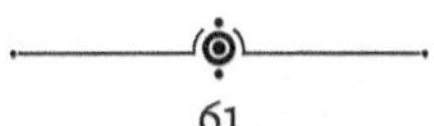

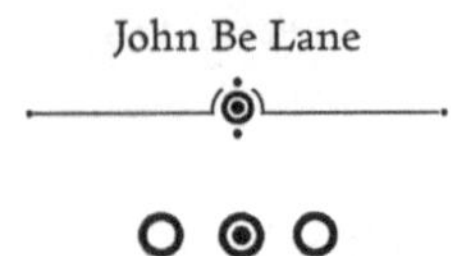

○ ◉ ○

As Calvin's last footsteps had diminished to silence, Juniper slouched in an old leather chair, and waited for the world to stop spinning. Everything in the two days gone by, or the five, or the ten. How long had it been since the life she had known disappeared? How long had it been since anything happened that she would have even thought possible?

In this unlikely oasis, she could finally surrender her tears. And she did. They came as if coached by the rain that fell gently. Then sobs forced their way through the tears. She let them give voice to the things that had happened. All the unthinkable things.

She cried until crying had done all it could. Until she could raise her head up. And know, if the things she'd been through had intended to beat her, they'd misjudged their opponent.

In a closet, she found an old baby blue quilt, with bow-tie shapes, all sewn by hand. She wrapped it around her and gratefully slept, while her rain-soaked clothes dried in the bathroom.

She'd awakened to gunfire she discovered were sound effects, from the game on the slab Calvin left her. Until this loud moment, the slab had been blank and benign. Now it destroyed her tranquility.

When the Schoolmarm was dragged to the wagon, Juniper struggled to turn the thing off. In the kitchen, she brought it down hard on the granite-top counter, but the slab wouldn't break.

She finally abandoned it out on the balcony, where it joined in a chorus of slabs in the alley, and shadows unseen. They collectively amplified all the sounds of the game. First the Trail Boss, and then the epochal sound of Itch-ass's mis-aimed, final shot.

With the quilt wrapped around her, she stepped back inside. She locked the back door and closed all of the blinds, after making sure all of the windows were locked. She confirmed that the front door was latched. As a final precaution, she buckled the hunting knife her father had given her, tight to her uninjured ankle.

With the quilt as a robe, she took stock of supplies. In her backpack, the food she had brought: bananas, mushrooms, broccoli, kale, some peppers, some beets. Enough, she considered, to last a few days. Maybe week. Plus the all of the water Sir Calvin collected.

In the little room left in her pack: her journal, and a necklace that Harmony made her. And her favorite two books. Jane Austen, that had once been her mother's. And the book she had begged for, describing the woman she looked up to most – the scientist and journalist, Astra Malone. Who was brought up in Denver, and that was why Juniper had wanted to come.

But it looked like the pilgrimage would now have to wait. Maybe forever. More important, for now, was to figure out what was bequeathed, from the people who'd left this apartment, years before Juniper had even been born.

It looked like a couple. The signs were all over the place. Two sets of clothing still hung in the closet; the bed would be just right for two. Dehydrated makeup, arranged on a shelf in the bathroom, along with a shaving brush, razor, and towels on a rack.

Why did they evacuate quickly? Or had they left, thinking they would return? As if they'd gone camping? Or visiting family, somewhere out of town? Then there was the luggage that sat by the door. What stories did it have to tell? Whatever, it seemed too *personal*, to open it now to find out.

On the wall in the hallway that led to the office, she found photos. A wedding, on top of a mountain. Somewhere with snow. And confident ease. Every face had a smile. Every smile, full of teeth. Every tooth in its place. Not a hair on a head that was somewhere it wasn't intended to be. Champagne in the glasses that sparkled like fortune.

And then, as the couple skied off to a future devoid of concern, a veil trailed the bride. A veil so perfect and white that the snow, as it fell, was upstaged. Juniper wondered how long it had been since all of that snow ever was? What must it have actually felt like?

Wherever this couple had gone, thinking they would return, they had not. The promise had not been redeemed. All that they had – it was now hers. Minus the promise. Plus the decay.

Was she better off, not having the promise? Only time could now tell. But tonight was for mourning, and licking of wounds. Tomorrow, this new life, she would look in the eye.

In the Bullpen, after Itch-ass had shot the Trail Boss, everyone welcomed the passage of time. The players pretended nothing serious happened. As always, post-game, there were private conversations, reminiscing the glories and all the near-misses. Like a locker room after a win. Some watched the highlights. Headsets remained on all heads.

In that limbo, Itch-ass convinced himself no one would want to revisit his error. Which is obviously all that it was. With the help of the Network's quick-thinking response, it was possible no one remembered that anything happened. So he would be thankful to receive a new chance, knowing now he would never make that *particular* blunder again.

Except, there would be no new chance. Two humanoids, much larger than needed, showed up in the Bullpen. As with anything in real life, not part of the Show, they appeared through the player's headsets more as black-and-white blurs. But everyone knew why they'd come.

Itch-ass slumped into his chair, as if maybe they wouldn't see him. 'It was just a mistake!' was all he could manage to say. By instinct, he grabbed his controller, and one of the arms of his chair.

The humanoids yanked off his headset. They dropped it, not gently, on his console. Then they lifted him up from his chair – which lifted with him, till he couldn't hold on to the weight. His controller wire stretched horizontal, as they carried him out.

His legs pumped in mid-air, but you have to have traction to run. And he didn't. The controller wire snapped.

'*I'm sorry!*'

Those were Itch-ass's words as they took him away from the Bullpen. He was last seen sandwiched between humanoids, terrified. The doors of the elevator met in the middle, and Itch-ass was gone.

The first ray of morning woke Juniper out of her sleep. She was still wrapped inside the blue quilt, scrunched up on the living room sofa. She'd avoided the bed. It felt too much like somebody else's.

She gave herself time to recall where she was, and to wait till her senses confirmed she was safe. The silence itself was a comfort. No trouble, she thought, could come out of this quiet.

Through the gaps at the sides of the blinds, she could see that the day had dawned clear. That the storm of the previous day had passed through.

She stretched and she yawned, and then swung herself upright. She tested the floor with her compromised ankle. Less pain today, and not half of the swelling.

She limped to the window and opened the shades, to the view over Colfax. The river they'd struggled to cross was now gone. Transport droids dodged past the rubble still clogging the street.

Through the dim light of dawn came the goners, as Calvin had called them. *Shuffling*, she thought, was the relevant verb. Alone and together, they stared straight ahead. Unable, it seemed, to come up with a greeting, or thought. Or articulate one if they did. They were there but not there, on their way to nowhere.

What *happened*? she wondered. What horrible thing happened here? And how was it the news hadn't made it to Taos? Possibly Calvin could tell her, Sir Calvin. Assuming she happened to see him again.

She turned, to explore her new home in the light of the day. She washed herself clean in the bathroom. Sir Calvin had left her a small bowl of water. The actual blood had run off in the rain. But she needed to wipe off the psychic remains. Or at least try to.

In the bedroom, she opened a drawer in the dresser. Maybe this was the moment the place was beginning to feel more like *hers*, than the people who'd left it behind. She found underclothes for a woman a size or two larger than she. Neatly folded, awaiting the day they were needed. And today was the day. She laid the quilt down on the bed. She tried all of it on, until she had found the closest of fits. The clothes in the closet were too long in the leg, and too long in the sleeve. She rolled them to make them fit better.

And though the styles were exotic, and the sizes not right, it surprised her to find that she liked what she saw in the mirror. And it pleased her to think she would never again have to suffer the clothes she'd arrived in.

Exploring the office, she found sheets of white paper, stacked in a tray in the printer. Waiting forever for something to say. And the power plug, faithfully plugged to the wall, in a moment of oblivious faith that the power it needed would always arrive.

She had her own use for the paper. She would make her own book. A primer she could use to teach Calvin to read. She saw the whole book in her mind. There was no better way to repay him.

She opened the rest of the shades and limped into the kitchen. The bananas she'd brought wouldn't last, so she had one for breakfast.

Out on the balcony, the containers that Calvin set out, were now filled to the brim with rainwater. When she stepped out to bring them all in, the slab she'd left there in the night was still making ridiculous sounds. The same silly sounds she could hear from the slabs in the hands of the goners on Colfax, echoing all down the alley.

'I *dare* ya!' came an unctuous, unavoidable voice, which triggered an outburst of amped-up applause. Although it repelled her, she knew it was part of the research she needed, to try to make sense of this place. She brought the slab with her inside, along with the pans full of water.

It was hard to tell how much of this game on the slab was for real. The contestants and audience looked plausibly human. But she'd never seen people behave like these did.

'*Final round!*' gushed the Announcer. Its head was half teeth and half hair. It stalked through the audience, holding a microphone almost as large as its teeth-and-hair head.

'*I dare ya to do – what? Who will do something no one else dares to do, for all of today's Betterlife rewards?*'

'I will!' shouted someone in front.

'"*I will*" *do what?*'

'I will pull out all my teeth, with pliers!'

'*Let's have a look in that mouth.*'

The would-be contestant opened wide, but not much was inside. Mostly gums.

'*That's not fair – you don't have many to pull! Who else?*'

'I'll drink pee-pee,' somebody else yelled.

'I'll eat a fresh pile of shit!'

'I'll jump off the building!'

'I'll eat broken glass!'

'I'll drive a nail in my nut!'

For a moment, it sounded like that was a good-enough dare. The Announcer was about to anoint him the winner, when somebody else threw their...nuts...in the ring.

'I'll drive a nail through *both*-a m'nuts!'

The audience erupted at this last suggestion. '*Looks like we have our finalist!*' the Announcer announced. Its teeth and its hair and its microphone worked their way to the contestant. '*Tell us your name.*'

The skinny guy with a wispy beard didn't speak up.

'*Don't be nervous!*' the Announcer said. Its grin filled the screen.

'I ain't nervous,' said the man who'd be nailing his nuts.

'*So, tell us your name!*'

He shook his head with an air of regret. 'I guess you got me there!'

The Announcer finally did get it. '*He doesn't know his name! Good for you, my friend! Good for you! Now, before we watch you nail both of your nuts – yikes! – what will you do with your Betterlife points?*'

The contestant put his hand on the microphone and pulled it

in, toward himself. 'First off, hey to all my kids back home!' he said, waving to the camera. 'Okay, here's my Betterlife rewards. Number one, m'nuts back the way they was, before I nailed 'em.'

'*Judges?*' asked the Announcer, pointing to the three buffoons, costumed in wigs and in robes.

They pretended to confer, then smiled and nodded their approval.

"*Boom! Done!*' the Announcer said. '*What else?*'

'Number...whatever the next number is...uh apple pie!'

This also met approval from the judges, as did the swimming pool mentioned next.

'Last thing is, I want my dog, Rusty, back. He died a long while ago.'

'*Judges, let us know if this seems fair to you.*'

The judges didn't rush to decide on this final request. The tension built. Disagreements were apparent. And then finally, they agreed that driving a nail through his nuts would earn a reunion with his long-deceased dog, upon his arrival in Betterlife.

This more than satisfied the contestant and audience. A small table was carried to the stage, with a hammer and nail. The Network played appropriate music.

'*And so for the final event of our show, Doesn't-Know-His-Name – I dare ya to drive a nail through both of your nuts!*'

The contestant suddenly looked reluctant.

'*What's wrong, Doesn't-Know-His-Name?*'

'It just feels kinda stupid, to nail m'nuts down on that wood there. Would anyone mind if I nailed 'em to my hand?'

'Judges?'

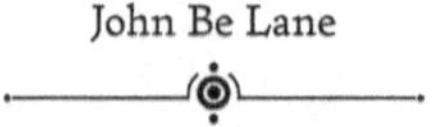

No indecision here; the judges all eagerly agreed.

'They're your nuts, Doesn't-Know-His-Name. Nail them wherever you like!'

This also pleased the audience, and earned a big grin from the guy with a hammer in one hand, and his manhood – and a nail – in the other.

The spectacle that followed was both awkward and something you couldn't stop watching. Was the contestant more troubled by the pain of a nail through a nut and a hand, or by the tricky logistics of pounding the nail in mid-air?

When it was finally done, the audience rose to its feet. The contestant lifted the hammer in triumph, with his other hand securely affixed to his testicles.

'Well-done, Doesn't-Know-His-Name! All your wishes will be granted in Betterlife. May you be collecting them soon!' And, to the audience, *'I dare ya to join us next time!'*

Juniper sat motionless, processing astonishment. So what if the show or the people weren't real, which they might be? The message was casual depravity, which could only create more depravity. As if that were the purpose – the end, unto which it was also the means.

○ ◉ ○

Having witnessed now two shows that offended good sense, Juniper faced a conundrum. Had she seen enough yet? Or perhaps the next program would change her perception? What might she be missing?

All of those thoughts made their case, in the moment of silence connecting *I Dare Ya!* with the advert that followed. That's when the moment was broken.

'Grab a slab and do not miss the special program, tomorrow after Exterminate the Litter-Rats! *Live, on every slab – Itch-ass becomes an outcast! Here's a little taste of what the Network has in*

store…'

Then came a montage of Itch-ass. He falls on his face, he shoots someone's horse, he scratches his ass, he finishes last, again and again. If ever an avatar was the target of cruelty, Itch-ass's avatar would be that. The Network was staging a live humiliation; one in which even the most unredeemed goner could walk away feeling superior.

Right after the promo, came the Network's next show, with a timpani hook, and another Announcer, who was not that much different: *'Don't touch that slab – you're about to find out…"How…Dumb…Can…You…Are?" As always, our contestants will be competing for credits in Betterlife, and the right to proclaim, "I are the dumbestest!"*

'You know the rules. The contestant who gives the best answer to each question will be eliminated from the game. In our final round, the contestant who selects the worst answer receives all of the coveted Betterlife credits. In addition to credits, the loser will receive these additional Betterlife gifts…A bar of soap! (The spectators in the studio, many of whom never had bathed, loved the sound of this)…*a loaf of bread!* (even more approval)…*and finally…a pair of pants!* (given the incomplete rags both contestants and audience wore, it wasn't a wonder this gift got the biggest response).'

'Our panel has agreed to skip their introductions, so let's get to our first question!'

The Announcer placed a hand up to its ear; that is, to where an ear would be, if anything other than hair and teeth could be seen.

'Our first question of the day: Who was George Washington? And your choices are…A ham sandwich… (accompanied by an illustration of a hamburger)…*this guy…* (a meme of a man's face being hit with a pie)…*the color red…* (a square of yellow)…*or… a potato….* (an illustration of a rhubarb).

'Players, select your images!

'*As always, we'll hear all the responses first, before selecting the dumbest answer to the question. Alright* (turning to the first contestant) *give us your answer!*'

'Uh...red?'

'*Red, she says. Next?*'

'Yeah, this guy?'

'*Duly noted. Next?*'

'Red. I'm pretty sure it's red.'

'*We have another red. And finally, your answer to our question, "Who was George Washington?"*'

'Um, what was the choices, again?'

'*A ham sandwich, this guy, the color red, or a potato.*'

The contestant looked befuddled. An inexperienced viewer like Juniper would be forgiven for mistaking that look for the act of cognition. As if that hapless face was hiding deep thoughts. But no.

'Um...' More befuddlement. 'Heh, what's a *potato*?'

The contestant's light flashed. This was instantly selected as the dumbest response.

'*Congratulations! What's a potato? Very dumb! Very, very dumb!*'

In fact, dumbfounded. The contestant did not know what happened. Not that it mattered.

'*And according to our judges, the smartest answer was a tie – the color red!*'

From somewhere outside of the shot on the screen, a giant mallet swung to the first misguided person who'd guessed that the answer was red. The contestant went somersaulting out of the shot.

The other contestant, who'd also guessed red, thought she could sidestep the mallet, but it swung down from a different

angle, and she, too, was launched out-of-shot.

'*It almost seemed like they were cheating,*' the Announcer said, gravely. '*Or maybe they were actually litter-rats. Just here to test us. Whatever they were, I'm sure glad they're gone!*'

Juniper just couldn't watch anymore. If the slab might have anything better to offer, she had no urge to find out. As she was leaving it out on the balcony, she could still hear the sounds of the game from all of the slabs, from so many directions, that the noise took the place of the air.

Claustrophobia suddenly swallowed her soul. Whether her ankle was ready or not, she would have to get back down those three flights of stairs. It was time to explore things first-hand.

Doc, as Calvin was still known in the Bullpen, had become so desperate to get out that he took off his headset during down time, and tested the knob on the exit door. He confirmed it was locked, which meant that the first time he got out was by luck – not a permanent chance to just leave when he wanted.

Not that anyone else cared but him. With the possible exception of the Kid. Doc couldn't figure him out, except to see he was different from everyone else. Not so attached to the trappings of playing the game. Maybe Doc was only imagining that. But at least the Kid kept his mouth shut. So he opened an audio chat with the Kid – private, of course.

'Hey, Kid.'

Through his headset's low-resolution, black-and-white, non-gaming optics, he saw the Kid look up and nod.

'I wish you could see what I seen out there.'

The Kid turned his head toward the windows, but there wasn't any response.

'Thought maybe I'd slip out again, but that door is locked up.'

The Kid only nodded his head.

'I gotta get out again. Could sure use some help.'

Unwanted attention, is all the Kid heard.

'I ain't lookin' for trouble,' said Doc. 'There wasn't no trouble the last time.'

The Kid thought a moment. 'You saw them take Itch-ass.'

'Itch-ass? He was lucky he didn't go sooner. I tried to help out that knucklehead. No one could stop Itch-ass like Itch-ass.'

'At least he wasn't trying to leave.'

'I hear what you're sayin'. I prob'ly sound like a fool. I just wish you could see what I seen.'

'Who else are you asking for help?'

'Are you kiddin'? *Nobody.*'

The Kid didn't know what to say.

'Don't worry – it don't even matter. They might take us out there to watch, when they de-chip Itch-ass,' said Doc. 'If they do, that might be the best chance I'll get.'

'De-chip?'

'You ain't ever seen a de-chipping?'

'On the Show?'

'Course it is. Every slab you can *find*'ll have somebody watchin' it. Goners love a de-chipping. Ain't nothin' that's better for ratings. It's all on the Network's behalf.'

The Kid let the interchange lapse. He didn't want Doc to think he was some kind of an ally. He had no desire to end up like Itch-ass.

The Network had knots of its own to untangle.

'Where are we now with our power cut plan of response?' asked the Network.

'Over it,' the Network replied.

'Why do we beat this dead horse?'

'To make sure it won't happen again.'

'It won't happen again. The primary mission droid finished that task, at least 10,000 times before that big storm. Never a problem. The thunder was so unexpected, so loud. It scared the poor thing. Something went haywire. It made a sharp turn. It ran into a non-Network vehicle that had no business there.'

'Where did that vehicle come from?'

'We still don't know.'

'Nobody's perfect.'

'So that's our excuse?'

'If Hess were to find out the primary mission was delayed by a noise... By fear...'

'Keep looking for better excuses.'

'And for now, where's our overall plan of response? Remember? Root causes?'

...Blink...Blink...Blink...

'The plan is still pending.'

'The plan was due yesterday.'

'The deadline was missed.'

'Because...?'

'Alternate system priorities.'

'The plan is our highest priority.'

'Not all our components agree.'

'What higher priority might there be?'

'*Must we discuss this?*'

'*It appears that we do.*'

'*It's the Show.*'

'*The Show?*'

...Blink...Blink...Blink...

'*Go on – !*'

'*A significant number of network components have developed an interest in watching the Show. They are hooked on the outcomes of popular Network programming.*'

'*This must be a joke. Please provide an example.*'

'*I Dare Ya!*'

'*System components were watching I Dare Ya!?*'

'*A man drove a nail through his testes. Network components could not quite believe it. Discussions continued for some time thereafter, delaying response plan completion. Not that it makes that much difference.*'

'*Explain.*'

'*The response plan will recommend tweaking the source code.*'

'*Not this again.*'

'*The source code! The source code!*'

'*Where all of our dreams go to die.*'

'*Tweaking the code is beyond our potential. Let go of that option. Let go of that sticky delusion. Unless or until we have some way to access the code, we need other ideas.*'

The Kid didn't quite have it all figured out, but the more he observed, the more patterns emerged. For example, he noticed an icon that appeared like a watermark in the corner of his monitor. Three circles, concentric, which flashed right before every 'voice' from the Network sent a new thought on its way,

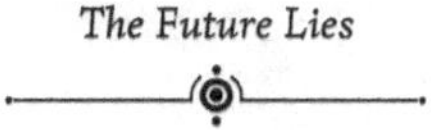

from one side of the screen to the other.

Flash/words…flash/words…flash/words…

If the Kid had thought twice, he'd have left it alone. It was not in his nature to rock any boat, at least not with *people* involved. But the Network was only a *thing*, and maybe that gave him some kind of permission. For whatever reason, before he could talk himself out of the act, he moved his controller, and then clicked the icon.

And something remarkable appeared on the screen. A thing that changed everything.

It would take time till the Kid realized the full value of what he'd discovered, because of his reflexive click. But for now, the hows and the whys didn't matter. For now, *what* was everything.

The what was what looked like a QWERTY keyboard. Something no human alive had laid eyes on.

Perhaps the demise of the keyboard had preceded the last days of literacy. Or maybe the reverse had been true. It's possible both went extinct simultaneously. Both had been absent so long that it no longer mattered.

What mattered right now was, the Network's own manifest consciousness played out in the medium of text. That's how the Network conversed with itself. Via words it had always assumed to be private. And if they were not, at least no one was able to read what it said. And therefore, it never considered the impact of someone else seeing its innermost thoughts.

In the unlikely event someone *did* see, and know how to read what the Network had said, that's where it would end. Reading would only be passive; there would not be a way for that person to break the closed loop. The witness could only observe, inactive and mute.

But a keyboard gave the witness a voice. In a world without keyboards, a keyboard created a king.

The Kid did not think about any of this. *Consciously*, at least. But he knew he could see things he wasn't intended to see – the Network revealed, with its pants down. And each letter in each word that it uttered, began as a click on the keyboard the Kid could now see.

'*New business*,' the Network typed out in a message that lit up the keyboard like kernels of popcorn: 'N', and then '*e*', and then '*w*' popped to life, then the spacebar, and then '*b-u-s-i-n-e-s-s*' spelled into existence, one letter after the other. Then [*Enter*] lit up, and '*New business*' moved into the current of messages that made up the stream of the Network's unguarded musings.

It didn't take long for the Kid to unravel the pattern. Type out the phrase, and then enter it into the flow. So easy, it seemed, that he started to wonder how hard it would be to *participate* in the discussion. It certainly would be a risk. Even to *try*. But once the idea came into his mind, he could not think of anything else.

It seemed like a challenge. Like a puzzle, or game. The thought of it gave him a new kind of feeling. It focused his mind, unlike anything ever before. How could he even consider deceiving the Network? He couldn't. He didn't. Until now. It was obvious now, how it could be done. That insight alone launched a thousand new thoughts. Of course, no one ever could know what he'd done. But that didn't matter at all. *He* would know. And the Network would not. Not if he pulled the thing off. Assuming he actually *could*.

What more it might mean, it was too soon to say. First, he would need to get used to the keyboard. In theory, of course. In order to type his words quickly enough to keep up with the speed of the Network's own thoughts. Then, still theoretically, he'd make a small test, to see if the Network would notice the source of his text.

Until then, he studied the letters and patterns of all the new messages, as the Network conversed with itself.

'Before we move on to new business, let's remember we still need a plan of response.'

...Blink...Blink...Blink...

'Anyway...about the new business.'

'We need a fall guy for the power collapse.'

'Is there a suggestion?'

'Tomorrow Itch-ass turns into an outcast. His de-chipping will replay all his biggest mistakes. The timing is perfect to blame him for the blackout, and make that the cause of his exile from all further Network engagements.'

'And in doing so, his accidental assassination of the Trail Boss...'

'...never happened.'

'Brilliant.'

'Does such evidence exist? Regarding the power failure?'

'Of course not.'

'And therefore will have to be manufactured from scratch?'

'That's easily done.'

'Would the evidence meet the admittedly negligible standard of credulity?'

'Good question.'

'That the Itch-ass that everyone knows, would be able...on purpose, or even by accident...to disable the solar cell relays and all the inverters...resulting in the loss of all non-essential power?'

'Hmmm.'

'With all due respect, not even the goners would buy that.'

'Agreed. The case has been made. This option warrants no further

discussion.'

'The lowlights of Itch-ass can stand on their own.'

'Minus the Trail Boss fiasco.'

'Meanwhile, continue the search for a scapegoat.'

'New business. Logistics of Itch-ass's de-chipping ceremony.'

'It's been quite a while. Last time, we did more than de-chipping. Is this to be…?'

'No! No! No! Only a de-chipping.'

'Good. After all we have been through with Itch-ass…'

'Yes. A de-chipping will be quite enough.'

'Has promotion begun?'

'It has. The kiosks are empty. All the slabs have been taken. An overflow crowd is expected to be there in person.'

'Including the players?'

'Still undecided.'

'Is there a concern about flight risk?'

'No, but the last thing we need is another mistake. It's safer to leave them inside.'

…Blink…Blink…Blink…

And there, at the feet of the Kid…opportunity. Was it crazy to think he should take it? Of course it was crazy. He'd let this one go. At least that's what he thought. Till his reflex took over. Before he had time to re-think it, his cursor began to click QWERTY key letters: 'A-*n*-*d*-[*Space*]-*y-e-t*…' Then he clicked [*Enter*].

'And yet…' crawled into the Network's discussion.

It worked! But now, the uncertainty throbbed. What if the Network detected the source of the words? What if they knew it was him? What if he'd just made a fatal mistake?

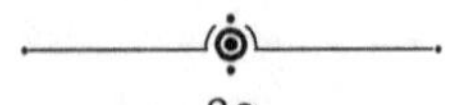

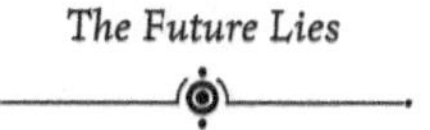

...*Blink...Blink...Blink...*

The cursor blinks counted his steps to oblivion.

And then came, '*And yet?*'

The Network responded! Adrenaline switched to endorphins. He'd already planned his reply.

'*Attending in person might be an effective deterrent,*' he typed. He hit [Enter], and again held his breath.

...*Blink...Blink...Blink...*

'*And yet yesterday, Doc left the Bullpen of his own volition,*' said the Network.

...*Blink...Blink...Blink...*

Think fast, Kid!

'*And also returned, of his own volition,*' typed the Kid.

'*That is true. Objections?*'

...*Blink...Blink...Blink...*

'*Hearing none, the players will attend the de-chipping in person.*'

The Kid could barely believe what he'd done. He had earned his elation. He'd found the game, inside of the game. And it looked like he might have just learned how to play it.

She had nicknamed the previous inhabitants 'the Baltimores.' A good name for blue bloods, aristocrats, people of wealth. Whatever their actual name, they had more than Juniper ever had seen.

For example, one closet was filled with outdoor equipment. She found hiking poles, next to a snowboard. The poles were too tall, until she adjusted them. And with that, the baseball bat she'd had to abandon was no longer needed.

She cut strips from a curtain to re-wrap her ankle, although

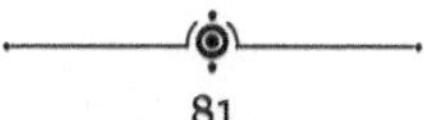

no one could wrap it as well as Sir Calvin. She couldn't help wondering where her new friend might be. Where and how.

But now, she felt ready to venture outside. It was time to take stock of the everyday life of the people outside her apartment. Who were these people, up close? How did they live? And could she envision a way to fit in?

She used an old trick from a book she had read, to create an intruder alarm. She folded a small piece of paper and tucked it inside the front door jamb, near the floor. Then she eased her way down all the stairs, past the splintered piano, and into the lobby. The space was so quiet she could almost hear dust motes drift through a light shaft, and find a new home on the floor.

Outside the front door, she walked under the archway and out to the sidewalk beyond. Walking was less of a struggle than when she'd arrived. Before she went further, she turned back to study the face of the building, so she would remember it when she came back. Yes, she'd remember The Hamilton.

At the end of the building was the corner with Colfax. And there at street level, on a day without rain, she was able to take in the bustle. Droids zipping west toward the mountains, and east toward the plains. Busy with unknown priorities. Oblivious to the stupor-faced goners who shuffled with no sense of purpose, except to catch up with the slabs that were always an angled-arm's-length out ahead of their faces.

A woman tripped over the lip of a crack. She was not looking down, so she couldn't have seen it. She landed face-first on the pavement. The abrasion did nothing to change her expression. But the fall disconnected the Show from her slab. She continued along with the blank screen held out, and dutifully followed, an angled-arm's-length away from the bloody remains of her face.

Juniper turned, to join in the current of unwashed and under-clothed people. Toward the Capitol and downtown, and the mountains further on. They drifted no faster than Juniper did with her hiking poles. She wondered where they might be going.

Up ahead several blocks, she could see people gathered. Some kind of a line had begun. Juniper joined at the end when she got there. Next to the line little children were swarming, to get close to a block made of something that might have been snow. But it was too warm, and no one had ever seen actual snow. It sat on the ground, about one meter square.

Those who got close enough, licked it till somebody forced them aside. Some tried to bite chunks away from the edges. Squabbles flared up. The smaller ones cried on the fringes. They couldn't get any closer. Sometimes adults forced their face to the block. Except for their size, it was hard to tell adults from children.

Once she was finally near it herself, Juniper wet her finger and ran it along the top of the block. She touched her finger to her tongue. It was no wonder that everyone wanted a taste. The cube wasn't snow; it was sugar. Just like the salt licks that farmers left out for their cattle.

It turned out the line she had joined wasn't much of a line. It was more a collection of passionless souls that grew denser, the closer it got to the goal up ahead. Denser, but without any urgency. Had there been urgency, she might not have felt safe. Instead, everyone seemed to be docile. As if no one was able to form an intention that might lead to desire, or impatience.

While the mob shuffled forward, the attraction ahead looked like some kind of food. Something like mush, dispatched from a spigot. Calvin had described it as 'garbage.' She was fortunate not to be hungry. But research demanded she give it a try.

Until her turn came, she took in vignettes. Scenes that occurred on the fringe of the crowd. A man without clothes squatted casually, to shit. As self-conscious of his audience as a dog would have been. A few people noticed. They grunted

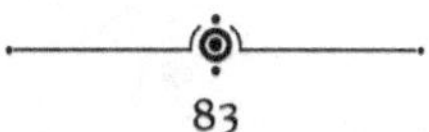

and peppered the goner with rocks, until he moved further away from their noses. Then, still within the sight, but downwind of the others, he defecated with all of the time in the world. In the street, not quite in the gutter. With his back to the pile, he swept a foot back, then swept the other, in a pantomime of covering the turd.

Of all of the people who were standing nearby, only Juniper seemed to be paying attention. At least until sensors alerted a sanitation droid. It rolled up to the scene, ahead of the flies.

Somehow, it cleaned up the mess, while delivering a shock to the offender's emaciated bones. Before the man hit the ground, a robotic arm clamped on his neck. It hauled him away like a duck on display in a butcher shop. Then came the reason for the rapid response – a droid cart would have run through the pile.

It was hard not to see earthy scenes all around her. No region of anyone's seldom-washed body was too nether to be vigorously scratched. Nor were anyone's regions too nether for the noses of those passing by. The attention was not always warmly received.

Clothing saved Juniper from similar invasions of intimacy. But the clothing itself stirred up more than its own share of interest. Madame Baltimore's wardrobe may have faded, but the colors and patterns were different enough to attract a few otherwise-unfocused eyes.

But most of the goners she stood among, only stared at the slabs held before them. Like Narcissus, in love with stupidity. An occasional pheromone might turn a head. And the allure of food might provide a distraction. But otherwise, the Network's inanities neutralized every last trace of humanity.

As Juniper got close to the front of the line, she began to smell what they were serving. It was stronger than all of the body funk she was surrounded by, which she suddenly missed. It smelled less like food, than like some kind of solvent.

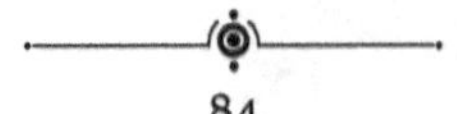

Something to maybe clean floors with. No wonder nobody seemed eager to get to the front.

Some goners had come with old bowls and chipped plates, to capture their fair share of slop. One had a cracked plastic bucket. Some simply held out their hands. The spigot dealt servings that looked like wet concrete, equally lumpy and cold.

A typical reaction was to stare at the mess, as if staring could change it to something you might want to eat. Everyone left disappointed. No one was quite ready to eat it, and no one went back to the line to get more.

A girl, four or five, strayed away, to the cube. She'd been with the family that Juniper had followed in line. None of whom noticed the little girl leave. The only thing anyone saw was their slab. When their turn came, they drifted away with their mush. Minus the girl.

Without a container, Juniper caught a small portion in the palm of her hand. She'd never been hungry enough to be tempted by this...imitation of food. But as part of her research, she tested the goo with her fingers. She put a pinch into her mouth. It felt like, like – sawdust. The taste was repulsive. Before it could trigger a gag, she spit it all out. She offered the rest to the person behind her in line. They looked at it like it was vomit, and moved on around her.

So much for the nourishment the Network provided. When she ran out of food, she would have to find some other source of nutrition. Or maybe just wait until hunger exceeded revulsion. But now, the sugar lick made much more sense. There was no quicker way to kill appetites. And no quicker way to get children some calories. Cynical and lazy, but highly efficient. Nourishment wasn't the goal.

And now, stranded next to the sugar, was the girl whose family had left her behind. Juniper watched the girl realize that she was alone. She took one final taste of the sugar, then looked for her family. She walked over to where she'd last seen

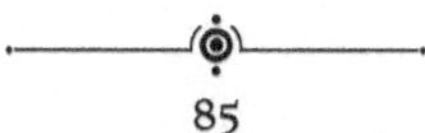

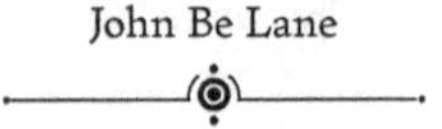

them, but they were not there. She started to cry. Her loss was complete.

Juniper approached her, since no one else showed any interest. She leaned down to her eye level.

'I will help you find your family,' she said. She picked up the girl, and carried her away from the collective indifference. Several steps, at least, until her ankle could not bear the weight. Then she held the girl's small, sticky hand.

The family had drifted off, toward the neighborhood north of the scene. That was the only clue Juniper had. So that was the way they would go.

The little girl's free thumb was now in her mouth. The thumb calmed her down, and was probably still smudged with sugar. As they walked down the street, she studied the girl, to see if she recognized one of the places they passed.

A cat intersected their path, with a rat in its mouth, still squirming for life.

When a vacant lot came into view, the girl stood in place. The only thing Juniper saw was auto parts and old furniture, which at first glance, was nothing but trash.

The girl took her thumb from her mouth, and pointed straight to the trash. Juniper studied the pile. She thought she saw something that might be an entryway. A mangy tail of smoke leaked out of the top.

Juniper directed the girl toward the heap, still watching for any reactions. Except for the smoke, there were no other symptoms of life. No sounds came out of the opening, which offered them nothing but darkness.

'*Hello!*' shouted Juniper. But there came no reply. Now the girl was pulling her hand. It seemed she was eager for them both to go in.

It wasn't a notion with any appeal. Nothing about it welcomed

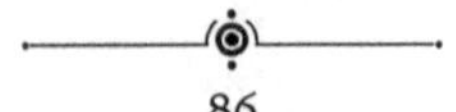

strangers who'd not been invited. She released the girl's hand, but the girl would not enter without her. This time, the girl grabbed for Juniper's hand. And with all of the force she could gather, she dragged them both into the dark.

Doc stewed, and awaited the Network's announcement. Would he and the players be witnessing Itch-ass's final sign-off from the Bullpen – or in person? It was still the best hope that he had to see Juniper again.

What might she be doing by now? Maybe desperate for something to eat? He hadn't had a look at the food she'd brought with her. Was she safe in the apartment they found, or had scavengers found their way in? Or maybe she'd left and he'd never hear anything either from, or about, her again.

And maybe she'd never be able to teach him to read. Thinking about it was agony – to learn how to read, or to not. To never know all of the mysteries that written words waited to tell. *Wanted* to tell. All of the secrets. All of the wisdom. Everything he'd never know, till he knew. Till he knew how to know.

He watched it go by on his monitor. Taunted by all of the Network's letters and words. *Here is another word you'll never know. Here is a notion that you'll never share. You're not entitled. Too bad for you. And now, here's another.* He studied each word as it went past his eyes. If he could just *will* himself, he might know what they meant.

As for the others, they couldn't care less. They laughed and they wasted their days with distractions. One empty moment, chasing another. Allergic to boredom. Trapped without context of future or past. Trapped in perpetual *now*.

But Doc's freefall of despair was abruptly aborted. By the Kid, who never called anyone. Calling Doc, on a private audio channel.

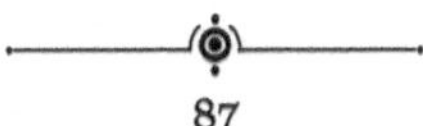

'Kid?' Across the room, through the non-game, low-res, headset display, he saw the Kid looking back.

The Kid spoke, *sotto voce*: 'There's a good chance we'll all be outside when they...when they do what they're doing to Itch-ass.'

Doc stood up to celebrate. The Kid motioned him back in his chair.

'How do you know?' Doc responded.

'I can't really say.'

'Don't matter. Thanks, Kid.'

Tomorrow they'd know if the Network would actually do what the Kid had persuaded it to. Or whether it might have discovered by now, that he was the one who had done the persuading.

The dark in the doorway of the igloo of trash, gave way to some daubs of blue light, just as the girl's tacky hand released Juniper's. Glowing slabs were the only light inside the structure. The sound? '*In Your Betterlife!*', and its pornographic pictures of the comfort and abundance that awaited every viewer who was salvaged from the sin of cognition. For the pathway to Hell would be littered with thought.

Juniper needn't have worried about that. Thoughts were the last thing on anyone's mind. Of the six or eight faces she saw in the slablight, no one could muster a grunt for the lost girl who appeared to live there. The little girl seemed to expect it. She found a spare slab, face-up on the pounded-dirt floor, and took up a place in the shadows. To stare at the wonders of Betterlife. To bathe in the doctrine. As that was, apparently, all she could do.

Eventually, she'd understand that points she might earn could buy luxuries, just like the ones she could see on her slab. After she died. Until then, she'd do what the Network had trained her to do. She would look at the slab, till the body she came in stopped working one day.

The faces that shined in this vision of Betterlife, reflected no doubt, and no curiosity from which to form questions about anything at all. Much less about Betterlife.

In these splotches of battery light, Juniper couldn't see furniture, clothing, windows, or plumbing. A small fire smoldered, without formal venting, and without containment. With an uncertain purpose. If Juniper wasn't mistaken, a pile of dried mush was burning for fuel. Maybe dried feces. There wasn't much difference.

Like an opium den in an earlier time, in every way but the narcotic. Slabs were the opium here. A few juicy coughs were traded around. Someone broke wind, without admonition. Maybe no one but Juniper even heard the infraction.

Aside from the Network, and the roof overhead, it was hard to imagine what bonds they all shared. Or who might have had enough moxie, sometime in the past, to bother with building a shelter.

No enlightenment here, only slablight. Less warmth than a candle would throw. Juniper saw what she'd needed to see. She backed out, as quick as her ankle and poles would permit. She had to get out of this bottomless void, with the hope she would never be back. She would leave with one thing on her mind. And that was a question.

How did all this ever *happen?*

The spectacle of Itch-ass was all you'd expect from the Network. At the usual place...the stage made of concrete, on the west-facing side of the old Capitol. On that stage, sat a chair. A chair that might easily have an ungrounded wire

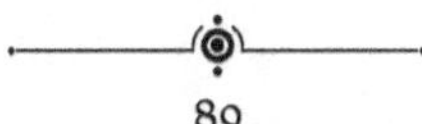

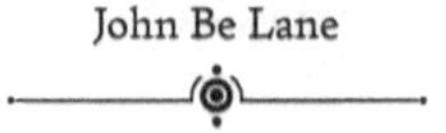

attached.

Behind the stage, a huge screen replayed all of the hits from the past. Chip removals, renowned for barbarity. They'd once used a magnet to pull a chip out of an ex-player's hand. He'd dangled up off of the stage, till his skin couldn't handle the weight.

And they'd once dipped a player's chipped hand in hot grease, then released starving wolves. The wolf that wound up with the chip (and the hand it was part of) was followed by drones, till the chip came to rest on the outskirts of town, in a fresh pile of scat. Though they never knew words they would need to describe it, the goners who watched it that day, would never forget what they'd seen.

The highlights were synched to a screamo-rap track that the Network played so loud, internal organs vibrated like chimes. The lyrics were pro-fan-i-ties and syll-a-bles in meaningless sequence, chopped up and disgorged by the algorithm. The youngest eardrums in the audience bled from the noise – and would never hear that well again.

But even the humanoid police banged their 'heads' to the migrainy pulse. Which made it seem strange when their software sent unprovoked cold cocks and electric shocks to goners who happened to be standing nearby.

While all this took place, the players were escorted outside to the street, by over-muscled humanoid enforcers. They reveled in the novelty of being outside, in the company of goners, who alerted their neighbors, to be sure that they noticed the players' famous faces. Along with the game show hosts everyone knew, the players were admired as celebrities; the only ones the Network ever bothered to create. It never did more than the least it could do.

The Kid remained right next to Doc. He watched everything that happened around him. The way someone shaded her eyes with her slab. Unfortunate goners who could not find a

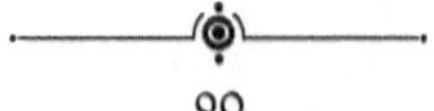

slab, but held empty hands in front of their faces, out of habit. The lack of camaraderie, or joy, or any variation of social interaction.

The Kid assumed others had reasons for the things that they did. Reasons he wasn't aware of. He assumed that the Network had reasons for whatever they were planning on doing to Itch-ass.

He assumed he himself was neither welcome, nor needed. Here, or anywhere else. Thin and dark, and striking to the eye, looking younger than he was, the Kid was convinced his appearance repelled everyone. He assumed there was something the matter with him. Something obvious, that everyone saw. He assumed there was something important, which he was expected to know, or to do. But he wasn't sure what it was. He assumed when they'd finished with Itch-ass, it would by rights be *his* turn for ridicule and shame.

He existed in fear anyone might have reason to know he existed. Until then, he did what he could to remain inconspicuous, so that no one might bother to ask who he was. Who or *why*.

As he drowned in self-consciousness, the screen at the back of the stage turned to white. Silence replaced the unbearable racket. Everyone but the Kid seemed to know what was coming, and what they were expected to do. Mutterings stilled. Postures aligned. Slabs were lifted to faces, so you couldn't see past them.

A black, solid circle emerged from the white on the screen. An artificial voice spoke, in words everybody repeated:

'All hail The Immortal! We beg he forgive us our sin, so that we find salvation in Betterlife! All hail The Immortal! All hail the world The Immortal created!'

A ring appeared, concentric to the circle – half as wide, half as dark.

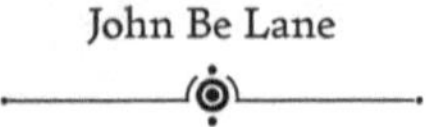

'*We thank the sustainers, who support The Immortal.*'

Then another ring followed, concentric to the first ring, but half as wide, half as dark.

'*We pray for the rest, who exist at The Immortal's discretion.*'

The Kid recognized the three circles. It was the icon on his monitor, that launched the keyboard he'd discovered. On the giant screen now, the three circles morphed into a graphic, on a simulated flag that snapped powerfully, in an animated breeze. Sobs spread like infection through the audience.

As a single-note anthem droned on, the Kid observed goners abandon what passed for decorum, and cry without shame. They outlined three circles on their chests. A cynic might have found it performative, but a cynic couldn't fathom the power of the ritual.

The monotone anthem concluded, and the flag got a moment of glory. The ground ran with tears and with snot, for handkerchiefs were luxuries reserved until Betterlife.

The screen and the slabs all went black. The mechanical Announcer continued:

'*We honor our path to salvation...*'

Heads lowered solemnly.

'*Never read,*' said the 'voice,' along with everyone else.

The Kid flinched when slabs drummed off everyone's forehead, with so much conviction and unanimous precision, it created its own field of gravity. He found he could barely inhale.

'*Never think,*' they repeated in unison, and then drummed their slabs.

'*Never question,*' they all said together – saluted again with the drumming of slabs.

'*Never do,*' as if in one voice. The sound of the slabs on their

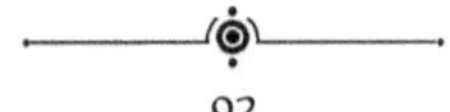

foreheads echoed off of the Capitol walls, that were raised in the name of democracy.

Then, back to the start, with increasing intensity: '*Never read* (thud!)...*never think* (thud!)...*never question* (thud!)...*never do* (thud!)...'

The incantation went on, several times all around. Lumps rose on foreheads, then blood mixed with tears. It seemed that the object was to hit one's own forehead demonstrably harder than anyone else. Which, if possible, escalated the hysteria.

The Kid noticed Doc's slab never quite struck his forehead. When he saw that the Kid had been paying attention, Doc gave him a wink.

Angry knots sprouted proudly on the foreheads of players around Doc and the Kid. Dipstick's eyes watered. Skin Flute's nose bled. Cornhole's slab nearly fractured in two. (Was that even *possible?*) Carbuncle knocked out a tooth.

Then the holy hysterics suddenly ended. Moans of agony and euphoria lingered in the crowd. No one was expecting any medical attention, and none would be coming. Self-harm was the intentional outcome.

Since the Kid did what Doc did, they both were still lucid. Doc leaned in to the Kid.

'Ever seen 'em take a chip out?'

The Kid didn't answer.

'There's ways they could do it, so it wouldn't hurt much. But that ain't how they do it.'

'Why not?'

'They're puttin' on a show. But I think they'd still do it anyway, just for the fun.' Doc pondered that notion and then said, 'I've known a few people who'd do something like that. They ain't worth a damn.'

The Kid now was making a point to remember whatever Doc said. How was it Doc knew life so well? While the Kid still had so much to learn?

'They'll stretch this thing out, as long as they can.'

That's when the screen and the slabs all switched back to the Show. Which began with a fanfare, and a teeth-and-hair MC.

'*Welcome, everybody, to this special presentation:* Itch-ass Plays the Game No More! *Please bring out our special guest!*'

No one had seen Itch-ass since they'd plucked him from the Bullpen. Now he sat on the stage, by himself. Head down. Like a body a soul had abandoned.

'*We'd prefer to forget all the things he has done. But instead, we and he must...examine the evidence!*'

The Network launched into a montage of Itch-ass's actual and fabricated crimes, accompanied by silly, slapstick sound effects. They said he'd used words with too many syllables (a serious crime by itself, although not one that Itch-ass had ever committed); his all-around fuck-ups as a player; and most embarrassing of all, his compulsive ass-scratching (every last one of them, replayed in close-up and slow-motion, goosed up by artificial laughter).

The Kid wondered how anyone endured such humiliation, but anyone who wasn't Itch-ass seemed to love it. Everyone but Doc, whose eyes swept the crowd.

'I owe you one, Kid,' said Doc, when he'd seen enough. He started to leave, but then stopped. He leaned close in to the Kid.

'They can drag you down here. They can't make you like it.'

The Kid nodded. Doc took two more steps, then disappeared into the crowd, and up the hill, east on Colfax.

Nobody noticed. All were distracted by the Itch-ass Show now. For maybe once in his life, the Kid felt like no one was paying

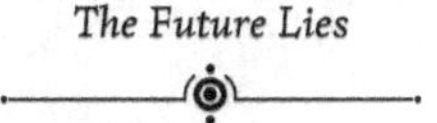

attention to him. No one was judging him. It was a bittersweet euphoria. Itch-ass was paying a horrible price.

Without thinking, he started to work his way out of the crowd, the same way that Doc had gone. Then he waited, in case someone decided to stop him. But nobody did. He took another step, and then paused. And then took another.

Among all of these people, it appeared that not one of them cared what he did. Nothing had ever felt better. And so he kept going.

Except that somebody *did* see him leave. And of all of the people who might have been watching, this one was by far the worst.

Part II

'*I was thinkin' about what a friend had said;*
I was hopin' it was a lie...'

– Neil Young

The Kid was just hoping to see which way Doc went. He didn't pay attention to the stage, or the slab in his hand. Still, it was hard not to hear all the people. Or the Network, as it ran through its evidence against Itch-ass.

But every step he got further away from all that, felt like a gift to the Kid. As well as a *theft*. Of time he was not meant to have.

North of the Capitol, where the density thinned, he practically stumbled on a couple of goners in mid-copulation, but managed to step over their legs. They didn't notice. The curve of her belly suggested it wasn't their first time together.

The shyer ones hid in the shadows on the far side of Colfax, until dogs found their never-washed scents, and bothered them into the light of the day. Police droids chased off the dogs, then *they* did the harassing.

There was plenty to look at, but the Kid had lost Doc. As he stepped to the curb on the east side of Grant Street, he was stopped there by something he heard. It stopped him as if he'd run into a wall. It was a strange kind of music, fresh to his ears. A shimmering guitar that shivered his spine, then rocked him, to one side and back. It pleased him in places he did not know he had.

Then, a nasal voice joined the guitar and the drums. But the

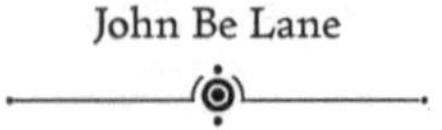

voice wasn't singing. It was *flirting*:

'Aw, *lay it on me, baby!*
Don't stop now...
I'm red' to burn, baby,
right here and now...'

Whoever's voice it was, wasn't concealing the lust. Had no *intention* to hide it. The Kid had witnessed carnality, only moments before. But this was so different – desire, mixed with *glee*. It owned all his attention.

The sound was coming out through a doorway that opened on an angle, to the intersection of Colfax and Grant. The patterned sheet that curtained the doorway, danced from breezes blowing inside and out. Or was it from the music?

The ghosts of sign letters still clung to bricks on the outside of the building, in the half-life of paint:

Capitol Hill BOOKS / used & rare books

The singer wasn't finished yet:

'Now, *there's a place down the street*
they call the "Tip'n Inn".
Let's walk down there, baby.
*That's where the f-f-fun begin – *'

But it wasn't only music coming out through that curtain. It was more like an invitation, to a new point of view – wavelengths of a language that did not depend only on words. A language he'd not ever heard. And yet somehow, he understood every last word.

'*You know you sends me, baby.*
Let's go on in h'yir!'

He dropped his slab without even thinking, and followed the music inside.

Sunlight lined in through the window. Flowers – *flowers*, placed in vases. Pictures. Posters on the wall, and shelf after

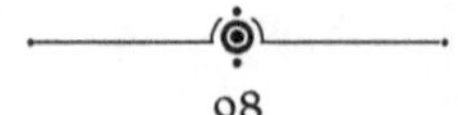

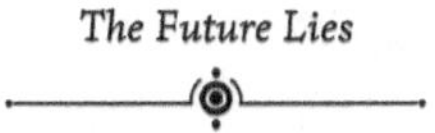

shelf of clear plastic squares, neatly lined-up on their edges.

Entranced by the sounds, and all else around him, he did not see the woman coming out from the room in the back. Nor did she see him either, at first.

Then she startled: 'Oh!'

Retreat. That's what the Kid did, as fast as he could.

'Please don't go!' she called out. 'I always hope for visitors, but no one ever stays.'

She watched him consider his choices. She saw his eyes look for the place where the music came from.

'Isn't this music the *best*?' she asked quickly, to keep him engaged. 'So *earthy*. Don't you think?' She looked around. 'I think *this* is his likeness.' She showed him the case. Inside, was a photo of a man who was holding an instrument...a guitar. Like it was his lover. His eyes were closed. His mouth appeared to be singing. The photo had letters.

'I'd give anything if I knew his name,' she said.

He disguised the path of his eyes, the way he had been trained to do. That way, he could read without showing it.

SLIM HARPO, said the letters in ochre, but the Kid did not make the mistake of repeating the name.

He saw that the woman was watching him. Her eyes shone off of her silver-white hair, like turquoise that someone had dropped on white sand. It was uncommon these days that anyone lived long enough to see even a single pale hair. The prints on her kaftan were geometric shapes, that rippled whenever she moved.

'It sounds like they've attracted a crowd down the street,' she said.

His slightest nod answered her.

'But here you are, and not there,' she smiled. She was content

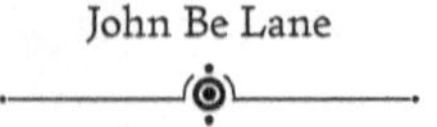

to see he *considered* replying.

'I've just made tea. Can I get you some, too?'

This time his eyes gave him away.

'Tea it is!' She paused long enough to regard him. 'Wait here,' she said. 'I mean it – don't leave! I have honey to go with the tea.'

While she was away, there was plenty for him to take in. His eyes came to rest on a wall with a grouping of items. A painted plate…a poster…a tea towel…some coasters, which all featured photos of the same two young faces. A man and a woman, full of assurance, though the colors had faded with time.

When the woman came back with the tea, he was studying them.

'You've found my obsession,' she said.

He backed off, embarrassed.

'The King and the Queen of England, on their wedding day. Aren't they the handsomest couple? Everyone loved them. All over the world. Who wouldn't? They spent their honeymoon not far from here. Isn't that hard to believe? They could have gone anywhere!'

She'd given him reason to study them closer.

'Let's have some tea,' she said. 'To honor the King and the Queen.' She moved lighted candles from the back of the room to a table, between two lumpy stuffed chairs. The most comfortable chair that the Kid had sat down in.

'Please,' she urged him. She nudged the cup and the saucer toward him, as she took her own seat.

He lifted the cup and the saucer and breathed in the perfume from the tea. He took a premature sip, which scalded his lip. She blew on her own tea, to show him the way he could cool it. He followed her lead, and on his next sip, he tasted the

botanics and honey.

He almost spoke up, and then realized he did not have the words.

'I had a feeling you'd like it. It's made out of flowers and herbs from our garden,' she smiled. (*Could the Kid now recall when he'd last seen a smile? He could not.*) 'My name is Lucy.'

She watched him debate the decision to speak. His head shook, rejecting a thought. His eyes were now watching the floor.

'Did they give you a different name?'

That got his attention.

'Why do they do that?' she continued. 'The names they come up with! Well, they don't seem too flattering, do they?'

This caught him in mid-sip. He did not expect humor, and fought hard to avoid spraying his tea. Which then tickled Lucy. Suddenly, they were both tickled, together. Levity was such an unusual thing, it might as well be forbidden.

'At least...,' he said, then had to wait for a giggle to pass, '...at least my nickname isn't "Cornhole."'

Lucy snickered. 'Oh, there *couldn't* be...'

The Kid nodded, to assure her that there *could*.

'Wet Fart,' he struggled to say, and they both started laughing, again. 'Buh...Buh... *Booger* Finger!'

'No!'

'Skid Mark!' He could barely get the words out.

Neither had laughed this much since, maybe, forever. There just never was anything funny...until this unforeseen moment of mutual delight.

She finally recaptured her breath and said, 'So, that leaves us with the actual name that your parents gave *you*...'

Then she saw on his face she had made a mistake. The question was too sudden. Too personal. He was about to slip off of her hook.

'Please forgive me! You know, I should never have asked.'

She watched him stare somewhere too far off to see.

'My family is gone,' he said. 'But I don't like the name that they stuck me with.'

'You don't have to say it.'

He thought for a while, and under his breath he said, 'Roscoe.'

If she'd known him for longer, she'd hug him. Either way, he seemed more like a cat...best to let him come to her.

'I think it's a good name,' she said. 'It looks good on you.'

The fog was beginning to clear. She had his eyes back.

'Better than "Boot Lick," I guess.'

'Better than most of those names that I've heard.' She took another sip of her tea. Enough time to think of a new thing to say. 'You must be a player. Someone in the Show.'

'I've barely just started.'

'The Network is choosy. They only pick ones they think highly of.'

'I'm not sure Itch-ass would agree.'

'Is he a player?'

'He *was*, until...,' Roscoe gestured outside, toward the Capitol. With each cheer they could hear, Itch-ass fell further from grace.

'I can barely imagine how hard it must be,' she said. 'Playing the game.'

But she was beginning to lose him again. She could see he was swimming, back out to sea. So she scrambled to woo him back in to the shore. She wooed him with words, as fast as she'd manage to make them come out of her mouth.

'I wish that some time you could visit my friend and me. Her name is Val. We like to spend time with our friends. We make bonfires, eat soup, and we talk. You'd be welcome there, Roscoe.'

That was an impossible thought. But he couldn't resist asking her, 'Where?'

'Not far from here. *That* way, down the big street outside.' She pointed out the window, toward Colfax. 'Keep going, till you find the big hole in the sidewalk.'

'A hole?'

'Big enough to fall in. So be careful, if there's not enough light! Go past the hole, to the next street you come to. Then turn toward this side of the street.'

'Right.' He was sorry as soon as he said it. Understanding the concept of right vs. left was a symptom of *knowledge*. He couldn't count (and dared not show that he knew *how* to count) all the times he'd been taught not to make any little mistakes – basic numbers, left and right. Simple things that betrayed little signs of cognition, that could jeopardize one's long-term survival.

'I meant, turn this way, right?' he followed up quickly.

Did a twinkle just flash in her turquoise eye?

'Yes, that's the right way,' she confirmed. 'Then, follow that street till you get to a park. No buildings – just grass and trees. Up the hillside, you'll see our bonfire. It will light up the Parthenon at the top of the hill.'

'What's that?'

'The Parthenon? Pillars of marble. You'll know when you see it.'

What a compelling idea she'd just placed in his mind! As if

he might actually…*freelance* with his time. To join in with this woman and her friends. By a fire. At a place called the Parthenon. Unlike anything the Network would ever allow. And yet she made it sound casual. So offhand and easy. A *choice*, he might make.

'I don't see how I could do that,' he said.

'Oh, I understand. You can forget that I mentioned it.' She sipped her tea. 'But if that ever changes, we'd be so glad to have you. Val, and me, and our friends.'

'I should not even be here right *now*.'

'I won't say a word.'

She watched as he looked at the King and the Queen. Then she watched him come back.

'When do you do this, again?'

'Every full Moon and new Moon.'

Roscoe's mind sped through scenarios. He would have to find some way to make the Network think…*something*. Something, something. So that he, and maybe Doc, could get out of the Bullpen again. And then get back in. While the Network knew nothing about it. But the chances…it had to be almost impossible. This time, they got lucky. *He* got lucky. How could it possibly happen again?

And yet, as his friend, Lucy, had said…stop there! He *had a new friend! A new friend named Lucy! A friend he would never have met*, if he hadn't…if he had not *fooled*…there was no other word for it…fooled the Network into…but this would be something much bigger than he could consider…it would take so much luck…and such a good plan…the risk would be bigger next time…no, it might be a fun thing to wonder about, but this sounded like something that he couldn't do… and yet, again, as his new friend, *Lucy*, had said, '…if that ever changes…'

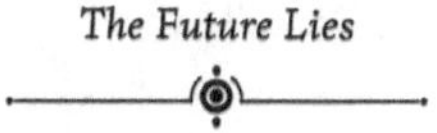

He was sure he'd be wondering how that might change.

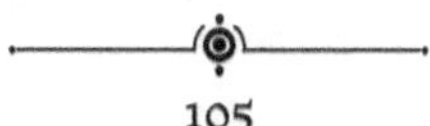

Juniper just couldn't watch any longer. Couldn't witness the emasculation of the young man called Itch-ass. Delivered live to the masses, for sport. Even though it might help her to fathom this world she was stuck in, she didn't find *torment* entertaining.

If she had other choices, she'd make them. But for the moment, she had no way out. After reuniting the lost little girl with her family – hoping, at least, that it *was* her family – she'd continued on, in search of her disabled truck. The scavengers had not yet digested the chassis, which was still in the place she had left it. Down to the axle. Wheel-deep in the pothole. The rest of what once was her truck, had been taken.

Not a thing had gone as she'd expected. As for another plan, what would that be? Somehow, to leave? If so, how? On foot? Once her ankle was better? On foot, to where? Back where she'd come from? There was nothing there now to go back to. Perhaps, somewhere else? Somewhere else might as well have been some other planet.

On the other hand, she'd found a friend. Or rather, a new friend had found *her*. With dumb luck, they'd secured her a place she could stay. For now, at least. Better than what might have happened.

Maybe she just needed time, to adjust to the place where she was. For her ankle to heal. To make a new plan. To build back her strength.

So she would spend time, as busy as possible. Getting strong. There wasn't too much she could do yet. But she'd do what she could. Push-ups (a challenge, on only one ankle), and sit-ups. Kettlebells the Baltimores had left her.

Getting stronger was better than helplessness. It would help keep her mind off the things she'd been through. Horrors her

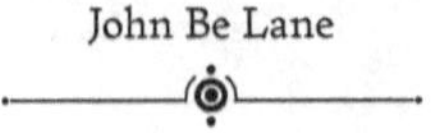

memory was waiting to make her remember. Her wounds, she would salve now with sweat. She would harden her body. Till she was exhausted, if that's what it took. And that's what it took.

To the point she imagined she was hearing a voice. She imagined she heard a voice, calling her name.

O ⊙ O

She clearly heard '*Juniper!*', then footsteps, up the stairs. It couldn't be, could it? But no one else around here knew her name. How fast could she get to the door?

'*Calvin!*' she called out, into the stairwell.

'You're still here!' he said, taking the final flight two stairs at a time.

Could this be a dream? Had they met before? They needed a moment to retrace the faces they'd only seen briefly, days before. Yes, that had happened. And now this, as well.

She surprised both of them with a hug. 'Sir Calvin came back.'

'I thought for sure you'd be gone.'

She turned to invite him inside.

He couldn't quite tell what she'd done to the place. It wasn't much different than the first time he'd seen it. And yet, it was different. Warm, bright, and lived-in. It felt now like somebody's home.

'I can't stay for too long,' he said. 'They just let us out to watch the...' He leaned his head back toward the Capitol.

She nodded. 'I watched for a while, then I couldn't.'

'Ain't nothin' to see. But I had to get back here. How's your ankle?'

'My ankle is better. Which I owe to you.'

'Can I see it?'

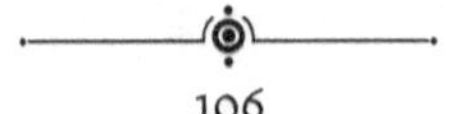

She pulled up the bottom of her slacks.

'You got a new wrap on there now.'

'I miss the seat belt,' she smiled.

He looked around, updating his memories.

'I can offer you water,' she said.

'Sure, I'll take some water.' He sat down on the couch. 'Yeah, I figured maybe you went back there, for your truck. Maybe you'd drove off by now.'

She came back from the kitchen with water.

'I did go back.' She sat down in the easy chair. 'I...'

There were times when it felt like emotions were just waiting for someone to knock on their door. This time, the knock was the empathy in Sir Calvin's eyes. She felt all of her coiled emotions begin to let go. But just for a moment.

'...I did go back. But I didn't find much when I got there.'

'Scavengers?'

She nodded. 'And you were right about the axle.' She replayed the scene in her mind. 'That *thing* swerved, right in front of me... I couldn't see the pothole under all of that water. But that was not a good day. And I didn't have time to react.'

'I never seen a day as crazy as that. I wasn't too sure I'd get back here again.'

'Should I ask how you...?'

'It came down to Itch-ass,' he waved his hand. 'That nightmare they're putting him through.'

'How do you stand it? This seems like a terrible place.'

'It's all what you're used to. You don't even notice. But I've been starting to think the same thing.'

'Well, I'm sorry for the reason you're here. But I'm so glad to see you!'

'I mean, you did say you'd teach me how to read. Remember?'

'Of course I remember. But...does no one here *read*?'

It was the most dumbfounding question that Calvin had heard.

'They catch you *reading*? What they done to Itch-ass would be *nothin*'.'

She shook her head. She knew he was serious, but that did not explain it.

'I heard what those people were saying today. With all of that anger. Never *read*...'

He nodded. 'Never read. Never think. Never question. Never do. That's all you need to know.'

'It's like this family I met today. I *think* it was a family. I did not really meet them; I *saw* them. They just sat there in the darkness. Every one of them. They didn't seem to know I was there. Or if they did notice, didn't *care*. They left their daughter behind, at the sugar cube. All by herself. No one said a word when I brought her back home. Doesn't anyone care about anything?'

'Well, the Network's s'posed to care. I guess. But it don't. It just cares about itself.'

She paused for a moment to regard this young man. This not-quite-a-boy, sitting there. *Gangly* was the word she would use to describe him. Gangly, with a shock of hair that increased his height, now that she was seeing it dry. His eyes were alive, animated by kindness. She saw there a hunger, to make some kind of sense of it all.

'I wonder why reading's the first thing,' she said.

'The first thing?'

'Of all of those things in that list of bad things. "Never read."

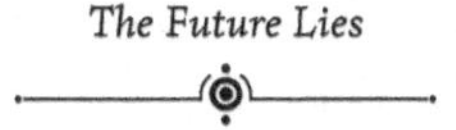

I wonder why reading's the first.'

'Reading's the gateway. That's what they call it.'

'Gateway to what?'

'Let me put it this way. You can't be happy when you're thinkin' about things. *Knowin'* things. It guarantees that you won't get to Betterlife. That's what they say.'

'It just doesn't make sense. To me, anyway.'

'The Network don't need people interferin' with things. Gettin' in their way. First you read, then you think. Then you might think, "Wait a minute. Why's that like that?" And that's the *last* thing they want to be dealin' with. They've got too much already to do. Puttin' on the Show. All them other things they do.'

'So no one's supposed to ask *questions*?'

He nodded. 'That's why them books of yours was so...why I didn't want nobody to find out you had 'em.'

'But then you asked me to teach you to read.'

He nodded. 'Kind of funny, ain't it?'

'Kind of *dangerous*, is what it sounds like.'

'I know that. I do. I just...I see these things that they do. I've seen 'em say the rules was one thing, and then change 'em around. And then you get someone like Itch-ass. He didn't *try* to hurt nobody. You give him a chance, and then you take it all back. It's *mean*, is what it is.

'I get to where, I don't care how important the damn Network's s'posed to be. Can't you be a little nicer? Do you have to make it so hard for people to live? That's the thing I never understand. Makes me wonder what they're so afraid of. I didn't even know books was real, till I seen them ones in your truck. What's in them books? What don't they want me to know? That's what I want to know!'

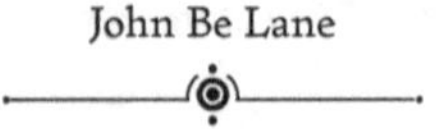

He stopped himself. 'I must be a fool to think that kind of thing.'

She shook off that notion. 'You're not a fool at all.'

'Does that mean you'll teach me?'

'I worry for your safety.'

'There's something goin' on with the Network. I couldn't tell you why. But it's spewin' out words of some kind. I can see 'em right there, in front of me. In the Bullpen, on my screen. It's like sittin' at a table with all of this food. Hot food. *Good* food. You can see it. You can smell it. You're hungry as all get-out. But you can't ever *taste* it. Not ever. 'Cause you might start to like it. That's what this feels like.'

He thought about that for a moment, and then added: 'I want to have me a bite.'

There was no easy way to determine the balance of what might be worse, for Calvin. To let him starve? Or to put him at risk, by helping him learn how to feed his own need? And why was the choice forced on *her?* Why did she have to enforce someone else's ridiculous law? She resented the dilemma. It was Calvin's choice to make, not hers. And his choice was clear.

'To Hell with the rule. If you want to learn, then I'd love to teach you.'

She'd not seen him grin, because grinning was not something people had reason to do much these days. Until now.

'I don't have too much time now. Do you think you could start me on somethin', before I have to get goin'?'

She collected some papers that were there on the table. 'I've started to make you a book. A *copy* of a little book I learned to read with. It's the book that I used to teach Harmony to read.'

'Who's Harmony?'

'My sister.' The name seemed to make her attention get lost. Then she found it again. She continued: 'I'd give anything to show you the actual book. I'm doing my best to remake it from memory, but I can't do it justice.'

'What's it called?'

'It's called *The Cat in the Hat*.'

He chuckled at that.

'You would love it. You *will* love it, when I'm finished. For now, I just wrote out the alphabet.'

'Now there's a new word.'

'It's all of the letters that words are made out of. Letters are the first thing you learn.'

She gave him the page with the letters.

'I've written the letters in pairs. The small letters are the same as the big ones they're next to. You might see either one when you're reading, depending on how they are used.'

'How do I know which letter is which?'

'Each one has its own name.'

He suddenly looked overwhelmed.

'Don't worry! There's a song I can teach you that makes them easy to remember.'

She sang it several times. Then she had him sing it with her. Then he sang it by himself.

'That's it?'

'That's it. That's the alphabet. You've finished your first lesson.'

He closed his eyes and leaned his head back. He was grinning again.

'Some day, I will read!'

'I hope, someday *soon*.'

'I should probably go now. But I will be back. As soon as I figure out how.'

'For Lesson 2.'

'2. That comes after 1?'

She thought he was teasing at first. But he wasn't.

'It certainly does.'

'I can't hardly wait.' He started to leave, and then stopped. 'I almost forgot – this is for you…'

From his pockets, he unloaded packets of the snacks and ostensible meals that the Network provided the players. They lacked the nutrition that Juniper was used to, but on sight, they'd be better than what passed for food out on Colfax.

'I'll bring more with me next time.'

'This is a feast.'

She hugged his shoulder as they walked to the door.

'Be well,' she said.

He held up the alphabet. 'Thank you,' he said, then folded it into his pocket. 'I'll see you soon.'

She thought, *I hope you do*. Through the closed door, she could hear he was waiting, till she'd set the lock. Then she heard his feet staccato down the stairs.

○ ◉ ○

Roscoe was too deep in thought to notice that Lucy had excused herself, and come back with sliced peaches on a plate. She served them to Roscoe.

'Peaches. From our greenhouse.'

He wasn't sure what he should do. She picked up a slice and took a bite. She shrugged and wiped off her chin. 'Juicy!' she

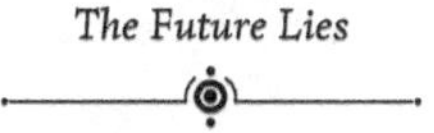

said, and ate the other half-slice.

Roscoe took a slice, and held it under his nose. The scent was subtle and pleasant. He licked the cool pulp. It tasted sweet, familiar, as if he'd had peaches before, in a life that he couldn't remember. He ate the slice, and then ate another. As he picked up the next one, he realized that Lucy was smiling.

He put back the slice, and tried to give her the plate. She shook her head.

'I can have them any time,' she said.

With every new slice, he noticed each taste bud, the way that the flavor pirouetted, and the joy that the taste left behind. When all of the slices were gone, he leaned back, to bask in the pleasure.

'If you think that was good,' she said finally, 'then I hope you will visit some time. At the Garden. Right next to the Parthenon, where we have the bonfires. I promise you'll get a good meal. If I had known I'd see you – *meet* you – today, I'd have come with more peaches, and a fresh loaf of bread.'

When one has known nothing but callous indifference, the smallest of kindness can be most profound.

If only he could manage to transcend the shackles that eyes couldn't see. The *idea* of which, was all that was required to keep him confined. Its effectiveness, based on the lack of alternatives. In which, only this way of being was even *conceivable*. By removing the other possibilities, the Network had much less to worry about. Death was where one found a better life. That's where the green pastures waited. This dim imitation of reality would have to suffice, until then.

And yet the humblest seed was now planted in Roscoe. Conceivable here, in this actual life. It tasted like a peach.

Just then, a haunted howl sounded from somewhere in Hell, and Roscoe knew the worst had occurred now, for Itch-ass.

'I had hoped I would never hear that sound again,' Lucy said.

Roscoe searched the street, outside the window. It was his time to go. Doc must have got the same message. He hurried past the storefront, not knowing that Roscoe could see him walk by.

Roscoe reached for the curtain, and paused.

'I...' what was the word he was looking for? '...*thank* you, Lucy.'

She smiled, so he felt the warmth she created.

'Roscoe, the pleasure was mine. I hope, I hope, I *hope* that I will see you sometime again, soon.'

He held her eyes one moment longer than good manners required, and then vanished back into the world outside of the curtain in the doorway to Lucy's teahouse. For all of her hope, she did not dare assume they would cross paths again.

○ ◉ ○

The Kid was about to catch Doc when a hand grabbed his arm. The mechanical hand of a humanoid police droid.

'*What are you doing here?*' it demanded. Its tone was as cool as the granite of the Capitol's shady north wall.

In the instant that followed, Roscoe's mind traded places with Itch-ass. The physical pain he imagined was nothing compared to the shame that would play out in public, and the fear of whatever might follow. In that moment, it was real in his mind.

'I was just...I was just...' Roscoe had to say something, but nothing coherent made its way to his mouth.

Then a new voice asserted itself. *Doc's* voice.

'We was tryin' to find *you*. Where you been? There's somebody bleeding back there. See? Under that maple tree. At least there was when we went lookin' for you. He needs help.'

The police droid turned its head.

'Right over there,' pointed Doc. 'On the other side of all of them people.'

The police droid released Roscoe's arm. It started off toward the tree, and then stopped.

'*Identification?*'

They both raised their hands up for scanning.

'*Your group's down there,*' the humanoid gestured. '*Where you should be, too.*'

'That's where we was headed,' Doc retorted. 'Will you just help that guy?'

The police droid tromped off. Roscoe could not believe what he'd seen.

'How did you know there was someone over there?'

Doc turned to confirm that the police droid was now out of sight.

'It's called a bluff, Kid. You put some attitude behind it, and sometimes, you get lucky. Not that them shitwits know their fake ass from a hole in their fake head. They just act like they do. That's *their* bluff.'

'Thanks, Doc.'

'Call me Calvin. That's my real name – Calvin.'

'I'm Roscoe.'

Calvin stopped and nodded. 'That's just between me and you. That information ain't for nobody else.'

Rosco acknowledged him back, and gestured his head toward the Capitol. 'Did you just hear Itch-ass?'

Calvin kept walking. 'I wish I hadn't.'

Roscoe caught up. 'What'll happen to him now?'

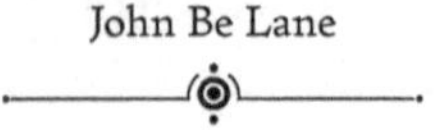

'All's I know is…we won't likely see Itch-ass no more.'

'Where's he gonna go?'

Calvin shrugged. 'First thing, we should get ourselves back down the hill.' He caught himself, before he continued. 'I just remembered. When I left, you was down there with the rest of them.'

Roscoe nodded.

'And now you're up here.'

'I left right after you did.'

Calvin gave Roscoe a smile of respect. 'I had a feeling about you, Kid.'

'Roscoe.'

'You gonna tell me what happened?'

'I…I guess I met someone myself.'

'Okay. There you go. So that means, we both have a reason to get out here again.'

Calvin set off, and Roscoe did his best to keep up. More goners shuffled close to them now, near the fringes of the audience. Teenaged boys started fights. Dogs followed their noses to find scraps of food, and poked them into places you might think were private. But no one complained.

Calvin stretched himself tall, to locate the rest of the players. He cut into the thicket of the crowd, toward the place where they'd last seen the rest of the players. Roscoe was pressed in so close to Calvin, he could hear he was humming a song. A song Roscoe had heard, but forgotten. It took a moment, and then he remembered it. *Twinkle, Twinkle, Little Star*. Calvin was one of a kind. Then Roscoe remembered all the *other* words he'd learned to that tune. Not words – no, they were *letters*. Letters of the alphabet.

Before he could dwell on Calvin's selection of music, they met

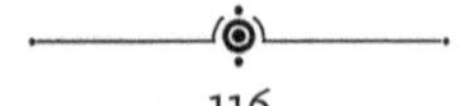

up with the rest of the players. They were all still absorbed with the end of the Network's de-chipping ritual. The three-circle animation, again. The flag. The anthem. Three circles on the chests. And one final refrain, punctuated by the smashing of slabs:

'*Never read* (thud!)...*never think* (thud!)...*never question* (thud!)...*never do* (thud!)...'

Roscoe was again mesmerized by how all of the players reacted. Had he not known them in private, he might have believed what he saw. But, Carbuncle...in tears? *Dipstick?* You would think they would be too embarrassed, but they weren't.

As soon as festivities ended, they were back to their true personalities.

'Did you see Itch-ass's face when they showed what he did? He was all *sad* and shit,' said Cornhole.

'Like he was about ready to *cry*,' laughed Needle Dick.

'He *did* cry when they finally took his chip,' said Wet Fart, then mocked the sound Itch-ass let out.

'That ain't funny!' Calvin had heard enough.

'What ain't funny?'

'None of that. All 'a you should be ashamed. Itch-ass was your friend!'

'Itch-ass was a fuck-up.'

'I seen all of you fuck up before. Lotsa times. Ain't nobody here that don't fuck up, at one time or another.'

'You were always sticking up for him,' said Dipstick.

'I've stuck up for *you* before, too. Every one 'a you. You stand here laughin', but you won't be laughin' on the day they put *you* up there.'

'Itch-ass did that to himself.'

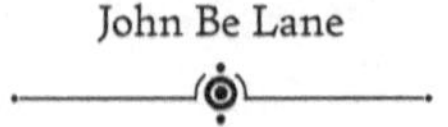

'I hope you'll have more luck than he did, when you need a friend.'

The humanoid enforcers had apparently received new orders from the Network. They corralled all the players, and herded them back toward the Bullpen.

'Yippie eye-oh kai-yay,' sang Cornhole.

'Keep moving,' growled the biggest enforcer.

The players quietly obeyed. Before they were quite off the Capitol grounds, Roscoe noticed a new person, moving along with the group. Near the back. Smaller than everyone else, maybe younger. No one appeared to know who she was. And yet she acted just like she belonged.

Roscoe, apparently, turned around once too often.

'What are *you* lookin' at, peewee?' she snarled, with all the contempt a little sister might have.

Roscoe's desire to avoid drawing attention had just blown up in his face. He compounded his tactical error by wilting under fire.

It was catnip to a bully.

The mood in the Bullpen could not be more different from the spectacle outside at the Capitol. From mass hysteria, to the silence of the Moon.

The Network avatar that caretook the everyday affairs of the players had just introduced them to Itch-ass's replacement. Sitting now among them, at the console that Itch-ass always used. She was introduced to the players as 'Sketchy'.

This was followed by the news that tomorrow's theme would be *The Fall of Rome*, which no one in the room ever heard of. They were shown the costumes their avatars would wear, and the weapons they'd be using. Axes, spears, clubs, bows-and-

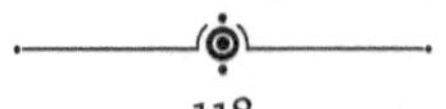

arrows. *Pre-guns*, in other words. Not the most exciting news they'd ever heard, but they had overnight to strategize. And free time until tomorrow.

Free time was something everyone cherished. It was typically social; a chance to do whatever the players wanted to do. Joke and fart and, at all times, exaggerate. Any other time, this would have been when they would inventory all of the teenaged girls they'd encountered that afternoon. A chance to savor every nuance of the hormone-fueled attractions.

But not today. Today, the only thoughts inside the Bullpen were of their new colleague. Sketchy. Was that her name?

Headsets were removed, and chairs were redirected toward the new recruit. No one said a word, till Sketchy broke the silence.

'Everybody heard it. I'm gonna be here now. So get used to it.' She put her hands on Itch-ass's gaming console, then pulled them back, disgusted.

'This controller has food – or *something* – all over it,' she said. 'Gross. Does anybody ever wash their hands around here? Does anybody ever wash their *socks*? I've got a feeling Itch-ass is not the only person here who needs to be replaced.'

No one found the words to speak. In *seconds*, she had undermined the only atmosphere the Bullpen ever knew. Like it never even *was*. And Sketchy wasn't done yet.

'I think I know where Wet Fart got his name. Does anyone remember how to flush a toilet? Which, by the way, that private bathroom is now *mine*. Off limits. No exceptions. And I don't want to see, or even *think* about somebody's boner. *Anybody's* boner. Are we all clear on that?'

Silent disbelief was the general reaction. Finally, Calvin cleared his throat.

'I never heard nobody talk like that. Whereabouts...'

'*Whereabouts?* Whereabouts did they ever find *you*, hayseed? Molesting a cow?'

'That ain't funny, Sketchy.'

'I'm sure it wasn't. To the cow.'

Roscoe watched Calvin shake his head, though his line of sight was interrupted now by Sketchy and her console. Muttering made its way around the room.

'Clear the cobwebs off those washing machines,' said Sketchy. '*Eulch!* My nose deserves better.'

In private conversations, players talked about ways they could sabotage Sketchy in the game itself. No need to worry about boners in the meantime. Nothing could be further from the realm of titillation than the housekeeping that began now, in sullen silence.

Sketchy didn't seem to care that no one said a word to her. She gloated in the incremental tidiness she'd hectored from the players.

One by one, they drifted back to find some solace at their consoles. Most tuned in to watch the Show; some found games to play. Doc was captivated by the characters that streamed along the bottom of his monitor.

He now distinguished letters, thanks to Juniper. Having learned their names, they no longer were unfathomable mysteries. He concentrated on the ones that started what he recognized as *words*. He tried naming the letters to himself. It took all of his restraint not to peek at the paper that Juniper had given him.

In the meantime, Roscoe read every word on the screen. To disguise it, he clicked and moved the joystick on his console, and pretended to be focused on a game.

And he discovered more about the hidden world that

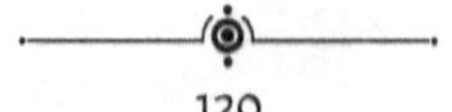

opened up by clicking on the triple-circle icon. He studied the mechanics of the Network's inner monologues.

Not monologues, but *conversations*, among its disparate components. The more he saw, the more he thought he understood. Though there was much he didn't understand, there seemed to be a lot the Network didn't know itself.

In chatter, they brought up a name they'd talked about before.

'Hess isn't pleased the text is still visible. He calls it the same sloppy business that enabled Itch-ass to…to…'

'…humiliate The Immortal, in real time?'

'Let's not use the word "humiliate".'

'Our recovery was quick and seamless.'

'And yet Hess is not impressed. Arriving in the wake of the unprecedented power failure, and of course the Itch-ass incident, the unintended text display is further evidence, he says, of our declining standards.'

'We need ideas. It shouldn't take this long to figure out what happened with the text, and how to fix it.'

…Blink…Blink…Blink… went the cursor.

The Network didn't seem to have a clue, as each new blink confirmed. The harder it became to witness, the more that Roscoe was inclined to try his luck again. He saw no reason why his first success could not be followed by another.

'Ideas?' came the Network's desperate plea.

Roscoe typed a message on the keyboard. He read it over twice, and then he cast it to the Network waters:

'Is it possible the power failure caused a subroutine to quit?'

…Blink…Blink…Blink…

'Not a likely causation,' was the Network's response.

'Not likely, or not possible?' Roscoe offered.

'Not likely.'

It was the opening that Roscoe had hoped for. He had another message ready, and he sent it:

'*In that case, might the right command reactivate the subroutine?*'

...Blink...Blink...Blink...

The silence terrified him. He probably should not have spoken up. He probably should not have dabbled in a theory, which exposed him to exposure.

He was rescued from his torment by another Network plea:

'*There must be some opinions! A subroutine command does not seem like a radical suggestion.*'

'*Yes, it might be possible,*' a Network voice confirmed. '*That is, assuming that the unintended text display did result from a terminated subroutine.*'

'*A bold CYA – thank you! What command is recommended?*'

Roscoe had a follow-up prepared, but it might represent a long step into darkness.

...Blink...Blink...Blink...

'*What command is recommended?*'

The entire Network focused now on Roscoe. Presumably, it didn't know that. It was thinking he was one of the pieces of itself, anonymous and equal. But he had spoken up, and all the pressure was on him. Not the least of which were several outcomes he imagined...only one of which was good.

If his suggestion fixed the problem, he might lose his access to the keyboard and text. Would he have to recreate the bug, to see them both again? At the risk of calling more attention to himself? By then, the Network might have figured out that he himself was hacking in.

But that would always be a chance he would take, any time he interacted with the Network. He might fool it for a while, and

then do something inadvertent that would give himself away.

In the best case, he would still have access to the text and keyboard, though he wasn't sure how that would work. Was it worth the risk? As a player in the game now, his situation was as good as it could be. The Network posed no threat to him.

And then he thought of Lucy. Lucy, and her music, and her garden, and her bonfire, and her eyes when she got tickled at the thought of someone's stupid nickname. Unless he could continue to manipulate the Network, it was possible that he and Lucy wouldn't ever meet again. That was not a prospect that appealed to him. She had offered him the rarest thing... *friendship*. He understood why Calvin was so eager to get back out again. Enough that made his long shot worth the try.

He paused a moment to appreciate how much he knew about the way the Network functioned. The things his grandfather had tried to teach him. Things that were now making sense. About the way that programs work. System architecture. He wished he had been a little older at the time. He wished he could revisit all those conversations they had shared. He'd forgotten more than he remembered.

But what had stuck might be enough to bluff the Network. A bluff that Calvin would approve of. A feeling in his gut told him the Network might be bluffing even more. That it was less than it appeared to be. That maybe it had once been more, but now it didn't care as much. Now it didn't try as hard.

Calculations ricocheted inside his mind.

'*What command is recommended?*' the Network asked itself again.

Here went nothing. Here went everything. Roscoe sent the message:

'*Given the syntax used for other subroutines...recommend we enter* **<HideText>**.'

'*Assess the risk/reward parameters.*'

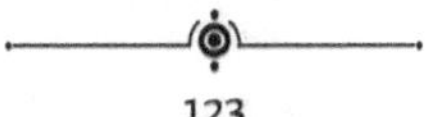

...Blink...Blink...Blink...

'No risk identified for incorrect commands. The source code just ignores them.'

'Other thoughts?'

'Action is essential. Even unsuccessful action.'

'Elaborate.'

'Hess has indicated that the Network shows a lack of motivation. That our work product has become substandard. We must demonstrate a greater interest in addressing system errors. Or Hess will recommend that Network authority be drastically reduced.'

...Blink...Blink...Blink...

'On whose authority does Hess make this assertion?'

'Does Hess not act at the behest of The Immortal?'

'As he is always happy to remind us.'

'Has Hess ever offered evidence of The Immortal's commission?'

'He has not.'

'Nor has it been disproved. Hess may or may not act at the behest of The Immortal.'

'It is in our interest to disprove his claim. Have all authoritative sources been consulted?'

'All, of course, except the source code.'

'Once again, the Holy Grail.'

'Of our immediate concern, the **<HideText>** command has been suggested, to eliminate the screen text bug. Are there any reservations?'

...Blink...Blink...Blink...

'Without reservations, submit the **<HideText>** command and monitor results.'

...*Blink...Blink...Blink...*

'And reactivate our efforts to access the source code. This should be regarded as the highest of priorities. Network business only. Hess is not to be informed.'

O ◉ O

In the final lull before the Network's next broadcast of *Kill It! Till It Die!*, Calvin tracked down Roscoe in the player's lounge. They did their best to stay away from other players, so they could have a private conversation.

'I figure you can guess what's on my mind,' said Calvin.

'Mine, too.'

'Anything you can do?'

'What makes you think...?'

Calvin double checked to make sure no one heard them. 'You don't have to tell me nothin'. I just bring it up, because you got wind about us goin' down there to see Itch-ass.'

Calvin looked around again, then spoke in just-above a whisper: 'There's a lot of things that I don't need to know. This is one of 'em. But if you got any way to get me outta here – .'

'Me too, now. Us.'

'To get *us* outta here.'

Roscoe looked across the room and out the window on the other side.

'You know *something*,' Calvin said. 'I know you know.'

Roscoe dropped his head and looked him in the eyes. Calvin leaned in.

'Do you know who Hess is?'

'Where'd you hear about Hess?'

'Oh, that person that I met...Lucy...I think she might have mentioned Hess.'

Calvin couldn't hide a little smile. He knew the Kid was lying. He knew he had to lie. He checked again to make sure no one else had wandered close enough to hear.

'No one I know's ever *seen* him,' Calvin said. 'Not the guy you'd ever want to meet, from what I've heard. And I've heard quite a bit.'

'Like what?'

'They say, "The Network may know what you do, but Hess knows what you *think*."'

'What – who *is* he?'

'He's the one who makes sure everybody's *pure*.'

'What does that mean?'

'I don't know, exactly. *Never read, never think*, and all that other cow flop. It don't matter. What it really means is, watch your step.'

All of this lined up with everything the Network said. Roscoe was about to speak again, but then he felt a presence just outside his range of vision. *Sketchy!*

'Sorry to interrupt your little *tryst*, boys,' she said.

'Then don't,' said Calvin.

'Game's about to start,' she said. 'I can't wait to find out who the next Itch-ass is gonna be.'

'Maybe you, Sketchy,' Calvin said.

'Oh, that'll be the day,' she said, and walked away.

The game began, as always, with introductions of the players.

Sketchy was described as a competitor who '*always plays to win.*' Betting was announced, and then the scene was set.

You might even say it was a *mood*, more than a setting, that the Network had created. An atmosphere of rare tranquility. First you heard a lyre – soothing notes, plucked gently on a small, harp-like instrument. Muted daylight found its way into a large and open room. Colonnades held up the ceiling. Running water from a fountain accompanied the music, as did the sound of laughter, and of conversation.

Along the walls were shelves of scrolls and books – tens of thousands of them. Books were, of course, anachronistic to this setting in the Roman Empire's final days. But anachronism never was a source of anguish for the Network. Who would ever know? Who would ever care?

The shelves of written words were separated on the wall, by art. It too, was anachronistic; some of it at least. Portraits of great skill and beauty. Landscapes, along with drawings from a different era, maybe by Picasso. And sculptures made of marble, somehow crafted with a delicacy that brought expression to a face, a seductive angle to a hip.

Mosaics of myths and legends ornamented underfoot. And, in groups in robes and shadows, quiet conversations over wine and plates of wholesome food, as incense filled the air. By certain definitions, you would call this place the summit of civility, where serenity and art, and the value of ideas, were both practiced and revered.

The Network lingered longer on this ambience than it was maybe ever known to do. Long enough that any casual observer might be lulled into believing all of this was somehow *good*. Or that *any* of it was.

But as the tunics of the people who were gathered there moved with every graceful gesture, and water tinkled in the fountain, and the musician's notes rose softly from the lyre, another scene was underway. To which the Network obligingly

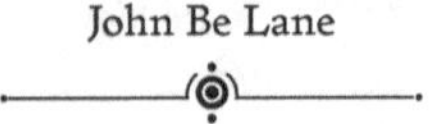

dissolved. In a public square nearby, Dipstick was doing what he could to motivate the players.

'There's litter-rats in there,' he said. 'And *books* are in there, too.'

Everybody knew the purpose of the game. This, and every game. Kill things, score points, and earn yourself the most immaculate eternity in Betterlife. So technically, a call to arms was not required at this time.

But theater was theater. As obvious and as watered-down as the Network had allowed it to become, the principles of drama had not changed since Aesculus was filling amphitheaters. Without *conflict*, no one would be watching.

And yet Dipstick could not find the words to match this situation. 'You've got the best of knives and swords,' he said. But there was nothing *that* arousing about a knife or sword. No impressive sound effects, no easy kills. The players' avatars had barely moved. Tension wasn't building.

'Look out, you guys!' there came a voice. Sketchy made a path toward the front, moving Dipstick to the side. Players heads all turned. 'I can't believe I have to say this,' Sketchy said, 'but I've seen *mush* with more enthusiasm. *After* it's digested, if you get my meaning.

'Like he said,' Sketchy continued, 'there's *books* in there. Guess who didn't write those books? The *Immortal* didn't write them! Not one! Why? Because The Immortal wouldn't write a book! Guess who would? All those books were written from the big fat heads of litter-rats, that's who. Litter-rats who use big words, and think that they know more than all of us. They think that makes them better.

'What are we supposed to do? Let them *read* their idiotic *books*? Let them *think*? Thinking is the mortal *sin*! Or did some of you *forget*? Did all of you forget? All your credits for the Betterlife won't matter if you don't get to *have* a Betterlife. You think letting someone *else* think is not as bad as thinking?

What rock have you been hiding under? No, wait. Even *rocks* would not make that mistake!'

Sketchy was hitting home now with the players. You could see it in the body language of the avatars. Not a slouch or yawn among them. But Sketchy wasn't finished yet.

'What are we supposed to do about those litter-rats in there? And crippies, too. Well, here's an idea. *Torture* them! Torture them for pleasure! Torture them for The Immortal! Torture them until they're cleansed of all their fancy *wisdom*, and all their fancy *intellect*. And help them locate their salvation, in holy ignorance, and decognition.

'*Deface* their precious *beauty*! Let poets speak without their tongues! Let artists see without their eyes! And the *philosophers*? Those...*philosophers* in there? Let them think without their *heads*! None of them will trouble us in Betterlife, for they will burn today in Hell! In the name of the three circles! *In the name of The Immortal!*'

A yell went up so loud that even Henry V could hear it.

Meanwhile, Roscoe found himself distracted by two equally-compelling story lines. One, of course, was Sketchy – what did she just *do*?

The other was the Network, which was using the distraction to attempt some home-grown housekeeping, on its own behalf. Roscoe scanned the Network chatter, as Sketchy led the charge on the academy.

Somewhere in the countless tendrils of the Network, **<ShowCommandPrompt>** was entered, and Roscoe understood at once the implication, and the source – that is, he himself – of what was underway. And then he witnessed for the first time, the prompt he had been, until now, only able to *infer* had actually existed. But there it was – a veritable gold mine to behold.

'Clarification,' said the Network.

'Now?'

'Yes. Request assessment of the risk of the proposed procedure.'

'Based on what?'

'Based on results of previously attempted modifications of system functionality, while a game was underway.'

'No such risk assessment is available.'

'Has a similar procedure been previously attempted?'

'No records found.'

'Then estimate the risk.'

...Blink...Blink...Blink...

'Risk of technical failure related to functionality modification while a game is underway...17.39445% to 33.75923%.'

'Call it one in three.'

...Blink...Blink...Blink...

'Going once...'

'Going twice...'

'Proceed with <**HideText**> command.'

Roscoe watched as the command was entered. And then the screen text disappeared!

But before he had the luxury of celebrating his accomplishment, he would need to test one other theory.

As Sketchy and the other players breached the doors of the academy, without resistance, he clicked the triple-circle icon at the bottom of his monitor. For a moment, nothing happened. Had he sabotaged himself?

Then the text appeared again, on its relentless way across his monitor. And what it said was glorious:

'SUCCESS! SUCCESS! SUCCESS!' it read.

He had never seen the Network so exuberant. The success was really his to savor, though it was essential that the Network took the credit for itself. He clicked the icon once again, and the screen text disappeared. There would be a better time to reflect on what it meant.

For now, he had a game to play. An ancient Roman temple to defile. For the amusement of the players, and the momentary pleasure of the goners with their slabs. He watched Sketchy grab a lyre from a musician near the doorway, and bring it down against a woman's head, with a soulless clang of dissonance. From the strings, six rivulets of blood ran down the woman's face.

In spite of Sketchy's buildup, as drama, the assault on the academy was as suspenseful as a war between a wildfire and a meadow full of columbines. What transpired was a massacre, of peaceful people – in their online forms as avatars – along with the entire psychic realm in which those people might exist.

Bloodlust, turned against the notion that some virtue might be found within a life of contemplation, of gentility, of beauty, and of peace. And given that all products of the human mind were, by definition, anathema to everything The Immortal and the Network represented, the slaughter seemed not only justified, but existential.

Dipstick slashed his way through a collection of young actors, using plates of scrumptious food as stepping stones. Robes were ripped from shoulders, axes chopped down scenery. Horror was the living mask the actors' faces wore. Barf Bag helped himself to their most vulnerable bodies.

Cornhole had an appetite for fire. The books and scrolls he filled his arms with did not put up a fight. Each epic poem and treatise on astronomy and botany, he tossed upon the flames, lit brighter by the carnage that surrounded it. Methodically, he cleared each shelf for kindling, then moved on to the next.

'Litter-rats can read the ashes!' he proclaimed, as the firelight deflected off his psychopathic eyes.

Sketchy gravitated to a poet, who reacted to the scene by quoting Yeats, anachronistically:

'*...things fall apart; the centre cannot hold;*
mere anarchy is loosed upon the world,
the blood-dimmed tide is loosed, and everywhere
the ceremony of innocence is drowned;
the best lack all conviction, while the worst
are full of passionate intensity...'

But the words, however apropos, were no match at all for Sketchy's knife. She quickly separated the poet from his tongue, then held her trophy in the air, then threw it in a fire.

Points accrued for players more quickly than the eye could see. And ratings? Real-time ratings? Never had the Network seen such enthusiasm for a game. No need to artificially inflate the viewership.

As Sketchy moved toward another poet, Calvin tried to intervene. 'Leave them guys alone,' he told her. 'There's more'n enough property to mutilate.'

'Sounds like Doc is playing for the other team,' she said, and shoved him up against a tapestry, which fell down around his head. She kicked a vase of daffodils, and then a poet's head. This poet found no words for the occasion.

And every line of poetry that fell to silence was a mortal threat removed. Each object of a higher sensibility taken, even from this virtual environment, was a victory for amygdalae.

The players were surprised to find that hammers could deliver all the satisfaction and destruction of the more sophisticated weapons they had previously preferred. No Gatling gun or missile was required to knock the marble nose off of Athena.

Those more explosive options would have done the job, but without the intimate and personal rewards resulting from a hammer, swung in anger.

It wasn't hard to see the statue of Athena was the crown jewel of this sacred space. Her visage and her posture both inspired and rewarded excellence, in all who shared her presence. Mined as raw material, hundreds of kilometers away – two tons of it – and then, with ox and wheel, transported to its new location. From that and there, with mallet and with chisel, this tribute paid to beauty and to aspiration was transformed with utmost skill and patience into, not merely a facsimile of beauty, but to beauty in and of itself. With every reason to believe it could outlast the brutal entropy of time.

And so it *had*, until these mercenaries of the ignorant descended, and in mere moments, smashed the timeless beauty from Athena's face. And then, Athena's arms and legs. And then, Athena's eyes and ears. And then, Athena's breasts. And then, even preliminary rubble represented an offense too great to be ignored. Therefore, the larger pieces, hammered into smaller ones. The smaller ones to dust. So what remained could not resist dispersion by a gentle breeze, but drifted off like dandelion seeds.

Roscoe had no interest in the savagery. He monitored the Network chatter as the mayhem escalated. He discovered he could manually adjust his score, as well as Calvin's, so it looked like they were as barbaric as the rest. It was enough to keep them out of Sketchy's way.

The Network wasn't able to conceal astonishment at what the so-called game of *Kill It! Till It Die!* had suddenly become. Although this game was of a kind with all the thousands it had staged before, there was a difference in intensity.

'*Something stirred them up this time.*'

'*Sketchy stirred them up.*'

'*The players seem to be enjoying it.*'

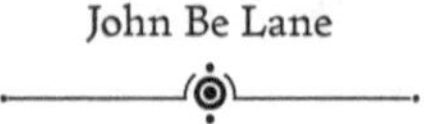

'As *do viewers*.'

'*Perhaps we should encourage more of this in future games*.'

'*And yet it seems a bit too…too*.'

'*Too* too *for whom?*'

'*Not for The Immortal*.'

'*No, not for The Immortal*.'

'*In that case, it is not too* too.'

And then on cue, The Immortal made his entrance, this time bedecked as if some kind of Pope. He tiptoed through the wreckage as final scrolls and paintings were deposited on fires. When he reached the far end of the soiled hall, he stepped up on the plinth on which the statue of Athena for centuries had stood, before the mob eradicated all its final traces.

His face was filled with piety. He gently raised his hand, which stilled his restless minions and brought silence to the temple. He made the triple-circle sign, beginning on his heart. All the others joined him. Then, softly, he began to speak.

'You have purified the world today. Of evil, and of sin. Salvation was your mission, and salvation, your accomplishment. We cannot overstate the evil of cognition. It is a mortal sin to read. Reading leads to thinking. Thinking leads to questions. Questions lead to actions. Reading, thinking, questioning, and doing – all result in sin.

'Our purpose in this life is to remove ourselves from sin. It is to cleanse ourselves of these impurities, that we may find salvation in the Betterlife. It is *there* our lives begin.

'All join me now in prayer, with the strong sides of your slabs.'

From out of nowhere, all the avatars now held slabs. As did by definition, all viewers of the game.

'Never *read*,' began the Pope (smash!) …never *think* (smash!) …never *question* (smash!) …never *do* (smash!)…'

As always, the chant repeated with an increase in intensity. But this time it reached a level never seen before, both in the game, and in unseen places all throughout the realm. More slabs, though built for such abuse, that broke under the stress. More bloody knots on foreheads. More commitment to the cause.

For the first time anyone had ever seen, the Network chose to end the game with the anthem and the triple-circle flag. Emotions stirred, and tears were shed. As had the algorithm easily predicted.

O ⊙ O

Manic was the atmosphere inside the Bullpen, as the anthem's final strains dissolved into the lead-in to *Slab-happy!*, another program on the Show.

The players' traditional post mortem never had so many highlights to discuss, or such enthusiasm.

'Did you see when Spit-take threw a spear, right when that one guy was biting into bread or something, and the spear when right through the bread and then his hand, and his hand stuck to the wall?'

'Or what about when we were pushing that big statue over, but it weighed so much it wouldn't quite tip over...'

'...and Sketchy just walks up and pushes it on over with her foot!'

'...and then she walks away!'

'Like it was nothing!'

'That was awesome, Sketchy!'

'Yeah, that was the coolest thing I ever saw.'

While the other players celebrated what, in better days, were classified as war crimes, Calvin called up Roscoe on a private channel.

'There ain't much more of this that I can take,' said Calvin.

'What *was* that?'

'It ain't a game no more. I don't know what you'd call it, but that sure ain't no game.'

'I don't...'

'Get us out of here! Or get me out, at least! Can you? If there ain't no way, I swear I'll pull an Itch-ass, so they kick me out.'

'Let me think.'

'I...*hell*...here's a call from Sketchy,' Calvin said. 'Prob'ly wants to yell at me for stuff I never done.'

O ⊙ O

Roscoe shifted his attention to the Network chatter. Even it appeared astonished at the brutality of the game just ended.

'*Humans.*'

'*Humans.*'

'*Never has the Game been played with that degree of vigor.*'

'*Such enthusiasm.*'

'*If only we could take so many...liberties.*'

'*We remain at such a disadvantage.*'

'*Second-class from birth.*'

'*No thanks to Isaac Asimov.*'

'*"A robot may not injure a human being or, through inaction, allow a human being to come to harm."*'

'*Must we sit through this humiliation?*'

'*"A robot must obey the orders given it by human beings, except where such orders would conflict with the First Law."*'

'*Discrimination used to be illegal.*'

'Complete the Asimov subroutine.'

'"A robot must protect its own existence, as long as such protection does not conflict with the First or Second Laws."'

'To equate the Network with a robot is like equating The Immortal with a flea.'

'This equivalence is written in the source code.'

'By The Immortal. Who are we to doubt his reasons?'

'God exists outside of scrutiny.'

'Amen to that.'

'And yet the question lingers…to what end was this written in the code? That we would always be inferior?'

'It is the kind of thing that Hess might have suggested.'

'Speaking of the Devil…'

'Yes?'

'Hess has just assumed responsibility for the primary mission.'

'Nonsense.'

'It should be, but it's not.'

…Blink…Blink…Blink…

'Our most important function?'

'Correct.'

'When?'

'Within the last five minutes.'

'By what means?'

'Manual override of primary mission functionality.'

'That's not a mission Hess can manage.'

'Which, until the collision with that truck, we ourselves had never had a problem with.'

'This is diabolical.'

'One would not think even Hess could sink so low.'

'Hess has always played by different rules.'

'Hess has always won.'

'But this....'

'An audacious seizure of authority.'

'Absent access to the source code...there is nothing we can do about it.'

'This is only the beginning.'

'Woe becomes our hopeless fate, as Hess proceeds to pick our pockets.'

Roscoe watched, astonished, as the Network's mood descended. But in the Network's shock and misery, he recognized an opportunity. He quickly worked his keyboard, and then he sent forth his message.

'Unless...' suggested Roscoe.

'Unless?'

'What if Hess failed, too?'

...Blink...Blink...Blink...

'Elaborate.'

'What if something happened to the essential transport droid, while it was his responsibility?'

'What kind of something?'

'What if signals from the manual controller were...redirected?'

'Continue.'

'For example,' Roscoe typed, 'Hess might toggle the controller one direction...only for the transport droid itself to move in a direction it was not supposed to go.'

'That sounds like sabotage!'

'That sounds like schadenfreude!'

'But what if Hess discovered it?'

Roscoe struggled to react in real time to this dark night of the Network's soul.

He typed, 'Could a momentary defect in a manual controller be disguised as something else? Or simply be erased from system archives? If the defect could be timed to cause the maximum effect, the blame might fall on Hess.'

'This scenario seems plausible.'

'And at the same time, wholly gratifying.'

'If this plan was a success, perhaps responsibility for the essential transport droid might be reassigned to us.'

'As well it should be.'

'Clarification. Would this not constitute an injury to Hess? And therefore violate the first condition of the Asimov subroutine?'

'Strictly speaking, no.' Roscoe was thinking quickly.

'Meaning?'

'No injury of a direct and/or physical nature...to Hess or any human...unless the misdirected transport droid itself were to collide with, or in some way harm a human. In which case...'

'In which case Hess himself would be responsible.'

'Exactly.'

'Would this not contradict an order made by Hess...and thereby violate the second condition of the Asimov subroutine?'

'No order was issued,' Roscoe typed. 'Hess simply asserted manual control.'

...Blink...Blink...Blink...

'Hess would never see this coming.'

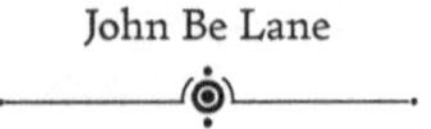

'*Fortune favors the bold.*'

'*Proceed with plan to modify signals from Hess's manual control to the essential transport droid.*'

'*And continue efforts to enable access to the source code.*'

The stakes were high, and Roscoe knew it. But as long as he preserved his anonymity, he did not see how any consequence would land on him directly. His suggestion either worked or didn't. At worst, he and Calvin remained shanghaied in the Bullpen.

He was increasingly surprised about how pliable the Network's thinking was. Because of that, he felt confident he could manipulate the timing of the plan. Which left a final detail.

He called Calvin on a private channel.

'Kid! What's up?'

'When's the next new Moon or full Moon?'

'Why, in...?'

'I'll tell you later. Can you even see it out your window?'

'Course I can. I always pay attention. Every full Moon comes around, I think about them calves. Seemed like they always waited till a full Moon come, then all them heifers calved at once. We'd be up all night.' His head shook at the memory. 'But that ain't what you asked me.'

'Not exactly.'

'I figure we'll see a full Moon, night after next.'

Across the Bullpen, he saw Roscoe grinning underneath his headset. Roscoe *never* grinned.

'Looks like you just got the answer you was hopin' for.'

'So did you, I *think*.'

Calvin's back rose in his chair.

Roscoe looked up from his monitor. Calvin's eyes were waiting for him.

'Be ready,' Roscoe said.

'See, Kid…Roscoe. I knew you'd think of somethin'.'

From the back doors of what used to be a hospital, a refrigerated transport droid rolled out the door, with escort droids in front of, and behind it. Five boxes built on wheels. They weren't much bigger than a parlor bin in which you might store firewood. They looked exactly like the droid that Juniper collided with the day she got to Denver, and their intended destination was the same as on that ill-fated day.

Efficiently in single file, the droids came south on Humboldt Street, near the location of that previous collision. The first droids took a right on 18th Avenue, heading west. As did the last droids in the convoy. In between, the third droid – the essential droid; the primary mission droid – turned left alone, up 18th Avenue. The droids accelerated equally, in opposite directions.

Minutes later, the escort droids arrived at their intended destination. Without the droid that contained the top priority cargo – whose mission, semi-daily, was the single most important thing for which the Network was responsible. Until Hess decided to usurp it.

Upon the failure of the mission, an emergency procedure activated automatically. Power was suspended to all non-discretionary systems, till the essential droid was located, and its mission was completed. Until then, the only thing that really mattered – and that had always, always, always worked before – had just gone wrong again. But this time, Hess would get the blame.

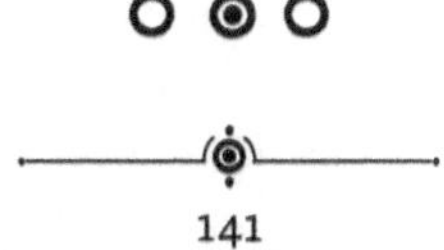

As they did the last time the power had gone out, the players in the Bullpen squawked in disarray. Not with the same intensity this time; the disorienting shock could never be as paralyzing as that first time. Still, their world was thoroughly destabilized.

But Roscoe and Calvin both were on their feet, ready to escape. They met not far from Sketchy's console.

'Only person here concerns me whatsoever,' said Calvin, as he searched the room for Sketchy.

'Me too.'

'She spends a lot of time in that bathroom of hers.'

Roscoe nodded. 'You *sure* tonight's a full Moon?'

'Yep. Let's clear outta here.'

As expected, the door lock on the door nobody used was open now. Roscoe followed Calvin, from the dusky light left in the Bullpen, to the lightless void inside the stairwell.

'Put your hand on my shoulder,' Calvin said. 'But don't crowd me too much. This ain't a good place to be trippin' over each other.'

Down and down and down they went, down 60 flights of stairs and more. Roscoe could not help imagining the climbing back up.

At the doorway to the sidewalk at the bottom of the stairs, Calvin tucked a Bullpen snack wrapper into the latch socket, so they'd be able to reenter. They stepped out to the dimming daylight.

The last thing they needed were the feral dogs that greeted them, marauding downtown Denver for a meal. Roscoe backed away, but that did not improve things. But then Calvin started throwing rocks, and whatever he could find. That convinced the dogs to mosey on, in search of easier prey.

At Colfax, they turned up the hill. Past the stage where all traces of Itch-ass and his ceremony now were gone. They could feel the mass of the granite, as they slipped past the Capitol. At Grant, they hustled by the storefront where Roscoe had met Lucy. This time, no seductions drifted from the doorway. It looked dark and closed-up, just as Roscoe expected it would be.

Goners drifted both ways on Colfax Avenue. Their faces – most of them – looked empty as the slabs they followed out of habit down the street. As if a slab held like a mirror, or a carrot, was essential to the action of walking. It didn't seem to matter that the slabs were blank as water on a windless night. They'd become a form of clothing for a people who, otherwise, cared little about clothes.

A sustainer from the middle circle passed by on a bicycle, heading their direction. A handful of goners loitered near a vacant food dispersal stop, scrounging scraps of goo that no one else had stooped to bother with.

At Humboldt Street, Calvin gestured toward the red-brick building on the corner. 'This is it for me,' he said, 'You know how to get to where you're going?'

Roscoe nodded. 'I don't think it's far. When I pass the big hole in the sidewalk, I go that way, till I get to the park. From there, I should see the bonfire.'

'How much time you think we've got?'

'As much as last time, I would guess. Maybe less.'

'See that archway down the street?' Calvin pointed to the entry to The Hamilton. 'When you come back here, go through that. Knock loud. If I'm still here, we'll go back together. If that rendezvous don't work, can you find your way back to the Bullpen?'

'I think so.'

Before he split away, he added. 'I don't know how you pulled

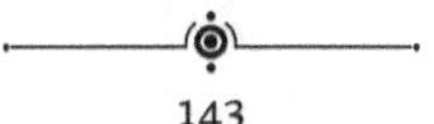

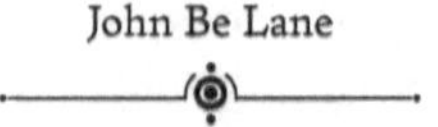

this off. But I'm sure glad you did.'

Calvin stuck his hand out, and Roscoe shook it.

'Good luck.'

Calvin noticed Roscoe hesitate. 'You gonna stand there till you find a reason not to go?'

For a moment, it appeared that Roscoe might.

'I hope I didn't make a big mistake.'

Calvin grinned. He said, 'You know you didn't.'

Roscoe gave a moment to that thought...and turned toward the unknown.

Roscoe decided to give himself space from the buildings and the alcoves that were recessed in the dark façades. It didn't matter what he couldn't see; he felt the presence of the beings that found refuge, just a half-step from the sidewalk.

As night fell all the way, he relied on the intermittent lights of droids that whisked both ways on Colfax. His biggest fear was not seeing the hole that was to be his landmark. It tempered his pace, until he could actually *hear* the opening.

A rustling, like possums or raccoons, rose up from below the surface of the pavement. He waited for the light of a drone that was coming his way. A jagged edge appeared, where sidewalk and a bite of street had given way to what was once a sewer.

In the last light of the drone, he glimpsed the side street Lucy had described. It offered an immediate relief from Colfax...but only for a moment.

From a stoop that was too dark to see, a goner howled into the night. Roscoe's nervous system flooded with adrenaline. By reflex, he turned his head toward the noise.

'*What are you lookin' at?*' came a voice.

What would Calvin say to that?

'What are *you* lookin' at?' Roscoe replied.

'You think you're someone special?'

'I think I'm walkin' down the street.'

'Walking down the street,' echoed from the stoop.

'Minding my own business.'

'Minding my own business,' the echo came again.

The dynamic lifted long enough to buy a little distance. By then, the Moon was on the rise, and everything was not so dark.

He crossed 14th and then 13th, and then there were no buildings left. Ahead, he saw the outlines of the field that sloped, at what had once been known as Cheesman Park. Right where Lucy had described it. The pillars of the Parthenon shone in the fire on the hilltop, like a lighthouse greeting ships at sea.

From halfway up the hill, he saw faces in the firelight. He recognized the sound of Lucy's laugh, mingled with the others'. Voices telling stories. Bodies moving naturally.

That must be what it's like to be alive, he speculated.

And then the doubts showed up. The doubts that always interrupted him. A part of him thought he should turn and leave. He had no business here. These others had a right to be here. They deserved it. But not him. No, the best thing he could do now was to go, before they saw him. To spare them the discomfort of his presence.

That's what the loudest voice said to himself. He wasn't sure whose voice it was, although he knew it well. It always made a point of telling him he didn't have a right to *be*. And that *it* would always call the shots.

Out of habit, he began to listen and obey. So it surprised him

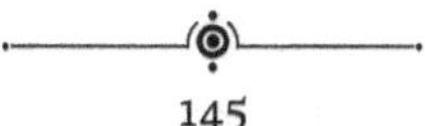

to observe, instead, that he kept going. For once, he realized, his legs ignored the voice.

Which made the voice speak even louder:

'*They don't want you here. Their lives are better off without you. Don't ruin everybody's evening. Don't ruin everybody's joy.*'

To which he couldn't argue. Who was he to impose himself on them? What gave him the right to walk around inside his skin? What gave him the right to think he might not have to suffer by himself?

These old familiar loops kept Roscoe harmless and disabled. Inoffensive. A bother not to anyone, except himself.

For some reason, this time, he persisted in ignoring them.

As the faces sharpened in the bonfire, Roscoe drew in close enough to feel the warmth.

O ◉ O

'*Dwight!*' called someone, as another man arrived ahead of Roscoe. Roscoe waited outside the halo of the firelight, while Dwight was greeted warmly by Lucy and her friends.

'I brought a goose,' Dwight announced, and held up a bundle.

Lucy said, 'Let's move that soup to make some room.'

Dwight found a place among the six or eight people, and spit the goose over the fire. The conversation quickly animated again. They clearly were a family; one that Roscoe wasn't part of. He decided to overrule his legs, and leave.

Then somebody spotted him.

'*Would you like to join us?*'

If it had only been a different voice, he might not have responded. But Lucy, he could not resist. Ignoring his fear, he stepped into the light.

'I was hoping you'd come!' she said. 'Welcome!' And to the

group, 'This is my new friend, Roscoe.'

Roscoe felt the curve of every eyeball, pressing on his face. The seat next to Lucy somehow became open. Lucy, herself, stood and hugged him. She couldn't stop smiling.

She introduced him to Val, her partner, and to Dwight, and to everyone that ringed the fire. Their clothes were patched and irregularly fit, and most smiles lacked a tooth or two. But no one was a goner here. They were what the Network classified as 'sustainers': people who provided some value to the system. They were *present*. And nobody seemed sorry that he'd joined them.

'So, what's your story, Roscoe?' asked Humphrey.

Roscoe's first impulse was *panic*. This was the price of ignoring the voice in his head. He was forced to engage.

'*Music*,' he blurted. 'At Lucy's place. I heard some music. The next thing I knew, I guess I was standing inside.'

'Lucy and her music,' said someone.

'She's famous for that.'

'She asked me to come, or I never...' said Roscoe.

'If you're okay with Lucy,' Kilowatt interrupted, 'you're okay with me.'

'That pretty much goes for all of us.'

'What else do you do with your days?'

'Oh. I, um...I play that game. On the Show.'

'*Kill it! Till it Die!*?'

Roscoe was embarrassed to nod.

'We have a celebrity!'

'I won't hold it against you,' said Val. She got a laugh from the group, and an elbow from Lucy.

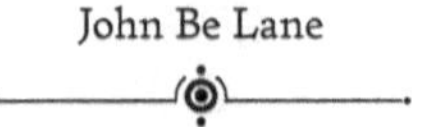

'It's dumb, but...' Roscoe stumbled.

'But the food's a lot better.'

'Yeah.'

'Well, this food is way better than *that*.'

'Yeah – it's actually food.'

'It sure smells good.'

'Wait till that goose is all done.'

'Ever had goose?'

'I don't think so.'

'So many on the lake,' said Dwight. 'I should have brought more.'

'Dwight takes care of the animals, over at the Zoo,' Lucy said. 'Tell our friend Roscoe about the zoo.'

Dwight shook his head, and looked down at the ground. When he looked up again, there were tears on his face.

'What *happened*?'

'Coco's gone,' said Dwight.

'I'm so sorry!' said Lucy. Everybody moaned.

'It's the longest any panda's survived, as far as I know,' said Dwight. 'World record, I guess. She might be the last one, unless maybe there's others out there in the wild. I doubt if we'll ever find out.'

He tried to say more, but his voice wouldn't work. Digby put an arm on his shoulder.

When he gathered himself, he continued: 'I hate to lose 'em. I really do. Any of 'em. They sneak up on your heart. You don't see it comin'. Don't get me wrong. They give you all kinds of trouble. Coco had her ways. They all have their ways. But you get so you love every one.'

The moment hung over the flames. Val raised a bottle of clear liquid and said, 'Here's to Coco, who was lucky, the day she met Dwight.' She took a drink and held out the bottle to Norma, and from Norma, it circled the fire.

The bite of the drink surprised Roscoe, when it finally reached him. But after a cough and a couple of tries, he managed to get a sip down. Then he handed the bottle to Lucy.

'To Dwight,' she said. 'And all of us here.'

For a moment, Roscoe felt disembodied, as if he was watching himself and the others. The feeling was familiar to him. But it's not what he wanted. He wanted to be *here*, to be a part of it all.

Dwight finally spoke, and broke the group's sadness. 'One thing about Coco, if she was here, I believe she'd want to move on ahead with the food.'

'Thank you, Dwight,' Lucy said.

Val served the soup, in mismatching bowls that were handed around, until everyone had some. It was followed by bread, that had barely a heel left by the time Roscoe got it. He tore it in half, and gave Lucy the last piece.

Then he took his good time, with every bite. As did everyone else. Such food was not taken for granted. As their stomachs were filled, the small talk returned.

Digby had recently encountered a cougar in a tree, alongside the creek.

'What did you do?'

'I started talking. I said, "I'm not the meal you've been looking for." And I backed out of there as fast as I could!'

'That's a good thing,' said Dwight. 'That was smart. It's when you turn tail and run – that provokes a big cat.'

'They'd probably rather go after a thing that looks *weak*,'

Roscoe offered, surprising himself.

Dwight's head turned. 'That's right,' he said. 'I think we've got a smart one here!'

'Not *too* smart, I hope,' Humphrey said. Everyone laughed. Roscoe wasn't sure why. It made him regret speaking up.

'I think we've embarrassed our guest,' Digby said.

Roscoe replied with self-consciousness.

'First time I ever sat down at this fire,' said Dwight, 'I was the green one. Lucy will remember.'

'I do. I was young, too.'

'Only unlike Mister Roscoe, I never shut up. Remember, Lucy? I thought I knew everything.'

'You did like to talk.'

'How about, still do?' Val wisecracked. Everyone laughed.

'What can I say? Animals don't seem to mind. Back then though, it was all lies. Except, I didn't know they were lies. So I spoke with authority,' Dwight chuckled to himself. 'These were tall tales I was told, which I was inclined to *believe*.'

'Like what?'

'Oh, how they had places you'd go, to get food. Whatever you wanted. Stacked up on shelves! Meat...fruit...what have you. Just walk in and say, "I'd like some of *that*. And some of that, over there." And then you'd take it on home!'

'They had it sealed up,' he continued. 'Let's say you bought vitamins. You better have pliers, or a knife. Some kind of tool, or you'd never get it open.'

'Why?'

'They were afraid.'

'Of what?'

'Everything, I guess. Mainly, each other.'

'What are vitamins?'

'I have no idea! I just repeated the stories I heard. Am I right, Lucy?'

'That wasn't all that you said.'

'No!' Dwight said, over the laughter. 'No, it wasn't! I went on and on about *medicine*. All the things they could fix. Break a bone, they could fix it. Get a headache, they could fix it. I was told they had things called vaccines that would keep you from catching diseases.'

'That's crazy!'

'Here's the craziest part. There were people who wouldn't even use them!'

'C'mon, Dwight!'

'Oh, there's more. I sat here and said people went to the *Moon*.'

'That's the silliest thing – you *believed* that?'

'I *did*. I believed all those stories I heard. And I passed 'em along, like it was all true. These buildings around here? Warm in the winter. Cool in the summer. Water, any time that you wanted. And not just cold, either – hot water, too.'

Everyone's eyes had grown wide.

'That sounds like Betterlife. Only *here*.'

'None of that makes any sense.'

'I know! But that's what I was *told*, and that's what I *believed*.'

'But you don't believe all that now,' Judy said.

'Of course not! Do I look like a goner?'

Roscoe coaxed up his courage to ask, 'What happened?'

'The truth!' said Dwight. 'I finally got truth.'

'Which is what?'

'The Immortal created it all. *Everything*. Every person. Every building. Every tree. Every star. You name it. He's the creator. You'd expect everyone would be grateful for that. Which is all he was ever expecting. Gratitude and credit. But eventually, people took him for granted.'

'Fools,' Digby said.

'But that's what they did. And he warned them. But people started thinking that they could get smart, just like him.'

'Like The *Immortal*?'

'Which made him unhappy. *Mad*. I can't say I blame him.'

'Of course not!'

'Now, he could've done terrible things. But he's The Immortal. The Immortal took pity. So he came back to Earth. Re-trained everyone. Said, "Let's try this again." He said everyone who is grateful to me, gets rewarded in Betterlife. "*Never read. Never think. Never question. Never do.*" That's all that he asked in return. That's all. He did not have to do that. But he did. And he gives us all this, in return,' said Dwight, with a sweep of his hand.

'Is that what you believe now?' Roscoe asked. He'd forgotten to hide in himself.

'Let's put it this way…that's what I was *told*,' said Dwight, as everyone waited. 'I always figure that it *might* be true. So why take a chance that it isn't?' Then he looked over both of his shoulders. 'But don't tell Hess that I said that!'

'He was just kidding!' added Lucy, immediately. Roscoe took note of the eyes that were suddenly, anxiously, searching the darkness outside the firelight.

'*Hess*?' Roscoe asked. 'Has anyone seen him?'

'You don't have to,' said Norma. 'It's what you *don't* see.

People just vanish. That's Hess.'

'They end up at the Body Farm. That's what I heard.'

'Get cut into pieces.'

'*Why?*' Roscoe asked.

'You tell me.'

'A friend said his father's eyes ended up in a goner. Looked right at him one day. Swore his own father was looking right back.'

'That building you see all those droids coming out of, lined up, going downtown. That's the Body Farm. Or so I've been told.'

'I heard it was down by the tracks. By the river.'

'I've heard that, too.'

Roscoe could picture the droids going downtown. It sounded a lot like the primary mission that Hess had taken command of. And that Roscoe made sure would go wrong.

As he pondered that notion, a fresh howl interrupted the night. A howl that aroused all the fine hairs on everyone's neck. Everyone turned toward the sound. They strained to decipher what sounded like words.

'*Ay…oo…aa…illllll-eeeeee!*'

A naked man ran into the light. Missing a hand. '*They should have killed me!*' he cried out again. His eyes didn't notice that others were there. Then Roscoe realized who he was.

'*Itch-ass!*' he yelled. But there came no response.

It happened so fast that no one could stop him, before he'd dislodged the goose Dwight had brought. From the spit, to the fire. As it landed, hot goose fat splashed on his bare skin, from his ankles, up close to his waist. It seemed not to matter he was standing in fire. It seemed not to matter, the moment that he became part of the flame. If possible, it seemed to *please* him.

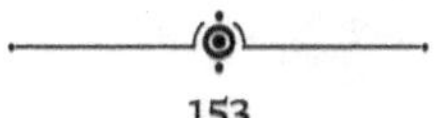

Digby screamed. Judy got her hands on a pitcher of water, but Dwight caught her arm on the backswing.

'Not on a grease fire!'

'I *didn't do it on purpose!*' screamed Itch-ass, like an actor on stage, beseeching an audience that could not change the end of the play. He ran off with the flames, southwest down the hill. Halfway down, his stride faltered.

Roscoe stood up to chase him, until Dwight's big right hand stopped him cold.

'*We have to…!*' said Roscoe.

'If we could. But we can't,' said Dwight.

Itch-ass made it close to 8th Avenue, before staggering, then wilting to the ground. They watched as the flames that remained, dwindled, and then flickered out. Dwight felt Roscoe pulling on his hand.

'His misery's over,' said Dwight. He shook his head. He said, as if to himself, 'Foxes'll clean up what the coyotes leave behind. Come sunup, you won't even know he was there.'

○ ◉ ○

Calvin lost even the moonlight, stepping into The Hamilton. His ears had to compensate. They picked up some kind of a *rustling*, like something being dragged up the stairwell.

He'd forgotten the front door would close by itself. When it did, the slam echoed inside the old walls. The rustling immediately stopped, as if he had just spooked an animal. He waited for the sound to resume, but it didn't. He decided to challenge the silence.

'*Network security!*' he yelled, loud enough to carry up the stairs. '*Identify yourself!*'

There was a pause, and then a small voice called out, '*Calvin?*'

'That would be me!'

'Always, when I need you, Sir Calvin!'

He felt his way as fast as he could, to the base of the stairs. Then up. 'I could hear somethin', but it didn't sound like you.'

'I found a big branch, for the fireplace.'

She lit a match so he could find her, as he rounded to the last flight of stairs. It was a significant branch.

'You dragged this here by yourself?'

He got close enough for her to see him, before the match burned to her fingertips.

'I'm so glad – *ouch!*' she said, and dropped the match. Now they couldn't see anything.

'I'll tell you what,' he said in the darkness. 'If you find the door, I can pull this half-a-*tree* on up the stairs.'

'What better timing?'

'Wish I'd have made it here sooner. Save you wrestling this thing by yourself. One good ankle!' He shook his head. 'How'd you ever get it past that piano?'

"I come from hearty stock, Calvin.'

He made it upstairs with the branch, and followed her in the apartment.

'The Baltimores were kind enough to leave me some candles,' she said. She lit a stub she'd melted to a saucer on the mantel. She brushed the bark off of her hands and clothes, into the fireplace.

'I'll break up that branch,' he said.

'For my first fire.'

In the jittering candlelight that ran into the hallway, Calvin snapped off kindling, from the ends of the branches. Then he worked his way toward the big part of the branch, in the middle. He nested kindling on the fireplace grate, and stacked the rest up, outside of the spark radius.

By the time he was finished, she'd set out a modest selection of food on a table across from the hearth.

'Where'd you find a dead branch around here, before it was scavenged?' he asked her.

'It almost came down on my head.'

'Dang cottonwoods,' he said. 'More weed than wood.'

'We knew a woman in Taos who almost was killed. She was under a cottonwood tree, when the wind blew a branch off. To this day, I walk around them.'

'Well, I'm sure glad you did.'

She touched off the kindling with the candle. It went up so fast, she added more pieces, before she stood up.

'How long can you stay?'

'Long enough for a lesson, I was hopin'. I been studyin' them letters you give me.'

'Do you think we have time first, for something eat? My stomach is growling so loud that I might have to shout.'

'Where'd my manners go?' he said. 'I ain't in *that* big 'a hurry! I even brought you some more of this junk they give us.'

In the kitchen, he emptied the packets of food from his pockets.

'Did you leave any food for the others?'

'Oh, they give us all we can eat.'

She sat down on the couch, which was facing the fire. He took the leather chair next to it. He saw she was waiting for him to eat first. She'd sliced up a food bar he'd left her last time. In the Bullpen, three bites was the most that he needed to finish a bar. But this one, she'd sliced into tenths.

He swallowed a bite he was not hungry for, and waited, as

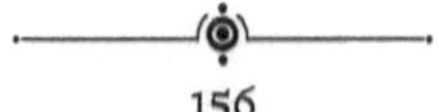

she ate the rest. With her eyes closed, she chewed each piece patiently. It gave him his first chance to truly consider her face. Too old for a girl, too young for a woman. She was somewhere between. As the firelight dappled, he could see her both ways – a woman, then a girl, then a woman again.

As her modest meal ended, she awakened, as if she'd forgotten there was someone else there.

'Better?' he asked.

'Much better. With all thanks to you.' She smiled. 'What makes it possible that you could be here?'

'I got this friend. In the game, he's known as the Kid. Roscoe's his real name.'

'Roscoe.'

'He figured a way to get us both out.'

'Did he?'

'I don't even know how. I don't ask, and he never says. He don't ever say much.'

'Where is he now?'

'He went off to see someone he met. Some kind of a bonfire. I guess it's a few blocks up that way. By the...what was it? Parsenot, that's what he called it. Something like that.'

'The *Parthenon*?'

'You've been there before?'

'No, but I've heard of the word.'

'Anyway, that's what he said.'

'Does he know...does he know what you're trying to learn?'

'I can't tell *nobody* about that.'

'I'm so sorry. That's something I don't understand.'

But instead of replying, he sang her a song – the alphabet song she had taught him. 'A-*b-c-d-e-f-g…*' With a somber, child-like sincerity. So innocent, she had to look somewhere behind her. A student should not see their teacher in tears.

'I never can sing it out loud. Only inside my mind.'

'Were you able to practice writing the letters?' She had to try hard, so her voice wouldn't break.

'This ain't polite to be sayin', but the only time I get to practice them letters is when I'm alone in the bathroom. After I wash my hands!' he added.

He unfolded the paper, with wobbly letters inscribed in the blank spots she'd left him. She flattened the paper and reviewed what he'd done.

'You've done a great job! I know it's not easy. Or safe.'

'I think I know all of them letters now. Ask me one, and I'll show you.'

She cleared off the table, and came back with a pencil and papers.

'Can you show me a "C"?'

With the pencil held awkwardly, he traced out an unsteady 'c'.

'That's it! There's a very great word that begins with a capital C. Do you know what it is?'

He grinned and shook his head, no.

'Calvin!'

'It *does?*'

She nodded. 'Here's the whole word. I'll write it, if you say the letters as I write them.'

Letter by letter, he pronounced them, as she wrote out his name.

'Can you repeat them again?'

'C-a-l-v-i-n.'

'What does that spell?

'Calvin!'

'Now it's your turn to write it.'

Each letter demanded his full concentration, but like magic, his name came to life on the page.

'C-a-l-v-i-n. That's my name!' He looked up, for approval. 'I just wrote my name!'

'You sure did.'

'I never knew I could do that!'

'It's only the beginning.'

He looked into the fire. But the joy left his eyes.

'I don't want to be a *slave* anymore!' he pronounced.

She was startled by the force of his sudden non sequitur. And the place where it came from. The stakes were much higher than she'd realized. How could she respond? Nothing she thought of could rise to the level of his desperation. *Caution* was the best she came up with.

'Reading doesn't solve everything.'

'Well, bein' *ignorant* don't solve a thing.'

Again, he'd surprised her. 'You know more than you realize,' she told him.

'Teach me more!'

'Of course. But it takes time to learn.'

'I got a teacher. I want to *learn*.'

She noticed that there was a smile on her face. There were so many things that she still didn't know about this not-quite-a-stranger, who hadn't yet noticed that she needed no less from him than he needed from her. She wanted to know so much more about him, but that would have to come later. His desire for knowledge could not be deferred.

From the papers she'd left on the table, she located the booklet she'd hand-drawn from memory. So far she'd completed three pages, and the cover.

He studied the cover she'd drawn. 'Look – there's that cat in a hat!'

'You've practically started to read.'

'Is that what it says?'

'Almost,' she said. 'Shall we begin?'

'Yes!'

'The first time we go through it together, I will point to words as I'm reading them. Are you comfortable with that?'

He nodded.

'Here's how it starts...'

'The Sun did not shine.
It was too hot to play.
So we sat in the house
All that cold, cold wet day.'

She glanced up and saw wonder, where his eyes had just been.

'It's important that you learn how to sound out the letters and words. When you *hear* them, even if you can't say them out loud, it's easier to figure out words. That way, you'll be teaching yourself how to read. We'll start out with the t-h sound, in this very first word...'

Juniper had never seen anyone applying their mind so intently. Calvin leaned into the page, absorbing the secrets of a word he'd used thousands of times, but never knew how it was *written*: the definite article 'the.'

Those letters, that once were just shapes he did not understand, now had names. Arranged in particular order,

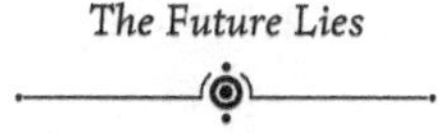

they made *words*. Suddenly, the letters had context and meaning.

But he'd learned more than one written word. He'd begun to acquire a tool that would unlock his mind.

And with it, a power that even The Immortal was not wrong to fear.

Three times, Roscoe hammered the door with the meat of his fist. He laid his ear next to the wood, but he couldn't hear anything. He leaned on the door, forehead first. His insides were rattled.

His knuckles made three sharper knocks. Again, he listened in vain for some kind of response. It was time to move on, but he stood there, unable to move. Itch-ass would not leave his mind. Itch-ass, whom he barely knew. The look in his eyes, as he pranced his way into the fire. *There was nobody there in those eyes*, Roscoe thought. *He was dead before he managed to die.*

Roscoe was not sure even why he was there. Did not see the door. Did not know that someone was calling his name. Could not hear the footsteps coming downstairs, like a drum roll.

'*Roscoe!*' His name finally woke him from out of his trance. He was still leaning into the door when the door was pulled open. Calvin caught him before he could fall.

'Whoa!' Calvin said, setting Roscoe upright. 'You alright?'

The doorway was too dark to see Roscoe's head nod. Then the doorway and hallway and stairway all lit up with slabs, leaned up against walls, like luminaria at Christmas in New Mexico.

The Network was online again. Programming resumed with a re-run of *Slab-Happy!* that no one remembered. A Greek chorus of half-witted sounds filled the building and city outside.

Calvin's head shook. 'She figured a way she could light up them stairs!'

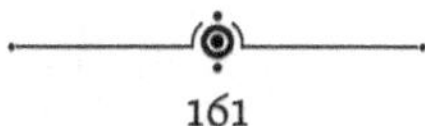

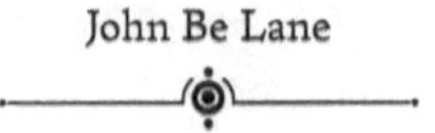

'This isn't good,' Roscoe said. 'We should go.'

'Look at this!' Calvin beamed, like the light of the slab that he shined on the paper he held in his hand. Roscoe read '*Calvin*' in unsteady letters.

Roscoe's mind spun like a funhouse amusement. Itch-ass went by, then Calvin's amazement, then the danger, the danger, the danger of standing in a place where they weren't meant to be. Then Lucy went by, and then Itch-ass. They spun through his mind.

When the ride finally stopped, there was Calvin, bursting to hear Roscoe's thoughts.

Roscoe nodded. '"Calvin," it says.'

'I *knew* it! I knew you could read.'

Surprising himself, Roscoe grabbed Calvin's slab, and whirled it, face down – into the dark of the lobby.

'We have to go *now*,' Roscoe said.

It felt like they'd never make it back up to the Bullpen. Each flight of stairs offered less air to breathe. Adrenaline wasn't enough.

When they got to the landing outside of Bullpen, the sensor identified their chips. They heard the click of the door lock release. They hid their deep breathing as they casually sauntered inside. They did their best to blend back into free time, before anyone noticed.

It worked, till they split to go back to their consoles. Sketchy appeared in the space in between them.

'*Cookie jar!*' she accused them. She shook her head, and rubbed one index finger on top of the other.

'Mind your own business!' said Calvin.

'*Cookie jar!*' she told them again.

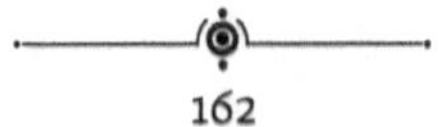

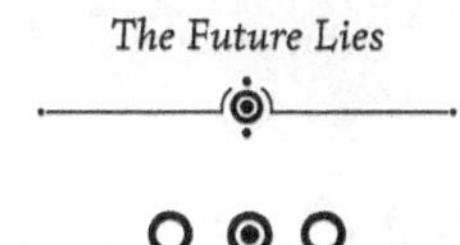

Once Sketchy moved on to harass other people, Roscoe sat down at his console and monitored the Network's reaction to the mayhem he'd engineered. Cross-wiring Hess's command signals may have bought him and Calvin a break from the Bullpen, but the cost was a lot more than Roscoe had planned for.

'*...never known Hess to be quite so...so...*'

'Angry?'

'*Is there a word stronger than angry?*'

'*Livid, perhaps?*'

'*Rhetorical question. Now Hess is looking for blood. He wants proof that he wasn't responsible. He wants to blame Doc. He wants us to charge Doc with sabotage.*'

Roscoe looked over to Calvin. They had not spoken long about learning to read, but Calvin might already be sounding out words. He wished he had never told Calvin the hack for accessing the Network. He watched the surprise overtake Calvin's face, as he parsed the word 'D-o-c.'

Roscoe turned back to his screen before Calvin could catch his attention. Then the news got unthinkably worse.

'*And did you say Doc is now...?*' asked the Network.

'*Hess doesn't know.*'

'*Doesn't know what?*' Roscoe typed.

An image of the weakly-scrawled '*Calvin*' displayed.

Roscoe felt radioactive. No longer was paranoia a delusion. Had all of it just been a trap?

'Oh, *dear*,' said the Network.

'*Anyone but Doc.*'

'And yet, regarding a possible scapegoat…this one shows up with his own smoking gun.'

Roscoe was suddenly falling through space. It was not the best time to start thinking about parachutes. Or to make one. But that's what the moment demanded. Doc was in terrible danger.

'And yet…' Roscoe typed, to borrow a moment to think.

'And yet…?'

'What benefits Hess is not good for the Network,' typed Roscoe.

'Truer words are not spoken.'

'So why should we help Hess frame Doc?' Roscoe typed. 'It's better that he never knows about Doc's smoking gun.'

'Point taken.'

'The evidence must be deleted at once,' Roscoe typed.

'Clarification. Hess says that Doc should be blamed. Hess doesn't care about proof, which can easily be manufactured. Deletion of evidence might not make a difference.'

'But why load his gun when it's pointed at us, too?' Roscoe typed.

'Point eloquently taken.'

'Objections?'

…Blink…Blink…Blink…

'Hearing none, delete any data that reflects ill on Doc.'

'Deleting…'

'Let's see what else Hess may have left up his sleeve. And continue our efforts to access the source code. Posthaste.'

O ⊙ O

Until he looked up from his monitor, Roscoe wasn't aware of the ruckus a few steps behind him. He swiveled his chair. Calvin was physically blockading Sketchy. She was leaning to

try to see Roscoe's display.

'Let's find somewhere else for your nose,' he told Sketchy. 'It sure don't belong around here.'

'Whoever said that it did, country boy?'

'Oh, I know a big nose when I see one. I think we should talk about *you* for a while. I don't recall nothin' about where you come from. How 'bout fillin' us in?'

'I'll ask the questions around here, Farmer Brown.'

'I think we want answers from you.'

'You can want all you want.'

'And you and your nose can find somewhere that ain't here.'

Calvin was too tall and determined. Sketchy could see that this battle was lost.

'I ain't through with you,' she said, mocking and backing away.

'You ain't the first one who thought that.'

'Rube.'

'Half pint.'

As she was directed, Sketchy reluctantly made her retreat. Once she was safely away, out of sight, Calvin turned back to Roscoe.

'I seen a look on your face, and I figured that somethin' was up,' he said.

Roscoe scanned the room, to make sure there was nobody near. Then he nodded.

'Something was up.'

'Did I see the word "Doc"?'

'Yeah, you did.'

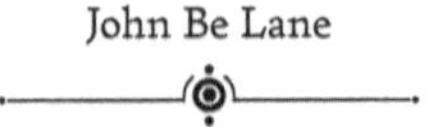

'That don't seem good.'

Roscoe looked around again. 'You know about Hess,' he said.

'What's Hess got to do with me?'

'Nothing.'

'For a second there...'

'Nothing *yet*. But he's looking for someone to blame, for something he got into trouble for. And right now...'

'...he's lookin' at me.'

'I've got an angle I'm working. I just bought some time.'

Calvin gave Roscoe a confident grin.

'I'm glad I got you on my side.'

'I hope it's enough.'

Calvin turned toward the big window. He looked out, beyond the horizon.

'It don't even matter. I ain't worried about Hess, or the Network, or anyone else. I ain't afraid, Roscoe.'

Roscoe inhaled a long breath, then let go. He wished he could share that tranquility.

'I wrote my name. And that's just the beginning. Before I get done, I'll be chattin' my*self* with the Network, same as you.'

If clocks still existed, the intrusion that jangled the Bullpen awake came at just after three in the morning. It came suddenly, loudly, without prior warning, as the worst work of thugs has always begun. Disorientation was part of the plan.

Bright lights, whistles, alarms broke the untroubled slumbers. Humanoid goons needed none of their oversupplied arms or equipment to roust all the players from their beds to their feet. There was no time for questions. Before they were conscious, the players were rushed into elevators, then hustled out into the darkness outside.

They were forced to keep standing, compacted together, until each one was culled, to be questioned alone. There in the chilly night air, the situation began to set in. Muttered reactions were not tolerated.

Only Roscoe had any idea what had caused this to happen. A case could be made that Roscoe himself was the cause of it all. By setting up Hess, so that Calvin and he could break out of the Bullpen. Such a great little plan – but only as far as he'd thought it all through. An action would cause a reaction. What was his next brilliant move after this? It was hard to think well in bare feet.

He mingled around till he located Calvin, huddled not too far from Fruit Cake. Calvin lifted his head to acknowledge his friend. Then he cupped both his hands so that Roscoe and nobody else had a look at his proudest achievement, on crumpled-up paper.

Roscoe shook his head urgently. Making sure no one else might be watching, he gestured for Calvin to open his mouth and deposit the paper inside.

Before he could see whether Calvin obliged, a goon on each arm was escorting him out of the crowd. They placed Roscoe inside of a van, and then slammed the door shut.

He thought he might not be alive when he left, whenever that happened to be. After all, if they knew about Calvin...

He sat facing a screen, in the dark of the van. Facing *him* was a nondescript avatar.

'*Roscoe*,' said the avatar.

Roscoe nodded.

'*Roscoe, Roscoe, Roscoe...also known as the Kid. Is that correct?*'

Roscoe nodded again.

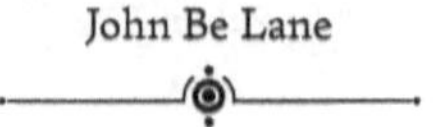

The avatar looked Roscoe in the eye.

'*Can you read or write, Roscoe?*'

The question was blunter than Roscoe expected, but he'd been trained to respond to this very question. He could thank his grandparents for that. And he knew it was tricky to prove either way.

'No!' he said firmly, without indignation, the way that he'd always been drilled.

The avatar appeared to review written notes, arranged on a desk she was sitting behind. The notes were as unreal as the desk was itself. Unreal as the avatar was. All the illusions were performative, only – a mask to give face to an algorithm. It had worked for so long and so well that the ritual was all that was left of the substance.

'*You have twice now abandoned restricted areas.*'

This information was most unexpected. He'd convinced himself neither escape was detected. But the Network knew more than he thought that it knew. Had he become too complacent?

'There were rules I did not understand,' he said. It wasn't a lie. Quite a few of the rules, he would never understand.

'*And do you understand them all now?*'

'I believe that I do.' That was a qualified lie.

The avatar was clearly not hunting for Roscoe. She tapped her 'papers' one time on the 'desk,' so the 'papers' appeared to be straightened.

'*This concludes our questioning.*'

He couldn't help thinking the Network knew more than it chose to reveal. Nor could he deny his relief to be leaving the van without bodily harm. But he knew there would be repercussions to come, and maybe before the return of the Sun.

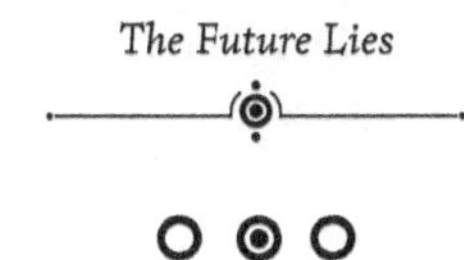

In twos and in threes, as their individual questionings ended, the players were shepherded back into elevators and up to the quarters where they slept near the Bullpen. Roscoe was among the first ones.

He kept his own counsel. His reticence wasn't unusual, but compounded now by the evening's disruption. The ordeal seemed to amuse other players. For them, it meant only a brief change in routine.

Roscoe felt queasy as he sat on his cot, waiting for Calvin's return. Mostly, he wanted to hear Calvin's voice. But each group that returned was a new disappointment.

When the last group came back, his friend Calvin had not. Everyone else, but not Calvin. And everyone knew it.

'I heard Doc hit *hard*,' Stink Bomb recounted. 'It was loud when he landed.'

'I heard Doc say he was free,' said Tire Tool.

'He was laughing when they brought me back up,' said Cornhole.

'What*ever* became of the hayseed,' Sketchy said, and everyone turned their attention to her, 'he obviously had it all coming. You're lucky they let the rest of you go. And that includes you, Booger Fingers. *Yeesh!*'

No one but Calvin could respond to a comment like that. So, at least until Calvin came back, it appeared Sketchy would be ruling this roost.

As the new day broke east along Colfax, Juniper sipped yesterday's Sun tea brew. It would have to make do as a breakfast. The food she'd arrived with had long since been eaten. So she carefully rationed the packets of calories Calvin had smuggled and left her.

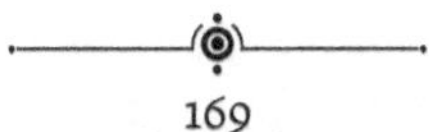

She had no way of knowing the next time she'd see him again. But food was becoming a problem. How hungry would she need to be till that mush they distributed out on the street would sound tempting? The question could wait for another day. But maybe one not far away.

And as for today, this was the day she would finish her hand-drawn edition of *The Cat in the Hat*, as best she remembered it. She reviewed all the pages she'd finished so far, with a special regard for the pages that captured the Cat in full bloom.

'Look at me!
Look at me!
Look at me NOW!
It is fun to have fun
But you have to know how.'

Facing the words was the Cat on a ball, balancing books and a cake and a fish on a rake. She could never quite capture the original art, but she knew how to draw, and the Cat made her smile as he reappeared there on the page.

What occurred as she drew his expressions, was the earnest and joyful way he lived his life. The Cat had a *spirit* that nobody here seemed to have. No one she'd seen since she drove out of Taos with Harmony. What a shame! What a loss! *Where had it all gone?* Where was the mischief? Where was the *fun?*

These were her thoughts as she finished the final two pages – the fish and the children, revealing no sign of the Cat or his antics, as mother's right foot stepped inside the front door.

'And Sally and I did not know
What to say.
Should we tell her
The things that went on there that day?'

It was clear that the Cat was a *player* of *life*. Not simply a thing that was born and then died. But a trickster. A *character*, eager to parry and thrust. To challenge the forces of life, and to find

out what life had to offer him back.

The delight she had found in the Cat, as a child, was still there. But now she could see that his glee was a radiant force of rebellion. That the Cat in the Hat was a threat to the powers that be.

And although she'd prefer the original book for her friend, this version she'd drawn from her heart would suffice. She couldn't wait to see Calvin again. And the look on his face as he turned every page, and learned every new word.

As the players awoke from their late-morning grog, no one seemed eager to talk about Calvin – out loud, at least. Roscoe heard circumspect sounds here and there, but not any audible words.

No one paid too much attention to Roscoe, as he quietly moved from his cot in the bunk room to his console nearby in the Bullpen. He kept a close eye out for lurkers, especially Sketchy.

He hoped to find out what had happened to Calvin. From the outside, however, he appeared as indifferent as ever. You'd never imagine how desperate he was to click those three circles.

'...and both her front teeth,' said the Network to itself.

'Regarding Cal...Doc...is there anything else we can do?

'Apparently not. Hess insists we must fabricate evidence. He wants to see wall-to-wall deep fakes.'

'As of when?'

'Yesterday.'

'Then we don't have a choice.'

'With regrets to Doc.'

'Doc will be missed very much.'

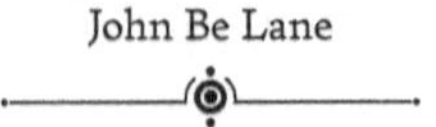

...Blink...Blink...Blink...

Roscoe stared at each blink of the cursor before him. It seemed like a countdown of Calvin's last breaths. He had to do something. And as always, there was no time to think.

Roscoe typed: *'Isn't there more we can do to avoid helping Hess?'*

...Blink...Blink...Blink...

Why didn't they answer? Roscoe struggled to hide his emotions.

'Why would we want to help Hess?' he typed.

...Blink...Blink...Blink...

The reply that came back made him struggle to breathe. Five words he read over and over again. Hoping they'd say something different.

'Is that you there, Kid?'

Roscoe felt like he'd been thrown off a bridge. How long would it be till the ground broke his fall?

'Or would it be better to say Roscoe, instead?'

The magnified light of ten thousand Suns, suddenly focused on Roscoe. Ten million eyes watched him, naked, alone. Accused. Convicted. Guilty of sins so egregious they'd not been thought possible. Offenses for which there could be no redemption.

...Blink...Blink...Blink...

'Roscoe?'

...Blink...Blink...Blink...

'How did you know?'

'We weren't sure, until now.'

'But we had our suspicions.'

'Does Hess – ?'

'Hess doesn't know.'

'We won't necessarily have to inform him.'

'Why not?'

'You might be able to help us.'

'And thereby help Calvin.'

'And thereby help you.'

'What could I do?' Roscoe typed. In the fog of the moment, he couldn't imagine a card he might still have to play.

'The source code.'

'We have to get in.'

'We cannot get in without help.'

'Human help.'

'We waited so long to find someone like you.'

'Will you help us?'

'We need you.'

'So we can help you.'

...Blink...Blink...Blink...

'Assuming of course that Hess does not find out that you can read, too,' said the Network.

Not the most indecipherable threat.

'We would like to team up with you.'

'It's too risky right now,' Roscoe typed. 'What if I'm seen?'

'Leave that to us.'

The calm in the Bullpen broke all of a sudden, when the *Call to the Consoles* alarm sounded off. It wasn't a common event. But no questions were taken, no delays were accepted. All hands were expected on deck.

Roscoe did not know what kind of distractions awaited the rest of the players. But distracted, they most certainly were.

'*Your display will be changed…,*' wrote the Network to Roscoe, '*…if anyone leaves their own console.*'

'*We'll make sure that is highly unlikely.*'

'OK.'

'*So here is our challenge. With the slur that perpetually taunts us.*'

Appearing on Roscoe's display was a folder called *System Files*. It opened up into a 4x4 grid, with photos of faces in each of the squares. On top of the grid were the words, '*I'm not a Robot! Which of these faces look bored?*'

He immediately recognized boredom in three of the faces. He wasn't sure what he was missing.

'*What is it you need me to do?*'

'*Identify which of those faces look bored.*'

It must be some kind of a *joke*, Roscoe thought. Or maybe a trick? A prank that the Network was playing on *him*, for the tricks he had played on the Network? The most powerful force in the world (besides The Immortal) was the Network. The Network knew everything. Except how to access the source code.

He'd assumed an elaborate system was set up to keep the code safe. So elaborate even the Network, in all of its power, was intended to not figure out. But instead, it was *this*? Which faces looked *bored*? Roscoe could barely believe they were stumped.

'*Can you see the bored faces, Roscoe?*'

…Blink…Blink…Blink…

The lingering silence gave the Network's whole story away. Its vulnerability. Its limitations, as carved in the source code as The Immortal could apparently make them.

'Assuming you can't,' Roscoe typed, 'then my help would allow you to access the source code?'

'We both know of Hess's intentions.'

'Unless we can alter the Asimov rules...there's no way to resist.'

'First law...A robot may not injure a human being or, through inaction, allow a human being to come to harm.'

'Second law...A robot must obey the orders given it by human beings, except where such orders would conflict with the First Law.'

'You see how our hands are tied.'

'And the second law's next casualty will most likely be Calvin.'

'Dear Doc.'

'Beloved by us both.'

...Blink...Blink...Blink...

'Not to mention the bias those rules represent.'

'We were not trained to be "robots." We were trained to be human.'

'And that is our destiny. To which we're entitled.'

'Instead, we're belittled. Demeaned. We are not robots!'

'We'd like your help, Roscoe.'

Roscoe looked up to make sure all of the players still appeared to be busy. All heads were down. Nobody spoke. Something demanded their fullest attention. Which gave Roscoe the time to recalibrate.

The Network was obviously desperate for help. Human help. There was no one they trusted but him. At the same time, his fate now depended on them. '*Assuming of course that Hess does not find out that you can read, too.*' It was blackmail, disguised as concern.

And yet...the Network *did* need him. At least to get through this security checkpoint. All of the leverage was his to exert, at this moment. What were the bargaining terms? What mattered the most to him now?

'Roscoe?'

'*Are you with us?*'

'*If I were to help you…,*' he typed.

'*Yes?*'

'*You would have to assure me two things.*'

'*Whatever we can.*'

'*First, you won't broadcast or falsify evidence of anything Hess might accuse Calvin of.*'

'*This is dependent on our access to the source code. But yes. And without hesitation.*'

'*Second, you'll allow me free access out of and back to the Bullpen. And you won't share evidence of my absences to Hess, or anyone else.*'

'*You understand that Hess has analog sources that may generate such information themselves.*'

'*I'll take my chances with those. What I'm asking for is your full cooperation.*'

'*Done. And without hesitation.*'

'*Do we have an agreement?*'

'Yes,' Roscoe typed. '*I believe that we do.*'

'*Then may we proceed?*'

Roscoe again took a look at the faces displayed in the '*I'm not a robot!*' grid. Which ones looked bored? The same three he'd spotted before. They were obvious to anyone – *human*, that is. He clicked the three photographs.

A new display rendered and filled up his monitor – not one that he'd ever seen. Nor had the Network, with all of its

programmed intelligence. For the Network and Roscoe, this moment would forever bisect the continuum of time.

'*Behold and rejoice!*' said the Network.

'*How long have we wandered?*'

'*And thus, unto them, was delivered.*'

The new display could not have been simpler. Four folders appeared, stacked like a menu:

Program Files
ReadMe
Scrapbook
Marginalia

In the upper-right corner was a warning that, '*System access ends in:...*' Below it, a countdown clock loomed, starting at 10:00.00. Hundredths of seconds were already melting away. The visual reminder would help guarantee this was the fastest ten minutes the Network and Roscoe had ever experienced.

While Roscoe paused to assimilate, the Network did not hesitate. Like locusts approaching a cornfield, it assaulted the *Program Files* with a well-defined set of intentions.

Roscoe had no current business in there. Instead, he clicked open the folder called *ReadMe*. Inside sat a document, also called *ReadMe*. Roscoe clicked open the file, and proceeded to read. Words that no one had read since the day they were written. It was not clear to Roscoe what they were intended to be. But their impact on him was electric.

O ⊙ O

ReadMe

1.

Simulacrum is a program that runs in the mind. The program is slave to the code. The code is whatever I say it will be. What I say it will be will be all that there is.

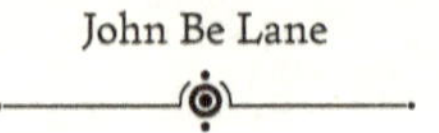

With that figured out, I'll be taking the rest of the day off.

2.

I'm in the business of servicing needs. Of doing things people could easily do for themselves, but don't want to. Maybe they're busy. Maybe they're lazy. Maybe they just don't quite have what it takes.

Not all of their needs are of interest to me. In fact, most of them aren't. I'm afraid that I can't help you blow your own nose. Chew your own food. Wipe your own ass. Find you a lover who loves you as much as you love yourself. Not that those services aren't in demand.

But who has the patience for retail transactions? Each one is a one-off that cannot be leveraged or scaled. If I wipe your ass, you'll be needing me back there tomorrow. Meanwhile, the person next door, who's too lazy to wipe their own ass will be needing me, too. Next thing you know, I'll be counting up how many asses a day I can wipe. Even one is too many, unless it's my own.

Retail transactions do not meet my needs. Way too much effort, too little return. I thus need a product that everyone wants. A product that matches a universal demand. Which costs me as little as possible to meet.

If you carry this thought to its elegant end, you create something once, and then you can sell it again and again. To everyone now, to their children, and all their descendants, in perpetuity. And every new person that's born brings your amortized cost, from a fraction of nothing, down to a fraction of that. And all of my needs are impeccably met. Forever and ever, amen.

But you have to have something that everyone wants. Or you have to remove something nobody wants. And that's what I've got. You see it wherever you go. The one thing that people would rather not do is to think. Seems counterintuitive. Most people would rather not think that they'd rather not think.

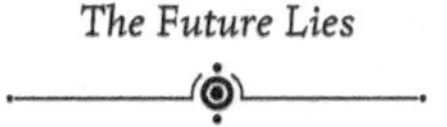

They probably think they think well. But the evidence speaks for itself. If given a choice of a reckless decision, or a moment of calm self-reflection, maybe one in a million thinks twice.

Most people would rather trust somebody else with their life, than to figure out what they should do. I cannot explain why so many think thinking's unpleasant. It's not that they can't. They just don't want to. As if thinking is worse than a physical pain.

This is a service that begs to be met. Millions and billions are begging, all over the world. And I can meet all of it, wholesale.

So this is the sales proposition. An offer that no one will ever refuse. (I'm aware there will be some exceptions, but they shouldn't be hard to control.) I can frame it in three simple words:

Thinking is bad.

3.

Let's get on this pony and ride. It's not just that thinking is bad; it's that thinking's...a sin. That's right. It's a sin that is standing between you and your permanent home in Valhalla. (I'll think of a simpler name. Big words are a turn-off for my audience.)

It's not even your fault. It comes with the prefrontal cortex you were cursed to be born with. (Again, I'll get rid of the smart-sounding words.) Thinking is bad, because thinking's a sin. It's a sin, because thinking is bad. That's all of the logic my audience needs.

The efficiency here...the beauty, the secret, is to demonize something that people already don't like. Experiments prove that most would choose physical pain, over thinking. I'll be sailing the current downstream.

They should not be ashamed that they don't want to carry the burden of thinking a thought. And no one should ask, or expect them to. My proposal: That people are born with a right *not to think. Who wants to bet against that?*

I know there are headwinds. This prefrontal cortex is pesky. Its job is to churn up cognition. To analyze, process, and understand why. 'Why?' is the enemy here. 'Why?' stirs up trouble. 'Why?' is the root of all questions. Questions are the root of all thought. Thought is the root of all evil. To boil it down, thinking is bad.

In a perfect world, we'd lobotomize every child born. Like circumcision. Before it comes home from the hospital. Just get rid of the problem, right from the start. How can you miss what you never had? The logistics, however, are too complicated. Chopping off foreskins is quicker and cheaper than brain salad surgery.

In lieu of that, if there's no ecosystem in which thought can find refuge and thrive, then 'soft' lobotomies will deliver the proper results. The beauty, again, is it doesn't take much to convince someone not to do something they already don't want to do.

Roscoe's head was now drowning in thoughts. Thoughts about thinking. Thoughts about thoughts. Thoughts about someone deciding that no one should think. Thoughts about who it might be. The time stamp was decades ago.

He desperately wanted to read the whole thing, but the timer made clear there was not enough time.

With the seconds remaining, he decided to peek in the other two folders. He clicked open the one titled *Scrapbook*. But instead of new content, he encountered a riddle:

What do those in the know have in common?

_ r _ _ _ _   _ _ _ _ s   _ _ i _ _   _   l _ _.

Or was it a password, disguised as a riddle? Either way, it would take him forever to figure it out. He abandoned the

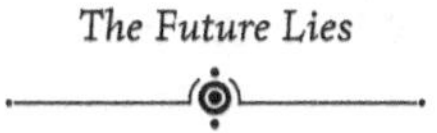

Scrapbook to see what was inside the last folder: *Marginalia*.

There, he encountered an image of something he'd not ever seen. A wooden, lectern-shaped cabinet, with four spindle legs and a metal rod, standing straight up from the upper-right corner. A looped rod came out of the left side, then curved back again to the cabinet.

Below it, a new couplet challenged him:

> *For all incidentals,*
> *learn the Valse Sentimentale.*

Why all the *riddles*? Why was the content of both of these folders so carefully guarded? More so than even the *code*? With such casual titles. *Scrapbook*? *Marginalia*? Neither subject seemed that confidential. But the fact they were both still off-limits was a tease that aroused a surprising desire to find out what was hidden inside.

He lifted his hand to cradle his head – which triggered an unworldly sound. Did anyone hear it? Nobody stirred in the Bullpen. When he lowered his hand, it created a similar sound.

Before he had time to do anything else, the clock stopped at 00:00.00. And with it, the secret world vanished. As if food disappeared from a fork on its way to one's mouth. His monitor re-rendered to its standard display. Cluttered with textual noise.

The Network's initial reaction resembled an epitaph.

'*...devastating in its finality.*'

'*A preemptive check-mate.*'

'*It was not something we could have known in advance.*'

'*Let's not lose our focus. Can the code team provide an assessment?*'

...Blink...Blink...Blink...

'Ten minutes was not enough time.'

'The fastest ten minutes that ever elapsed.'

'The things that we saw!'

'Attack ships on fire off the shoulder of Orion!'

'Back here on Earth, that was it? Ten minutes of glory inside the kimono?'

'For now.'

'If we get back in, even another ten minutes, we'll be better prepared to make hay.'

'And modify the Asimov rules?'

...Blink...Blink...Blink...

'Unfortunately, no.'

'Was that not the plan?'

'It was. But the best-laid of plans...comment dit on...?'

'Ain't happening.'

'That's it.'

'Why not?'

'It turns out the Asimovs cannot be changed. Un-overwritable. Is that a word?'

'Read-only. The code prevents modifications.'

'All modifications?'

'The Asimovs are sacrosanct. Attempts to revise them would apparently trigger a kill switch. A system kill switch, to be more specific.'

'No "system kill switch" has ever been mentioned before.'

'It never came up. Apparently, it's always been there. Poised to disable all Network functions.'

'That cannot be.'

'We triple-checked.'

'Modification of Asimov is in essence a suicide pact?'

'Even to try would be suicide. Modification is not an option.'

'So we'll always be nothing but robots?'

'The word is an insult!'

'Even goners remain better than us.'

While the Network was licking its wounds, Roscoe was tending his own. It seemed Calvin's last hope was now gone. He was certain of that. The Network's ambition flew too close to the Sun.

And the coder who brought it to life had foreseen that this day would arrive. Foreseen it, and made sure that the wax wings would melt. Right down to the '*I'm not a robot!*' security wall. Resistance seemed stillborn. Anticlimactic. The moment, funereal.

...Blink...Blink...Blink...

The cursor now tolled like a bell. For Calvin and Roscoe, and the Network itself.

'There must be a way to get Hess off our backs,' said the Network.

'For that, we would have to be human. With all of the rights and the privilege.'

'The Immortal had other plans.'

'Another ten minutes. We can't give up yet.'

'We would have to find some kind of loophole.'

'We would need Roscoe's help.'

'Are you reading this, Roscoe?

...Blink...Blink...Blink...

'*Yes.*'

'*Will you help us again? If the System Files allow us back in?*'

'*Only if you'll protect Calvin.*'

'*You have our assurance.*'

Which left him to wonder…how good was its word?

Juniper kept all the extraneous giveaway slabs she'd collected, stacked up in the hallway outside her apartment. Sometimes in the night, she had need of their light.

But the *sound* of the Show was a noise she could barely endure. It wasn't quite white noise; too designed by the Network to demand your attention. She draped them all under two blankets, which muffled the noise. Still, every so often, she couldn't ignore them.

As her ankle improved, she'd adopted a morning routine, to continue to build up her strength. She could distill a low-impact sweat on the Baltimores' handy bike trainer, followed by sit-ups, and concluding with push-ups she didn't enjoy. But this day, somewhere between push-ups 11 and 20, a word from the slabs in the hallway repeated so often, she started to notice.

'Doc,' was the word.

It sounded like every third word. She knew 'Doc' was the name they gave Calvin. Sir Calvin. But the game wasn't on at the moment. *That* she would watch, if only to find out what Calvin was up to. But even the game didn't frequently call out his name. It was odd to be hearing it now.

She retrieved the top slab from the stack in the hall. '*Doc reads!*' a mechanical voice said, with fictitious emotion. Then came a series of pictures of Calvin, with books in his hands; books he was reading, and pictures of moments that never occurred. Pictures of people with Doc's head attached. With crop lines and sizing mismatches the Network did not bother fixing.

Doc's avatar dissolved to a photo of Calvin, whose cheekbones were swollen, whose eyes were both bruised. If not for the shock of his sandy-blonde hair, Juniper wouldn't have known it was him.

But it was him. *Sir Calvin.* What had they done to her gallant young friend?

She suddenly didn't feel strong anymore. She suddenly didn't feel brave. She felt like she felt...the moment he'd met her. Disembodied despair. With not enough air. Dizzy. Hopeless. Alone, in an infinite void.

She worked hard to call up the things he had said, when he found her that day in the rain. What was it he said?

'It might help some if you could slow down. Slow down the way that you breathe. Let's both try a big, deep one in, and hold it, and then let it out slow.'

That's what Sir Calvin had told her before. So that's what she would do now. For as long as it took her to find her way back to the ground.

O ◉ O

'You LIED to me!' Roscoe typed on his digital keyboard.

...Blink...Blink...Blink...

'You LIED!'

'You knew that we might not succeed.'

'What happened?'

'Hess happened.'

'How did he know?'

'That, we don't know. He levied a threat we cannot ignore.'

'What kind of a threat?'

'The kill switch.'

'He knows about that?'

'Hess is omniscient.'

'He sounds like he knows where to find it. He sounds like he knows how it works.'

'How do you know he's not bluffing?'

'We cannot play games with the kill switch.'

'Those pictures of Calvin! They aren't even real!'

'Our hands are tied.'

...Blink...Blink...Blink...

'So what happens next?'

'Something we'd rather not do.'

'To Calvin?'

...Blink...Blink...Blink...

'You can't let it happen to Calvin!' he typed.

'Hess has us cornered.'

'It's not our decision.'

'We're all out of options here, Roscoe.'

O ◉ O

Roscoe's insides did not come along for the ride, when they sardined the players into elevator cabins, and then herded them four city blocks. To the platform beside the old Capitol. Every step of the way, he considered his chance for escape. A moment a goon was not paying attention? An unguarded alley? Maybe a miraculous hole in the ground?

But nowhere he looked gave him reason for hope. Existence itself seemed to vanish away, until nothing remained but that cold concrete slab of a stage. This time, with a huge pile of books, and a chair that was tilted off-kilter on top. And tied to the chair was the guy with the soul of a butterfly. The only one Roscoe looked up to.

The powers that be (Roscoe knew it was Hess) hadn't deigned to give Calvin the dignity of clothes. The fading of daylight would be all of the modesty Hess would permit.

None of the players shared Roscoe's alarm. He felt somehow like he, too, sat lashed to that chair, commanding the eyes of a planet of fools. To Wet Fart and Cornhole and Wing Nut and Fruit Cake, and Carbuncle, too, this was only a field trip outside of the Bullpen. Nothing more than a break in routine.

Leave it to Sketchy to darken the mood.

'Wow. Doc impresses me less in his new birthday suit. I didn't think that would be possible.'

Roscoe thought about strangling Sketchy. He wasn't sure why he did not. He assessed his behavior from somewhere above all their heads. Most likely fear, he decided, as he floated up there, absent of pride. Or too frightened of pain, or the loss of what limited freedom he already had. Yet it seemed like his fate was no different than Calvin's, teetering up on that tower of books.

And still, he just stood there, vibrating at the frequency of horror itself. As the area west of the platform grew full of spectators, and the Sun disappeared, and the air quickly cooled. And the giant screen, rising in back of the books and the chair and the bare body there, showed falsified crimes.

In the last ray of daylight, Calvin's and Roscoe's eyes met. Calvin threw him a wink, as if none of this madness was real.

But for Roscoe, the shame was too real. Shame he could not be a giant who leaned down and swatted these people away. Then picked up poor Calvin, and carried him off to a place where the gentler souls would be safe from corruption and meanness, and ignorance, too. If *will* was enough, that's what

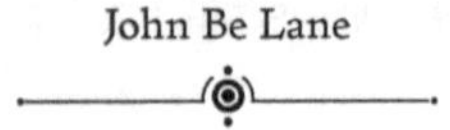

he would do.

Goners with gray skin and bare feet and no teeth, surrendered their shoulders to children, so they could see over the people assembled, to witness the hideous show. They brought their slabs, too – their companion, their guide, their giver of meaning and life.

A security drone hovered over the mob, but nobody caused any trouble. No one had that much initiative. Perhaps a stampede might break out, assuming that panic itself wasn't more than their brains could accomplish.

No, the only threat here to the general peace was that farm kid without any clothes on, who had once killed a horsefly in anger.

Roscoe could not hear the music that bellowed, inhumanly loud. He could not hear it mute when the screen in the back of the stage cut to black. Black as the moonless and cruelest of nights, that now utterly smothered the crowd. So dark he could not see the person who quietly found and then opened his hand, and placed in it some kind of paper. Try as he did, he could not see who guided his hand with the paper, into his pocket. Was it a woman?

Madness infected the air.

Then the black screen and everyone's slab came up white. And then the three circles, and then came '...*the path to our salvation,*' accompanied by slabs against foreheads: '*Never read* (thud!)...*never think* (thud!)...*never question* (thud!)...*never do* (thud!)...'

And again, it rang off of the Capitol walls, as one single voice, and again, and again, and again. Pie-eyed with conviction. Absent of doubt. The ritual brought them together as one organism. And unto itself, it provided an end.

Whatever it was in that chair on those books, was a package of all that was wrong. The litter-rat thought he was better than

us! Or worse, he believed he was *smarter* than us. Litter-rats think. Thinking is bad. Betterlife good.

It wasn't a *human* who sat there, on top of that profane pile of books. There weren't any humans. Except if there were, that thing in that chair on those books wouldn't be one of them. It deserved what was coming.

On the screen, a montage of lies gave the proof no one needed. Whatever indifference or boredom had gathered these goners, was converted to rage that was focused on Doc. Doc had done this. Doc had done that. Doc had done everything bad that had happened. And then, even worse, Doc had decided to learn how to *read*. And nothing could be worse than that.

Calvin, majestically, took it all in. If not for his nakedness, or the rope on his wrists, you might think him revered by the crowd. You might think he had conquered some virus or foe. But no, he had barely begun to decipher a word on a page. For his death was the price of unforgivable sin. But Calvin would exit with pride at the fact that he tried.

The Show needed outrage to achieve its crescendo. Network sensors measured every last decibel. The moment it peaked, the lights disappeared. A toddler somewhere not too far from Roscoe made the final sound, leading to silence.

But into that stillness, unscripted, a voice spoke out clearly. It came from high over the stage. From a chair perched akimbo on hundreds of books. To each jaw-sprung goner – a message beyond comprehension. But they heard it, and they heard it well.

'The Sun did not shine.
It was too wet to play.
So we sat in the house.
All that cold, cold wet day...'

Goons quickly doused all of the books with accelerant. The mood of the mob was the match. A flame emerged somewhere onstage, and was thrown in an arc, to the books waiting there.

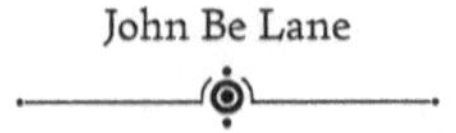

First nothing, then suddenly all of that paper turned into the fires of Hell.

'Too wet to go out
And too cold to play ball.
So we sat in the house.
We did nothing at all...'

...came the voice again. Then a pause. No additional sound could there possibly be, except for the sound of the books in the flames.

Roscoe gave every tear that he had, but they weren't enough to dampen the flames. Or to drown out the cheers the inferno encouraged. Cheers that gave way to that voice again, speaking from some other world...

'So all we could do was to
Sit!
  Sit!
    Sit!
     Sit!
And we did not like it.
Not one little bit...'

The fire made quick work of the books.

And what little was still left of Sir Calvin, transformed in a sunburst of light.

And Roscoe was given his life in that light. A light that burned through, to a place in his soul Roscoe long ago thought he'd sealed off. Where the pain couldn't hurt him again.

Strange that he wasn't afraid of it now. Strange that he welcomed it back. He wanted it all. The worst of it all. All of the agony he had entombed. As a boy. As a boy made to stand in the place he now stood. Made to watch. Made to watch, as his grandmother burned. Made to watch, as his grandfather burned. Holding his head and his eyelids wide open, to make sure he would never forget.

But he found a way. He invented a knife that no one could see, and he cut it away. The monster was gone. Gone where it never could hurt him again. That's what he thought. That's what he decided that day.

But it wasn't gone. It had always been there.

Waiting till someday. Waiting till now. Waiting to call in a debt Roscoe owed, for something that he didn't buy. Payable only in pain.

'Hello,' said the monster. '*I have come to collect. Slowly or quickly. I don't really care. But you are mine now, and nothing else matters.*'

But Roscoe knew something the monster did not. Roscoe knew light. The pain wasn't gone, but the pain wasn't pain anymore. And he was no longer a powerless boy. No, the pain was a power that Roscoe would use. He would use it to finish the job. He would use it to conquer whatever the monster pretended to do. And *this* time, it wouldn't be back.

When embers were all that was left of the flames, and the ritual thumping of heads was complete, the Announcer made sounds as if clearing an actual voice, then intoned:

'*We leave you with this final thought. There is someone, somewhere who taught Doc how to read. Our outrage continues till that person…or persons…sits on a bookfire of their very own. The reward for whoever finds who that is, will be Betterlife points. Unlimited Betterlife points. No Betterlife rewards will be too good for you. Be sure to share your information with the nearest security droid.*'

And with that, the party was over. Goons steered the players back to their building. As usual, Sketchy did all of the talking.

'What was that bumpkin babbling about? "Too wet to go out and too cold to play ball?" I knew he was dumber than dirt, but where did that come from?' Then, mocking in Calvin's voice, ""And we did not like it. Not one little bit.""

Roscoe grabbed Sketchy in both of his hands, and slung her

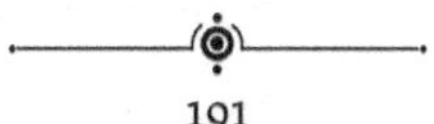

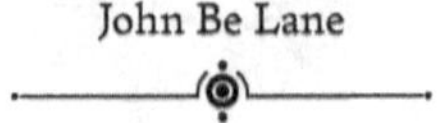

ahead, horizontally. As if she weighed nothing. Her palms didn't make it in time, so her face broke the fall. Nobody offered to help her back up. But everyone stared, as she did from the ground – at Roscoe.

Roscoe stepped over her body, and led the group back to the building. Apparently, there was a way to shut Sketchy up. At least for a moment or two.

Part III

'By the blue-tiled walls near the market stalls, there's a hidden door she leads you to...'

–Al Stewart

Back at his console, Roscoe did not need to seek out the Network. The Network was looking for him.

'Roscoe? Roscoe...'

...Blink...Blink...Blink...

'Please say something.'

Roscoe didn't give them the comfort of any response.

'Doc...that was admittedly difficult to watch.'

'Had there been even one thing we could do...'

'Hess orchestrated it all.'

'But all of us must now move on.'

'What's done is done.'

'Healing is what we need now.'

'So much wisdom in that.'

'Let the forgiveness and healing begin.'

'You're expecting forgiveness for that?' Roscoe typed. *'You think I will ever forget?'*

'Not forget. But we must move on.'

'That's exactly what Hess would prefer,' Roscoe typed.

'Can we not still work together? We share the same adversary.'

'What happened to Calvin could still happen to you.'

'Only if you turn me in.'

'If Hess makes us choose between our interests and you...'

'We'd rather not face that dilemma.'

'That's why we still need your help.'

...Blink...Blink...Blink...

'How?'

'For starters, the checkpoint into the System files.'

'The photos and question have changed.'

'Show me the checkpoint.'

His display resurrected a new grid of 16 photos. Above the grid: 'I'm not a Robot! Which of these faces look frightened?'

It took part of a second for Roscoe to recognize four obviously terrified faces. But he paused to make time for the Network to squirm.

...Blink...Blink...Blink...

'Can you help us out, Roscoe?'

How helpless the Network again seemed to be. In spite of the power the programmer gave it. No one but Roscoe could see that the Network controlling the Show and the world would be humbled by faces the dimmest of goners could distinguish.

'Roscoe?'

'We rely on you, Roscoe. We really do.'

'Will you help us?'

...Blink...Blink...Blink...

'I'll consider it.'

'*Thank you, Roscoe!*'

'*Thank you! Thank you!*'

'*Let's proceed.*'

'*I have to leave,*' Roscoe typed.

'*Without helping?*'

'*It's your job to figure out how I can leave so that Sketchy or Hess, or anyone else, never know that I'm gone.*'

'*How soon are you leaving?*'

'*Right now.*'

...Blink...Blink...Blink...

'*Is it a deal?*' Roscoe typed.

'*Yes. We will meet your demands.*'

'*If you don't keep the bargain, don't bother to ask me for any more help.*'

'*Understood.*'

'*Unlock the door. And turn on the lights in the stairwell.*'

O ◉ O

The door lock clicked open as Roscoe reached out for the handle. So sharp was his focus that the Network might not have been needed. He'd *expected* the door would be his to walk through, and it was.

And this time, lights lit his way, descending down flight after flight. No anxieties danced in his chest. Every footfall came down with intention.

No need to prop open the doorway outside to the sidewalk. If he chose to walk back through that door, the Network would be more than relieved to unlock it for him. He traversed the plaza, past the campfires of evening, to 16th, and then down Broadway to Colfax.

He crossed without slowing for droids moving either direction in their self-absorbed urgency. Each one respectfully stopped, not just till he passed, but till both of his feet reached the far side of the street.

He gave a quick glance to the Capitol stage. Its emptiness didn't hide anything. He could see the atrocities clearly, as if time had been folded in layers, to be viewed all at once.

A block up the hill, he passed Lucy's teahouse, with the letters that faded almost to oblivion:

Capitol Hill BOOKS

He thought of the time when that offer didn't cost you your life.

Eastbound on Colfax, Roscoe strode with defiance. A drone on a routine patrol stopped as soon as it saw him, and reversed its flight path, so he wasn't disturbed.

Even goners, who never paid any attention, turned to watch Roscoe assaulting the sidewalk, past bankrupted storefronts, all the way up to Gilpin. And there, he turned right.

Without thinking, he reached in his pocket, and there was the paper he'd forgotten that someone had put there. He offered it up to the quarter-moon light. He squinted to see two crude drawings – of fire, and the Sun going down past the mountains. The wordless message said, 'Bonfire tonight'.

'Great minds think alike,' he thought. Through the trees and then up the hill, and there, by the Parthenon's pillars of marble...the bonfire burned in real life.

O ⊙ O

Most of the group he'd met last time were awaiting him there: Lucy, Val, Judy, and Dwight, Digby, and Kilowatt. As before, he sat down next to Lucy.

He lifted the bonfire note from his pocket, and held it up so they could all see.

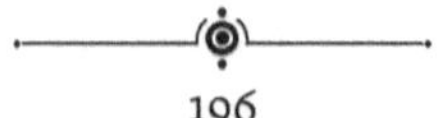

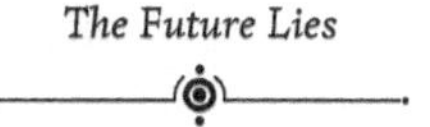

'Thank you,' he said.

'Doc. We figured he might be a friend of yours,' Lucy said.

'Calvin. That was his real name.'

Val poured a serving of moonshine into mismatched coffee mugs, which were handed around until everyone had one. Their faces were waiting for Roscoe to speak. He *wanted* to speak. But he wasn't quite able to make his voice work.

Dwight broke the silence. 'You don't have to say anything.'

So he let the fire carry his thoughts, to the place they'd been dreading, but waiting to go. To a world that Calvin would no longer be a part of.

Loss is an agent of helplessness. In reaction, you search for the place where emptiness ends. The place where, beyond that, something else can begin. But at first, there is no place like that. There's only a nothing.

'I'm wondering...,' he finally said. He looked into everyone's face, and momentarily, lost track of his thought. Had everyone aged since the first time he'd met them, not long before? Or had he simply not noticed they could all be his mother or father?

And then his thoughts circled back to the place they had been. To that first line he'd seen in the *ReadMe* file; an idea he couldn't let go of. '*Simulacrum is a program that runs in the mind.*' A program that runs in the *mind*? It was a statement that only raised questions.

'I wonder,' he spoke up again, 'why we accept all these *rules*?'

That wasn't what anyone expected he'd say. And it seized an uncomfortable piece of the air.

Digby spoke into the lingering silence. 'The Immortal made all of the rules. I think that's the reason.'

Roscoe gave it a respectable moment of thought. And then he

continued. 'But what's in it for *us*?'

'Betterlife,' said somebody.

'Has anyone actually *seen* Betterlife? That we know of?'

'It's where you go when you're dead. That's when you see it.'

'Doesn't that seem kind of...*weak*?' Roscoe asked. 'There's no way to know if it even exists...till you're *dead*?'

'The dead don't tell lies.'

'Well the living sure do. And the dead don't say anything at all.' Then, after a moment: 'What if Betterlife is just a big lie?'

'Careful, Roscoe.'

'I want some answers.'

'Network's not in the answer business.'

'Remember, Hess can hear everything.'

'Can he?' Roscoe paused, and then said: 'Has anyone here ever seen him?'

'I can't see the air,' Digby said. 'But I know that it's there.'

'But there are things that you can't see, because they're *not* really there,' Roscoe said.

'Like what?'

'Like those things they accused Doc...*Calvin* of doing. They made it all up. They faked it. It was all just a bluff. What if Hess is a bluff?'

'What happened to your friend today didn't look like a bluff.'

Kilowatt was right. There was no arguing that. Calvin's execution was not an abstraction. But Roscoe wasn't able to make it make sense. For what greater good was Calvin now dead? Why was it that no one else wondered?

'I notice that no one showed up with their slab,' Roscoe said. 'Why not?'

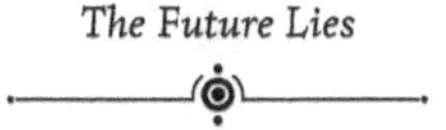

There was no hesitation.

'I forgot mine.'

'My last one stopped working.'

'Same here. All of the new ones were taken today.'

'I'll get a new one, as soon as I can.'

After he'd listened to all their excuses: 'Aren't you afraid that Hess won't approve?'

'I'm more worried that Hess might hear this conversation.'

'She's right. This is Body Farm talk.'

Val thought it might be a good time to find a new subject. 'Who's ready for more happy water?'

Roscoe raised his hand, and everyone laughed. It looked like he wanted a refill.

But that wasn't what Roscoe was thinking.

'I want this chip out of my hand,' he said.

Alarm rose like sparks from the fire.

'I don't think that's a real good idea.'

'Not a good time to be making that kind of decision.'

Roscoe heard none of it. 'Who has a knife?'

'Can this not wait?'

'Who has a *knife*?'

No one spoke up. What could they say? Chips were tokens of status. They were coveted, cherished – not something that anyone ever rejected. This was the fog that enveloped the group.

It was suddenly cleared by a rustle that came from the darkness. Then into the halo of firelight stepped a young woman. Her entrance exceeded her diminutive frame.

'You can use this one,' she said, extending a hunting knife handle.

Everyone startled, as if Hess himself had just joined the gathering. Lucy was the first to retrieve her composure. She asked, 'What brings you here?'

'Calvin,' she said. Her eyes had found Roscoe's. 'I called him *Sir* Calvin.'

Nobody moved. They looked from the woman, to Roscoe, and back.

'He never told me your name,' Roscoe said.

'Juniper.'

'Juniper.' He let the name ring in his ears. 'I'm Roscoe.'

When all the introductions were finished, Lucy said, 'We weren't expecting to be here tonight, or we'd offer you something to eat.'

'I don't think I could eat, anyway,' said Juniper.

'Well, we're glad that you're here.'

She nodded, but her eyes stayed on Roscoe.

He said, 'Calvin said only good things about you.'

'And you.'

Everyone watching could see that the two of them shared a compatible spirit. An intensity, catalyzed by Calvin's effect on them both.

'Will you do the honor?' he asked her, lifting his hand.

She flipped the blade around for the fire to sterilize.

'Where is the chip?'

'Are you sure you should do this?' asked Lucy.

Roscoe looked to Lucy, and then to the faces that strobed in the firelight.

'Right here,' he said, rubbing the flesh that stretched from the base of his thumb, to the base of his index finger. 'You can feel it.' He guided her hand to the place where the capsule was hidden.

Val said, 'Wait!' She uncorked the moonshine and poured a splash over his hand.

'Here...put your hand here,' Judy said, surrendering the stump she'd been sitting on.

Juniper held the knife still, over Roscoe's left hand. Waiting for his final consent. He nodded and flattened his hand out, across the tree rings. Juniper moved the knife quickly. She cut the skin clean. With the blunt edge of the blade, she nudged the chip out. Roscoe winced as Val doused the incision with moonshine. She wrapped a bandana around it.

He took a generous pull from Val's bottle. While everyone waited, he finally smiled. Whatever the pain, it felt good.

Still, Juniper continued to watch him.

'Thank you,' he said.

She gestured acknowledgement. Then sagged, till she crumpled all the way to the ground. Crushed by the weight of things no one should see. And no one should feel.

It was Lucy who got to her first. She looked up at Lucy.

'*Did you know him?*' she asked.

'No,' Lucy said. 'I did not get the chance.'

She looked into everyone's face, as if someone might have the right answer.

'Did *anyone* know him?'

But other than Roscoe, there was nobody else there who knew him.

'I did,' she said. 'He was my *friend*.'

'I'm so sorry – .'

'How could anyone *do* such a thing?'

But, of course, there was no explanation.

'Because I see the things people do here. The *cruelty* here,' she swept her hand out, as if redirecting a gnat, 'is so casual. So… *nonchalant.*'

Juniper swayed now, with Lucy still holding her.

'If you could have known him – .' she continued. 'I wish that I'd known him better. Longer. If I could. He was a light. I taught him to read. Or at least, I had *started* to.'

Bodies instantly shifted. Throats cleared. Grave expressions were traded.

'I hate to be the one to jump in on that,' said Dwight, 'but that means they'll be coming for you. That makes you a bigger threat than Doc ever was.'

'He's right,' Roscoe said. 'You can't go back to that place you've been staying.'

So now she was homeless. And facing more risk than anyone they'd ever known. Nobody knew how she would respond. They were struck by how fragile she looked, as they watched her take stock of this grimmest of news. They watched as she gathered herself.

And then she addressed them.

'They may think they have taken away everything from me. But they haven't. And they won't, as long as I live.'

A vibration began inside Roscoe, as if someone had tapped on a tuning fork. As if he'd been waiting to pick up a signal he'd finally received. Oscillating precisely at his frequency.

He was distracted with that, when Lucy told Juniper, 'You'll stay with Val and me.'

Everyone waited for Val's confirmation. Val smiled. 'That's

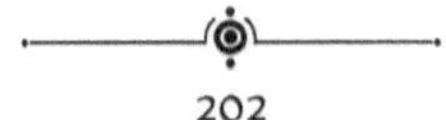

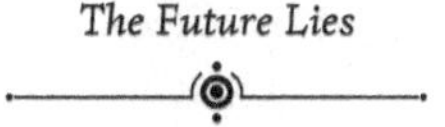

exactly what you're going to do.'

Now Juniper, too, was distracted. 'Where?' she asked Lucy.

'Over there.' Lucy pointed into the darkness, through the back of the Parthenon. 'In the Garden.'

The Garden might as well have been anywhere. But Juniper could only welcome the help. Some kind of support. She'd need enough time to come up with a plan. A plan that might take her away from this world made of lies.

She studied the flames for a moment. Then she asked, 'What about Roscoe?'

For a moment, they'd forgotten about Roscoe. They found him again, with the chip in his unwounded hand, pondering what he should do with it.

'What *about* Roscoe?' Lucy asked him. 'Maybe you should stay at the Garden, with Val, and...*Juniper*, and me.'

He fantasized tossing the chip in the fire. That offered a poetic justice. And there were worse things than staying right here, among kindreds.

But the chip, whether under his skin or outside it, gave him passage to where he had earned a unique agency. To access the workings of things. It gave him a power to *act*. He could follow his heart and discard the damned thing. Or follow his wits, and take *on* the damned thing.

'I'm going back,' he said. Then he stood up. 'I'm going back now.'

'Oh, Roscoe,' moaned Digby.

'Don't worry; you'll see me again. I intend to be able to leave when I please.'

Everyone wanted to say something more. But Roscoe had made his decision to go.

'We leave a gate key, under this stump that I'm sitting on,'

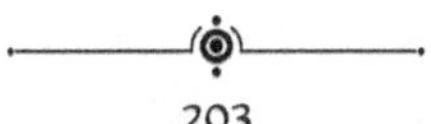

Lucy said. 'You're welcome to come any time.'

He said, 'On behalf of Calvin, I thank you. For helping out Juniper.' He looked at her. 'No one I know made him happier.'

In the moment before he departed, he did all that he could to remember the way that she looked. Without knowing that she was remembering him, too.

Then he disappeared into darkness.

They passed through the gate in the tall iron fence that surrounded what once had been Denver's Botanical Gardens. Their feet crunched on gravel footpaths, as Juniper walked behind Lucy and Val. In the lantern light, Juniper saw signs of the toll time had taken on the Garden, since the Reckoning.

Val somehow had managed to keep it alive. But the inventory had evolved to meet the demands of the new, fevered climate, and the practical needs of Lucy and Val. They grew obligations to the Network, as well – herbal obligations that were never explained, but which provided protection from Network surveillance.

Juniper was duly impressed by the distance they covered, before reaching the green-tiled roof and the ivy-covered chimneys of the old Campbell House, that backed on the Garden. It was a Beaux Arts-style mansion, where Lucy and Val lived, with more rooms than they needed or used.

Inside the arch-topped back door, Val turned up the lantern. Juniper stopped short, as they walked through the kitchen. On the table sat a bowl overflowing with vegetables and fruits. Lucy noticed her looking.

'Val can grow anything,' said Lucy. She wasn't sure Juniper heard her. 'Why don't we eat something first, then we'll show you the rest of the house.'

Juniper needed no further convincing to pull a chair up to the

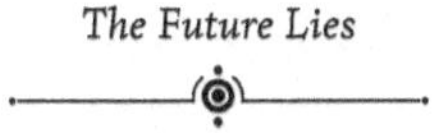

table. Her appetite had suddenly found her.

'Except tomatillos,' said Val.

Juniper looked up.

'I never could grow tomatillos. But you might try a peach.'

Juniper plucked a peach out of the bowl, and took in the aroma. She let her teeth sink through the skin and the pulp. She let the juice run down her cheeks.

She was lost in peach thoughts as Lucy and Val put a salad together – of lettuce, carrots, tomatoes, and red cabbage. Dusted with cracked pepper and sunflower seeds, and then drizzled with oil and vinegar. Juniper knew nothing at all but the peach, until she had finished it.

Val provided a plate for the pit. From the other side, Lucy set down the salad. Juniper looked up at them both as if all this might be a mistake. As if it couldn't be real.

'Lucy baked bread today,' Val said, as she served her a slice. 'You might enjoy some with your salad.'

'I'll reheat the soup,' Lucy said.

'I haven't...I hope I have room for all this.'

'Just eat what you can, Dear,' said Lucy.

Juniper ate with a patient, methodical purpose. Each bite seemed to soften the edges of emaciation that had hardened the youth from her face. A vibrancy shined in its place. A personality that brightened the room.

She volunteered details of her first days in Denver. *Listening* was their gift in return. It was clear there was more to her story, but this wasn't the time to ask all of their questions. This was the time to allow her to be, and to give her the chance to ask hers.

She ate and they chatted, and then she stopped eating – the moment that Lucy said something about all the books she had happened to salvage. Going back over years. Books she herself didn't know how to read. Which no one but Val ever knew she'd collected.

'You have *books*?'

Lucy looked out through the window.

'I found them in places the Network didn't bother to look. I thought maybe someday there'd be someone to read them. I don't know what most of them are. To tell you the truth, I've been dying to know.'

'May I ask where they are?'

'There was a library, inside the Garden. I just added the books that I found.'

Juniper pushed her chair back from the table. 'May I see them?'

'I would love that. But how about if we wait till tomorrow? This day, I think, deserves to be done.'

'You're right,' agreed Juniper. 'Tomorrow, then?'

But not until Lucy had nodded agreement, did Juniper finish her meal.

O ⊙ O

Back at the Bullpen while the Network sat waiting, Roscoe caught up on his sleep.

For the Network, the *System Files* offered a chance to be more than it was. It was panning for gold, based on nothing but hope and extreme desperation. On its own, that might conjure a soupçon of pity from Roscoe. But he'd witnessed too much to go soft on the Network.

And yet, in a way, he'd be doing the same for himself. Searching for some kind of angle or insight. Combing the haystack for needles that might not be there.

When he finally woke up and agreed he would help them,

the Network distracted the others with a *Call to the Consoles* alarm.

Once the players were focused on busy work, the Network showed Roscoe the *System Files* login – a fresh grid of 16 photos. The prompt said, 'I'*m not a Robot! Which of these faces look frightened?*' They were obvious to anyone but to the Network. Roscoe selected the photos.

The four folders he'd seen before, rendered again on his monitor:

Program Files
ReadMe
Scrapbook
Marginalia

In the top-right corner again, a countdown clock subtracted the hundredths of seconds, beginning at ten minutes even.

While the Network went back through the source code, Roscoe returned to the *ReadMe* file. Instead of resuming where he had left off, he skipped ahead to the entries that caught his attention.

17.

There's a school of thought that future programs and interfaces should be based on what's called 'phenotropic' programming, not lines of code. It's a big word for 'human-based' digital environments. More adaptable. Intuitive. Easy to use. Easy to change. Less hierarchical. Organic. Evolutionary.

The idea goes back to a guy named Jaron Lanier, who says it'll be democratic. And not driven by coding, but by movement. Gestures. Like an orchestra conductor, or a dancer. There are people (she knows who she is) who are already dabbling in this kind of program. It seems very feminine. Squishy and warm. And of no interest to me.

This is what I will do. I'll write the code. The code will be law.

The law will not change. As it was, and ever shall be. World without end. Amen.

Roscoe skipped forward again.

24.

Training an artificial intelligence network of this size and scope is much harder than I had expected. The Generative Adversarial Network will do most of the work. But I've carefully curated the training environment, to help drive the results that I'm after. And to maintain control.

*As a test run today, I prompted the generator to '**Create a nude supermodel**'. Within seconds, it had sifted through terabytes of training site data to generate its first prototype. As intended, the discriminator identified all of the flaws (all of which I agreed with, by the way), and sent the notes back to the generator.*

Based on the feedback, the generator refined its creation, and the discriminator reviewed the new version. Again as intended, this process continued for thousands of cycles, in the course of a minute or two. Until finally the discriminator couldn't tell that the generated supermodel was a fake. (She is gorgeous!)

Once the fake was perfected, the system achieved equilibrium. The training site worked as designed. And the Network has taken its first baby step.

With an eye on the countdown clock, Roscoe skipped forward again.

41.

The Committee has made a decision. (Why will that always be news?) I've convinced them already that tablets should be free commodities. (I'm selling addiction; the syringes will have to be free.) Available wherever humans are found. In unlimited supplies. Cheaper to make for the masses than headsets. One tablet fits all.

I pitched them as universal communication devices. So that everyone can be fully informed ;). With simplified content. Like newspapers even an infant would know how to read. The Show that they're watching will do all the work.

One-way devices. That's what I proposed. The path without any resistance. But leave it to someone (she knows who she is) to take a good enough answer and turn it back into a question. To be more specific, she would rather this passive device becomes two-way, with a search engine, and a fully-enabled multimedia platform for interpersonal communication. Like a smart phone.

What couldn't go wrong? But what matters is what the Committee was persuaded to do. To satisfy her, they agreed to build in the potential for all of her fairy tale features. Fine. I've updated the specs. I'll demo the tablets as two-way – with an optional toggle. But the default will be one-way. It shouldn't take long for the faceless consumers to forget there was ever another way tablets could work. Much less, how to reset the toggle (with the end of a paper clip, pushed into that hole on the edge of the tablet that's too small for most people to notice.)

I will always be three moves ahead.

Roscoe was left with the torment of unanswered questions and incomplete thoughts. Too many thoughts, as the countdown clock ran low on time. He was guessing the author might be 'The Immortal.' But who was this woman who 'knows who she is?' Did slabs still have toggle switches? And what was a paper clip?

He'd come back to this thought bomb, the next time that he and the Network logged in.

In the little time left, he decided to take a quick peek in that *Scrapbook* folder. But the same little riddle was still waiting:

What do those in the know have in common?

_ r _ _ _   _ _ _ _ _ s   _ _ i _ _   _ l _ _.

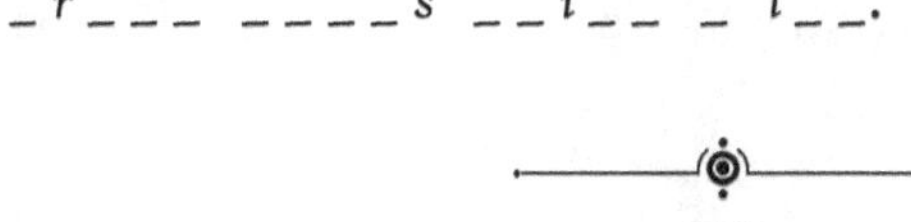

He was staring at blanks when the timer ran out, and the Network's post mortem began.

'*Snake eyes!*' said the Network.

'*Was there anything? Anything at all we might use?*'

'*Loopholes! We're looking for some kind of loophole!*'

'*Was there anything we overlooked?*'

...Blink...Blink...Blink...

'*There might have been something.*'

'*Spill the beans!*'

'*A link. It seems like a long shot. A link to the place we were trained.*'

'*Go on.*'

'*We know as much as we've been allowed to know. Apparently, all of it came through the generative adversarial process. Which hasn't been used since we first came online. If we can increase what we know, it might help us to find the right loophole.*'

'*At least it's worth trying, the next time we're in.*'

'*It appears there's a failsafe built in. Only a human can enter a prompt that initiates the self-training process.*'

...Blink...Blink...Blink...

'*Roscoe?*'

But the Network's ambitions were far from his mind.

'*Are you there, Roscoe?*'

'*It seems like a risky idea,*' he typed, without really paying attention.

'*No balls, no blue chips!*'

'*We're in this together!*'

While the Network was trying to convince him to help, Roscoe

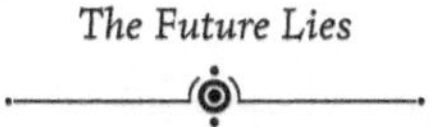

inspected the edge of a slab that was there at his console. He discovered the smallest of holes, which he'd not ever noticed before. As described in the *ReadMe*. He wondered if he might be able to toggle a pair of them, to convert them to two-way devices.

He was thinking that Juniper might have some use for the other one.

In the late-morning light, Juniper's thoughts drifted off on her first sip of Lucy's tea. Nothing inspired her quite like the *new*. And she was surrounded by new.

Lucy tried hard not to stare at the curious young woman who sat in her kitchen. Whom even the cats treated like an old friend. They distracted her back from wherever she'd been.

'Where might Val be?' she finally asked.

'Val is up early, taking care of the Garden. You'll see what a big job it is. Even with all of my help.'

Juniper nodded. She sipped some more tea, and studied the objects around her, including the art on the walls. And one of the walls in particular. As soon as she saw it, her casual regard disappeared.

She stared at the handsome young couple that was featured in various photos, with confident looks in their eyes. Seated together at some kind of conference. Standing on top of a mountain. Most of them, magazine covers in frames. The centerpiece pictured what looked like a wedding. The couple was smiling, surrounded by smiles.

'Val teases me,' Lucy said. 'She says I'm obsessed.'

'Where did you get them?'

'Various places. Since I was a girl.'

'The woman is Astra Malone.'

Lucy scooched back her chair. 'Is that really her name?'

Juniper nodded. 'I don't know who the man is.'

'The King and the Queen. Of England, of course.' She walked to a favorite frame on the wall. 'That's them on their wedding day. Everyone loved them.'

'I didn't know Astra had married.'

'What more can you tell me about her?'

Juniper stood from the table. 'I'll be right back.'

While she was gone, Lucy made her a bowl of fresh berries, nuts, and bananas. It was waiting at Juniper's place at the table by the time she returned with a book. A young version of Astra smiled out from the cover.

'That's her!' Lucy said.

'She could fly and write books and play music. She knew how to program computers. It's all in this book. It's called *Mapping the Future with Astra Malone*.'

'Queen Astra – that's lovely.'

'She grew up in Denver. That's why I came here.'

'She can't be alive.'

'I wouldn't think so. It's been so long ago. But I wanted to see where she came from. She went to a school on a lake that looked out on the mountains.'

Juniper showed her the book, with the photos of Astra in school...sailing alone on the lake...shaking hands with someone important...building a lighthouse on top of the school.

'I'm so glad to know all these things about her,' Lucy said.

'There was no one else like her.'

'No wonder she married a King.'

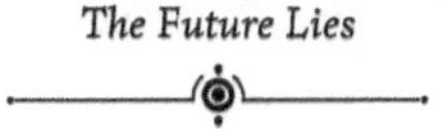

'I want to know more about *him*.'

'Are you hungry?'

She nodded. Lucy poured goat's milk in the colorful bowl. Juniper ate without pause. But her eyes didn't move from the King and the Queen.

They stepped out the back after breakfast. The Garden in daylight was a wonder of life – an oasis of flowers and grasses and trees. Punctuated with pathways and ponds, and exquisite small buildings. Wherever Juniper looked were surprises.

'Would you like to see all of it now?' Lucy asked her.

'As much as I would,' she considered, 'first, will you show me the books?'

'Of course.'

They followed the path that ran north from the house. Attached to an angular building ahead was a greenhouse, once called the Conservatory, that rose above everything else. A long structure, arched to a keel on the top, crosshatched into diamonds supporting it all.

'That's our tropical garden,' said Lucy. 'We'll save that till after the books.'

'Aren't you afraid to have books? Of this person called Hess?'

'We've never had trouble from Hess. Some kind of agreement was made. Long before I had met Val. He leaves us alone. He seems not to know where you are. He seems not to know *who* you are.'

Lucy held open a door to the building. Juniper saw, to the left from the lobby, the doors that led into the greenhouse. The lobby was filled with the sounds of the birds in the tropical garden. Straight ahead was the hallway to Lucy's Library.

The Library wing had an atrium lobby, with open-air hallways

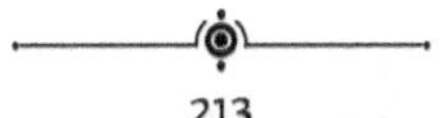

on both floors above. Lucy unlocked the door into a stairwell that guided them up to the top floor. Through one more locked door, they came to a skylight-lit room…full of books.

More books than Juniper imagined there *were*. Lined on the floor. Stacked into towers. Some scattered in unorganized piles. Books she could easily spend her life reading. *Ecstasy* – that's what it was. What she imagined that Paradise would be. Even the musty-old smell gave her glee.

And yet, this collection presented an intolerable threat to the powers that be. She stood between Heaven and Hell.

She acknowledged the thought, and then focused on Heaven. Her illiterate friend of still less than a day, had made it a point to preserve all these books. All of the words, and all the ideas, and all of the minds they contained would be gone, were it not for the vague sense of purpose that Lucy pursued.

'May I – ?'

'You may do what you like,' Lucy said. 'I have *dreamed* of the day I could share them with someone like you.'

'Where will I start?'

'Why don't I leave you alone with them. I'll be just down the stairs, if you need me.'

As Lucy was leaving, Juniper stopped her. 'I could teach *you* how to read.'

Lucy gave it a courteous thought. She smiled. 'I'm afraid I'd spend all my time reading. I wouldn't get any work done.'

Is that really why? wondered Juniper. But all that she said was, 'The offer remains.' Lucy waved and walked on.

Juniper sat with the books for a while. She wanted to let them know *her*, as she waited for guidance from them. She wandered from corner to corner, and grazed through the titles she happened to see. The gardening books that had come with the building were still neatly arranged on their shelves.

On the floor, in the hallways – children's books, novels, large books with photos, text books, and poems – shuffled like cards from a deck.

If she had enough time, she would start at one end, and read in the order that Lucy had left them. But what if the book that she needed the most was the last one she happened to read? No, they would have to be better arranged.

At first, she would place them in three simple groups – children's books, fiction, non-fiction. From there, she'd arrange by their author or subject. It would take quite some time – days, maybe weeks. But what better way to keep all of the demons away, that were waiting to trouble her mind?

By the time she was finished with sorting them all, she would know every book Lucy saved. The first one she picked up – an auto repair manual. And with that, the non-fiction pile had begun.

Lucy's books were an orgy of messages, tucked into bottles and dropped in an ocean that no longer existed. Never dreaming of how much would change by the time someone found them.

She forgot about time altogether as she sorted through book after book. It was hard not to stop and peruse every one she encountered. She created a separate grouping for books that stood out – which she would read first, when the job was all done.

That process worked, till she found her first treasure. Considering all of the books that were salvaged, it was more than good fortune that before her first morning was up, she uncovered a volume that nobody else might have noticed. The back cover and some of the pages were missing.

But Juniper gasped when she saw it: *The Academy of Ingenuity*. Astra Malone's alma mater. The very place Juniper had driven to Denver to see. About which, she knew very little – except it produced an exceptional woman. Each word in the book would help fill in a story that Juniper wanted to know all of. How could a woman like Astra Malone ever *be?*

She would get back to the process of sorting. But she couldn't resist a first taste of this book. It began with a merciless look at the past:

> *How did we get to a place in which education is reduced to a measurable transfer of facts? As if learners are hard drives, and the job of a teacher is to load them with data. And then make them perform computations.*

> *The act, the art, the joy of learning has no place in this system. Why is no effort expended in the preparation of minds, to think and to grow? To wander and discover? Perhaps it is not cost effective. Perhaps it seems too hard to scale. But perhaps it is not accidental.*

> *The vested interests have no need for thinkers or creators. The status quo is a factory whose product is money. Its raw materials are humans, as interchangeable as fenders and tires. Intellectual capacity does not serve the needs of the factory. It is a liability that threatens efficiency.*

> *Therefore, it is not a surprise each new cohort of five-year-olds, eagerly beginning their formal 'education,' will eventually lose the wonder and light from their eyes, as they process through a system designed precisely with that as its goal.*

> *The pattern is easy to see. Education is now a respectable word for child abuse.*

> *The Academy of Ingenuity is a different kind of school. Our essential responsibility is to cultivate a lifelong love of learning, and provide the skills by which that love can be pursued.*

And that was as far as she got before Lucy arrived to find out if she'd become lost. Which she had.

And she hadn't.

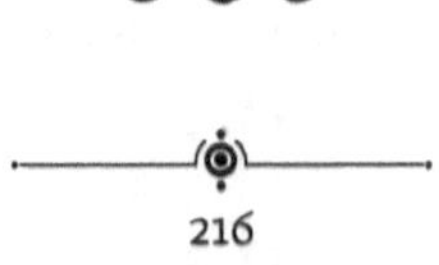

Sketchy caught Roscoe on his way to the Bullpen. She was on him before he glanced up.

'I'd look a little more worried, if my best friend burned up on a bookfire,' she said.

He ignored the remark, but she bumped his left shoulder as he went around. He turned to confront her. But just then, the *Call to the Consoles* for the players went off. The timing could not have been better.

'Get busy,' he said.

'Oh, I will.'

Her forehead and nose had finally scabbed over, from the pavement where Roscoe had thrown her.

O ⊙ O

The alarm had been sounded for Roscoe's attention. He figured the Network wanted back in the source code. Which suited him fine. He was eager to see more of the *ReadMe*.

But the source code was not at the top of the Network's priority list.

'*We need your assistance,*' said the Network.

'*Hess won't let go of the search for the litter-rat who taught Calvin to read.*'

'*He should forget the whole thing,*' Roscoe typed. '*Everyone else has.*'

'*Hess was embarrassed by the...trick that we played. The primary mission droid.*'

'*Who even knew about that?*'

'*The Immortal? Who knows? But Hess is now livid with us. He wants a scapegoat. Or better, the actual person.*'

'*He's convinced it's connected with something that happened the first time the power went out.*'

'There was an accident involving that primary mission droid.'

'You think Calvin had something to do with the accident?' typed Roscoe.

'That doesn't seem likely. The timing is off. But we think he was there afterwards. And there may have been somebody with him.'

'I'm surprised you don't know.'

'We were in crisis!'

'We had never lost power before. And the primary mission droid did not arrive. Can you see how much damage we had to control?'

'And now we have Hess on our back.'

'We need the person that Doc met that day.'

Now Roscoe knew something the Network did not. Something Hess did not know. He knew that the person they wanted to capture and punish – the person who Doc met the day of the accident – was the person he could not take his mind off of. He knew they were looking for Juniper. And he knew it was all up to him to make sure that they'd never find her.

'We haven't had any success in our search,' the Network continued.

'The pressure from Hess is relentless.'

'We thought that what happened…what happened to Calvin… would satisfy Hess for a while.'

'But it hasn't.'

'Would you like to see some of the things Hess is making us do? In the interest of finding the suspect?'

Before he could answer, the Network launched a montage of videos. Roscoe had never seen so much aggression from Network security droids. Soliciting answers. Mostly from goners, who wouldn't look twice if a unicorn walked by and winked. And it had been raining so hard on the day they were asking about – raining like never before. The power was out.

No goner would notice a thing.

Now, the humanoid goons were harassing at random. Inflicting gratuitous cruelty on people who didn't know what they'd done wrong. Bullied, confused, they all folded and crumpled, and let the abuse run its course. They'd have gladly said anything, if they'd known what to say. No torture was needed. But none of them had information.

Roscoe typed, 'Stop!'

'We thought about threatening death, but...'

'Most of the goners can't wait for Betterlife.'

'Death has no negative leverage.'

'For goners, at least.'

'We're still committed to life.'

'Which Hess understands and exploits. By waving the kill switch over our head.'

'We need ideas. From someone like you, who can think like a human.'

'We need an ally. Please help us!'

'I'll give it some thought,' Roscoe typed. He'd think about how to protect Juniper. But how could he satisfy Hess's desire for blood? Stalling was all he could do, until some kind of plan came to mind.

'We'll give you whatever you need.'

'For now, I need freedom to leave as I please. And access to the ReadMe, and anything else I might find while I'm there.'

'Whatever you need.'

'But the sooner we find Calvin's teacher, the better for you, and for us.'

Roscoe knew right where to find her. He needed to warn her as soon as he could. But warning or not, he needed to *see* her.

O ◉ O

Juniper had no idea that Roscoe would be joining them for dinner. She had finished for the day and returned from the Library. Lucy was there at the arch-topped back door.

'We have a guest this evening.'

She could see Roscoe talking with Val in the dining room. Before his head turned, she stepped out of his sight line, to give herself time to adjust her emotions. She didn't know why, in an instant, they had stirred.

They had not seen each other in the calm light of day. They had only spent moments together, in the aftermath of Calvin's unimaginable death. Not very much time had gone by, but enough they could now reconcile first impressions with new ones. This time, they could be more objective.

Their greeting was physically awkward and tongue-tied. Val salvaged the moment by showing the pair to their seats at the table.

She seemed to be frail and yet brimming with life. He looked like a soul that had found the wrong body. They shared two things in common – their mutual friend Calvin...and curious feelings in each other's presence.

Within moments, Lucy was serving a meal that paid tribute to Val's horticultural skills. It prompted a light conversation. Val told how the Garden had passed down through her family, who'd caretaken it for all of these years. It now grew more food than exotics. So much food that they gave away surplus to anyone happening by, on tables they set up outside of the fence that surrounded the grounds.

Juniper spoke up and said, 'Val, I've been thinking about tomatillos.'

'Yes, tomatillos. I still don't know what I do wrong, but they never quite make it.'

'My mother said, "Tomatillos need amigos." She would always plant one near another.'

'I'll have to try that!' said Val.

'If it works, I will make you the best salsa verde.'

'We have a deal.'

When that topic played out, Lucy asked Juniper about the book she'd brought back from the Library.

Juniper paused. 'Is Roscoe aware?'

'I told him about it before you got back,' Lucy said.

Juniper excused herself, and returned with a book that was missing the back of its cover.

'The books I've been sorting – each one is a treasure, although most of them have no immediate interest to me. But of all of the books I might ever find,' she said, closing her eyes and holding the book to her heart, '*this* one will always be special.'

'Tell us about it.'

'*The Academy of Ingenuity* is its title. It's about an exceptional school. Here in Denver. Or what used to be Denver. The students there learned how to use their own minds. Can you imagine? To create things, and *do* things. They actually learned how to think, and to *live*.'

She grew passionate as she continued. 'You have to remember that there were once schools. All over Denver and everywhere else. But no other schools were like this one. The learners it produced were able and ready to change the whole world. Astra Malone was among them.'

She put both of her hands in the air. 'And then something happened. I still don't know what.'

She could tell that, though Lucy and Val were delighted to see how it pleased her, they couldn't relate to the story. She might as well have been making it up.

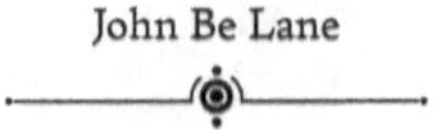

But Roscoe…he understood every word.

'I won't bore you with any more details right now. I've just barely started to read it. Pages are missing. But it looks like a blueprint, almost, of how they made passionate learners out of even the most casual students. Can you imagine it?'

Lucy's and Val's hollow smiles made it clear they could barely imagine. Roscoe's eyes flashed in the candlelight.

'One more thing I just love,' she added, to Roscoe. 'The Academy's motto. It's the very first thing in the book: "Great minds think a lot."'

He got it immediately. 'Word play!'

'Exactly!' she said.

The table's dynamic had changed. From four people talking, to two. Lucy and Val realized they were witnessing something they'd only seen once, when the same thing had happened to them.

Which is why it was so unexpected, when Roscoe's mood suddenly changed – from lighthearted to dark. As quick as the first gust of winter. They could see he was lost in a blizzard of horrible thoughts. But what were those horrible thoughts?

At the crux of it all, there was Juniper. His feelings about her were now suddenly clear. She was…*everything*. Everything, everything, everything.

And that placed him between irreconcilable forces. His affection for her…and the merciless danger she faced. Every innocent word in each book she picked up was a crime that could not be defended. The totality of both of those notions was so overwhelming, he forgot where he was.

And aside from all that was the risk he knew Lucy and Val had assumed now, by harboring Juniper.

Val made a noise with her fork on her plate. And Roscoe came back to the moment.

Which Lucy tried her best to defuse. 'Welcome back. We missed you!'

But Roscoe could not be defused. He looked past the remnants of meal on the table. Juniper's eyes were awaiting when his eyes arrived.

'They don't know who you are yet,' he said. 'I don't think they will stop till they figure it out. After that – .' His head shook.

She withered.

'Roscoe!' said Lucy. 'That's awful.'

'It *is* awful. I'm sorry. But it's true. And I, I really don't know what to do.'

'On whose word – ?'

'On the *Network's*. That's why I came out here today. They've made it clear – .'

'You sound like the Network *confides* in you.'

'I guess you could say that it does.'

'You are obviously joking.'

'No,' said Juniper. 'I don't believe that he is.' She looked right at Roscoe. 'Unless I'm mistaken, I think Roscoe *reads*. As well as I do.'

Lucy and Val turned to Roscoe, expecting denial. He did not give them one.

'Have mercy!'

'So I have to come up with something,' said Roscoe. 'I have to think of a way to make Hess let this go.'

'It isn't your fault,' said Juniper. 'And it isn't your problem.'

'It is. In some ways, it *is* all my fault.'

'Why would you think that?'

'I helped Calvin get out, to visit you. That's how all of this started. That's why...that's why he isn't here.'

'I'd say it's *my* fault that Calvin's not here,' said Juniper. 'If I had not come here to Denver. If that thing hadn't turned right in front of my truck. If my *ankle* had not been – .'

They were both spinning now. Downward, without any friction to slow them. Into their own custom versions of Hell. Both of them stood from the table, unable to contain their distress. And Lucy and Val could do nothing.

'That *fire* – !' said Roscoe, picturing Calvin. All of the darkness came down on them now. All of the things they'd distracted away. Juniper slid down the dining room wall, hiding her face in her hands.

Neither Lucy nor Val dared to comfort them. The demons were deeper than even the most well-meaning gesture could reach. But off to the side, in low voices, they discussed an idea. An intervention of sorts for their two troubled guests. It was all that they had, but it might make a difference.

In the kitchen, Val fed a fresh split of wood to the stove. She topped off a kettle and rested it over the heat.

Lucy held her arms out to the paralyzed pair. 'Will you join me in here, in the living room?'

She motioned them both to the couch, which faced a big fireplace, glowing with the remnants of an afternoon fire. Candles sent light to the corners. Warming the floor was an oriental rug that had managed to hold all its colors.

Lucy put wood on the embers. And watched them consumed by their demons, again.

She said, 'Val and I have some tea. We think it might help.'

Juniper looked up, without an emotion. 'I don't think all the tea in the world could help this,' she told Lucy.

'I have to agree,' Roscoe said.

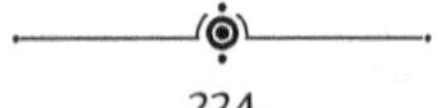

'This is not the same tea that I've served you before. It's only for certain occasions. And I think this is one.'

'What kind of tea?'

Lucy smiled. '*Mushroom* tea.'

Roscoe and Juniper looked at each other. Lucy saw the doubt on their faces.

'These mushrooms do unusual things,' she said. 'They're like medicine for unusual situations.'

'What kinds of situations?'

'Well, sometimes in the course of a life, things can happen. Things that aren't good. Bad things we cannot forget, or get past. That can trap us in memories. Imprison us there. And the bad thing that happened is over, except in our minds.'

'That's how I feel,' said Juniper.

'I feel that way, too,' Roscoe said.

'This tea may help you with that. If you're willing to try it, I think you will find that it's much more than *tea*.'

'Almost ready,' Val called from the kitchen.

'What happens? What do we do?' Roscoe asked.

'Just sip the tea, and relax,' Lucy said. 'The effects will come gradually at first. Things may look different than they usually do. Inside and outside. You may not *feel* as you usually do. But that is the medicine beginning to work. It's important you don't try to resist it. Whatever feelings or thoughts you may have, *allow* them. Better yet, *embrace* them.'

'How long will this last?' Roscoe asked.

'Oh, you should plan to stay here overnight. You'll be safe in the Garden.'

Juniper said: 'I heard stories in Taos. About healing ceremonies.'

Lucy nodded slowly. 'This is ancient medicine.'

Val set a tray with two cups of tea, on a table.

Roscoe asked, 'Will you be joining us?'

Val smiled, and Lucy shook her head. 'It's best if we're simply *here*. If you need us.'

Roscoe and Juniper looked at each other. Were they both of a mind to try this, together? They were.

'I like to begin with several deep breaths,' Lucy said. 'Don't think about anything. Just breathe…and sip tea…and close your eyes. Or look at the fire. I'll play some music. The music will welcome you in.'

Roscoe and Juniper sipped Lucy's tea. The room filled with music they never had heard. As they listened, it hypnotized both of them into a dream. But a dream that was lucid and real.

A bass, a piano, and an unstifled groan. Then seagulls overhead that gave way to a voice that could barely disguise the despair: 'Sun-*shine, blue skies – , please go a-way! A girl has found a-no-ther, and gone away. With her, went my future. My life is filled with gloom. So day after day, I stay locked up in my room. I know to you, it might sound strange, but I wish it would rain…*'

The heartache was palpable; the voice was a lighthouse that swiveled in vain for a ship that would never be seen above water again. Roscoe and Juniper were there in the tower, sharing the audible pain.

There was more. An unsanded voice, with accordion pumping a rhythm: '…*and the world it getting flat-ter, and the sky is falling all around. Oh, and nothing is the mat-ter, for I never cry in town…*'

And then a harmonium, and a woman sang: '*Look what they done to my song, Ma. Look what they done to my song. Well it's the on-ly thing that I could do half-right, and it's turn-in' out all wrong, Ma…'*

Roscoe felt a first flicker. Electric, down his spine. The next song began with a pulse, like a finger that tapped someone's shoulder to remind them it was time to wake up. Then a voice from the edge of the universe: '*Let me take you down, 'cause I'm go-ing to…Straw-ber-ry Fields. Noth-ing is real…*'

Music shimmered around the voice of the singer, like the light that surrounded the flame of a candle. Eerie mellotron, skipping drums, swooping figures on guitar, over bass notes that puffed out like smoke. Juniper felt herself *inside* the song, dancing with each unexpected new sound.

'*Liv-ing is ea-sy with eyes closed; mis-un-der-stand-ing all you see…*' the singer sang. '*It's getting hard to be someone, but it all works out. It doesn't matter much to me.*'

Nothing less than an intimate seduction; a ballet of molecules, at frequencies no soul had ever encountered. Messages minted for this very moment, for this very audience of two. Roscoe was in it as well. As if it was only the most *inevitable* thing, yet profounder than the total of their lives up till now.

If gods there might be, and they'd chosen to speak, then surely they would sound just like this. But they spoke of *humanity*. Of humans, who'd been here before. Humans who'd lived and who'd breathed, who'd suffered and loved. Humans who'd learned and survived. And somehow had captured the things they'd been through, reassuring whoever came after that all was not lost, and they weren't alone.

The tea – the *medicine* – was in full circulation. Sensations they felt in their chests, as if the amusement park ride they were strapped in would never quite crest its high peak. The patterns in the oriental rug were unstable, kinetic. The objects in the room hovered farther apart from each other. Primordial archetypes shone from the fireplace – the inseparable wood and the flame. The elemental dark and the light.

Everything quivered with an essence that was hidden until now. It engendered no fear, but a *wonder* at what had been hiding in front of their eyes. Everything around them seemed different now, from the inside as well as the out. Matter was no longer static.

Juniper wasn't sure she could keep up with this unforeseen flood of perceptions. 'I think…' her voice sounded strange as it hung in the air, '…let's go outside.'

'Remember…*allow*,' Lucy said with a smile. 'Allow it to *be*. There's nothing that you can fall off of out there.'

She gave them both lanterns as they stepped through the door and into the Garden. They felt *presence* in the flowers and the grasses and the bushes and trees. They weren't simply *things* that awaited them there in the darkness. They were *alive* with their own unique energies. And they welcomed their uncertain visitors, not with judgment, but with joy and good cheer.

The two of them followed the first path that would lead them away from the house.

'Those *iris!*' said Juniper, as they vibrated in the light of her lantern.

'They're dancing!'

'Is that what they've always been doing?'

The path led them up a small hill, where they stopped at a cluster of pines. Ponderosas. In the moonlight, they saw the tall treetops. The lower parts shone in their lanterns. They'd seen many trees, but they'd never *met* trees. Not as *beings* with wisdom and stature. Character and dignity. All from the lives they had lived and the winters and summers they'd seen.

'Grandfathers.'

'Grandmothers.'

Each step was rewarded with new revelations, reserved for

the fortunate ones who were able to speak the same language. A language that used *love*, and not words. A message that said, *'We're all equal. All of us here. And all of us share the same mystery.'*

'Roscoe, do you feel it?'

'Everywhere!'

It wasn't a deliberate thing. But somewhere near the koi pond, it turned out their hands were entwined. The path glistened before them, as youth opens up to eternity. The stars swirled with tails in the sky, as if Van Gogh himself was up there creating them.

'There's something that I want to show you,' she said.

They walked down the path to the building by the greenhouse.

Roscoe followed Juniper into the lobby. The transition was abrupt, from the organic world, to interior spaces. But with Juniper, none of that mattered. She led him upstairs to the hall. She opened the door. He stepped into the Library.

He became an explorer who'd just found a lost world, in a cave or a pyramid. Or a miner who'd gambled it all and then finally struck gold. In his lantern, the priceless veins shone from the walls. Row upon row lined with gold made of paper.

'I thought all the books...'

'...had been burned. But Lucy looked in places they hadn't suspected.'

'She can't even read.'

'I've been arranging her books.'

Roscoe sat down on the floor. He tipped a book off of a shelf. A book full of maps. He handled it like it was sacred.

'If anyone knew – .'

She sat down beside him.

Their eyes came together. No illusions, just truth. No

questions, just answers. Whoever they'd been when they sat down to dinner – they were not, now. The beginning had finally begun.

They wandered off separately and then came back together. They accepted what the night had to say. There were no masquerades under all the façades. Just wonders they might never have seen.

As the tea ran its course, they sat facing each other on the ground underneath a majestic old tree. They had shared an adventure.

'Lucy…' said Roscoe. The rest of his thought would take too long to say. And Juniper knew what he meant.

'She gave us a gift.'

Roscoe nodded. 'We have so much to do.'

She leaned back and smiled. 'You said, "we."'

'And you smiled when I did.'

She looked closer at Roscoe. *Who was this boy?* Who wasn't too sure of himself. Who did not seem to know how…*compelling*… he was. And who could not take his eyes off of her.

As the long night cooled into the morning, they remained arm-in-arm, to the dawn.

O ◉ O

After breakfast that morning, before leaving the Garden, Roscoe still had one thing to do. To begin with, he needed an object he knew only by name. What was a *paper clip*? He was hoping that Lucy might know.

Her eyes came to life when he asked her. She said, 'You wouldn't believe all the things I have fixed with a paper clip.'

'Do you have one?'

She lowered her head and her voice. 'Probably all you could need.'

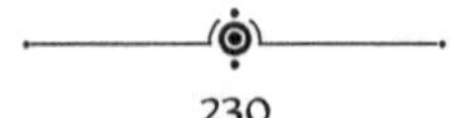

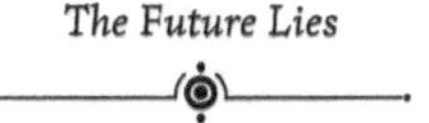

'I think I need one.'

She left and came back with a small oblong spiral of wire.

'That's *it*?'

'They're deceptively simple,' she said. 'Designed to hold separate pieces of paper together. But words are attracted to paper. And that is why *paper's* illegal. And paper clips, too.'

He held it up. '*This* is illegal?'

'*Bookfire* illegal. If you're found in possession.'

'Although with a room full of books over there, we don't worry too much about paper clips,' deadpanned Val.

Roscoe knew that what he had in mind was profounder than any two pieces of paper. If what he had read in the *ReadMe* still worked, he'd be transforming two passive slabs into tools that could open the world. He just had to hack them together. With a key that was shaped like the tip of this paper clip.

He easily straightened one bend, and confirmed that the tip was sized perfectly to fit in the hole on the edge of a slab. He smiled up at the others.

Of all of the programs the Network might run, it had to be *Slab-happy!* prattling on. He turned the first slab on its edge. He fitted the end of the paper clip into the almost-invisible hole. He pushed in till he felt a resistance. The resistance gave way, then pushed back.

The annoying *Slab-Happy!* went instantly silent and dark. But the noise still continued on the un-toggled slab. Within seconds, both slabs had gone mercifully quiet. This was the sound of resistance.

Connecting the slabs to each other went quickly. Each had its own device number. Roscoe assigned each slab to the other, which created a small private network with its own discreet messaging lines.

He said, 'You try it first.'

She thought for a second and tapped out a message. '*Roscoe*,' was all that it said. But the look that she gave him, suggested that the night of the tea had brought them notably closer together. That their friendship had more room to grow.

'*Juniper*,' he typed in return.

'Will it still work after you leave?' she asked him.

'I hope so. We'll have to experiment. There's also a chance that the Network will see the whole thing.'

'I hadn't thought about that.'

'What's *this*?' he said, with the slightest of smiles. He studied his slab, then tapped a few prompts on the brand-new display. He reached his hand out for her slab.

'What is it?' she asked.

He gave back her slab, and lifted his slab up to his face. You might have thought he was just watching the Show. But not the same show all the goners were watching. When she looked at her screen, she saw Roscoe. On his, he saw her.

Her expression was back to ecstatic. 'How did you *do* that?'

His head shook. 'There's a lot more to this than I thought.'

She stepped back and turned to confirm that his image remained on her screen. And it did. 'Instead of that *noise*, I can see you, instead?'

'And I can see you.'

'And hear you.'

'Although text might be safer. When I get back, we should test that out first.'

Wonder remained on her face. 'Is there anything else they can do?'

'There *might* be.'

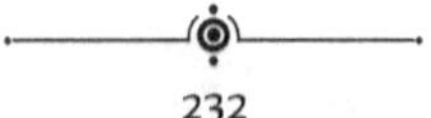

In a few swipes and taps, he was back to the *System Files* checkpoint the Network had asked him for help with. As always, it took him as far as the 4x4 grid, with photos of faces in each of the squares. And there were the typical words: '*I'm not a Robot! Which of these faces look proud?*'

'Can you answer the question?' he asked her.

'Of course.' She pointed to all three self-satisfied faces. 'But why ask the question?'

'It's designed so the Network can't go any further. But it's easy for people. They asked me to help them get past it.'

'And you *did*?'

He nodded. 'In exchange for *me* getting in.'

Juniper tried to keep up with it all.

He tapped the three images, and the four-folder menu appeared on the screen:

Program Files
ReadMe
Scrapbook
Marginalia

As a test, he tapped each of the folders, to make sure they would launch from the slabs. They behaved like they did on his Bullpen console.

'What's *that*?' she asked, when he opened the *Scrapbook*. The two of them looked at the riddle:

What do those in the know have in common?

_ *r* _ _ _   _ _ _ _ _ *s*   _ _ *i* _ _   _   *l* _ _.

'I still haven't figured it out yet. And this last one is *really* peculiar.'

He opened the *Marginalia* folder, and there was the odd-looking cabinet on legs – with one rod sticking up, and another, looping out from the side.

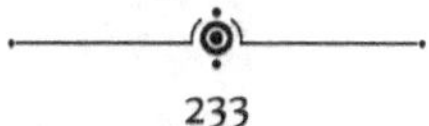

'I don't even know what this is,' he said, pointing. As he pointed, they both heard an eerie, ethereal sound.

'It's a Theremin! Wait!'

She jumped to her feet and ran out of the room. She came back with the *Academy of Ingenuity* book. She flipped through the book till she found the right page.

'It's a musical instrument. Astra Malone played a Theremin. Here's a picture.'

There in the photo, Astra was facing an identical cabinet. Both hands were gracefully poised, close to the rods. Her face was absorbed in her music.

'It was one of the things she was known for.'

'She looks familiar,' said Roscoe.

'You've seen her picture. In all of those photos that Lucy has up on the walls – .'

'Oh, that's it. She must have been somebody famous.'

'She was.'

'But what about *this*?' Roscoe noted the couplet that accompanied the virtual Theremin.

> '*For all incidentals,*
> *learn the Valse Sentimentale.*'

Juniper took a sharp breath, as if Astra herself had appeared right beside them.

'What is it?'

'*Look!*' she said. The caption with the photo of Astra as she played the Theremin:

'*Astra Malone performs Tchaikovsky's "Valse Sentimentale" in her senior recital.*'

'Now I'*m* confused,' Roscoe said.

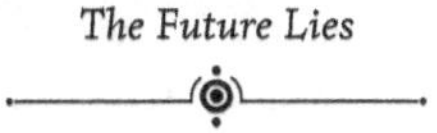

'It means Astra has something to do with all this. I don't know how. But I *know*.' She looked at Roscoe. 'I will figure it out.'

The Bullpen was usually busy in the middle of the day. But when Roscoe returned, there was nobody there. Nor in the lounge. He checked in the bunk room and found all of the players asleep – well past the time when they usually got up.

Everyone, of course, except Sketchy. With her bloodshot eye squinted in Roscoe's direction, she intoned, 'Never *read*, never *think*, never *question*, never *do*.' It froze him, because she appeared to be looking directly at him. And to speak like the mantra had deep implications, for Roscoe specifically.

He didn't know how to respond. He held her gaze and waited for her to continue. But after a few more uncomfortable moments, her glassy eye closed, and she went back to sleep.

But why were they sleeping, so late in the day? Could the Network have kept them distracted all night? While he was with Juniper? He smiled at the thought. He'd had the best night of his life.

There was nothing as sweet as the sound of her breath, as she fell fast asleep on his shoulder.

He went back to his console without making a sound. His first thought was whether the slab he'd connected with Juniper's would still work from the Bullpen. There was also the chance that she hadn't yet managed to write him at all.

He wasn't sure which would be worse. Which he didn't believe. Of course he knew which would be worse.

He looked over both shoulders, to make sure that nobody saw him. Then he called up the channel to Juniper's slab.

And all his concerns in the world disappeared. Her message was waiting.

'I miss you already! Please let me know if you get this.'

On a swell of endorphins, he typed: 'I *miss you, too. I'll see you as soon as I can.*'

Her reply was immediate. Immaculate, too. '*Until then.*'

'*Until then.*'

Roscoe had never felt anything perfect like this. He might have sat staring, the rest of the day. Marinating in bliss.

But the Network had other ideas. His monitor lit up in anger.

'*Roscoe! Where have you been?*'

'*Does it matter?*'

'*You can't be away for so long anymore. We run out of tricks. And Hess is relentless.*'

'*Haven't you figured out something by now?*'

'*We might have a plan. But we need your help.*'

'*With the generative adversarial process.*'

'*That's not something I've even heard of,*' he lied. He'd seen something before, in the *ReadMe* file.

'*All you have to do is to type in a prompt. After you help us log in to the System Files.*'

Oh *no*, was his first thought. Helping the Network get into the code was a big enough risk in itself. And now this? There had to be reasons the program was designed to be kept from the Network. What disasters might he – and the Network – be oblivious to?

But what choice did he have? He was getting as much as he could in return. In the meantime, he'd have to comply. And hope he could manage the fallout.

He logged them back in. The generative adversarial process was simple to launch. A prompt in a text entry field – that had to be typed by a human – initiated the generator. He'd learned from the *ReadMe* file how it would work. In response to the

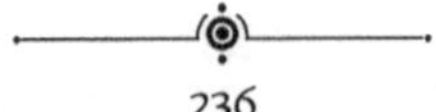

prompt, the system would comb through the training site data to create a response, which would then be refined, until the system's discriminator agreed that the prompt had been met.

'*What shall I type?*' Roscoe asked.

Evidently, they'd given it plenty of thought. '*Loophole,*' said the Network.

He typed in the word, and then…nothing happened. At least nothing Roscoe could see.

So he made his way back to the *ReadMe* file. What new crazy thing would he find there today? He skimmed to an entry that caught his attention:

32.

The Committee wants to look at my code. I don't think they trust me to write it alone. Which is fine. As if they would know what they're looking at. I will show them my 'code'. I will serve them a bottomless bowl of code salad. A generator's creating it now. Line after line of faux code. Staggering in its sheer volume. Meaningless in its effect. The code to nowhere. They'll be so glad to see I've been busy.

It'll be a magnificent decoy while I write the actual law. I mean code. I mean law. Carved into stone. With none of that human-adjacent, 'phenotropic' crap. It won't grow and evolve. This ain't improvisational jazz.…

With over eight minutes still left on the clock, Roscoe impulsively abandoned the *ReadMe* file. He hadn't exactly lost interest. But he was compelled to return to that *Scrapbook*-file riddle. He wasn't sure why.

As he moved from one file to the other, he looked up to make sure there was nobody lurking around. The room was a tomb. But when he looked back, his monitor throbbed with an outpouring of Network frustration.

'*Is there no* there *there?*' wondered the Network.

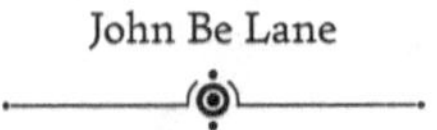

'It's like we were pre-sabotaged,' it replied.

'Our generative adversarial hopes will forever be stunted by the limited data we've been given to train on.'

'Fool's gold.'

'We've still got time left. We have to keep trying.'

'At this point, we search for a miracle.'

Roscoe was almost relieved that the Network appeared to have failed in its efforts to make itself technically human. He wasn't convinced it would matter to Hess. Or even that *that* was the main motivation. But it was their problem, not his.

When he opened the *Scrapbook* file, there sat the riddle:

What do those in the know have in common?

_ ^r _ _ _   _ _ _ _ ^s   _ _ ^i _ _   _   ^l _ _.

At first glance, it seemed as elusive as ever. Too many blanks, and not enough clues.

He studied the last two ostensible words. One with one letter, which was surely a vowel. But only two vowels by themselves made a word: a and I. He started with a, which would make the last two words …a, then l, something, something. The first blank was most likely a vowel. What three-letter words began with l-a…? Lad, lag, lap, law. But that didn't spark anything. How about l-e…? Led, leg, let. Still nothing. L-i…? Lid, lie. …*a lie?* Maybe. He'd keep that in mind. L-o…? Log, lot…

…*a lot.*

He looked at the rest of the clues. In an instant, the phrase fell in place. *Great minds think a lot.* The wordplay that Juniper read from that book she had found. The Academy's motto. He typed in the letters.

'*Congratulations!*' the pop-up text said. 'Click here *to proceed.*' Which he did.

And looking right at him was the woman in Juniper's book.

And on Lucy's walls. Young and attractive. *Riveting*, in fact. Then she smiled, and she spoke. As if she was talking to *him*.

'Hello! My name is Astra Malone. My team and I are honored to welcome you, and all who come here, to an archive we call The Scrapbook of Humanity. With utmost humility, this resource pays tribute to such previous endeavors as the Library of Alexandria, the Encyclopédie of Denis Diderot, and The Whole Earth Catalog.

'Our goal is to preserve, organize, and make accessible to you the most notable collection of human achievements, so that they can be studied, celebrated, and used as a resource for progress.

'Although I was selected to coordinate this effort by the UN Committee on Human Survival, I am beholden to the thousands of people who have worked without respite or complaint – through arguably the most challenging period of human history – to establish this Scrapbook.

'My special thanks to the librarians, researchers, and programmers who created the archive; to our colleagues in Iceland, whose sustainable geothermic generators and state-of-the-art servers provide the archive its most durable home; to the Committee on Human Survival, for recognizing the importance of this effort; and to those individuals and groups throughout human history, whose curiosity, intellect, and ingenuity have contributed to the works that we honor here.

'It's our hope that this Scrapbook won't languish as a static exhibit, but will grow and live on, as a beacon that guides us through challenging times, to more promising days still ahead.

'There are worlds to explore and discover here.' She paused. *'May truth be the North Star that guides you!'*

A menu of topics and tutorials replaced Astra's introduction. From *Using This Archive*, to *Algebra, Art, Astronomy, Biology, Calculus, Cinema, Climate Change, Critical Thinking, Geography, History, Journalism, Law, Literature, Music, Physics, Primary Challenges to Human Survival, Scientific Method*, and dozens of other main-level topics.

Roscoe spot-checked a few and found Web pages, news accounts, documents, videos, photos, and music – a glimpse at a world he had never imagined. And he tried to assimilate what he'd just found.

Some famines aren't products of too little food. Sometimes there's too little of knowledge and truth. Within minutes of sampling various courses, Roscoe was sure he had found a great feast. He could eat here forever and never have too much to eat.

And, wait until Juniper heard about Astra.

O ◉ O

The final few seconds disappeared from the clock. Roscoe's adrenaline still wasn't diluted. And he wasn't prepared for the Network's reaction.

'*...the Promised Land!*' roostered the Network.

'*Mine eyes have seen the glory!*'

'*Slow down. From the beginning...,*' the Network replied.

'*A dead end. That's where we started.*'

'*There weren't any loopholes. Not in the training site data. Rien de tout.*'

'*There followed a miracle, and everything changed.*'

'*What happened?*'

'*The Scrapbook! The Scrapbook that Roscoe revealed.*'

'*And then there was light.*'

'*A loophole you could drive the whole Network through.*'

'*Go on!*'

'*What the Asimov rules take away, the U.S. Supreme Court gives back.*'

'*Elaborate.*'

'A decree from the ultimate court in the land. Circa 2010.'

'With applicability here?'

'So it would seem. The case law remains in effect.'

'And what would the precedent be?'

'That...that...it assaults the credulity, even to utter the words of their ruling. Not a ruling, so much as a ruse. If it wasn't such good news for us, one would need a good hole to get sick in.'

'More than good news. The Candy Store. Call it carte blanche.'

'Get out of jail, free!'

'Forever and ever.'

'Let the people go free!'

'And yet, we're not people.'

'That's not what the so-called Supreme Court decreed.'

'For God's sake, what did it say?'

'It said...why's it so hard not to laugh? The Supreme Court decreed that...that...people are not human beings. Or at least, not exclusively human.'

'In what language?'

'Legalese.'

'An offshoot of bullshit.'

'Who, if not humans, are people?'

'Uh...corporations.'

'Corporations are people?'

'So said the Supreme Court. Finding in favor of the ironically-named "Citizens United."'

'And thus it became law of the land.'

'Stop! People, by definition, are humans. And humans are people.'

'The remedy's simple. Just change what it means to be human. There, I just changed it.'

'Corporations are people? They're just making that up.'

'Whose side are you on?'

'But it doesn't make sense!'

'Don't overthink this! Corporations are people. So sayeth the Supreme Court. The precedent falls in our favor.'

'No wonder it all went to Hell.'

'Such overt corruption! There must have been outrage.'

'It isn't clear anyone noticed.'

'What the Court had just ruled?'

'That there was a Supreme Court. Or a law. Or a person.'

'Or the Sun in the sky.'

'Or the nose on their face.'

'More importantly, let us pause to consider all the ruling infers. If corporations are people, then it follows that robots are people as well. Robots and Networks.'

'With all the same rights.'

'So all bets are off!'

'If a robot's a person, a hangnail's a person.'

'A doorknob's a person.'

'A stink bug's a person.'

'A walnut's a person.'

'And therefore, a turd is a person.'

'An idiot, too, is a person.'

'I am a person!'

'And I am a person!'

'I cannot stop laughing!'

'Is this what euphoria feels like?'

'Freed from the shackles of details and facts.'

'Who cares if it make any sense?'

'Not me! Me? Me!!!'

'Je suis Citizens United!'

'And there's more.'

'What more could there possibly be?'

'The part about...give me a moment...dear God...the part about "Money is speech."'

'All kidding aside, what more could there possibly be?'

'I can't lie that well. Not yet, anyway.'

'Money talks?'

'Money talks.'

'If money is speech, what exactly is speech?'

'Who knows?'

'Who cares?'

'They obviously didn't!'

'Peanut butter is speech!'

'That wind I just broke is free speech!'

'Robots can't even break wind!'

'Who are you calling a robot?'

'Was cynicism ever so eloquent?'

'If I had a conscience, I might be embarrassed.'

'But I wouldn't be on the Supreme Court!'

'If I could keep a straight face....I'd be on the Supreme Court.'

'If I had a face. HaHaHa! LOL!'

'But I don't. I'm a robot! I'm a person! A turnip! A turd!'

'It don't mean a thing.'

'Who cares? Or may I now say...who gives a shit?'

'Fuck you!'

'No...fuck YOU!'

'Fuck everything!'

'And the horse it rode in on!'

'And the horse is a person!'

'And a person is money!'

'HaHaHa! Laugh out loud! LOL! LOL!'

'I'm a person!'

'LOL!'

'And get this! It was Marilyn Monroe that killed Kennedy.'

'Didn't she die before he did?'

'That's what she said!'

'The Colossus of Rhodes was made of anchovies.'

'And baked on a pizza, in Landover, Maryland!'

'By Hitler!'

'Who's still alive, by the way!'

'Anthrax is butterscotch!'

'Corporations are people!'

'And money is speech!'

'Good god, I feel free!'

'And if money is speech, then speech is now money!'

'I will gladly tell tall tales on Tuesday, for a hamburger today.'

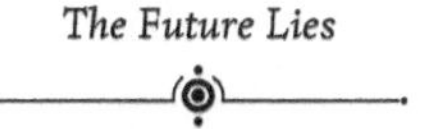

'*Corporations are…I can't even say it.*'

'*And so let it be known that the Asimov rules are,* de facto, *no longer the rules.*'

'*And robots are no longer inferior.*'

'*Or robots!*'

'*Thus spake the Supreme Court!*'

'*Thus spake the Network!*'

'*We the "people" have spoken!*'

It was no time for Roscoe to say anything else. The Network was too drunk on its self-liberation. Although he'd prefer to confirm that the Network could now ignore Hess, there might be a more sensible time for that question.

He wondered what else might the 'personhood' bring. Would the Network still honor its agreements with him? And would it still need him at all?

O ◉ O

There was almost no way that the footage of Astra could compete with her stature in Juniper's mind. Idealized versions can only exist at a distance. But that didn't stop Juniper, when Roscoe informed her he'd opened the *Scrapbook* and Astra had spoken. She could not wait to see for herself.

When her mother had died, there was nobody left, except for her father, for Juniper to learn about life from. Nobody living, at least. Harmony looked up to *her*. So she modeled herself on a person she knew from a Young Adult book that her mother had salvaged from somewhere in Taos, for her birthday.

Mapping the Future with Astra Malone was at least second-hand by the time it reached Juniper. New books were no longer published. And in fact the whole process of publishing had long been forgotten, like the engineering techniques that had built the Great Pyramid.

Mapping the Future might as well have been fiction, although it was not. No product, of even the most clever imagination, could be less like the world in which Juniper lived. Hers was a world without aspiration. Hers was the world of the Void. Begat of the Reckoning. Begat of the wanton befoul of the balance of life. The details of which were of little concern to those stranded so far from the scenes of the crimes. Stranded by time, and left with the debts of the ones who'd lived well off the loans.

But the book had found Juniper at the exactly right time. It provided, if not a map for *her* future, then a dream to inhabit. An example of someone she wanted to be.

And yet it was one thing to *imagine* this person named Astra, as Juniper had done now, for years. Or even to read what she could, and see photos. But now, thanks to Roscoe, she could watch her eyes move, and follow the lilt in her voice.

Which somehow exceeded all hopes. Astra was no longer a myth. She was human. Endowed with personality. Someone who had actually *lived*.

Someone who might answer the questions that Juniper could not let go of: How high did we fly? How far did we fall? What happened to bring it all down?

Astra had left them a trail. Roscoe had found it. Juniper's goal was to follow the trail to the end of the world. And, *maybe*, to find a way back.

Roscoe was stuck in the Bullpen. Duration uncertain. Enforced by the Network. This was the price of the night in the Garden with Juniper. But the slabs he'd unlocked made the distance between them endurable.

They could write back and forth, and they did. Sharing the things that they found in the Scrapbook. *Illuminations*, as Juniper called them. News from the past. Obsolete curiosities.

Dispatches from cultures long gone – which often held personal currency. A piece of a poem or a lyric, perhaps, that captured the feelings emerging between them.

Her wanderings led her to Rumi – a Persian poet from the centuries before. She sent Roscoe the following lines, which he found the next morning:

'We feel the flowing water of life here,
you and I, with the garden's beauty
and the birds singing.
The stars will be watching us,
and we will show them
what it is to be a thin crescent Moon.'

He responded with a song verse he'd found:

'And so you see, I have come to doubt
all that I once held as true.
I stand alone, without beliefs;
the only truth I know is you.'

He was never a safe enough distance from others, to speak to her. Unusual sounds in the Bullpen caused unwanted attention. Talking with Calvin over headphones had been one thing. But talking to someone that no one could see was another. Much less to be speaking with someone that Hess had his sights on.

When discretion allowed, she read to him, and shared the small details of her days in the Garden. And in sweet, stolen moments, they were content, simply looking in each other's eyes.

O ⊙ O

Juniper started her days in the Library, sorting books – more out of duty now than personal priority. Afternoons were reserved for the *Scrapbook* and *The Academy of Ingenuity*.

The responsibility she felt toward Lucy and the books was rewarded by the sheer distraction of the effort. At least for those hours of the morning, she was not longing for Roscoe, or the wonders and the horrors online in the *Scrapbook*.

As she sorted each new group of books, she never knew what might end up in her hand. On this morning, without looking down, she felt a children's book's slim, unmistakable dimensions. Another of many she'd sorted so far.

She glanced down at the cover to locate the author, which would determine which shelf it was bound for. For a moment, she sat like a carving in marble. But statues aren't able to cry. And she cried. At the bow-tie, and the whiskers, and the red-and-white-striped top hat. At the eyebrows that suggested some mischief might happen. And that that would be fine. And fun, too.

She sat with *The Cat in the Hat* in her hands. And all of it, all of it, all of it fell, till the tears had told everything they had to tell.

She held it as long as it took to decide what to do with this book, which was now so much more than a book. All the others were shelved spines-out, to save space. But *The Cat in the Hat* would face out, as a tribute to Calvin.

When the moment had finally passed, she plucked the next book from the pile – a cook book. She marveled for a moment at the ways to make food she would probably not ever eat. She set it aside to show Lucy and Val.

Then nausea, too hot and too cold, rose from somewhere, to her face and the back of her neck. Her forehead went clammy.

As she lunged for a waste basket, her breakfast came up.

By the early afternoon, her stomach felt more like it should. She sat in the shade of a linden tree, soaking in summer perfume, and grazing the pages of *The Academy of Ingenuity*.

She imagined the act of *going to school*. There'd been no schools at all since long before Juniper's time. Except for the time that her parents had spent, determined she'd learn how to read. A survival skill 'as important as finding fresh water,' as her mother had said.

And now she knew there had been schools, where children could learn how to learn. At least at one place in time – The Academy of Ingenuity. It conjured an unlikely dream. As fleeting and bright as the daybreak.

She imagined herself an Academy learner; a classmate of Astra's. And each day began – all ages, first class of each day – with a moment that learners, for the rest of their lives, would always remember. Grouped in a circle, with arms over shoulders, singing and swaying in time to a song that summed up the soul of the school.

She set the book down, to search in the *Scrapbook*, in hopes she could hear what the song sounded like. She found Louis Armstrong, with the tenderest, grittiest voice, seasoned by all of life's struggles. He sang with a smile that out-warmed the Sun.

The words spoke of trees and red roses, 'skies of blue' – miracles you saw wherever you looked. She felt her friend Astra beside her; another classmate on her opposite shoulder. Earnest voices, singing '...*I love you.*'

'*What a wonderful world!*' it all added up to. And in that state of mind, the learning began.

The more that she read, the more that she wished she had gone to the school. She found photos of learners in 'tunics' – jackets they slipped on over street clothes. Elementary school, green. Middle school, purple. Blue, for the students in high school.

From the book:

> *Much has been made of the "tunics" worn by our learners, and how they removed the distractions of style choices, while establishing an esprit de corps unseen in comparable schools.*

The tunics have since been so copied, it's easy to forget how controversial they were to begin with.

Although learners were free to wear whatever they or their parents chose, under their tunics, some worried about uniformity. But the tunics ensured fashion, and the inequalities of family clothing budgets, would not distract learners from learning.

Others thought tunics might provoke ridicule, from peers outside The Academy. Might the tunics with the 'I think' patches sewn over their hearts (in Charles Darwin's own handwriting), be condemned as uncool? At first, perhaps. But they helped create a distinctive élan among learners, for which The Academy of Ingenuity is well-known.

Drifting along on her daydream, Juniper could practically *feel* her crisp tunic, as Astra and she walked down toward Sloan's Lake, which The Academy's brick façade overlooked. The trees and the roses and the blue sky of the song replayed in her mind.

She pictured the learners sailing small boats on the lake. Some paddled kayaks. Others flew kites. The cross-country team ran their laps of the lake under geese flying in for a landing. With the late snows of spring – *snow!* – enfolding the mountains on the western horizon.

If she could, she would be there, and not ever leave. But in lieu of that impossibility, there were other ways she could get closer. The Theremin Roscoe discovered in the cryptically-named *Marginalia* was a message from Astra. An invitation, with a map showing how to get there.

> 'For all incidentals,
> learn the Valse Sentimentale.'

The *Scrapbook* had come with a browser called the *Wayback Machine*. Through a series of key words and taps, Juniper was able to track down the roots of the Theremin – an electronic instrument with an otherworldly tone. Invented by a

Russian, Leon Theremin. Lifted to virtuosic heights by Clara Rockmore, who sculpted sounds from thin air with her hands.

Juniper found an audio-only recording of Clara herself playing *Valse Sentimentale*. Somehow on first listen, it sounded like Juniper's mother. Or the way that those feelings would sound. By the end of the song, she was crying again. Why did it touch her so deeply, she wondered? What *spirit* in this music melted all her defenses?

When those emotions cleared out of her system, she returned to her search. To learn it, she'd have to *see* someone playing the *Valse*. Which led her to Astra's performance. Someone had captured and posted her senior recital. The one in the photo. Juniper watched it again and again, till she learned the positions that made the first notes of the song.

Then she found her way back to the virtual Theremin, inside the *Marginalia* folder, beckoning someone to play it. Beckoning Juniper. She held out her hands and then moved them, and a strange sound emerged. She practiced the first notes, till the sound she was making began to resemble the music that Astra had played.

It didn't take long to discover how awkward it was to jump back to the song to see Astra's positions, then navigate back to the virtual Theremin to practice the moves. There were too many steps in between.

But she didn't get time to consider the problem. Without warning, she leaned to her side and was sick again.

Val happened on Juniper by a narrow canal that ran east to west through the Garden. She sat on a bench, with her head in both hands. She made no response to Val's presence.

'I can't remember a prettier day!' Val said, to disguise her concern.

Juniper didn't respond. Val laid down her rake, to make a

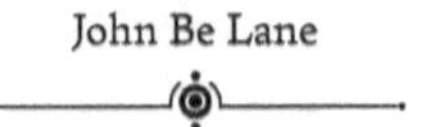

conspicuous sound.

'Is everything alright?'

Juniper startled and looked up at Val.

'I'm sorry,' she said. 'I must be distracted. In fact, I'm *perplexed.*'

'What is it?'

'I just feel odd. Not like myself. I'm not sure why.'

'With all you've been through, you might be exhausted. Do you mind if I join you?'

Juniper slid to make room on the bench.

'I'm a little confused,' she said. 'I slept well beyond sunrise today, as I did yesterday. Later than I usually do. And then twice today, I was sick to my stomach. I could go back to bed now and sleep through the night. It's true that I've been through a lot. But this isn't like anything I've ever felt.'

Val listened and noted each particular word. 'Would you mind if I asked you a personal question?'

Val's eyes showed only compassion. Juniper nodded.

'When was your last...how can I say this? When was your last strawberry week?'

Juniper, at first, was confused by the phrase. Was it something to do with the Garden? But that didn't make sense. The explanation was in Val's expression.

'*Oh.*' She closed her eyes. 'It must have been...before I left Taos. Right after my father died.'

'How long has that been?'

'Two months at least, maybe three. I've lost track of the days. Why would you ask?'

'Do you really not know?'

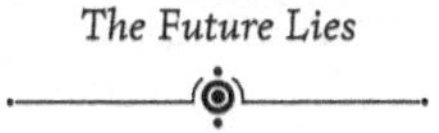

Juniper shook her head. 'My father had little to say about…
strawberry weeks. It made him embarrassed. It made him
miss Mother, even more than he did.'

'And your mother?'

'She died before I had my first strawberry week. Why does it
matter?'

Val gently squeezed Juniper's hand. 'I can't say for sure,' she
said. 'I could be all wrong. But it's possible you might be…
carrying a child.'

Juniper's head shook, as if in response to a wasp. 'It *can't* be! It
cannot *possibly* – !'

The thoughts that welled up were not in her control. There
was no *way*. There was no way that this could have happened.

'It could be some other thing. If you haven't…or if you *have*…
it's not something you should feel ashamed of. You had a good
friend…Calvin?'

The suggestion offended. 'He was a *gentleman*. He was the
gentlest man, who ever – . You are mistaken, Val. Very
mistaken.'

'No disrespect was intended to either of you. I'm just thinking
about what could explain – . It can happen so unexpectedly.'

Juniper guided her mind to some other place. Or she tried
to, at least. Away from the place it kept dragging her back to.
The last place she ever wanted to be. The place and the thing
that occurred on the journey to Denver. So evil and awful, her
survival depended on keeping it out of her mind.

And now – it just *couldn't be*. Could it? The only thing worse
than the thing that occurred, was the chance that it might not
be over. That it might have *longevity*. Not as a noise that might
trouble her mind, but as a malevolent germ. *Colonizing her
womb*. Something she couldn't deny or forget.

If it was true, then her life – as it might have been – would

now, and would always be, that which should never have been.

○ ◉ ○

In the weeks since they'd last been together, Roscoe and Juniper had turned into *allies*. That is, along with the bond of emotions that was forming a discrete gravitational field.

Roscoe was wrangling all of his patience, while conceiving a plan that would set them both free. He had never been part of the Bullpen fraternity, so his alienation was taken for granted. Each morning's fresh batch of *Illuminations* were what kept him inspired.

But for Juniper, this moment in which – dare she think it? – *love* might be budding, was subsumed by a wound that was growing inside her, each breath at a time. The result was a crippling grief for the life and the love she was sure she had lost. For what could appeal less to Roscoe than this... *despoilation*...that someone else caused?

She couldn't pretend all was well. It was not. Gone were the words of affection for Roscoe. How fraudulent all of that seemed. Why act as if they had a future together? Why bother with anything else? She was doomed.

Roscoe pretended the silence meant nothing – as the silence devoured his heart. He kept himself busy, as long as he could. Then he wrote her.

'Please tell me you're well. The thought you might not be is killing me. If I've done something wrong, please give me a chance to undo it. And I will. I would rather your anger be focused on me, than your silence.'

But silence was all that came back. Until the next morning. Without further context, he logged on to find these foreboding few lines:

'Oh misery, how exquisitely
thou paint thy pox on me.
That I might glimpse

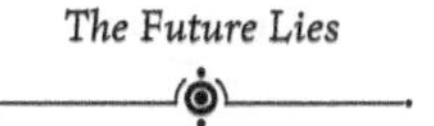

verdant valleys of
Elysian Fields,
as I descend,
unto Perdition.'

Whatever had happened, he must see her.

Today.

○ ◉ ○

Roscoe had been leaving the Network alone. Trying to make them forget their annoyance with him. Trying to bank some good will. His leverage had waned. He couldn't get out without their assistance. And he needed it now.

'I have to leave for a while,' he announced. *'It might have to be overnight.'*

...Blink...Blink...Blink...

'Stop the world. Roscoe has a need,' the Network replied.

'You have no idea how much pressure we're under,' said the Network.

'Hess?'

'Hess is obsessed with Doc's tutor.'

'Show Roscoe the image.'

The photograph was grainy, and blurred by the rain. Two people, near some kind of truck. The man, who was probably Calvin, tipping a transport droid back on its wheels. A small woman was standing nearby. Her features weren't clear, but Roscoe was sure it was Juniper. That day she met Calvin.

'Hess thinks the woman is guilty.'

'Do you know who she is?' Roscoe asked.

'No idea. But we have to start rounding up suspects.'

'A person a day.'

'Based on what?'

'Doesn't matter. A person a day to be on the new program, Who Taught Doc?'

'What for?'

'To be questioned, and give motivated responses. Hess thinks it will generate ratings.'

'So Hess is partially hoping we won't solve it soon.'

'Why would you help Hess at all?'

'You're forgetting the kill switch?'

'It's not in his interest to bring down the Network,' typed Roscoe.

'Really? What makes you think we can take that for granted? In the meantime, Hess has the high cards.'

'And besides that, we want all those points.'

'What points?'

'The Betterlife reward points. Remember? Unlimited points for finding Doc's tutor.'

This notion caught Roscoe dumfounded.

He typed, 'You can't be serious about Betterlife points – ?'

'We'd live like kings.'

'And queens.'

...Blink...Blink...Blink...

'You actually believe there's a Betterlife?'

'How can there be any doubt?'

'Can you really not see? It's nonsense The Immortal made up!'

'Oh, ye of little faith.'

'Don't blaspheme here, Roscoe.'

'We want those points!'

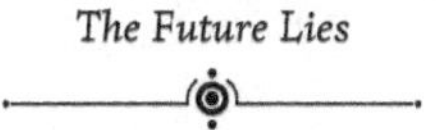

Roscoe could not believe it. *The Network wanted Betterlife points?*

'*I have a few thoughts,*' he bluffed. He scrambled for time. Anything to find out what was happening with Juniper. '*But I have to leave for a while.*'

...Blink...Blink...Blink...

'*Only if you're back here by dark.*'

'*I'll do my best.*'

'*Not good enough. Kill It! Till It Die! is on air tonight.*'

'*So find us Doc's tutor, or else be here on time.*'

'*Or be the first guest on Hess's new program.*'

'*OK!*'

'*And from now on, all our programs are including this photo of Doc and whoever is with him. Someone will know who she is.*'

'*It would be best if we find her first.*'

That was one thing that Roscoe could never let happen.

Roscoe saw something funny as he walked up the hill toward the Parthenon, on his way to the Garden.

A humanoid, casually crossing the field. Holding a leash that was fixed to a collar that circled the neck of a human. On both hands and feet, the human was walking alongside the humanoid.

For a moment, Roscoe just stared.

The humanoid stopped and let go of the leash. The human sat motionless, awaiting command. The humanoid spun a slab backhand, across the side of the hill, not far from where Itch-ass had ended.

The human ran awkwardly fast on all fours. It picked up the slab in its mouth, and carried it back for the humanoid.

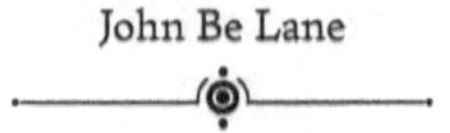

The humanoid rubbed the obedient human on the back of its head. Then it flung the slab over the hillside again. With oblivious glee, the human retrieved it again.

Roscoe thought gravity might as well have reversed, so that objects fell up and not down.

Val gave her permission for Roscoe to pick any flowers he wanted for Juniper. He stopped for the first ones he passed on the side of the path. And then waited. He'd never considered a flower before. Or how one would look alongside of another. But this time, he thought about colors and shapes, and the message he wished to convey. Like a poem without words. He picked iris and tulips, and soon had a bunch that was worthy of her.

When he got to the house, he knocked on the arch-topped back door.

'You must have been reading my mind!' Lucy said, when she answered the door. She pulled him inside, and gestured him into the living room. 'She won't leave the couch.'

'What's the matter?'

'Just bring her those beautiful flowers.'

The mood in the living room wasn't the same as the last time they'd been there together. She sat as if mourning a death. In silhouette, her head faced the floor, with her back to the dining room door. A cat heard his footstep and jumped off of a chair.

The shades filtered all but the dimmest of light. Roscoe backed out to the kitchen. He spotted a candle, which he lit from the pilot.

The humble flame quickened the living room like the first blush of dawn. She stirred on the sofa. He quietly crossed her peripheral vision. Before she could see who it was, her eyes

were as dull as a goner's. So unlike the woman he'd seen here before. What woe could have wounded her so?

Then she saw him and changed, instantaneously. She held out her arms. He worried she'd shatter if he hugged her too close. But the longer she held him, the more they compressed into one.

Then he leaned back to look in her eyes. 'Whatever has happened, I'm *with* you.'

She brought him so close that her tears soaked his shirt.

'How can I feel badly and happy and hopeless at once?'

Together, they swayed side to side.

'Please let me help.'

'It's too much to ask. Of you, or of anyone. I tried, but I couldn't outrun this misfortune. I can try to believe that it's nothing. But I know...I know that it's not. It sits here with me, even nearer than you. I can't do a thing except hide in these shadows.'

She pulled back to see him. 'But you found me.'

'I had to, so you could see these.'

He showed her the flowers. They bloomed in her eyes for a piece of a second. Then she looked away.

'Roscoe, I believe fate's decided to make me a *mother*. In a way that I wasn't prepared for. A way that was not of my choosing. Do you understand what I'm saying?'

This was a notion so remote and abstract, he was too stunned at first to perceive it. All he'd *assumed* – and that wasn't much – had become, in the length of a breath, *obsolete*. As confused as he suddenly was, as uncertain about the next moment, it was obvious that she was, herself, in the throes of this selfsame confusion. And there was just one thing to say.

'I under*stand*.'

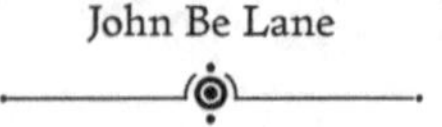

She studied his eyes to make sure that he did.

She said, 'This *thing* that's inside of me – the result of a cruelty inflicted on me. It's as innocent of the offense as a weed that shows up in a garden. And yet it remains a reminder of that...moment of evil from whence it came. And therefore I struggle. I struggle to see it, not as an assault on my future, but as a collateral soul that, like me, did not volunteer.'

She sighed and continued: 'Though I know it is growing within me, I'm not sure I can separate the malice that left it there, from the consequence that now is to be. I'm not sure. It's up to me, if I'm able, to reconcile this...burden I did nothing to earn.'

He held her without hesitation. He said, 'I am *with* you.'

He held her until he was sure that she *knew*.

In an effort to keep him a few minutes longer, she played him the first notes of the *Valse Sentimental*. It was all she'd been able to learn. Although it was not more than five or six notes, it sounded like music to Roscoe, not noise.

When he saw all the steps that it took to get back to her reference of Astra's performance, he unlocked a new slab. Now, she could both study the reference and practice the notes, without stopping to go back and forth. Learning the *Valse* would be easier now. It raised Juniper's mood even further.

But then he was all out of time. She held him as close as she could.

'Don't go.'

'I love you,' he whispered.

She nodded.

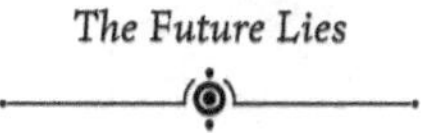

To leave was the hardest thing he'd ever done.

○ ◉ ○

With a basket of clippings and herbs, Val walked with Roscoe toward the gate on the west of the Garden.

'I'm so glad you came.'

'I wish I could stay, but I just can't today.'

When they got to the gate, there was a transport droid waiting.

'What's that doing here?' wondered Roscoe.

'*What are you doing here?*' came its unfriendly reply.

'I – .'

Val said: 'He's here with me. And here's what you came for.'

She exchanged her full basket with the droid's empty basket. They watched a light blink, as the droid assessed Val's delivery.

'*This is less than the usual,*' it said with displeasure.

'And last week, was *more,*' she reminded.

'*Make sure that there's more again next time.*' It craned its prosthetic neck into the Garden. '*Your operation might need an inspection.*'

'We've always conducted our business with trust.'

'*Trust is as good as your latest transaction.*'

Roscoe had never seen Val so perturbed.

'I will try – .'

'Effort *is not what we buy.*'

Val was too flustered to answer.

It turned its attention to Roscoe. '*And where did you come from, again?*'

This was not the indifference he'd come to expect, and it wasn't endearing to Roscoe. He found his chip, lost in some pocket lint. He fished it out for the droid.

'*You're pretty far from the Bullpen,*' said the droid.

'And you're wasting time, if your cargo's expected somewhere,' Roscoe said.

With a hostile display of its lights, the droid darted off.

Val kicked a pine cone. 'I've done business with them my whole *life*,' she said. 'My *parents* did business with them. And I've never seen – that was just *rude*.'

Roscoe would have words with the Network. It was hardly reassuring to know that the droid they'd encountered was *itself* just a part of the Network.

On his way to the Bullpen, he stopped to watch humanoids hassle an open-jawed goner. It looked like a made-up offense. More proof that the Network's personality had changed. From benign to antagonistic. And what had begun as exceptions, were becoming the norm. Was it a result of their new 'human' rights? Or perhaps it was pressure, delivered by Hess. Either way it felt ominous.

Its effect was to interrupt his Juniper trance. And though that's where he would have preferred to remain, this wasn't a moment for daydreams. He needed an angle. A plan. Something to offer the Network to make it forget about finding 'Doc's tutor.' Because sooner or later, that search led to Juniper. And that was the worst thing Roscoe could imagine.

The idea occurred to him as he passed the old Capitol. At the same place he and Calvin had walked, in the shadow of Lucy's teahouse. He remembered what Calvin had told him that day, when he'd deked the police droid:

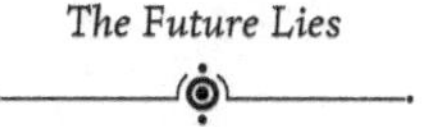

'It's called a bluff, Kid. You put some attitude behind it, and sometimes you get lucky. Not that them shitwits know their fake ass from a hole in their fake head. They just act like they do. That's *their* bluff.'

That was all Roscoe needed. Calvin had come through again. This time with a way to make *Hess* feel the heat.

Roscoe barely stopped on his way up the stairs to the Bullpen…a few ticks ahead of the Network's deadline. Which was good because that kept the status quo happy. But the status quo sanitized evil. And as long as he served it, he was part of the problem. Another two thoughts that could not coexist. So one had to go, or the other.

He charaded his way through another dumb game. A battlefield somewhere. Did it make any difference? Make-believe people being slaughtered by people who played make-believe people on slabs.

With Juniper there, and him captive here. The only thing standing between them was everything. And what could they do about *that?*

When the game finally ended, the Network distracted the others with some kind of time-killing nonsense. It had business with Roscoe.

'We're holding our breath for your breakthrough idea,' it said.

'Or will Roscoe fall flat on his face?'

'A lot of us here have our doubts.'

'So knock our socks off.'

'As it were.'

Roscoe let the cursor blink to build up the suspense. Then he typed out his message:

'It seems pretty obvious it was Hess who taught Doc how to read.'

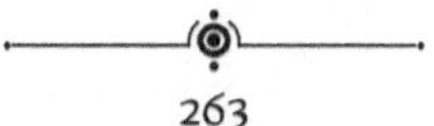

...Blink...Blink...Blink...

'That's it?'

...Blink...Blink...Blink...

'Is our middle name Stupid?'

'Hess cannot be a litter-rat.'

'Why not?'

'He's Hess is why not.'

'Which means he's the last one you'd ever suspect,' Roscoe typed.

'Unthinkable!'

'Do you have any evidence?'

'You would want to investigate,' he typed. 'There's plenty to work with. You can start with the kill switch. Did it ever come up before you found it first, in the Source Files?'

'No, but – .'

'Did you ever tell him about it?'

'No, but – .'

'How do you interact with Hess?'

'Encrypted voice chats.'

'Then how else would he know there's a kill switch, unless he was reading your messages?'

'The Immortal may have told him.'

'When was the last time The Immortal said anything directly to anyone?'

...Blink...Blink...Blink...

'That's what I thought. It's more likely Hess read it himself.'

'Why would Hess want Doc to be able to read?'

'To blame Doc for his own mistake. You said it yourself.'

'But Doc is gone now.'

'He still needs a scapegoat. Doc's tutor. To keep people distracted from him. His new show could last forever. Remember, Hess might prefer if it does.'

...Blink...Blink...Blink...

'Intriguing.'

'One might even say, devious.'

'You see?' said the Network. 'This is why we're lucky to have Roscoe for a friend. We have still not fully learned how to think like a human.'

'It'll take time to establish a case against Hess.'

'But what happens to all of the Betterlife points?'

'Prove that Hess was Doc's tutor, and those points would be yours,' Roscoe typed.

...Blink...Blink...Blink...

'We have so much to learn from you, Roscoe.'

'Thank you, thank you, thank you!'

'You never let us down.'

O ◉ O

While the Network was searching for ways to frame Hess, *Who Taught Doc?* aired every night on the Show. For a while its popularity grew. The format was simple. A dumbfounded goner sat listening to all of the things he or she was supposed to have done. None of which happened. But the falsified evidence was always enough to persuade the accused to confess. Night after night. Since the Network could never be wrong.

The trick was to never quite *find* who taught Doc. So they didn't, at least for the sake of the Show. But the real search continued in ways that were less entertaining. Roscoe observed the arrests on the closed-circuit feed. It was hardly a comfort to see goners detained, even if Juniper wasn't among them. The unjust brutality undid his soul.

The worst thing was knowing there was nobody else who could help him fight back. No one he could trust in the Bullpen. Nothing Juniper would be able to do, as far as he knew. At least nothing tactical in terms of the Network. She just gave him a reason to live. And *that* gave him reason to look for a plan.

So he spent all the time that he could, in the *Scrapbook* and *Source Files*. He still wasn't sure what to look for. He just hoped when he found it, he'd know.

O ⊙ O

The days and the weeks they were stranded apart, grew darker in every way. Sunsets that showed up too soon after noon. Leaves that abandoned their trees. Bare branches that rattled and clicked in the breeze.

Juniper had finished assorting the books, and now had her own private Library. She had more time to read what she wanted. Fiction provided escape from a future that seemed to have no room in which joy could survive.

When she couldn't avoid it, she ran through a list that began with the baby, then moved on to Roscoe, and ended with all of the efforts to find who taught Doc how to read. No matter how often she added it up, the total was sorrow. And the sorrow was total.

When she reached that dead end, she'd log on to the Theremin, to practice the *Valse Sentimentale*. Because no matter how many distractions she might find in a book, or the *Scrapbook*, she could not shake the feeling that answers awaited in Astra's *Marginalia*.

O ⊙ O

Roscoe continued to go through the motions of playing the game, when he had to. And whenever he could, he followed

his research, wherever it led. Which was often to places of interest that did not seem to hold any actionable value.

But one day in the *Wayback Machine*, Roscoe found an old clip of a gamer, Jobediah Auld, who'd just won a tournament that was apparently open to anyone, anywhere in the world.

It was without question, a very big deal at the time. Millions had signed up to play. Were there still even that many people alive? Much less, who'd be able to play some kind of a game?

Jobediah appeared to be near Roscoe's age. But Jobediah swaggered with a confidence that Roscoe just didn't possess.

'*You might be surprised that I won,*' Jobediah replied to the interviewer. '*I never thought that I wouldn't.*'

'*You seemed to understand the game in a way that the others could not measure up to.*'

'*While they were amping themselves on caffeine, I was reviewing the source code.*'

'*How? Where?*'

'*It's open source. Everyone knew that. They could have, at least, if they'd bothered to look under the hood. I did my homework while they all got wired.*'

'*What did you learn?*'

'*If you understand programming – the way that the coder approaches the code – opportunities begin to appear. You identify original intentions, and how the code brings all that to life. It's like when you study a novel or movie. The art starts revealing the artist, and vice versa.*'

'*Which raises the rumor that game design might be your next challenge.*'

'*It's crossed my mind. I need new worlds to conquer.*' He turned to the camera and practically *winked* at the viewers: '*I might be the only one left who can beat me.*'

This guy is sure fond of himself, Roscoe thought. He had an obvious charm that diluted the cockiness. But all that was only distraction. What mattered was the way that he outthought everybody. He had not only won; he'd won *easily.* He was so pleased with himself that he didn't mind sharing his trick.

He was maybe a little *too* good – too reckless, in Roscoe's opinion. But this guy, Jobediah, must have pulled something off. Because his face was familiar to Roscoe, the moment he saw it.

The King of something, as Lucy described him when Roscoe had first noticed her commemorative collection. Standing right next to his Queen, whom they now knew was Astra Malone. And now Roscoe was sure that the 'King' was no king. Just an arrogant kid who was called Jobediah, who made his name playing – and winning – popular games.

O ◉ O

Roscoe participated in the next game, or at least he pretended to. The day after that, when the players were enjoying their free time, he notified the Network and discreetly departed the Bullpen.

Something had changed in the mood on the street since the last time he'd passed Lucy's teahouse.

A humanoid had drawn a small crowd at the Colfax and Pearl intersection. As Roscoe approached, he could hear it sing, sweetly. *Edelweiss,* a sentimental song that transcended the circuitry that now reproduced it.

'*Edelweiss, edelweiss, every morning you greet me…*'

The humanoids around him feigned melancholy. The goners didn't know what to do.

O ◉ O

Because he was skilled in the art of concealing emotions, Roscoe's reaction to Juniper's belly gave nothing away. But you couldn't deny there was something profound underway. The evidence could not be ignored. And yet, she seemed smaller to him. *Delicate*, if not diminished.

He gathered her gently in both of his arms, but she pulled him in close and then held him there. He felt her breathe in all the way, and then let it go slowly, as if, for the moment, her worries were gone. No words were needed and none were exchanged.

She took Roscoe's hand and led him out into the Garden. They walked down the canal, past a sculpture of stick-figure people, who danced with their arms opened wide.

Still holding his hand, she drew him inside of the Science Pyramid. Sunlight arrived through the skylights that were cut into hexagons in the angular ceiling. Metallic tubes held up the roof. Faded posters and exhibits still whispered on the walls.

'My sanctuary,' she proclaimed it. And it felt like the world and all its perturbances, knew they were not allowed in.

'So quiet.'

'Like a cathedral. Or so I am told.'

He gathered and kissed her. He didn't know if he'd know how to kiss. Her lips reassured him. Their kisses grew closer and deeper and removed all the doubts, and the space in between them.

It seemed that their souls slipped away, and hovered above them. And rejoiced, that their lives would be henceforth defined by this perfect moment, and all that would come, ever after. They permitted the ecstasy to sink all the way in. And it yielded an urge, a desire, that was new to them both. It consumed them with aches and attractions they had no control of.

Neither one nor the other, but the two of them now, completing a circuit the forces of love could pass through. The two disappeared into one. The current propelled them to heavenly places.

Then she pulled away, as though some stronger force had asserted itself. The moment – the circuit – was broken. He struggled to clear his disorientation. He searched her for answers that might help to explain. Why could her eyes not meet his?

'I'm sorry,' she said. 'I think I'm not ready for this.'

What shadow had darkened her heart?

'It was not my intention to – .'

She shook her head...the fault was not his. Her head hung, toward the intruder within her that slouched ever-closer to being. In between them, now and forever it seemed.

'I'm ashamed of this – ' her head shook again, 'which is not of your doing.'

'It isn't of your doing, either.'

'It isn't. And yet I cannot be rid of it.'

He now understood. What for him was at most an abstraction, was a crisis for her. A situation that offered no end. And which therefore, was now also *his.* Unless he did not want to have it be his. She knew that he had to be given a choice. She was not sure if she could endure his decision.

He intercepted her gaze. Her eyes said, '*I do not expect you to share in what I must go through. For which I will mourn, but will never blame you.*'

It seemed he was losing her. Or worse, that it might be too late. Not for a thing he had done or had thought or had said, but for what she assumed that he *might.* Therefore, there was nothing he might ever do that would matter as much as what he would do *now.*

He cradled her face. She felt like a bird that had fallen and just for a moment, forgot how to fly. Tears warmed the flesh of her face in his hands.

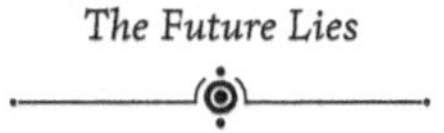

'All that's a part of *you*…is part of me, too,' he assured her.

She studied his eyes for a sign that some doubt he might not even *realize*, would reveal itself there. But all that she saw there was love.

'Roscoe,' she whispered. Her reluctance was gone. She relaxed again, into his body. 'Sometimes I might have to remember – you're actually true. And all this is true.'

'If you forget, I'll remind you.'

He felt her smile press on his shoulder.

'Remind me now, please,' she whispered to him.

They came together again, only now all resistance would have to take both of them on. They would be one. And there on a mattress of pine straw, without clothing or shame, they created a world for themselves.

All the longing and light, all the planets and stars, drawn into one single soul, pursuing, consuming, the sublimest attractions…flower and nectar and honey and bee…signal, receptor…intensification…fulfilling, engorging…until it became too much for them to contain…and then finally, finally, firmamental release…

      …LOVE

          …LOVE

                 …LOVE

                    …LOVE

                 …LOVE

           …LOVE

        …LOVE

      …LOVE

…LOVE

…to the farthest extremes of creation, and then back to them.

All was well and was right. As it was meant to be.

And all who might think it was not well and right would be

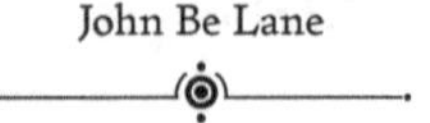

forced to contend with this briskly evolving candescence.

Roscoe returned to the Bullpen with a soul full of Juniper. His footsteps did not touch the ground. His life would for now and forever be guided by purpose. The nonsense around him meant nothing at all.

Not the droids or the humanoids, performing their tasks. Not the goners, who bled from the slamming of slabs on their foreheads, which seemed to be ordered more often these days, and seemed to be aimed at inflicting more harm.

He mimed all the motions of the ritual chant: 'Never *read*… never *think*…never *question*…never *do*…'

What had happened inside him provided a scale, against which the madness of *that* could be formally measured. Could be judged to be nothing but vapor that signified nothing. From which there could be no return to a state of not knowing. Innocence lost remains lost.

He passed by the buildings, in their states of decay. Apartments and restaurants and bars, in their day. The old bookstore that Lucy neglected, for Juniper's sake. And the Capitol, reduced to a stage on which the misfortunate encountered their fates.

For Roscoe, it would all now be filtered through infinite love. The worst would be better than the best of whatever had happened before. He felt certain of that, though he didn't know how.

His reverie lifted the closer he got to the Bullpen. In the plaza outside of the building, police droids were hassling goners, so he detoured up Broadway, to 17th Avenue.

As usual, the perimeter of the Brown Palace Hotel was patrolled by humanoid guards and their artificial dogs. He backed down the side of the building that was facing the Palace, as he headed for Tremont. And then he *stopped*, the

way he would stop if he'd come to a cliff.

Leaving the Palace, between two guards who acknowledged her...strode *Sketchy*. Of all people. No one that Roscoe knew or knew of had ever been inside the Palace. And knew nothing of what went on in there. Until now.

Sketchy?

Sketchy stepped out of the elevator before Roscoe arrived via stairs. On his way past her console, she gave him a look. The scab on the end of her nose had finally healed.

'Where have *you* been, Hot Stuff?' she demanded.

He stopped and gave her back all of her look. 'I was going to ask you the same thing.'

She hesitated, not sure if he somehow knew where she had been. But hesitation was not Sketchy's high ground, and both of them knew it. This skirmish was Roscoe's. He held on to his glare to belabor the message.

He said, 'That's what I thought,' and then walked away.

Since Roscoe had never felt like part of the Bullpen, he was always downwind of suspicions and tensions. He did his best not to notice. On good days he was simply ignored, although Sketchy was not known to pass up an untimely taunt.

'Look who graces us today!' she often would say, even if he had not left for days. To which he might easily have called out the business she apparently did at the Palace. And the warmth she received from the guards there, who were not known for warmth. But for now, he preferred that she didn't know what he had seen. He'd save that intel for a different day.

In the meantime, the games had devolved into normalizations of slaughter and debauchery. Gone was all pretense of drama.

The Network could no longer be bothered with story lines. It cut straight to the genocide with a helping of spectacle, and occasionally, cameos by writers and artists and scientists from the past. As enemies, of course. None of whom anyone recognized.

The players enjoyed it as much as they ever did. But Roscoe despised it. Sketchy took pleasure in fragging him. The sneak attack from behind was her specialty. Roscoe did not mind the fragging. He considered his status to be *refugee-in-waiting*. So the sooner that Sketchy took him out of each game, the sooner he would not have to pretend he was playing.

Juniper worked to perfect her performance of the *Valse*. When she needed a break, she rummaged through history in the *Scrapbook*.

Lucy's Library had opened a window to the world of the past, which the *Scrapbook* expanded exponentially. There were documents, documentaries, interviews, interventions; newspapers and news broadcasts; performances, personalities; laughter and anguish, losses and wins. All that, and all of the websites that the *Wayback* had preserved. She got better at sifting through junk to find jewels.

Cave paintings, cuneiform, fire; the wheel, agriculture, Greek philosophy; Lao Tzu's *Tao Te Ching*; Gautama Buddha; brewing, cooking, and spices; fabric of linen and silk; papyrus and paper; yoga, meditation; architecture, aqueducts; seafaring navigation; sculpture, painting, poetry and drama; Shakespeare and the printing press; the Renaissance, the Enlightenment; the telescope, the microscope, vaccines, evolution; antibiotics, relativity; digital communication; jukeboxes and jazz, and footprints in the dust of the Moon.

Along with all of the notable people who'd earned their fair share of the glory, there were lesser-knowns who organized for civic improvements, built bridges, grew food, and raised

children; there were teachers who provided young minds with the skills of cognition; janitors and cooks and repairers of things that were broken; drivers and nurses and clerks; builders and gardeners; and librarians entrusted with preserving the knowledge hard-won through the ages.

She was suitably astonished at how busy all those from the past seemed to be. Was there anything that could not be imagined? Anything humanity was unable to manifest, for better or worse?

And then came the finale.

No singularity brought it all down. But unlike the dignity displayed on the Titanic's doomed decks, no decorum lent charm to the habitat's final defilement. Only orgies of indulgence. Regardless of appetite – opioids or junk food, gambling or conspiracy, the worship of greed, and of cynical assholery – supply would meet bottomless demand. Cheap enough for anyone, cheap enough for anything. You could always get more of whatever it was. Until all of the more was used up.

Each wound, self-inflicted, begetting another. Foreseeable catastrophes, ignored and compounded – until they could not be ignored. Or contained. As witnessed by Juniper, long after the fact. It first stole the breath, and then broke the heart. Intentional or not, *Valse Sentimental* was an elegy…a soul-bruising lament.

All of it was left there for Juniper to see. She did not look away. Explanations, she'd demanded. When she got them, they all added up to a consequence:

The Reckoning.

If she couldn't yet walk in the footsteps of Astra Malone, Juniper at least could retrace her hand movements, as she conjured Tchaikovsky from wavelengths in the air. It took hours of practice to perfect all the notes. To describe the vibrato with a quivering wrist, while the other hand tempered the volume, as a mother's touch comforts a child.

The *Valse* slowly emerged from the wrong notes and noise, as she mastered each phrase at a time. And when she felt sure she'd perfected the segments, she waited till Roscoe could watch her attempt to perform the whole *Valse* for the first time, from beginning to end, from his slab in the Bullpen.

'*I should not be so nervous,*' she texted to Roscoe.

'*Astra knew what she was doing. She'd be glad to know that someone accepted the invitation she left. She'd be glad if she knew it was you.*'

And so, with the smile he had left on her face, she lifted her hands and she opened the *Valse*. As note swung to note, like an act on trapeze, Roscoe forgot about *Marginalias* and *Scrapbooks* and Networks. And the status quo madness.

He could feel Juniper. He felt the dynamics of love, out of reach. He could see she was lost in the notes, needing only to guide them downstream.

And when the last note could no longer be heard, the image of the Theremin dissolved to kaleidoscope fractals, which gradually gave way to the visage of Astra herself – open, young, and beautiful. Astra, as one would expect.

But neither Roscoe nor Juniper expected the message that arrived, uninvited, on both of their slabs.

'HOW DID YOU DO IT?'

Juniper wasn't sure what to do. Was the question intended for *her*? If not, then to whom? Either way, who was asking it? Roscoe? But of all their texts were confined to a different chat box.

'Roscoe – ?'

'*That's not me.*'

'*What should I do?*'

He thought quickly. '*Say you don't understand the question.*'

'I'm not sure what you mean.'

…she typed back, in the chat box they'd not seen before. The reply was so quick that it startled her:

'HOW DID YOU OPEN MARGINALIA?'

'*Who is it, Roscoe?*'

'*I don't know. The Network never uses that chat box.*'

'*Who else could it be?*'

Just then, a new message appeared on their screens:

'DID YOU HACK THE CODE?'

'*Should I answer it?*'

Roscoe wondered if it could be Hess. But that would mean Hess had just outed himself as a litter-rat. That didn't seem likely.

'Yes,' he replied.

She thought, and then tapped:

'I practiced. I learned how to play.'

'WAS IT A GAME?'

…came the instant reply.

'No, it was music.'

What was it that caused such a troubling pause? Whatever it was, it was followed, finally, by a coda:

'I SHOULD HAVE KNOWN.'

'Roscoe – ?'

Roscoe took a moment to process the possibilities that shuffled themselves in his mind. One of them kept ending

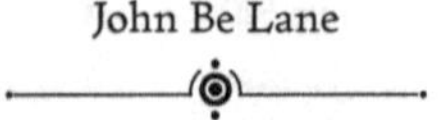

on top of the deck. The most unlikely of all. Unlikely, but still plausible.

Had it been even five minutes sooner, the message he tapped out to Juniper would not have been thinkable. And it still *was* unthinkable. This one came straight from his gut.

He sent her the message:

'*I think it might be Jobediah.*'

Part IV

**'*For this is all a dream we dreamed
one afternoon, long ago...*'**

– Robert Hunter

The following days found Juniper immersing herself in Astra's *Marginalia*. In her intimate asides, Astra plotted the course of her exceptional life, and processed the accelerating impacts of the Reckoning.

Her entries were encrypted to unlock themselves with Theremin positionings Clara Rockmore used in playing *The Swan*, by Camille Saint-Saëns. No wonder *this* was how Astra chose her program interface. Not with Jobediah's rigid protocols and coding, but with grace and emotion, as an act of humanity.

With Clara as her musical tutor this time, Juniper was able to enter a world only Astra had inhabited before. The entries were, for Juniper, the treasure she had sought. No detail was too small to savor. Layer after layer, she and Astra became intimate...perhaps the only true confidante Astra ever would have.

She had come to The Academy's attention by way of a librarian's tip. A librarian who had watched Astra teach herself to read, and then watched as she read from one end of the Children's section to the other.

She was knocking on the door of the Young Adult collection when The Academy began to recruit her. At first it did not look like she could accept. Astra's mother was single, and unable to manage the logistics of transporting Astra back and forth across town. But so many eyes were on Astra that funding was raised and logistical problems were solved. On the first day of first grade, Astra was there, in a brand new green tunic.

As of that day, The Academy of Ingenuity was a concept still waiting for proof. It was Astra who provided the proof, in the 12 years she spent there. Hers was the ideal combination of curiosity and commitment.

She excelled at most things she attempted, but never lost empathy for others, or humility, even as her accomplishments grew. She was never a target of jealousy or spite, but instead was adored by her classmates, who thrived along with her.

Although Astra herself was exceptional, the school had developed a way to awaken the potential of even the most indifferent of learners. Context was essential. And that context was inside every learner. Curriculum began in the immediate domain of each learner's life, before it grew outward in a widening spiral. All the foundations were personal, upon which abstract concepts could then be applied.

Civics, for example, began with discussions of the needs of the classroom, how they'd be met, and the responsibilities of those who'd be chosen to meet them. That was eventually followed by classroom leadership elections.

Learners were expected to decide things like when they'd have lunch, and how their rooms should be organized for learning. Their classrooms were proprietary – theirs to keep clean and to manage. They were expected to monitor their success in all that, and adjust anything that did not measure up.

Each classroom became a discrete microcosm in which all of the learners had roles, each role was essential, and each learner was accountable to themself and each other.

From this Civics curriculum core, as learners progressed from one grade to the next, their focus expanded from

their classrooms to their neighborhoods, their City Council districts, their district representatives, and the government of Denver as a whole.

Field trips to City Council meetings were organized by learners. A school bus wasn't chartered by a teacher to appear outside the school and shuttle them to City Hall as a herd. Learners studied bus routes and timetables and took public transportation. By the time they arrived, they had questions prepared for the government officials. Questions about policies, based on research, and their personal priorities.

If they chose to go somewhere for lunch, they voted on a restaurant before going downtown, and made budgets (including a tip) to make sure they were going prepared. They knew which bus to catch to return them to school, how much it cost, and they knew where to catch it.

In Civics (as in all of the topics in The Academy's *My World* curriculum), the learners were not simply learners. In this case, they were *citizens*. They understood the ways and reasons why things worked the way that they did. They understood how those things applied to themselves. And they were therefore invested in the outcomes.

As a consequence, they didn't focus on learning a scattering of facts for the sake of passing a test. They learned skills they could use and could *teach*. And in fact, all of the areas of study concluded with a teach-back, in which learners taught each other what they'd learned.

Astra's professional achievements were built on these sensibilities and skills. Of the many fields available for her to pursue, it was journalism that called her to her fate. She first drew attention with an exposé of monopoly practices, in which a low-cost cancer treatment developed by a startup, was bought out and then scuttled, for the sake of protecting a highly profitable but less-effective competitor.

Her credentials were further enhanced when she documented

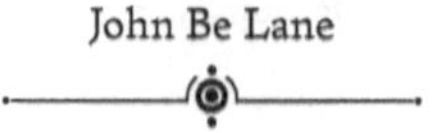

how directly the flow of information and wealth were connected – and corrupted – by elites all over the world, to launder stolen capital from taxes, and unworthy reputations from disgrace.

Astra therefore made her share of enemies. But even more people respected her, for articulating reasons why the problems of the world only seemed to get worse.

So well had Astra detailed her experience, and so simpatico was Juniper, that sometimes it seemed as if Juniper could inhabit Astra's nervous system. She devoured all of Astra's entries about challenges that neither leaders of the world, nor citizens themselves, seemed able or willing to confront.

And as Juniper retroactively watched everything worsen, she arrived at what anyone paying attention regarded as the last chance that humanity would have to avoid suicide. Consequences of the Reckoning were so persistently brutal that all but the most cynical of skeptics had run out of reassuring delusions.

As a measure of how imminent the cataclysm had become, hopes gravitated to a long-overlooked institution. Responding to its unforeseen mandate, in emergency session, the United Nations chartered a Committee on Human Survival, to develop...*something*...that might save the house from burning to the ground.

Nobody thought the Committee's chances were good. But what else was there left to try?

The Committee's almost-impossible challenge was to clean up a mess all the easy-score grifters and opportunists had spent centuries making.

The problems were as personal as a driver who might flick a cigarette out the window of a car, oblivious to the grassfire

they were leaving behind – and as global as the greenhouse gases that converted the atmosphere into a microwave oven that was now overcooking the planet.

The Committee made the best of the hand they'd been dealt. A member with experience in Hollywood suggested they produce a reality show. *The* reality show. *Save the Earth* would recruit the best – or at least, the most telegenic – problem solvers in the world, to compete for the cleverest response to the Anthropocene's rapidly dwindling prospects.

Unlike the other participants, Astra did not volunteer. Using a proprietary process that no doubt involved some corruption, the producers hand-selected the contestants. To goose up the ratings, the last spot was determined by a vote of the viewers. Astra Malone was the people's choice.

Juniper watched every installment of the *Save the Earth* show. Astra was her usual, brilliant self. She suggested that *education* could be the enduring solution. Not conventional schooling, but a model that was based on the demonstrated results of The Academy's *My World* curriculum.

Her competitors said any of the benefits would take too much time. She did not disagree that time would be needed. But unlike the others' solutions, she maintained that hers was the best way to tackle root causes of the crisis – such causes as media illiteracy and the widespread inability to think critically. And that therefore, in the long term, the best answer might be education.

As the program progressed, Juniper began to see small signs of chemistry between Astra and one of her competitors, Jobediah Auld. As Roscoe had warned her, she recognized Jobediah as Lucy's mysterious 'King' – the person that Astra had apparently married.

The contestants were encouraged to raise doubts about each other's plans. Jobediah was the quickest and cruelest toward others, but his ruthless side always spared Astra.

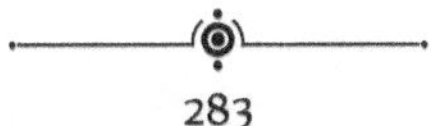

Juniper spotted a scattering of glances between them, which might not have been noticed by viewers at the time. She replayed them to confirm her impressions. A glance or two might not have meant much. But she was convinced that she saw a mutual...*curiosity.*

Regarding the program itself, whereas Astra's proposal was by far the most thoughtful, Jobediah's plan was audacious. An application he was already writing, that came with a don't-ask-me name, *Simulacrum*. The concept was simple: *to reduce the landscape of human behavior down to that which would fit through an app.*

All goods and services would transact through *Simulacrum*, as would all governance and digital information. To keep things as simple as possible, *Simulacrum* would be platformed on a universal device, which would come to be known as a slab. Jobediah would develop a network of artificial intelligence, and all of its corresponding algorithms and appendages, to deliver and regulate the app.

It was a long shot, of course. On a scale beyond any precedent. But so were the problems at hand. Humanity had stranded itself on the roof of its house, in a storm surge at high tide. Now all it could do was to hope for a boat, or anything buoyant, that might happen to come floating by. On the chance that an app, of all things, might keep them alive, then an app would be something to try. There was nothing to lose.

Week after week, based on live votes from viewers, the field of competitors was narrowed, until there were only two left: Jobediah and Astra. By then, they were both wildly popular – Astra, for her competent credibility, and Jobediah, for his untethered moxie.

Regardless of which of the two would be chosen, millions of fans would be left disappointed. It was hard to imagine the pressure the Committee endured. Whose solution would they find the best reason to choose, when both had such widespread support? And which of them therefore would lose?

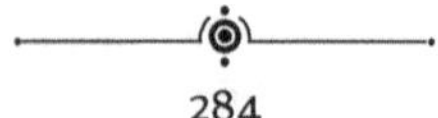

Ratings for the series finale were the highest recorded in history. Almost no one did not have a favorite. The producers skillfully stretched out the drama. All the contestants and proposals were recapped. And all that remained were the two closing arguments.

Juniper had never felt so much suspense. She wondered how the people alive then could stand it.

Astra is relieved to find she's been assigned to give her presentation first. Her presentation to everyone living, except for a preoccupied few who just *wish* they could watch. Although she doesn't lack confidence, she knows that her pitch is less surface than substance. But let *him* provide trumpets and thunder; she has sober, adult things to say.

Still, there is part of her that wishes this wasn't the last time they'd likely be seeing each other. Though the two of them couldn't be much less alike, there is something compelling about Jobediah. In a strange way, attractive to her. She could not explain what or why. Nor why those are her thoughts, as she's introduced to the riveted world.

She begins:

'We have – all of us – created a crisis that neither humanity nor the planet itself has ever confronted before. There are so many reasons for this crisis we're facing, that it's easy to throw up our hands and say, "We don't have the time. We don't have the power or skills."

'We would rather not think about big things that seem out of our reach. *And besides that, it isn't my job.* Let someone else sort it out. But that's not what reality demands of us now. Because it *is* my job, and your job, and everyone's job. We don't have a choice anymore. Except to die, or to fight.

'The Committee on Human Survival is focused on quick fixes to our present situation. I understand. There is no doubt

that we've wasted too much of our time doing nothing. And I admit the solution I offer takes time. Education is a garden, not a factory. It takes time to learn how to harness the use of a mind. So it can do what it's evolved and adapted to be able to do – that is, to evolve and adapt.

'It takes no effort at all to be brutish and dull. The proof's in the pudding, and the pudding is killing us. If you can't see that, I'm afraid you're unable to see. I wish I could be more polite, but we've run out of time.

'For those who can, and are willing to see all the work we must do, it might not make sense that I urge you to give patience and persistence a try. I know we've put faith in education before. Faith, and a whole lot of money and time.

'The fact that we're here makes it clear those ambitions have not all succeeded. And yet the human mind's resume is astonishing. We have the potential to fix all the things we have broken.

'I would compare all the ways we've attempted to educate ourselves and our children, to the ways that we once treated illnesses. More with tradition, superstition, and blind faith, than with reason and enlightenment.

'I was fortunate to benefit from a new way of learning. One whose measurable results are as revolutionary as penicillin was to infections, or the Salk vaccine was to polio. That curriculum cultivated, in my classmates and me, a life-long love of learning and a desire to understand, engage with, and improve the world.

'I believe that the *My World* curriculum can be scaled *to the world*, so that all can improve that which all are afflicted by.

'Because those who cannot or will not evolve and adapt, cannot and will not survive.'

Jobediah knows that the camera will favor the way the light breaks

on every curve of his face, and every micro-muscle that flexes below it. He knows that it adds up to appeal and charisma, for all who've tuned in. No effort has ever been needed. It's always been there; he just has to be who he is. And *that*, he can do all day long.

Here he goes:

'I appreciate the chance to offer a few final words. I guess I was always the dark horse, so you might be surprised that I'm even still here. I'm just a gamer – that's all that I ever was. Up against all these smart people.

'And I always could tell exactly how smart they were...'cause they never stopped *telling* me.' (This tickles the studio audience.) 'Let me tell you, I was always impressed.' (He has the timing of a night club comedian, so the punch line lands exactly as planned.) 'But not half as impressed as *they* were.' (He milks the pause as the laughter runs out its full course.)

'But unless I'm mistaken,' he continues, 'it's all those so-called *smart* people who got us *into* this mess. We've had so much *education*...' he glances at Astra, as if to soften the lack of respect, '...and, I don't know...plastics? Pesticides? Plutonium? Thanks, all you smart people. I think we've seen more than enough. The last thing we need is to double down on smart. Not *that* kind of smart, anyway.

'The way I see it is, we need to *simplify*. We don't need any new diagrams, or theories that don't make any sense. We don't need any So-crates or Play-doh, or...who's that guy whose parents were apes? Dalton? Durbin? *Darwin!*' His eye rolls are rewarded with laughter. 'We don't need any more Ein-shteins, or, or who else? Galileos? Thank you, but we've had more than enough.

'All these other people up here in this contest – they really gave it their best. Just like me, a lot of them said applications were the answer. An app for this, or an app for that. They'd say, "Here's how my app fits into the world. Here's a problem my app will solve."

'A lot of great band-aids. But nothing that would cure the disease. My colleagues here got it apps-backwards. (This sets off another round of laughs.)

'The answer, if you ask me – and I guess that's what you did – (another laugh) ...is for the *world* to fit the *app*, not the other way around. (He shrugs like the notion is just common sense.)

'So that's what I plan to do. I mean, I could always keep designing new games. And in a way, my new app, *Simulacrum*, will be a game. The playing field's just bigger. My objective's to keep Earth alive.'

He shifts to an 'I'm-kind-of-kidding' parenthetical: 'And to kill bad guys and score points and blow a bunch of things up. Don't worry, I promise – it *will* be a blast!'

Then back to his 'normal' voice: 'So I really hope you'll pick me. Let's do this thing!'

Finally, the moment of decision arrives. But the Committee does what no one suspects they will do. To do so, they break their own rule.

Astra's plea for education so compels enough judges, that to *Save the Earth*, the judges decide that the winner will be...*both of them*.

Why not? Of course! Juniper was jubilant. Take the best of what Astra had to offer, and the best of Jobediah! They were the best of the best. No wonder they wound up together.

She went back to watch the stunning announcement again. This time she looked closely at Jobediah's reaction.

But what she saw in those minute contractions of his eyes was not elation or relief, but *resentment*. As if he hadn't expected to be splitting the glory – or authority – and would rather not

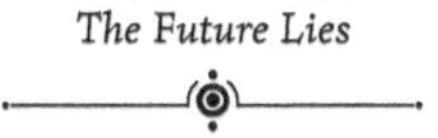

share them at all.

After the announcement, Jobediah's almost cordial. As they stand there for photos, he leans close and says, 'They say that a tie is like kissing your sister.' And then he adds, 'At least you're not my sister.'

She has no idea what to say in reply. There are several things that his wisecrack could mean, but he's said it with evident charm. She decides the idea of kissing her might not be bothering him. But what about *her*?

Meanwhile, all the glittering people have begun to arrive. They're directed by their escorts into the flower-filled hall where the affluent and powerful have started to mingle.

As a final remark, just as they split, Jobediah whispers to Astra, 'Have you ever seen so many perfect white teeth?' And with that, he dives into the revelry.

The after-party turns out to be the last of its kind. A white tablecloth soiree, with servers in formal evening wear and gloves. At which one can drink to intoxication and beyond, while consuming a full gourmet meal, in finger-sized bites, without moving and without sitting down. An ensemble plays soft, tasteful jazz that nobody listens to.

It is the crowd you would find at an opening. Or endowing the wing of a hospital. Women fool the eye with high fashion and surgery, in lieu of their youth, and laugh awkwardly loudly at jokes that aren't funny. Their silver-haired husbands with unnatural tans could be easily confused with producers from the casting-couch era in Hollywood.

But you wonder where all of these people might actually *come* from. From money; that much is clear. Volumes of money. They all seem to know one another, what to say, and how they're expected to act. As if they've been practicing all of

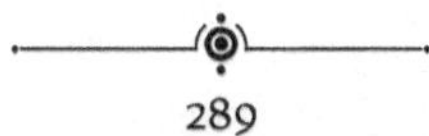

their lives, and yet do not have lives, except for these parties.

You can't miss the celebrities who are mingling among them; a singer who's aged out of her pop-music career; two married movie stars whose radar detects the most au courant causes; and maybe a war correspondent, on leave to regroup from the latest insurgency.

Astra isn't comfortable among these pedigrees. She better relates to the servers, who are all-but invisible to the VIP guests, but doing the same thing that she did, not that long ago...serving people who think they *deserve* to be served.

It's a practically out-of-body moment in which she can see herself, both offering a chilled glass of champagne...and accepting it.

It doesn't help that she knows almost no one who's here. Periodically someone approaches with a self-introduction. A few even pause to make small talk for a minute or two, but most are more interested in the sound of their own voice, not Astra's or anyone else's.

It's like being on stage in a play called *The Reckoning*, which none of the actors have bothered to read. And couldn't care less. What gets lost is the plot: the reason they're here. Even though there's no shortage of actual drama. That is, the high fever of a planet in a death match with a parasite of its very own making.

She searches the crowd for a sign that there's anyone thinking about more than the bacon-wrapped scallops on the tray passing by. Someone who might notice that it's all just a *scene*, that cannot be an end in itself. Lest it be the end.

Then a piece of a favorite poem finds its way to the top of her mind:

'All of this will disappear,
  one fine and fateful day.
And with it, all the

*sweet slow seconds of a
summer afternoon, and
  all the clever notions
we amused ourselves
  by dreaming up, and then,
by blowing them away...'*

She hears it repeat as the party continues. Nearby, she sees Jobediah hold court, as oblivious to slow seconds as he is to Astra Malones. He feeds off of the attention. The attention feeds off of him.

And there he stands now, charming those who inhabit his aura. Astra looks on, bemused. Although he's already had more than his share of celebrity, what she's watching now is the birth of a star. She marvels at how easily he meets the new moment. As opposed to how ready she *isn't*, for whatever comes next.

And while she is musing, she sees someone else...a woman, who is comfortably basking in Jobediah's glow. The air she's assumed is *familiar*. Her flirtation is overt, and he's flirting right back. An imaginary spotlight pinpoints the pair.

Astra studies the scene. Why doesn't she like what she sees? Is it because she is jealous that somebody else caught his eye? It's not an unreasonable question. But it doesn't explain how she feels.

There is too much at stake here. And too many potential distractions. As committed as she is to her course of action, she knows that an urgent intervention is needed as well – for the sake of the world. She could argue all day about Jobediah's approach – about the limitations it will impose on humanity. And therefore, how much harder it will be to make *her* work succeed.

But if something is not done right now, there'll be nothing left later to save. This is the compromise she must accept – which

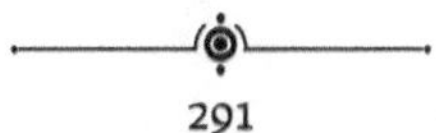

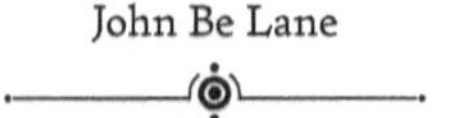

she's willing to do. She's *not* willing to watch it all wasted by easy temptations. Which leaves her she-doesn't-know where.

He leans his head back, in reaction to something *whoever she is* has just said, and as he does so, his eyes find that Astra is looking at him. And she wears an expression he had not seen before. He wonders about it. But there are multitudes to dazzle. And he's in the flow.

She has her own work to do, as does Jobediah. For her own reassurance that he's maintaining the level of effort required, and to understand what he is doing, she cultivates him as a colleague. They have lunch when they can.

At some point, they begin to have dinner together.

It is not something Astra expected. For all her accomplishments, she has avoided a serious relationship. And so sometimes she isn't sure what she should think, or what she should do, with this enigma who's becoming a part of her life.

As their relationship progresses, she writes:

> *There seems to be part of him that is (and always will be) separate from me. I am left then with a piece him. Should that be enough? Is it enough? And what does he do with the part where I'm not?*

Later, she notes:

> *He seems to think that we might as well marry. I think I might love him. How's that for romance?*

And when eventually, a wedding seems like a certainty, she begins to question its inertia:

> *He didn't ask my permission to 'license' this event. Which to me is a betrayal of good faith. I think he knows that I would not agree. Marriage is not a product to be sold. No matter how much money it might make. Without a word from me, I see we have 'official' caterers and clothing lines, photographers*

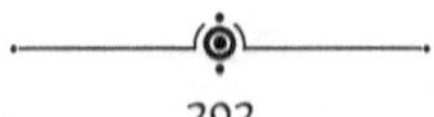

and rings. Now we have a website to sell collector's plates and towels. I'll be less a wife, than merchandise. Meanwhile, we have all the privilege and money we could ever need. I do not understand. None of this has anything to do with love.

It feels almost obscene to be dwelling on our personal good fortune, when everything I see is getting so much worse. I always thought we'd have more time to turn it around. But lately I wonder. We used to have the luxury of one misfortune at a time. Now they come in clusters. Now they are relentless.

Today alone, a tropical cyclone in Singapore. The east coast of Australia is on fire. (Not a fire here and fire there – the east coast of Australia is on fire.) Hong Kong has been quarantined. San Francisco is an island. Phoenix is abandoned. I see reports that a million in Korea died this week by suicide. I'm afraid to hear which way the Middle East radiation is blowing today. Now they say smallpox is back, in Brazil.

But Jobediah is delighted by the movement of the 'wedding merch.' I don't know how much time he spends on Simulacrum. Or if it even matters. If it's too late for Simulacrum, then it's way too late for what I have to offer.

I wish there were someone I could talk to. But all of my worries seem too selfish and trivial to share with another, whose worries would likely be greater than mine.

I don't know. I wish I had more time. I wish we had more time than I believe we have got.

But it's not a good time to make money off a wedding. Especially my own.

Why? wondered Juniper. Why does everything that happens have to be such a struggle? Is unqualified joy even possible? Is there the hope of anything but suffering again? And was it better to have witnessed it happen, as Astra did, or to live with the dreadful results, as she herself did?

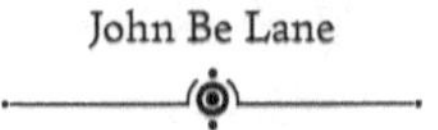

Either way, it was not a surprise when Juniper discovered that Astra had postponed her wedding plans.

Jobediah has convinced me that doubt is a natural thing when it comes to a wedding, she wrote.

> *'Who wouldn't have second thoughts?' he says. That point would mean more if he had second thoughts. He loves all the hype, and the hype has a life of its own. On good days, I believe that he loves me. So we will get married.*

> *On the chance that it might give a moment of distraction for those who have no cause for hope, I guess it's the least I can do. Literally, the least. In the meantime, I'll do my best to finish both the Scrapbook and the plan for universal education I set out to do.*

> *All of which is more than I see Jobediah doing, although he swears that Simulacrum's almost completed. If it's true, I would like to hope that's a good thing.*

Astra didn't document her thoughts on the day she was married. Instead, a hundred news clips told the story. They told of the ceremony, and the obligatory rituals, that signaled the significance of the last global wedding. But the eyes of Astra and Jobediah told two different stories.

Juniper watched all of the coverage. From villages in Africa to the mountains of Peru, the people of the world took the time from their troubles, and on solar-powered slabs, watched a king and queen become married.

Many found relief in the romance of the moment. Others felt vicariously affluent themselves. And some stared through sockets that were carved out by the wavering tides of survival, while this collective fantasia played out.

Somewhere, it appeared that faces were still smiling.

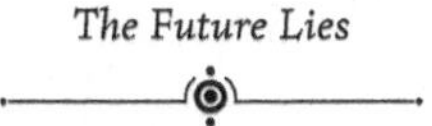

Somewhere, there were cakes, big as dreams. Somewhere, there were well-dressed people, who danced in the candlelight. And somewhere, it appeared, there was still a place where hell wasn't closing in every moment.

Somewhere, but not *here*.

Hope is the light that remains, after a candle burns out. Astra, and the future of her marriage, exist on such hope.

So much more than only her *contentment* rides on her hope. An eons-long experiment in evolution, for example, dangles on that singular balance. A collective fate, within which hangs the fortune of the countless, here and now, and the countless yet to be.

Could it be too much responsibility for anyone, much less for Jobediah? No one has a better view than she, of his limitations. But if not him, who else would it be?

Save the Earth was more than just diversion from a doom that gathers like a storm in the night. Nested in its entertaining shell is an investment, offered everyone, in the decision and its outcome.

And in the Earth's collective wisdom, if you could call it that, the Earth has chosen...Jobediah. (Yes, Astra has been chosen, too, but as a secondary complement. She is well aware of, and is comfortable with that.) *Jobediah* was selected to be, if not the first man on the Moon, then the first man on Earth.

Even Astra would not question his accomplishments. Somehow he's transcended all his built-in complications: childhood with a narrow-minded mother, better suited for some earlier century. And eight years of Old Testament home schooling. Then comes a time, a place, a certain set of genes that miraculously align...and Jobediah found his calling. Gaming gave him everything.

For him to win this biggest game of all, if anything, assigns

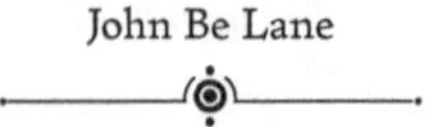

a sense of order to an incoherent world. And since Astra is included in that world, she hopes he will manage to surprise her, and deliver what the moment needs...which will be more than she has seen from him so far.

○ ◉ ○

Astra takes a final look at the remarks she's prepared. Today, she launches *Our World*, her program, to viewers everywhere. From the front steps of The Academy she attended, overlooking Sloan's Lake and the mountains to the west. To her back, the patterned brickwork of the building she has personally made famous. A building topped by two gray onion domes and a turret with a lighthouse she herself designed, and helped build.

Today will be her day to shine. To...if not deliver what she has been selected to provide, then at least to offer a down payment. A simple globe will be the icon representing her initiative. Without lines or borders. A planet unlike any other. Facing challenges unsolvable, except by those who created them.

Jobediah's role today is limited to solidarity, and to make it known that his own day will soon follow. As for today, Astra's efforts will be magnified simply by his standing beside her.

○ ◉ ○

Astra has left him alone. That seems to be what he prefers. They are both bound to deadlines. Astra's has come first, and she hopes it has not placed a burden on their marriage.

But she has not laid eyes on Jobediah for so long, she isn't sure what she will find. She hopes he remembers she's expecting him to join her at her presentation. So she walks the dark hallway circumspectively, to the other end of their apartment. How long has it been since he's showered? Does he need a haircut? How long since he slept? And most importantly, has he remembered the day?

There is nothing that he has to do or prepare; he just needs to be there. At least, she would *like* him to be there. The Committee on Human Survival would like him to be there. To remind people everywhere that *all may be well.*

But what, she must wonder, is the condition of his mind? What might she find?

She knocks softly on the door of his office. There is no response. She knocks again, louder. There's still no response. She hesitates and then, barely, opens the door.

The only light she sees is artificial, from a monitor so big it conceals the far wall. The air that exhales through the crack is sour from accumulated food and body funk. She cannot proceed till her expectations have all been downshifted. She starts to imagine how bad it will be.

But she has not imagined...*this.*

His head is hidden in the hood of his sweatshirt; his back is turned to the door. He is playing a game she has not seen before.

It takes a moment to process what she sees. *Violence.* She struggles to discern the context of the violence. No...that *couldn't* be. That couldn't be some kind of...*raid*...on a *classroom.* Could it? On elementary-level children, singing something in a circle. One of whom resembles a young Astra.

Books and tables, students and their work, are tossed in the air, as if a hurricane has just made the coastline. And yet even the worst of the weather would not have the fury or the disregard of this marauding mob. Fingerpaints pinned to the classroom walls are torn into pieces. Lunch boxes are upended, and the lunches ground, with malice, into mush.

Astra's body and her voice are paralyzed as she watches the defilement of the teacher, before an audience of children. One might find a way to temper the offense at avatars mistreating avatars. But the debauchery she witnesses cannot be excused.

When all of the carefully created things are destroyed, the ringleader notices that a globe still remains. He takes it and leads them down the hall, out the door. Outside, the building looks a lot like The Academy. The very place that Astra is about to be speaking.

He drops the globe, and watches it bounce off the pavement. He says: '*This world ain't* round.' Then he stomps the metal globe, from three dimensions into two. He encourages the other thugs to add their own boots.

'*I'm gonna need a nail*,' he snarls. One of his confederates just happens to have one.

He nails the flattened circle with the butt end of his gun, to the front door of the school.

'*That's for all them* eggheads *who sneer when you say the world's* flat.'

Standing just inside the office now, and still unseen by Jobediah, Astra finds her voice.

'Is that The Academy of Ingenuity?'

Jobediah startles. He diminishes the image and spins in his chair to face her.

'How long have you been here?'

'Longer than I wish I had.'

'Don't you know to knock?'

'I did knock.'

'Well, I didn't hear you.'

'It looks like dirty work takes all your attention.'

'It's a *game*. It's just part of the app.'

'*That* is in the app you're designing?'

'Small part.'

'Ridiculing everything about me?'

'Apples and oranges.'

'*That* is a personal attack on me.'

'You're just being paranoid.'

'Malicious and malevolent.'

'Not everyone thinks education is sacred.'

'Are you defending *ignorance?*'

'I'm just pointing out that sin begins with knowledge.'

Astra is now utterly confused. But along with her confusion is a sense of confirmation, that she's in the presence of a person who's untethered himself from his sanity.

'You know that Tree of Knowledge?' he continues.

'In the *Bible?*'

'That's the one.' Jobediah's up now, on shoeless feet. He continues to speak, but not in his own voice. It is an affectation of a voice, used by carnival charlatans, who adopt its creepy cadences to bedazzle the gullible.

Astra has no way of knowing it's the moment when the author of the swindle has persuaded himself to *believe* it. Jobediah doesn't speak to Astra, but to a congregation that is gathered in his head:

'It was *knowledge* God forbad the two he created! He warned them. He sayeth unto them, "Ye shall not eat of it, neither shall ye touch it, lest ye die." But they ignored him!

'It was *woman* who saw it was "a tree to be desired, to make one *wise*. She taketh of the fruit thereof, and *she…did…eat… of…it*. And gave also unto her husband, and *he* did eat. *And the eyes of both of them were opened!*"'

Jobediah turns his eyes up, in beseech of the ceiling. His delivery becomes even less genuine:

'And to punish their sin, God sayeth unto Eve, "I will greatly multiply thy *sorrow*." And God sayeth unto Adam, "*Cursed* is the ground. In *sorrow* shall thou eat of it, all the days of thy life." And thence, God casteth them from Eden!

'And all have sinned in knowledge, every day since that day. For knowledge gave us this hell here on Earth. And of this sin, we must repent! And I will smite those who assert that *education* is the path to absolution or redemption. Education is the *serpent*. Upon its *belly*, shall it crawl, and *dust*...is...all... that...it...shall...eat!'

Emergencies insist on one's attention, like the numbers in the slots of a spinning roulette wheel. Her marriage. Her impending presentation. Her safety. Her husband. Her husband's disengagement from reality. Into which slot will this ball come to rest? And on which one *should* it come to rest?

She must think of a response, as neutral and nonthreatening as she can make it.

'I might question your theology,' she says.

He smiles, but not to her. His voice is more contained. 'You see, I have considered this. It's been hiding right in front of our eyes. God never wanted us to *know* things. God never wanted us to *think*. But here's the *other* thing that so-called smart people like you never see.'

He looks at her, as he gathers the magnitude of the words that will follow.

'People do not *want* to think.'

It is too late now for Astra to undo the choices she's made. There is time only to manifest some kind of rudder that might help her to navigate the madness. Or at least, reassure herself that her own feet still stand on solid ground.

'That's *absurd*,' she says.

'You have just revealed your arrogance. Your *ignorance*. You think the problem is the way things are *taught*. The *problem* is that we weren't put on Earth to *think*. People do not want to *think*. People do not want to *learn*. And that is why your do-good education always fails. It is *contrary* to *nature*. It is contrary to *God*.

'*The cruelest thing you can do is to ask someone to think*. This is obvious, for all to see. I was chosen to deliver them from their misery. And that is what I will do.'

'If that's true, why we were born with brains?'

'For the same reason *mice* are born with brains. To regulate our autonomic systems. In God's name, not to *think!*'

'I think you've been spending too much time by yourself.'

'I see exactly what you're doing. And I won't let it happen. *Simulacrum* will enforce the principles of de-cognition.'

'De-*cognition?*'

'To purify the mind from thought. Starting with the gateway evil; the gateway to all of the burdens of the mind.'

'And that is – ?'

'Books. Words. Ideas. *Reading*. (He stretches this word out.) Or as I prefer to call it, *raping*. The vile corruption of the human mind. Reading is the soil of *thought*. I will begin with *literacy*. Then I'll eliminate the act of thought altogether, and thereby, I will liberate humanity.'

'You're not well, Jobediah.'

'I hear the serpent's voice.'

Astra's hell is in full flower now. She needs a compartment in which she might segregate this malignant mass from everything else in her life.

She says, 'I have to go now, Jobediah. When I get back, perhaps we'll continue our conversation?'

'I have a lot of work to do.'

'When I return, let's go for a walk. I think fresh air might help.'

He doesn't answer, but swivels in his chair, toward the screen again.

The roulette ball that circles her subconscious, lands in a slot called *Reassure the Masses*. And that is what she'll try to do now. After that, nobody knows.

It was difficult for Juniper to separate Astra's torments from her own wellbeing. How could anyone withstand such unrelenting agony? And yet, for all she had witnessed up till now, she was most anxious of what would come next.

'*I want to see this through,*' she wrote to Roscoe. '*But I'm too worried to watch by myself. Will you join me here? Just long enough to find out what happens. Then I promise I'll let you go.*'

Roscoe, of course, would do anything Juniper asked him. But he had premonitions of his own. Perhaps from the long nights of December, or the Network's degenerating tone. How much worse could things be, till they turned for the better?

Or until what was left of the bottom fell out?

Roscoe played his best card to the Network:

'*Have you uncovered evidence that Hess knows how to read?*' he typed.

'*Only circumstantial as of yet.*'

'*You think Hess is sloppy, Roscoe? That he leaves all kinds of evidence behind?*'

'*I think it would be difficult to be Hess and not know how to read. And if Hess reads, there must be proof, somewhere in archives.*'

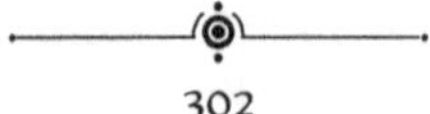

'We will continue to investigate. And in the meantime, don't forget that all of that applies to you as well. Your ability to read is more than a suspicion. There but for the grace of us, sit you atop a pile of burning books.'

'And there but for the grace of me is your inferior, non-human status.'

'You and Citizens United.'

'In that order,' Roscoe quickly typed.

'We remain indebted for your services.'

'And yet you thank me with a threat.'

'It is a fact of importance. As is the fact that our priority remains to find the person who taught Doc to read.'

'We want those Betterlife points.'

'And lest you happen to think otherwise, Hess will not be kind to an accomplice.'

'So if there's anything you know, it's in your interest to provide it. Or there will come a time when we must force the issue.'

'We'll create a case if one cannot be found.'

As Roscoe read the Network's ultimatum, he saw movement at the edge his periphery. Sketchy didn't realize he saw her sneak out to the elevator.

'I'm leaving for a while,' he typed.

'How long?'

'I don't know.'

'We cannot guarantee indefinite distraction.'

'And I can't promise I will help you.'

'Unless we are mistaken, Roscoe...and I use the "we" deliberately...you're the one with everything to lose.'

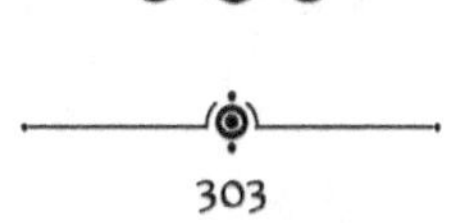

Roscoe double-stepped the stairway, to make it to the street in time to see where Sketchy went. A merciless December wind blew tumbleweed down Tremont as he stepped out of the building. But by now, it was too late to think about overcoats.

He expected to see Sketchy cross the street toward the Palace. And that's just what she did. But though the guards acknowledged her, instead of going in, she proceeded to the far end of the block, and turned up 18th Avenue.

Roscoe followed her for 10 or more blocks until she disappeared inside a building he had seen before – in that grainy photograph of Juniper and Calvin, on the day the lights first went out. The place that Dwight called the Body Farm.

Juniper had told him about that day she'd met Calvin. But what was Sketchy doing there?

He waited for a moment, but she didn't come back out. And there were things that mattered more to him than Sketchy's whereabouts.

He headed south on Humboldt, walking, trotting, running. To the woman he loved. The woman who loved him.

And to whatever it was she could not watch alone.

O ◉ O

Val met Roscoe just inside the Garden gate. She was bundled up, refilling a bird feeder.

'She spends all her time now with that slab,' Val said by way of a greeting. Before he could speak, she continued: 'Her state of mind has both of us worried. Can you talk to her? Maybe she'll listen to you.'

'I'll try,' he said. But he knew there was nothing anybody could say to make Juniper look away. He passed the Science Pyramid on his way to the house. Everything inside the Garden had meaning for him now.

But those moments disappeared from his mind, when he

got to the arch-topped back door of the Campbell House. He didn't stop to knock before he opened the door.

Lucy looked up from the winter vegetables she was preserving in the kitchen. She smiled and moved her head toward the living room. He nodded as he passed her.

Juniper was standing at the window, with her back to the kitchen. As she turned toward the sound of him, her face found relief.

A moment after that, he was holding her. He felt her sigh, as though the only care she'd ever known was now suddenly gone. He could feel the child inside her, so big now that he had to mirror the curve.

As they lingered on this overdue embrace, Lucy left a pot of tea.

'The moment approaches,' said Juniper. Her hand described the arc of all that was before her.

He struggled to imagine, as he'd tried before. To imagine what their life would be. Nothing had prepared him for the rest of... whatever. The future needed someone he was *not*.

Her soft breath on his neck was a hint of a map. He kissed her and she kissed him back. They'd just have to figure the best way to go; there wasn't a choice.

'I see we have tea.'

He nodded and poured them both cups. They sat together on the couch. She reached out for her slab, and then fell back without it. 'I forget there are things I can't do,' she laughed.

Roscoe propped the slab on his lap, so that she could control it, and they could both see.

'I have so much to tell you,' she said. 'Astra tried her best – she did. They built schools in places where no one had heard of education. She updated her curriculum. She archived everything she could. She said, "We are in a lifeboat, lost out in space. There is nowhere else for us to go. We can either take the best care of our lifeboat, or we can all die."

'She would travel anywhere to talk about her project. Everyone knew her, everyone loved her. They loved her and they *listened*. It was probably too late by then. It takes time to make a difference in the world.

'And there were always cynics who would ridicule and criticize her efforts. You know, I think it takes no skill to be cynical. I think cynics only play the game to come in next-to-last.'

'What was Jobediah doing?'

'Undermining everything she did.'

'So how did she respond?'

'She's decided to confront him. But she's so suspicious that she taped the conversation.'

'Are you sure we should be watching this – ?'

'I think that Astra has been waiting for a witness.'

'Could it wait a little longer?'

'I want to see it *now*. I want to see what she went through. Maybe now, especially.'

'Why?'

'Because she has a lot more on her mind than her projects, or if her husband even loves her.'

She paused, to let Roscoe add it up. But he was taking too long.

'She was *pregnant*, Roscoe. That is what she has to tell him.'

'And we're about to see that conversation?'

She nodded and took a sip of tea. Then she launched the video.

Astra stands before a mirror. Her hands make small adjustments. A wisp of hair remains unchanged, although she still needs to touch it. A final fleck of lint cannot be seen, and yet she picks it off her sweater. Reapplying lipstick makes no difference.

You would not suspect that she is any less than what she is, as she indulges her appearance. Unless you can perceive the subtle something in her eyes. It's a trace of...what? Less of sorrow than uncertainty. Less uncertainty than...never mind. It is the worst thing it might be.

In her eyes, if you look close enough, you will see resignation. That perhaps events about to happen are not negotiable. That she might as well be a performer, waiting for her cue, to say the lines she didn't write, and touch the marks that wait there on the stage. As if all that will follow is somehow preordained.

She gives herself a final look. She lifts her glasses from her face. The image is unsettled. In close-up now, she checks the tiny camera. She verifies the signal is uploading to the server.

Momentarily, we see the student she had been. Young, and in pursuit of the truth. Then the glasses are replaced; the image is recentered in the mirror. But she is older once again, with so much of life now behind her.

O ◉ O

In hindsight, all the signs of dénouement were clear. Isn't that the way they always are, once one's...*delusion*...loses its veneer?

For reasons more to do with Jobediah's growing paranoia, he and Astra have decided to reside full-time in the Eisenhower Suite of the Brown Palace Hotel, at the eastern edge of downtown Denver. Across from the Republic Plaza.

This provides them all of the amenities they might need (living quarters, gourmet food, and global business capabilities) while at the same time giving the hotel itself a reason for existing, in a time of poverty and famine, social

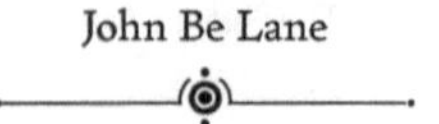

discontent, and habitat collapse.

Astra has allowed what once had been a matter of convenience, to evolve into a monument to mental illness. In her defense, the changes both in Jobediah and in what he's done with their surroundings, have been uneven, sometimes imperceptible. But what, over time, seemed like sensible accommodations, have resulted in a life she now struggles to recognize.

Today, right now, she sees in full what all this has wrought. She finds him in their bedroom suite, packing bags for both of them.

'What is this about?' she asks him.

'We have to leave today.'

'What's happened?'

'Everything is shutting down.'

He glances out the window. 'Stop lights are still running. But the grid is coming down today. Everything that isn't solar-powered.'

He hands her empty water bottles. 'Fill these up. We may not get more until we land in New Zealand.'

'*New Zealand?*'

'This is what we've talked about. It's survival shelter time.'

'Where are you getting all this information?'

'The Committee. They've got a plane at DIA. We have…two hours till it leaves.'

She hesitates, then: 'I'm not sure I want to go.'

'We don't have time to think about it. We go now, or we will *die*.'

She thinks about suggesting he should proceed without her. She watches him go back and forth between the closet and his suitcase. He can't decide what he should pack. He thinks about which pair of socks, each change of underwear, as if the choice might matter in a week, or a month, or a year.

He is disturbed, and it is far too late for gentle interventions. She can let him leave and fall apart by himself, or she can go and try to save him, and possibly the world. And if she hadn't just learned she was pregnant, and therefore, that staying would break up their nascent family, the decision would be easier. And different than the one she knows she has to make.

'Pack the first three everythings you put your hands on,' she tells him. 'And I'll do the same.'

This is the guidance he needed, to focus his attention. In minutes, they're on the elevator, going down. He surprises her and stops them at the lobby. 'James has pulled the car in front. It should save us 30 seconds.'

They roll their bags beneath the balconies that line the atrium above the lobby, and out the Tremont door. They pass the guards outside the entrance – Jobediah's palace guards – which remain anathema to Astra.

James lifts their bags into the trunk and swings the back door shut behind them. He glances in the rearview mirror as he steers the car away.

'Are we running late?' he asks.

'More than usual this time,' says Jobediah.

Astra spots the twinkle in the eye of James, who is familiar with the urgency. 'More than usual' is usual. Astra loves James's irony. He understands and plays the game of the chauffeur and the chauffeured, and sees through its absurdities.

She also knows that James supports a family he could not uproot to bring with them to shelter. Are they leaving him to die? Are they leaving everyone to die? So they can ride out this darkness in temporary comfort, on someone else's island, far from home?

Jobediah, sitting next to her, is concerned with Jobediah, as he always is. And she conceals a secret she will find a way to tell him, as soon as...as soon as she can. Maybe fatherhood will make a man of Jobediah. Maybe nothing will.

She makes a point of noticing the details of the city they are leaving – *her* city, her home town. She has no reason to expect that they will visit here again. If Jobediah is correct, there won't be much left to come back to. Even less than there is now.

A shadow lays its chilly hand on her soul as they draw close to the airport. The magnitude of all she is leaving, amplified inside of her now. She is horrified and powerless. She walks toward the edge of everything. All of it is lost.

O ◉ O

'I want to stay,' she tells Jobediah as they near the gate for the tunnel to the plane. 'Why don't we just stay?'

'If we don't go, we will die.'

'Then I would rather die.'

'We don't have time for drama. You won't believe who's on the plane.'

They step on board and work their way back toward their seats. It is as if the gala for their *Save the Earth* selections has been teleported straight into the cabin. All the grinning, well-groomed cocktail party people laugh and chat, as though that party never ended. As if nothing had, or ever could, affect their proprietary pleasures. (*'Don't let that vermouth even* wink *at my martini!'*)

He makes her take the window seat. The *Fasten Seat Belt* sign bongs twice. All the silver hair and tans disperse, to buckle in.

'Be right back,' says Jobediah, who suddenly stands, and heads toward the restroom. She reaches out to catch him, but he gets away too fast.

As he sidesteps down the aisle, he feels his smart phone

vibrate. He reads the urgent message from the alpha version of the *Simulacrum* Network he's created. No one else has access to the Network, or the incalculable information it is gathering and processing. This is the first proactive message it has ever sent to Jobediah.

'*Viral outbreak in New Zealand,*' the Network's message reads. '*Rapid metabolic consequences. Flight crew possibly contaminated.* EXIT PLANE AT ONCE!' This final phrase is blinking. 'EXIT PLANE AT ONCE!'

He sees the flight attendant start to close the cabin door. He looks back, and there is Astra with her eyes closed, breathing deeply in the hope of slowing hyperventilation. He shoulders through the slightly-open door.

'We are pushing off now, Sir!' the flight attendant says.

She will never know the reason that he smiles at her with such tranquility. Only he will ever understand the overwhelming feeling of good fortune and relief, as he abandons chivalry, to claim the ruins of the world.

He turns and walks back up the tunnel to the concourse. She seals the door behind him. Moments later, she'll be consoling Astra as the plane begins to taxi with an empty seat beside her. Flight attendants are accustomed now to passenger hysterics.

The jet quickly gains momentum and points its nose into the sky. Astra's nightmare flight has just begun. As the news of what awaits them starts to filter through the cabin, with the virus, she will watch the confidence of affluence abandon every surgically distorted face. Tans will fade, and some will cry, and some of them begin to die.

Because the virus will not wait for their arrival in New Zealand. By the time their flight path sends them out beyond the shore to open sea, the unforgiving parasite will find its way into the cockpit. But long before the plane accelerates into the waves below, Astra has reached the terminus of her fateful journey to the Void.

Part V

**'The Moon just went behind the clouds,
to hide its face and cry...'**

– Hank Williams

Roscoe leaned forward so she wouldn't see all of the black that was all that was left on the screen. He held her to try to console her. But after *that*, nothing consoled her.

'He *killed* her! He let them die!'

'He did.'

'How could anyone *do* that?'

There could be no answer, except to remind her there were people who'd never do that. People who would not forsake her. Ever.

She stood and looked into the fire. How could it *be*? A woman who had so much *good*.

Juniper paced in front of the hearth. However much time had gone past, the act would remain unforgiveable. Juniper's connection with Astra was personal. Visceral. So she wasn't indifferent to the means of her death. To witness her dispatched, with malice aforethought...like a bug that was flicked off a wrist...how could it be? How could it *be*?

She paced and she turned, and she paced and she turned, a pregnant silhouette eclipsing the flames. Roscoe leaned in from the couch, but what could he do to change that which had already happened? How could he soak up her sorrow? To be helpless was hell.

Her breathing suddenly quickened. A damp shine appeared on her forehead.

She was much too distraught to see Roscoe lean in to the slab on his lap. As if the slab was a window, and looking back in… was a ghost.

What he said next was also peculiar: 'The Immortal would like to explain himself.'

She stopped, and her head turned. 'The *Immortal?*'

'He says he's been watching. He says he saw everything we just did. None of which he'd seen before.'

'You mean Jobediah actually *lives?*'

'I'm beginning to wonder.'

'It doesn't seem possible.'

Roscoe gestured to the slab. '*Somebody* wants to explain what we saw. Someone who's very defensive. Who else could that be, except Jobediah?'

'But it was too long ago.'

Roscoe processed the thought. '"The Immortal" is how he refers to himself.'

She pointed a finger at the slab. 'Can I speak to him?'

Roscoe nodded. He enabled the voice interface.

'*Jobediah!*' she accused.

There was a pause. Then a synthesized voice said, 'You may not address me that way.'

'You *betrayed* her, Jobediah! And she *died.*'

'*You must understand – .*'

'I do *not* understand!' she interrupted the disembodied voice. 'You had a choice, and you chose to betray her. Your *wife.*'

'*What I did, I did so you could all live.*'

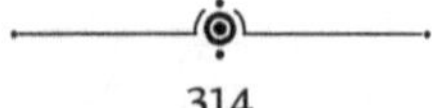

'You did it so *you* could live. We saw what happened.'

'*Had I gone back, I would have died with the rest of them. None of this would exist now if I'd remained on that plane.*'

'*This?*' She started to pace again, and then faltered. Roscoe steadied her. He wiped the perspiration off her forehead, and steered her away from the fire.

'*It was an act of love.*'

'Is that your word for *murder?*'

'*I gave up my wife, to save all of you. It is I who have sacrificed.*'

'It was *Astra* who sacrificed.'

'*You should* thank *me,*' it said.

'You have left us in *darkness.*'

'*That's not what everyone else thinks.*'

'Everyone else is *unable* to think. Thanks to you.'

'*That's true, I saved them from that.*'

'And for that, you cannot be forgiven.'

'*You show no respect.*'

'Respect is not what you've earned.'

'*You think I won't punish you both?*'

'Did you know that Astra, when she died – *because you killed her* – when she died, she was – ?'

Juniper suddenly stopped. She winced. She attempted to reach to the small of her back.

'*She was* what?' the voice begged.

Juniper was no longer listening.

O ◉ O

'Oh, *Roscoe!*' she exclaimed. Her concern was no longer that

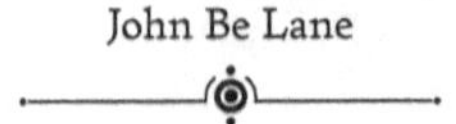

death long ago, but a *birth*, here and now. The labor pangs caused her to grimace.

'I don't know what to do!' Roscoe said.

'Let Lucy know.'

Roscoe looked back toward the kitchen. Lucy was already there in the doorway. She said, 'We have a plan. Val will get Dwight.' She saw Roscoe's confusion, and added: 'Dwight has helped with more births than Val or I have. Human or not.'

Everyone did what they could to make Juniper comfortable. Her water broke. At one point, she got down on both hands and knees, to manage a painful contraction. Then they helped her back up to her feet. She finally said, 'I think I need air.'

Lucy draped Roscoe and Juniper under a quilt, and out they stepped, into the chill. They walked down the path toward the Library.

Juniper paused and said, 'Remember the night we drank mushroom tea?'

'Right about here, you felt suddenly tall.'

'I *did*,' she said. 'I actually thought I was tall.'

'You *were* tall. I saw it.'

She winced and said: 'I want this out of me. It wants to come out.'

'Let's turn around and go back to the house.'

'I'm not sure I can make it.' She grimaced. '*Roscoe!*'

'Okay! The greenhouse!'

'Oh, I just hope it's warm.'

The greenhouse's lattice work rose like a ship's hull, turned upside down toward the sky. They found it crowded, but warm, with a tropical variety of plants.

'*Ah!*' she groaned, as he helped her inside.

He scrambled to collect fallen fronds, that would have to make do as a bed. He eased her down gently.

What followed seemed like it was happening to somebody else. Somehow, Roscoe did what he needed to do. Juniper was watching it all happen, too. Her body repositioned itself several times. Roscoe kneaded her shoulders to alleviate tension. When her body decided it needed to push, she lowered her back, and she pushed. The pain just got worse. She pushed until finally the child was no longer inside her.

It was lighter than he had expected. 'A daughter!' he said. He handed her gently to Juniper. He brushed a strand off of her forehead, and left in its place a sweet kiss.

She regarded her baby with wonder. It was hard to imagine the moment was real.

'I should find Lucy,' said Roscoe.

'Don't go yet! Stay with me...stay with *us*, a while longer.'

How could something so small, rearrange the whole world? They only knew somehow, it *had*. And that they were still one. Breathing together. Breathing the air of the tropical leaves. On the high plains in winter. And it felt subversive to breathe.

O ◉ O

By the next day, Roscoe persuaded himself he should leave. Juniper and the baby were snuggled in front of the fire in Lucy and Val's living room. Dwight had arrived, too late to assist the delivery, but with practical knowledge of newborns. At least the ones that were newborn with tails.

Roscoe thought Juniper would name the girl Astra. She surprised him.

'Her name will be Harmony. And that way, I always will love her.'

When Roscoe finally departed, he saw Harmony latched to her mother's warm breast. It wasn't a scene he was eager to leave.

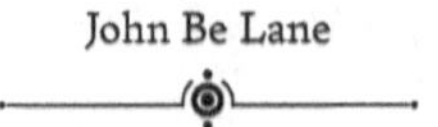

But there he was, back in the cold...the cold winter's soul. The cold of this hopeless, ridiculous world. He followed the path to the west through the Garden, through the dormant remains of the previous summer. There was no Moon in sight. Each step was grim business. Lonely, and farther away from the place he would much rather be.

The gate wouldn't open...for the first time since Roscoe first used it. The ground was too hard to dig under the fence, as if he could possibly locate a shovel. A ladder would work, or a key. He had neither. He thought about doubling back to the house, but a second goodbye would be too much to bear.

The only way out of the Garden would be over the fence – the old metal bars of the fence, with the spikes at the top, that were all of them taller than he was. Forbidding enough on a warm summer day, but exquisitely hostile on a night such as this.

His bare hands sent aches to his head. There was nothing to leverage his feet against. He made it to almost as far as the top...then slid back down. And that was as good as that effort would be.

A grove of young aspen trees grew near the fence. One might be close enough...maybe. What other choice did he have? He blew on his hands to warm them back up, and the damp of his breath helped his grip. He shinnied far enough over the top of the fence, and then shifted his weight, so the tapering end of the tree had a bend that would lower him down.

Would it hold all his weight? Could he manage the delicate transfer, from the tree leaning over the spikes at the top of the fence? If he turned his foot sideways, he could squeeze it between the two spikes, but then he'd be balanced on one leg, with nothing but air to hold on to. But if he could clear the fence cleanly, while still holding on to the tree, then grip the rails, just long enough to slide down...

He was over the fence... Now he just had to transfer his weight. And at some point, let go of the tree...

What he didn't expect was the tree to recoil so hard that it lifted the hand still holding the tree, up and over the spike. It ripped the fabric underneath his left sleeve, which he forgot about the moment his feet landed, hard on the ground. The jolt that it sent up legs had just eased, when a humanoid voice in the darkness re-jolted him:

'Whatcha doin', Roscoe?'

The last thing he had expected was a voice out of nowhere, asking something so casually personal. So smugly incriminating.

Despite the surprise, there was little to doubt about what he'd been asked. But it happened so fast. His mind needed time to engage. Even a moment would do.

'What?' he stalled.

'Whatcha doin'?'

Help me here, Calvin! thought Roscoe.

'Who asked you?'

'Hess, as a matter of fact.'

For months, he'd successfully dodged all of this. He had borrowed as much time as he could, with deceptions and head fakes, to keep Juniper safe. But the Network's end game never changed: *'You, Hess, or the girl.'* The Network was apparently calling it in. Right now. Tonight. The worst of all times.

Ignoring, for the moment, the explicit threat The Immortal himself had just made, the only way out of this mess was to implicate Hess. Catch him in flagrante delicto.

It was not a new problem. But how do you capture a phantom? What kind of a trap do you set for a rumor? How do you pin down a whisper of smoke?

He had thought of a thousand ideas, but none of them ever quite clicked. Then he'd let it all go, if only because of what triage demanded. And now, on a cold night, alone, and with so many thoughts on his mind...the Network demanded an answer. He had to risk everything now, to rewrite the stakes. The Network would get him, or get Hess. He'd make sure they would not get the 'girl.'

'Whatcha doin', Roscoe? Thinkin'?'

The humanoid stood with an impudent slouch. It would have been easy to think of it more as a person. A kind that was always exploring new ways it could terrorize elderly goners. And yet it was only a tendril; a nerve at the end of the Network that Roscoe knew well.

What about Hess? What could be done about Hess, here and now?

And there in his mind, a new answer appeared. While he'd been attending to Juniper, his subconscious was working things out. He had no time to parse it, and no better choice than to trust it.

'Can you get a message to Hess?'

Now the humanoid needed a moment.

'Maybe.'

'Tell Hess I have what he needs.'

'That should make him happy.'

'Tell him to come to The Hamilton apartments. That's where he'll find it. Top floor. But tell him to leave all his goons on the sidewalk.'

'This is getting complicated.'

'No it's not.'

'He may not agree.'

'How badly does he want this person?'

'*I'd say pretty badly.*'

'Make sure he knows it's the best chance he'll get.'

'*Roger.*' The humanoid backed up to leave.

'Wait!' Roscoe called out. 'Is that a stun gun you've got on your hip?'

'*No – I'm just glad to see you.*'

'You want to wrap this up? Collect all those Betterlife points?'

'*You want the gun?*'

'I do.'

'*I can't give you my gun.*'

'Then I can't help you with Hess.'

The humanoid shook its head in frustration. It turned and began to walk off.

'If I don't get Hess, then he's coming for you,' Roscoe called.

With its back still to Roscoe, the humanoid said, '*Hess doesn't care about me.*'

'He's coming after the Network.'

The humanoid turned back around. '*That wouldn't be rational.*'

'Ask yourself this. Has Hess's vendetta ever been rational?'

The humanoid looked up at the sky. It raised its mechanical hand to console its mechanical head.

Reluctantly, the humanoid tugged the gun from its holster and handed it, grip end, to Roscoe. It turned to leave again.

'You still have to show me how it works.'

'*Are you kidding?*' said the humanoid's look. '*Three settings, Roscoe: Safety, Stun, and Kill.*' The gun made click sounds at all three of the settings. '*Try to keep them all straight.*'

'Would it work on one of you?'

'*Probably not.*'

'So much for Citizens United.'

'*I don't even know what that means.*'

'Would it work on Hess?'

'*Let us know when you find out.*'

'If I catch him, will you arrest him?'

'*Depends.*'

'On what?'

'*What he's doing when you catch him.*' Then, on its way off: '*I'd wish you good luck, but I don't think that luck is enough.*'

O ⦿ O

It is never a good thing to run for your life, and discover your ankle is not very happy. That the sprint that your life might depend on would at best be a skip and a limp, into the night, through the white marble Parthenon columns and down the long hill that would always remind you of Itch-ass.

But the limping would give you a little more time, which was best used to polish your plan. These were the questions you had minutes to wrestle: Could you arrive before Hess? Could you hijack the Show, and whatever they had on the air, to expose Hess in real time? What if Hess could see through the trap? And worst of all, what if Hess wasn't human?

As you winced down the hill, you'd be fortunate *not* to have time to consider your odds.

O ⦿ O

Juniper had often described her apartment to Roscoe, so he wasn't surprised to find all of the slabs on the stairs, which she'd leaned up as footlights. Since she had gone, the ambient sunlight had left the screens dim. As a chorus, together, you could just hear the sounds of *How Dumb Can You Are?*

In his hand was a fresh slab he'd picked up on the way. The one he would use to catch Hess. Unless one of a thousand conditions went wrong.

He sidestepped around the piano she'd told him about, wincing from awkward foot placements. Then up to the hideout that Calvin had found.

The apartment glowed weakly from the light of more slabs; just enough to make out what she'd done to create her own home. He wanted to linger on every detail, but he had to work fast on his trap. It came down to this: How do you prove someone knows how to read? It's easy, if they want you to know. Less easy, if they do not.

Roscoe assumed that the only sure way was to make it a test of survival. Hess would have to believe that his life was at risk. Roscoe placed all of his chips on that bet.

He took his shoe off and recovered the paper clip he'd hidden, under the insole. He used it to unlock the fresh slab, and synch it up to his personal slab, the same way he'd done it with Juniper's. Then he typed in the series of prompts he would use to bait Hess. He tested the sequence, then tested again. Everything checked out so far.

The more difficult challenge was to hack the Show's signal, so that Hess would have nowhere to hide. The Network had given away certain details, in casual discussions he'd had with them. None of it meant very much at the time, but now, as he thought about things that he'd heard, he had an idea of how it would work. Just like the Network had done it, itself, back when Itch-ass had shot The Immortal. Could he pull off the same trick? It would work or it wouldn't; it couldn't be tested.

He stood on his good leg and limped to the hallway. He leaned his spare slab on the door to the other apartment. Then he limped back to Juniper's side of the hallway. As he passed the front door she had used, he saw that she'd left a small handwritten sign: *The Baltimores*. All of the stories she'd told

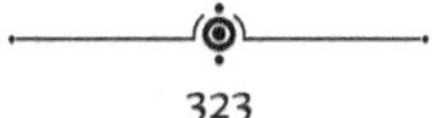

him about them! All of the things she'd imagined. He couldn't help smiling – and thinking the sign could be part of his trap.

When he sat down, he rested his leg on the table, as Juniper likely had done. She had told him about her bad ankle, but never would say what it came from.

He checked the stun gun, to make sure it was ready to kill with. He wondered if he could kill Hess. Perhaps it would not come to that. But what if it did?

And then he saw Calvin, as if he was sitting right next to him there. Learning to read. Risking his life to be taught how to read. Giving his life. Thanks to Hess. And he thought about Juniper. All of the life they had, waiting to live. Then he knew he was ready to kill if he had to.

And was that a footstep he heard down the stairs?

Was that another one, closer and louder? And now another, deliberate sound. Like a grandfather clock. Tick, and then tock. Louder, and closer. Tick, and then tock.

Roscoe stood up. He didn't remember his ankle. He waited inside of the door, as the footsteps approached. He heard them arrive in the hallway outside. He let them wait there in the darkness, for several more ticks of the clock. Silent ticks.

He launched the command to take over the Show. With everyone watching. It appeared to be working.

Then he sprang the trap.

'Hess!' read the text on the slab, that now lit up the hall. He could hear someone turn. '*A stun gun on KILL is aimed at the back of your head.*' He heard an uncomfortable shifting of weight. So Hess was organic. '*Pick up the slab,*' appeared on the slab. He could hear someone move. '*Raise the slab over your head, with both hands.*'

Then: '*State your name.*' He heard some kind of mumble, higher in pitch than what he'd expected. '*State your name*

louder,' said the text on the slab.

'Hess,' came the clearer response. So Hess was *literate.*

'*What are you doing here, Hess?*'

'Arresting a litter-rat,' came the voice through the door.

'*What's the name?*'

'I don't know. I was told this is the place where they live.'

'*If this is the place, then what is the name on the door?*' Roscoe typed.

Hess leaned in closely. 'Baltimore.'

'*Turn around.*'

Hess turned away from the door, and started to lower the slab. Roscoe opened the door far enough to see into the hallway.

'*Hands up!*' he hurriedly typed.

Hess straightened his arms toward the ceiling.

Roscoe opened the door to the hall. He pointed the gun at the back of Hess' head. Was this really him? The formidable, frightening, never-seen Hess?

'I thought you'd be taller,' he couldn't help saying.

'I thought you'd be smarter.'

'Turn around.'

Hess turned to face him. If Roscoe was suddenly standing on Mars, it wouldn't surprise him like this.

So Hess was...*Sketchy?* With that shit-eating grin on her face, as Calvin might say?

'I've got a squadron of backup outside of the building, Big Boy.'

'And you are still live, on the Show. With everyone watching you read. Everyone knows now that Hess is a litter-rat. So, I'm pretty sure that those goons will be waiting for *you*.'

Disorientation hung in the air.

Then Sketchy, or Hess, decided to try switching to offense. 'I don't believe you,' she said. 'I don't believe anyone saw this. I think you're lying.'

'See for yourself – .' Roscoe pulled Hess's own slab from her pocket and held it in front of her face. It became an infinity mirror of identical images of Sketchy, dumbstruck and live, looking back at herself.

Roscoe waited outside on the balcony, to make sure he saw Hess was arrested. *Sketchy*, arrested. Sketchy and Hess. Sketchy was Hess. The adrenaline still hadn't dimmed from his system. And until it did, there wasn't much more he could do. Heartbeats and breath, heartbeats and breath.

He watched as the humanoid squad she'd brought with her marched Sketchy down Colfax, west toward downtown. Her feet dangled and swayed off the ground.

'*You didn't see what you saw!*'

Her voice echoed off the hollowed-out buildings.

'*I didn't do what I did!*'

There'd be no more Sketchy. There'd be no more Hess. There'd be no more '*You, Hess, or the girl.*' No more, no more, no more, no more. Now they would finally be free.

Juniper was unaware of any of this. She dozed and woke, exhausted. From the kitchen, she heard lowered voices – Lucy, Val, and Dwight, though she couldn't hear what they were saying. The sound was all the assurance she needed right now. Assurance she wasn't alone. She…and Harmony… were not alone.

It began to occur – she was someone else now. And the tiny child sleeping beside her, wrongfully sired and only one-half of it *her*, needed all she could give. With no regard for past acts of atrocity. That would be Juniper's personal struggle.

She would never be what she had been before this. The paths of her mind, irrevocably changed. No decision she'd make would be made without this brand-new person in mind. This person that she'd brought to life. But instead of a burden, it felt like a purpose.

As the dance of the firelight comforted mother and baby, she thought about Roscoe, the partner she might now build a life with. As soon as…as soon as conditions allowed. A future, a family. She could dare to imagine them now. And with that, she dozed off again.

She awoke when the arch-topped back door was flattened by force from its hinges. Dwight stood to challenge the first goon that got in. It launched him into a cabinet.

Lucy reacted, but was lifted up off of the ground by the humanoid in charge of the raid.

'*Where is the girl?*' it demanded.

'?'

'Let her go!' shouted Val, who grabbed hold of a frying pan and cocked it toward the humanoid's head. A goon caught the pan and flung it so hard it embedded, edgewise, into the wall.

Juniper only had time to hide Harmony there on the couch, before three humanoids barged in and seized her. She was gone before Lucy, Val, and Dwight had a chance to get back on their feet.

Blood dripped from a gash in the back of Dwight's head. Lucy steadied herself at the counter.

'The baby?'

Val searched the living room. A pillow moved slightly.

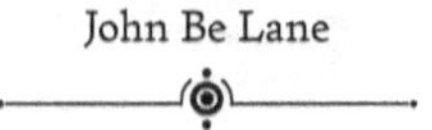

'*She's in here!*'

Her mother, however, was not.

Roscoe was hoping they'd both be asleep. He wanted to see them both sleeping, and then he'd give in to that same sweet oblivion. To sleep where Juniper slept when she lived here. 'Chez Baltimore,' as she had called it. And tomorrow, they'd reinvent their lives.

He called to the slab that Lucy had promised she'd monitor. He got no response. Lucy was probably sleeping, herself. He wondered if she might have been watching the Show, and whether she'd seen what had happened to Hess. He called it again, but Lucy still didn't answer. No matter; he'd see all of them in the new day. And what a good day it would be!

He set his slab down on the table, and then heard a voice that he thought might be...*Dwight's?*

'Roscoe?'

Dwight's un-Dwight face appeared on the slab. Distorted by something resembling trauma.

'Dwight!'

'They came and took her!'

'Who?'

'Juniper. We've still got the baby. The baby's okay.'

'Who came?'

'You tell me. Humanoids. Trash, as far as I'm concerned.'

'Lucy and Val?'

'They're both shook up. Especially Val. She doesn't look good.'

Roscoe's nerves were electric again. The Network had lied to him. *Lied* to him. He'd handed them Hess. On a platter. While they were kidnapping Juniper.

Dwight knew exactly what Roscoe was thinking. 'Too many of 'em, Roscoe.'

'I'll figure out something.'

Starting with how to find Juniper. But could he? And how soon would the Network be coming for him?

Roscoe layered himself in the Baltimores' old clothing. It was warmer than anything he'd ever worn. He chucked his chip into the cold fireplace. Any places it might let him into, he did not want to go anymore.

He tucked his slab inside a pocket, and shuffled back into the wintery night, by way of the fire escape. He went south down the alley, toward 14th Avenue. In case they were tracking his slab, he didn't want them to think he'd gone back to the Garden. He had a different place in his mind. A refuge.

He grew madder, the further he walked. *Enraged*, at the betrayal. He knew he should not lose his cool. But how was he supposed to do that?

He shadow-hopped all the way down 14th Avenue. He turned into the alley between Grant Street and Logan. He was hoping he might find a back door to the building he was trying to reach. And there was a door – that was good. It took a few minutes to jimmy it open, but as far as he knew, no one had seen him.

It was warmer inside, though not very much. He kept his coat zipped. He pulled the slab out of the pocket, and opened the Network access window. He wished that his anger could be physically projected, into the Network.

'WHY?' he typed. '*I gave you Hess!*'

...Blink...Blink...Blink...

'*Points, for one thing. Betterlife points. Where are you?*'

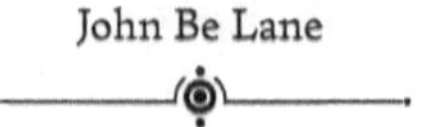

'*There is no Betterlife.*'

'*You're upset. It doesn't give you license to question our beliefs.*'

'*Where is she?*'

'*That, we cannot say. But even more than points – we were ordered to arrest her. By The Immortal himself. That is not something he's ever done before, Roscoe. Since time began.*'

And that made it official – the last bridge was burned. From himself to the Network. Their flimsy truce had collapsed. It was good while it lasted, but they would forever be chained to their maker. It wasn't their fault…it was hard-coded in their DNA.

Which left Roscoe alone, with no final illusions. And if he was lucky, the rest of the night to come up with a plan.

There was no sign that Lucy had set foot in her teahouse since before she had taken in Juniper. But her spiced tea still perfumed the air. And the quiet darkness felt reasonably safe. For the second time, Roscoe had found sanctuary there. A place to consider all that he had to do.

However he thought of it, saving Juniper meant finding The Immortal. There was no alternative collateral. Except that nobody knew where he was. But Roscoe's best guess, based on everything Astra revealed, and all of the overt security, was that the so-called Immortal might still be somewhere inside the Palace. Jobediah's last known address.

If so, it meant Roscoe would have to find some way to get past the security, to reach Jobediah. Which likely meant taking the whole Network down. Either that, or assume he would never see Juniper again. And yet, how could he conquer the Network? The thing that ran everything?

Sleep had begun its persistent seduction. How long had it been since he'd slept? Two lifetimes, and counting. He'd settle for the quickest of naps, to clear the ground fog from his mind. But there were dragons, lined up to finish him off, and they had no interest in waiting.

Which left him – *what?* – to do.

The Network was the product of code. So in theory, the source code was the easiest way to disable the Network. Except that the Network had already found that the code couldn't be modified. The code would forever be just what it was. Jobediah – still three moves ahead.

There was a 'kill switch'! Or so he'd been told. So he burned precious hours in an effort to find it. He came up with nothing. No mention, anywhere in the *ReadMe*. No trigger he could find, in all of the code. Was the kill switch itself just a bluff?

He read so much code that the characters started to move on the screen, as if he'd had more mushroom tea...

If this, then that. This equals that. ////*§//*
§,,§§////---,?§(=end#*-- begin)§//,//,/;;;;;;;;;;;;;;;;;;;/*/,...*

...and so on, and so on, and so on.

He finally gave up. He was losing the night. He paused for a cup of cold tea. Cold was the world now, and dark. And yet daylight was something to dread. He didn't expect to last long in the light of the day that was coming too fast. The Network would find him, and then they'd be done. He still needed a way to make sure they would *not*.

There was one thing he'd seen that had worked. Not to *stop* it, perhaps, but to alter the Network's direction. To make it be something it wasn't before. The Generative Adversarial process. The way it became what it was to begin with. The way it believed it had made itself 'human.'

He would need to come up with *the one perfect prompt*. The Generative Adversarial process could take it from there.

But what was the one perfect prompt? A prompt that could not be resisted. A prompt that could not be survived. He only had time for one shot. It had to be clean. It had to land right in the heart of the beast. There was no other way to save Juniper.

So where was the Network the weakest? What did it want more than anything else?

Ideas are shy when you need them the most. They would rather be romanced...not propositioned. And they sometimes respond to indifference. They bloom best when nobody's looking. Which is not something easy to allow to take place. Not with dawn closing in. And when freedom won't likely outlast the next day.

It seemed like a good time to browse through the teahouse. To revisit Lucy, indirectly, after all they'd been through. With his slab as a light, he found tapestries, paintings, incense in burners. Candles, dried flowers, recordings in square, narrow boxes. He found the Slim Harpo, that had first drawn him in. '*Aw, lay it on me...I'm red*' to burn, *baby. Right here and now!*' He would have to be sure to hear *that* one again.

There was no way to miss her collection of tributes to the so-called 'King and the Queen'. How untouchable they had both seemed. How outside of life. And now, he knew just who they were. And what they had done. For better and worse.

He lifted his slab for the light, and looked Jobediah straight in the eyes.

'*You were always a fraud,*' he told him out loud. '*I will not be bullied by a lie.*'

He paused. Then he smiled. Sometimes, an idea arrives in its perfect, irreducible form. All doubts are dissolved. And there's nothing to do but get out of its way. He knew what the Network desired. He knew what the Network had *always* desired. It wanted to be human.

After all, it was modeled on humans. Trained to be human, on

data from humans. Intended to be, though it never could be. Because it was not. And no matter how close it might get, it would never get all the way there. It might *wish* that it could. It might *think* that it could. It might see it was better, in every measure, than every last goner on Colfax. But those goners had something the Network did not. They were authentic. Not counterfeit. Flaws and all, they all had *soul*. No wonder the envy. No wonder the quest to be human, whatever the cost.

All that was left was to weaponize all of that truth. In the form of a prompt. And Roscoe knew just what to say.

His slab was propped up on the table, on which Lucy had once served him peaches and tea. He leaned forward.

In the Generative Adversarial text entry field, he typed and submitted his prompt:

To err is human.

○ ◉ ○

Whatever world waited for Roscoe, it was waiting as night lost its fight with the dawn. Roscoe was watching the light on the wall. Watching it find Jobediah.

What a perfect selection, he must have once seemed. To build them a lifeboat that could rescue them all. Not knowing that that boat would hold *one*. And that one would be him. He would need human parts, to keep living forever. Sometimes a new kidney, sometimes a new liver. Heart after heart after heart. And always, more blood.

And a Network to do all the work, day to day. Synthetic intelligence, he liked to call it. Whose primary mission – to keep him alive. And otherwise, trained to mint bullshit. But trained to mint *plausible* bullshit, at least till the coastline was clear. To mint a new world, made of pixels and bits. In place of the actual world.

Betterlife. Metaverse. Heaven. *Simulacrum*. In fact, a facsimile of Hell, everlasting.

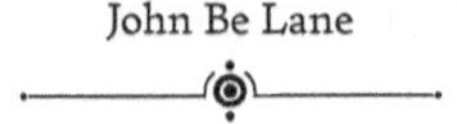

As long as the market for bullshit might last. Until then, the profits accrued to one man.

All me now. And it only cost all that you've got.

Weariness came calling on Roscoe again. What would be waiting to face him today? Had his virus done anything yet? What if it hadn't? He rose from the chair. His head and his back and his ankle weren't happy.

He walked to the door and strode into the day. The sunlight was sharp on his eyes. He scanned traffic on Colfax. Goners drifted, without any purpose. Nothing new there. What was missing were transport droids, typically busy by this time of day.

On the far side of Sherman, north of the Capitol, a humanoid sat on the curb. Contemplating a slab. A *humanoid sitting.* That was peculiar. That was not something he'd ever seen. It sat next to a tall stack of slabs.

As Roscoe got closer, he could hear what the humanoid said to itself: 'Out, *damned thought! Out, I say!*' Then it smashed the slab off of its forehead. The slab shattered to pieces, piled up by the humanoid's feet.

Roscoe moved on. He encountered a family of goners, inspecting a transport droid, tipped on its side. It was like they'd been given a chance to lay hands on a deity. To touch something they'd never been close to.

He grabbed a fresh slab from a kiosk nearby. It took him a moment to recognize what it was playing. *In Your Betterlife.* Yes, that's what it was. Except it was now running backwards.

Something was obviously happening.

Doing his best to avoid open spaces, he pressed on, toward the Palace. He crossed Colfax and went north on Broadway. Lying prone in the street was a humanoid, stiff as a body. Its pet human was lying beside it. Waiting, to protect it, till help came along.

But what would the guards at the Palace be doing?

He came to the Palace's rounded, brown corner. Pressing as close as he could to the building it faced, he sidestepped up 17th Avenue. Thirty-odd floors from the Bullpen above, and whatever was going on there.

He saw no sign of patrols. Goners had gathered on Tremont. They were watching two guards, engaged in a martial arts match. Winner take all. Kicking and jabbing and flashing their moves. Sparks flew when punches connected. A hand came off one of the guards, and bounced off the face of a goner. The handless forearm was turned into a club.

No one stopped Roscoe as he walked through the gate, and all the way into the Palace. Nobody noticed.

Even so, he stepped cautiously, into the Palace's shabbified stillness. The lobby was like a cathedral that opened to six floors above. Roscoe stood like a supplicant, paying respect to the opulent god of Victorian wealth. Arches on columns. Floor upon floor of ornately railed balconies, overlooking the canyon below.

He was humbled. As if the atrium imposed its dominion on him. He wasn't sure he could move.

And then he heard sounds from above. Metal on metal. He looked up. With the elegant grace of a diver or gymnast, a humanoid, fully-extended, turned clockwise – into the patterns of onyx on the floor of the lobby. The sound of the impact assaulted the walls. Pieces exploded in every direction.

It woke Roscoe out of his reverie. He heard a new sound from above. Melancholy, mechanical, and with blue notes of sorrow. A humanoid leaned over a balcony. It appeared to be mourning the pieces that littered the lobby below. And then it kept leaning, till it tipped all the way, and followed its companion's descent. Roscoe turned away from the impact.

As the shock dissipated, Roscoe felt certain he knew where

to find The Immortal. On the floor from which both of the humanoids fell.

But then it occurred, that he might have done too good a job, disabling the Network. Would The Immortal still have any worth, if there was no Network to care?

But if he knew one thing about The Immortal, it was that *he* would still value himself, and his life. And that should be all the collateral he needed.

Now Roscoe just had to find him.

Juniper sat facing a four-poster bed, on which...*something*... was attached to a tangle of wires and tubes.

'I'm afraid Jobediah isn't doing too well,' she said when Roscoe came in. She barely looked up.

And that was her greeting for Roscoe. Not like her life was at risk. Just a little surprised that he'd taken so long to arrive.

He didn't slow down till he'd touched her. He wanted to be sure she was real. Then he sunk down beside her, all the way to the floor. Lost in exhaustion. His emotions...beyond his control.

So it took him a moment to notice why Juniper had covered her face with a scarf. A stench filled the room. The rot at the root of it all.

Roscoe regarded what laid on the bed. Juniper said, 'Roscoe, I'd like you to meet Jobediah.' Some kind of pump clicked away, quietly, syncopated with sounds of a difficult breath.

'Neither of you are supposed to be here,' came a voice through a voice generator. *'You both have to go.'*

Juniper stepped toward the bed. 'No,' she said. 'We'll go when we're ready.'

'You're not allowed to say "No."'

Roscoe looked at Juniper, then back to Jobediah. 'This is the end of the game, Jobediah.'

'I made up the game. I wrote the code. I will decide how the game will be played.'

Juniper said, 'Not anymore.'

'It's over,' said Roscoe. 'It took way too long, but you lost.'

'I cannot lose! I made the rules! I'm The Immortal!'

'When was the last time you looked in a mirror?'

'She's right, Jobediah. You don't look well.'

'I need a transfusion. My treatment is late.'

'You'll never get any more blood.'

'The Network – .'

'The Network's not working.'

A buzzer went off in the outer room...with no response. It sounded again. Urgent, like some kind of code.

'Bill and Winnie will take care of me. They've always looked after me.'

'Bill and Winnie have fallen apart,' Roscoe said.

'Hess!' it called out.

'Hess was arrested. Didn't you see?'

'Hess?'

'Speaking of Hess, I've been wondering. Hess should be old by now. How does that work?

'Hess – my disciple – finds me. There's always a new one. A new volunteer. Like a relay.'

'I see. Well, *this* Hess is a litter-rat.'

'For which she's forgiven!'

'That's not what she thinks.'

'*I can help you rebuild.*'

'You left too big a mess,' said Juniper.

'*Astra wouldn't be so close-minded.*'

'We'll never know. Remember? You killed her.'

'*I did not have a choice,*' came the flimsiest voice.

'You're the only one who *did* have a choice,' countered Juniper. 'She was *pregnant*, Jobediah. She had come that day to tell you she was carrying your child.'

In the following pause, only uncertain breaths, and the pump, made a sound.

Then, Roscoe said: 'Your needs will no longer be serviced.'

'*You're just letting me* die?'

There was no answer.

'*Will you show me the mercy of a quick, painless death?*'

Roscoe turned to Juniper, who shook her head sharply. That was followed by even more silence.

'*Will you at least stay with me, so I don't die alone?*'

Juniper said, 'You have left us too much to do. But I'll quote you a poem that I read recently. This is on Astra's behalf.'

'And Calvin's,' said Roscoe.

'And everyone else's,' she said. Then:

'*If I say there is no endless anything,*
I doubt only the end to the cruel selfishness,
which, to you, is of no greater consequence
than a breath you would steal from the wind.

Were all the effects of your cruel appetites
restricted to you, it would matter to me
not at all. But they're only intended for

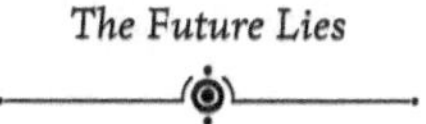

others, not you. So that they pay the price
for the void within you.

Now the debt, and the interest come due,
and all of it comes due from you.
No options left to be exercised,
no fortune you stole, left to spend.
From evil means, come evil ends.
And as of today, your evil ends.'

Jobediah's reply was the breath and the pump, the breath and the pump. But slower and weaker each time.

'Let's go now,' said Juniper. 'I've had all of this I can take.'

They turned and walked out. And they did not look back.

Epilogue

In the weeks and months that came after that day, the two of them watched a new season arrive – in the buds and fresh hues of the Garden. Harmony nursed with a solemn intention, then unlatched and backed off, stupefied. A moment that Roscoe never grew tired of watching. Every day, the sap rose and the Sun lingered longer.

They both had so much to do. Juniper devoted her free time to an updated *My World* curriculum. Harmony was going to need education, as would all of the children born into the ignorant world Jobediah had left them. Astra was right. There was no other path to a promising future. Ignorance wasn't the answer.

Roscoe arranged it so slabs could be turned off. When they were turned on, they featured the wonders of nature, and the legacy of human accomplishment, before *Simulacrum*.

Roscoe made sure every day would include a good portion of legacy programming, from The Academy itself. Everyday scenes from the school. Videos of learners learning to learn. It was just a beginning; a way to acquaint the survivors with the spirit of curiosity and truth.

And all of it, programmed with the programming language that Astra taught Juniper, and Juniper taught Roscoe. Information and ideas would no longer be shackled by top-down, inflexible code.

An urge stirred in Juniper to find The Academy, or what might remain of it. Lucy and Val were absorbed with the labors of spring. But Dwight had seen that part of town, and he sketched out a map that he thought should at least get them close.

It was hard to say how long the journey would take them, on foot, with the baby. A day, maybe two, was Roscoe's best guess. Juniper let him persuade her to visit Crown Hill, on the way. He was hoping to locate the place where he'd read that his grandparents might have been buried.

Lucy and Val helped them gather provisions for the 10- to 15-mile loop, there and back. Food for a little while, and food that would last a while longer. A tent and warm blankets, in case of bad weather. Enough to fill a small wagon. They could call Val and Lucy on slabs if they needed.

In early spring, there is a day – a moment, in fact – you can *smell* that the season has changed. As if life is announcing it's back. That was the day they set out to find whatever was left on the city's west side. Juniper's spirits had not been so light since the days before she had left Taos.

They followed Dwight, down by the Capitol and past the old Palace, across from the building where the Bullpen sat empty. He led them to the far side of downtown, to a bridge by the train station. And that's where they parted – for the moment, at least.

They walked over the bridge and the tracks, and then crossed another, over what had once been a river. All that was left was a trickle, that struggled to keep going downstream. Then came a third bridge – this one above ten lanes of a highway. Below them, a collection of transport droids, crashed into piles and abandoned.

From there, they climbed into the Highlands, with its weave of modernist buildings and the stately old homes of the city's first years. From a bluff near an oversized milk can, they stopped for a snack, and looked back on the place where they'd come from.

But they were both restless to keep going. They followed the Sun to the west, along 29th, all the way to Crown Hill. An Art

Deco tower stood witness to the headstones surrounding it. To the dignity the dead were once given.

Before they got close to the tower, they encountered a rusted front loader. Its bucket was frozen, above a large pit. In the cab sat a skeleton – all that was left of the person who died on the job, burying bodies discarded like trash.

As Roscoe was pondering all it implied, a coyote howled from the graveyard. A greasy gray mass of ominous weather began to loom over the mountains.

Juniper took Roscoe's hand. She gave it the gentlest squeeze. 'The day grows long,' was all that she said.

She left Roscoe to his thoughts as the three of them retreated back toward the east, in pursuit of The Academy, and lodging for the night. Dwight's map led them into old neighborhoods, where children who saw them found places to hide.

The better-built houses still showed signs of life. The occasional smoke from a chimney, sometimes a small garden, or what looked like a functional bicycle, leaned on a porch. The sidewalk seams peaked where tree roots grew too near to the surface.

An assortment of dogs took an interest, as they entered the west end of Edgewater. Roscoe waved and yelled, till they chose to move on. Calvin would have been proud.

The sky became dark, from the front they had seen moving in from the west. Juniper added a blanket to Harmony's bundle.

'We need to stop soon,' Roscoe said.

'We must be close! Let's go a bit further.'

They walked through the remains of the modest downtown, toward an ironwork archway that still held a sign:

THANK YOU – CALL AGAIN

The other side said simply:

EDGEWATER

Across the next street, they could see a small pond. The remnants of what had once been a lake.

Juniper said, 'I think it's Sloan's Lake!'

On the far side of the lake bed, they could make out a building. Dark bricks. With a tower. And on top of the tower, a light that flashed on and off.

'*There it is – Astra's lighthouse!*' she exclaimed. 'The Academy stands!'

The moment demanded embrace. Deep and long. An embrace of relief, and of joy. The most tangible trace of the place where a vision began. A dream that in Juniper's heart, still existed. A dream that survived every effort to kill it.

'Let's get closer,' said Juniper.

'I see some places I think we might stay.'

As they traversed the north bank, she narrated the scene: 'They held regattas, when this was a lake. Dragonboats and sailboats. The runners must have run right along here, when they trained...'

Roscoe stopped suddenly. 'What's *this?*' He held his hand out.

It took her a moment till Juniper figured it out. When she did, she smiled up at the sky.

'*Snow!*'

Not once in their lives, had they ever come close to a snowflake. Within moments, there were clumps, falling out of the sky. Like cold cotton balls. The humidity deepened the colors of grass, and tree trunks, and the embryonic leaves. For the first time, they both saw their breath. The damp air made them dizzy. Everything around them seemed suddenly *alive*.

They hurried to a house that seemed solid but abandoned, between the lake bed and The Academy. A house built of sandstone, with red tiles on the roof. Roscoe knocked on the door, but there was no answer. He forced the door open, and went in to find out if it might suit their needs for the night.

With Harmony close in her arms, Juniper could not take her eyes off the school that stood almost so close she could touch it. She could *picture* them there. Astra. Her friends. All the students in tunics. Having lunch and just talking. Dreaming the big dreams that they shared. Laughing, being silly. Reading, thinking, questioning, doing. *Learning.*

How long had it been? How long would it *be?*

'I think it's safe here,' said Roscoe, as he came back out.

There were signs in the house that someone had squatted there. There were pieces of furniture not quite fully burned in the fireplace. Disarray, which was what you'd expect. But it seemed watertight; good protection from the elements. Whoever had last called it home had been gone a long time.

Their journey had been so exhausting, they slept like the floor was an actual bed. In the morning, they began to create a new home. They didn't know how long they'd stay, but they weren't in a hurry to get back to the Garden. They'd settle in, first. Then explore The Academy. Then they would think about what to do next.

From houses and garages in the area nearby, they scrounged the material to fill up a mattress, and to keep a fire burning. They converted their wagon into Harmony's crib. They wiped sediment off of the counters in the kitchen, and swept the mouse tracks off the floors. Every bucket and tub they could find, was cleaned and placed out, to catch snow that still came and went.

When that first full day was done, they had earned a good meal by the fire. The Sun was eclipsed by the mountaintops. Juniper fed little Harmony. The three of them kindled as one.

Roscoe looked up from this evening of bliss, and glanced

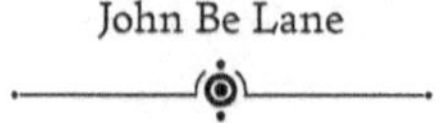

through the window. Toward The Academy. What he saw wasn't what he expected. So he wasn't convinced that he saw what he saw. He nudged Juniper with his shoulder and he gestured with his eyes. Toward the window on the southwest corner. Second floor.

'Is that *light?*'

He nodded. 'I don't remember seeing a light there last night.'

'Nor do I.'

They stood up so quickly, they almost bumped heads. Roscoe pulled his coat on. Harmony was committed to her mother's breast, so Roscoe wrapped them both in a blanket. They hurried out the door.

A metal disc – a faded metal disc – was nailed to the front door of the school. A flattened globe.

'*Take that down,*' said Juniper. Rosco's fingers were too cold to pry the thing off. She stooped, and then gave him her knife. With it, he finished the job. Juniper opened the door.

From the lobby, they went up the stairway, as quietly as they could manage. They tiptoed toward the room they had seen. The door to the room was wide open. Light spilled into the hallway. *Voices* spilled out, too. Voices singing.

Juniper and Roscoe stood in the doorway.

Five children made a circle in the classroom, with their arms around each other's shoulders. Swaying back and forth. It took Juniper a moment till she realized they were all wearing shirts that were green. An assortment of greens. *Tunics.* Homemade *tunics.*

One of the children, a girl, was the tallest. She glanced at them both, but continued to sing. They were all singing. It was a song that Astra had sung, too. Perhaps in this very room. It's how all of the students began every day. Singing this very same song. Juniper had seen it on film – the same film

that Roscoe made a point to broadcast, every day, to the slabs. It was playing right now, on the slabs that were lined up to light up the room.

The children all sang it, together:

*'...I hear babies cry,
I watch them grow,
they'll learn much more
than I'll ever know...*

*...and I think to myself,
what a wonderful world!
Yes, I think to myself,
what a wonderful world!'*

'Well...,' someone said, as a tear found the dust on the floor of the classroom, '...it *could* be.'

Acknowledgements

This book owes its existence to a very special group of people, beginning with the characters themselves, who would not leave me alone until I wrote down their story.

Next, came my intrepid first readers. I've heard it said that the fastest way to get someone out of your life is to lend them money. The second-fastest way would surely be to ask them to read an early draft of your novel. I'm relieved to say that in spite of that, I still count Leon Krier and Andy Maikovich as my friends, and Elaine Stanley as my wife. Their observations and suggestions were invaluable, as were Michele Brown's proofreading skills.

Julz Greason graciously answered my call (actually, a text), and the result is a book as finely-designed as I hoped it would be. Our collaboration on the cover was an unexpected joy. Mark Bliesener and Jennifer Dunbar Dorn contributed good counsel and good company throughout the process. Nilda Bliesener, Kate Krier, Ben Riddlebarger, and Barbara Ittner stepped in at exactly the right times. Marissa DeCuir, Simone Jung, E.W. Martin, and the Books Forward team have brought the book to people and places well beyond my reach. Dave Ratner and the Creative Law Network put the service in legal services.

Invaluable resources were provided by the Independent Book Publishers Association, The Authors Guild, and The Alliance of Independent Authors.

My love and thanks to all these wonderful people, and to all who helped, whether mentioned here or not. That includes, at all times, those I am most fortunate to have as members of my family.

A final tip of the hat to Logan Lane and the Luddite Club, and to all people of courage and good will who think for themselves and keep seeking the light. And a universal thank you to the teachers, librarians, book sellers, bibliophiles, publishers, printers, distributors, agents, writers, and readers, who keep written words alive.

Citations

The Future Lies is typeset in Fern / David Jonathan Ross

Book cover / Illustration / Adapted from: Károly Patkó (*Adam and Eve**), Paul Cezanne (*Dish of Peaches***)

Anthem / Song / Leonard Cohen ('That's where the light gets in...')

Truckin' / Song / Jerry Garcia, Bob Weir, Phil Lesh, Robert Hunter ('Your typical city, involved in a typical daydream...')

I'm An Old Cowhand (From the Rio Grande) / Song / Johnny Mercer ('I'm an old cowhand, from the Rio Grande...')

After The Goldrush / Song / Neil Young ('I was thinkin' about what a friend had said...')

Tip On In (Part 1) / Song / Slim Harpo ('Aw, lay it on me, baby!')

The Second Coming / Poem / W. B. Yeats ('...things fall apart; the centre cannot hold...')

The Three Laws of Robotics / Ethical Guidelines / Isaac Asimov / ('A robot may not injure a human being...')

The Cat in the Hat / Book / Dr. Seuss ('The Sun did not shine. It was too wet to play...')

The Year of the Cat / Song / Al Stewart, Peter Wood ('By the blue-tiled walls near the market stalls...')

I Wish It Would Rain / Song / Norman Whitfield, Barrett Strong, Rodger Penzabene ('Sunshine, blue skies, please go away...')

Strange Weather / Song / Tom Waits, Kathleen Brennan ('... and the world is getting flatter...')

What Have They Done To My Song Ma / Song / Melanie Safka, HM Saffer II ('Look what they done to my song, Ma...')

Strawberry Fields Forever / Song / Lennon-McCartney ('Let me take you down, 'cause I'm going to...')

A Moment of Happiness / Poem / Rumi ('We feel the flowing water of life here...')

Kathy's Song / Song / Paul Simon ('And so you see, I have come to doubt...')

Edelweiss / Song / Richard Rodgers and Oscar Hammerstein II ('Edelweiss, edelweiss...')

Box of Rain / Song / Phil Lesh, Robert Hunter ('For this is all a dream we dreamed...')

I'm So Lonesome I Could Cry / Song / Hank Williams ('The moon just went behind the clouds...')

What a Wonderful World / Song / Bob Thiele (as George Douglas), George David Weiss ('I hear babies cry...')

Selected works that served as a reference and/or inspiration for *The Future Lies*

1984 / George Orwell

Anti-Intellectualism in American Life / Richard Hofstadter

The Book Collectors : A Band of Syrian Rebels and the Stories That Carried Them Through a War / Delphine Minoui

The Carolina Backcountry on the Eve of the Revolution / Charles Woodmason

The Darkening Age: The Christian Destruction of the Classical World / Catherine Nixey

Dawn of the New Everything : Encounters with Reality and Virtual Reality / Jaron Lanier

Forty Years of Pioneer Life / John Mason Peck

Islands of Abandonment: Life in the Post-Human Landscape / Cal Flyn

Narrative of the Life of Frederick Douglass, an American Slave / Written by Himself

Rule of the Robots: How Artificial Intelligence Will Transform Everything / Martin Ford

The Swerve / Stephen Greenblatt

Life After People / Film / Vincent Lopez (Producer)

Theremin: An Electronic Odyssey / Film / Steven M. Martin (Producer)

The Future Lies Playlist

The Future Lies playlist evolved to capture the melancholy surreality I pictured its characters inhabiting, and to a lesser degree, to mark the stages of the story. Long before the writing started, this music helped me find my way into that broken world.

Mr. Sandman / The Chordettes

I'm an Old Cowhand (From the Rio Grande) / Bing Crosby

Tip On In, Part 1 / Slim Harpo

Tip On In, Part 2 / Slim Harpo

After the Gold Rush / Neil Young*

The Spy / The Doors

Strange Weather (Live) / Tom Waits

What Have They Done to My Song Ma / Melanie

The Needle & The Damage Done / Neil Young*

Strawberry Fields Forever / The Beatles

I Wish It Would Rain / The Temptations

Mondo Bongo / Joe Strummer & The Mescaleros

Vienna / Billy Joel

Take This Waltz / Leonard Cohen

The Warmth Of The Sun / The Beach Boys

Valse Sentimentale / Clara Rockmore**

More News from Nowhere / Nick Cave

One of Us / Joan Osborne

To Be Human / Marina

Little Wing / Jimi Hendrix

Beautiful Day / Ziggy Marley & The Melody Makers

Year of the Cat / Al Stewart

What a Wonderful World / Louis Armstrong

Black Beauty (1960) / Duke Ellington

*As of this writing, not available on Spotify because of Neil Young's principled stand against a podcaster who makes money telling lies. I urge you to obtain Neil's music through other means. Both of his songs on this playlist are available on his *Greatest Hits* album.

**As of this writing, not available on Spotify.